D0431239

Oh My Stars

Oh My Stars

A NOVEL

Lorna Landvik

BALLANTINE BOOKS

NEW YORK

2006 Ballantine Books Trade Paperback Edition

Copyright © 2005 by Lorna Landvik
Reader's guide copyright © 2006 by Random House, Inc.

Published in the United States by Ballantine Books, an imprint of The Random House Publishing Group, a division of Random House, Inc., New York.

BALLANTINE and colophon are registered trademarks of Random House, Inc.
READER'S CIRCLE and colophon are trademarks of Random House, Inc.

Originally published in hardcover in the United States by Ballantine Books, an imprint of The Random House Publishing Group, a division of Random House, Inc., in 2005.

Library of Congress Cataloging-in-Publication Data
Landvik, Lorna.
    Oh my stars : a novel / Lorna Landvik.
        p.   cm.
    ISBN 0-345-46836-8 (pbk.)
    1. Women travelers—Fiction. 2. North Dakota—Fiction.
3. Depressions—Fiction. 4. Musicians—Fiction. I. Title.
PS3562.A4835O37 2005b
813'.54—dc22   2005041163

Printed in the United States of America

www.readerscircle.com

9   8   7   6   5   4   3   2   1

Book design by Lisa Sloane

In loving memory of my mother, Ollie Landvik, who read a book a night and was especially thrilled when one happened to be mine.

Acknowledgments

I would like to thank Gina Centrello, my publisher, and everyone at Ballantine Books, especially Linda Marrow, an editor who asks the right questions and literally gave me the shirt off her back. To Kim Hovey, with whom I share news of hockey tournaments, and to Marie Coolman, for your hard work on my behalf and for booking me in all those swank hotels. Thanks to Peter Weissman for his sharp-eyed copyediting and to Arielle Zibrak for helping me with my computer illiteracy.

To Suzanne Gluck, my agent; thanks for your wise counsel and sense of fun. I hope we can have theater dates for years to come.

Many thanks to my friends Wendy Smith, Judy Henegan, and Kimberly Hoffer for consistent laughs and good times; a big thanks for joining me at the state capitol on my birthday with protest signs and a desire to better the world.

Speaking of a better world, I hope our government will realize the inestimable value of its libraries and adequately fund them. I will always be thankful for my favorite branch libraries in Minneapolis (now only open part-time), which have been oases since I was a kid. If they managed to stay open during the Great Depression, surely we can figure out a way to keep our libraries open now.

I am grateful to be a member of WWW, a group of writers who appreciate words, wine, and the importance of dessert after dinner. When are we going to figure out our secret handshake?

Thanks to the Riverview Theater for its real-butter popcorn, its wonderful aesthetic, and its cheap tickets.

I had finished this book before my mother died and she knew that its title came from her favorite saying and that I had named the North Dakota town of Pearl after her middle name. Still, more than anything, I wish she were here to read it. I could always count on her for a good review. Thanks to my brothers, Wendell and Glen and my sister-in-law, Cindy, who gave me strength and help through this big loss; thanks too to my nephew, Adam, and his wife, Amy; my nieces, Nichol and Daisy; and their mother, Debbie.

Thanks to my aunts, uncles, and cousins for their support and for singing "Beautiful Savior" at Ollie's funeral. The person who remarked "they sounded better than the Von Trapp family singers" was right on the money.

As always, thanks to Chuck, Harleigh, and Kinga for everything you are to me.

Oh My Stars

Prologue

TAKE A LOOK AROUND THIS DINER. SEE WHAT IT SAYS ON THE laminated menus that are propped between the salt and pepper caddies and the sugar bowls? *The Off-Ramp Cafe;* rightly named, tucked as it is beside a snarl of highway cloverleafs, the rumble of traffic laying down a bass line to every song the jukebox plays.

See the sullen waitress entranced by her fingernails, who acts as if a request for more coffee is a personal insult? See the trucker in the corner booth spanking the bottom of his ketchup bottle like he's mad at it? And the guy at the end of the counter, see him studying the sports page like a code breaker trying to decipher a secret message? And look at the cook behind the order window, who seems to think nose-picking and food preparation have a right to coexist in the same kitchen.

See anything else? The smudged dessert carousel making its lazy rotation with only a piece of lopsided lemon meringue pie along for the ride? The coffeemaker piddling decaf into a glass pot? The fishbowl of business cards gathering dust by the cash register?

The Off-Ramp could be anywhere at all, in Anytown, USA. All over the country, from Seattle to Selma, from Bangor to Boise, there are truckers burying their burgers in ketchup, salesmen sulking behind news-

3

paper curtains, waitresses scribbling orders on pale green pads in handwriting worse than doctors'. That's what I love about diners; they're as familiar as a next-door neighbor's house—one might be cleaner than the other, one might have a better cook, but in general you know what to expect. Don't even get me started on franchises; I avoid them like the plague, which I believe they are.

And the old lady at the counter? Well, thanks for noticing. Let me tell you, old ladies are the ghosts—boo!—of American culture; only a few people actually see us. Of course my arm usually does cause comment, but the way I've got my coat sleeve arranged, I'll bet you didn't even notice it.

Excuse me for saying so, but you look sort of lonesome—how's about you park your caboose next to mine and I'll buy you a cup of coffee and throw in a story to boot?

I want to tell you how I came into the Off-Ramp Cafe on this cool rainy night that smells of diesel fuel and lilacs. I want to tell you how a person can be almost drowned—and glad of it—and then be pulled up into sky so blue and sun so sparkling that the allure of those dark suffocating waters evaporates in an instant. I want to tell you how a person weighed down with bitterness heavy as lead can be filled with the lightness of a song. I want to tell you how the real kings of the world are more than likely to be sitting in the cab—or the bed—of a 1932 Ford pickup than on a throne.

Tomorrow night I'll be having dinner at The Waldorf-Astoria, where my story will be indirectly honored, but to tell you the truth, I think flown-in-from-Holland centerpieces and fancy linen and heavy silver impedes the storytelling process, don't you? People can't tell their real stories when they're afraid they might spill bouillabaise on their designer gown, when they're worried they might use the wrong fork.

That's the beauty of a diner, wouldn't you say? Diners—and especially their counters—are the indoor version of a campfire; people like to sit around them and tell their stories.

Mine's about miracles—I even have a daughter named Miracle, which gives you an idea of their importance in my life.

Aw, settle down and quit your squirming, I'm not witnessing for any Reverend I. M. Aphraud or Swami Fulla Lotta Bologna; I'm not one of those bothersome lackeys out to fill my quota of converts to the Church of

Perpetual Possibility or the Temple of Unending Yakety-Yak. I am the salt of the earth, and I do not believe in the ninety percent rigmarole that is organized religion. But miracles? Miracles, my friend, are a different thing entirely. From what I can see, miracles are built from love, and as far as love is concerned, I am a true believer.

Chapter One

ON HER SIXTEENTH BIRTHDAY, VIOLET MATHERS NEARLY BLED TO death in a thread factory. The "incident," as it was referred to in the company's 1935 logbook, happened on the graveyard shift, just before break time, when the pounding and the whirring and the squeaking of the machines had crescendoed into a percussion concert conducted by the devil himself. Lamont Travers, the foreman, told her later in the hospital that the worst accidents always happen before break; people can't wait to smoke their cigarettes or drink their coffee and talk about whose man or whose woman had done who the wrongest. Violet hadn't cared about any of that; she wanted only to cut into the marble cake RaeAnn Puffer had brought, wanted only to hear her co-workers raise their tired, smoky voices in a chorus of "Happy Birthday."

Excited and jumpy as a puppy with a full bladder, the birthday girl broke the cardinal rule of the Marcelline thread factory, the cardinal rule printed in capital letters on at least three signs posted on the dusty brick walls: DO NOT ATTEMPT TO CLEAR OR REPAIR THE MACHINERY WITHOUT FIRST TURNING MACHINERY OFF.

She was running the Klayson, a big reliable machine that

sweat oil as it wound and cut dozens of spools of thread. There were women who were possessive of their machines (Lula Wendell even named hers and explained that whenever the machine spit out thread or overwound, it was because "Pauletta" was on her monthly). Violet had formed no deep attachments to the masses of metal, preferring the job of "runner" and working whatever machine needed running. When she ran the Klayson, she felt as if she was wrangling a harmless but stubborn old cow, and it was almost with affection that she scolded the machine when it huffed and burped to a stop.

"Now, come on, gal, I ain't got time for this," said Violet, and with one hand on the Klayson's metal flank, she stuck the other up into its privates, feeling for the tangled clot of thread.

There was a yank then and the benign old cow turned into a crazed bull, sucking her arm up between its jaws.

A flash fire of shock and pain exploded at Violet's elbow joint and in her brain, and just as red-hot was her outrage: *But it's my birthday!*

RaeAnn, who was next to Violet on the floor, screamed, and Polly Ball, the only woman on the floor to have gone to college (she would have graduated from UNC-Raleigh with a degree in art history had she not been summoned home after her father died), thought: *that's the scream in the Edvard Munch painting.*

Violet too heard the scream even as she fainted, even as the weight of her falling body helped further tear skin from skin and bone from bone. When she woke up in the hospital, her stub-arm wrapped and bleeding like a rump roast in butcher's paper, the screaming was still inside her head—was in her head for more years than she cared to count.

When the morphine curtain lifted on her consciouness, her first thought was: *some sweet sixteenth.*

Violet should have known better; in her short history she had learned that expectations only deepened the disappointment that inevitably stained every special occasion—not that many were celebrated. In excavating her mind for memories of parties and presents, she'd only been able to dig up those concerning her sixth birthday, when her mother baked her a yellow cake iced with raspberry jelly and gave her a real present to unwrap. It was a rag doll Violet immediately christened Jellycakes, commemorating what she told her mother was "the best birthday cake and the best birthday doll ever ever ever *ever* made."

The remembrance of that lone celebration was ruined by what her mother did three days later, which was to run off with the pharmacist from Henson Drugs. Considering her robust good health, Erlene spent a lot of time at the pharmacy window; every other customer walked away tucking green or brown bottles of tonics and pills and elixirs into their purses or pockets, but all her mama left the drugstore with was a flushed face and a soft dreamy look in her eyes. Violet liked Mr. Gladstone, the pharmacist—he gave her root-beer barrels, and once a Henson's Drugs ("For All Your Drug & Sundries Needs") calendar with a picture of a kitten on it—but after he robbed her of her mother, Violet came to think of the druggist as the criminal he was; a man guilty of grand theft. She was a child at the time of the crime, hadn't even started the first grade yet. Ten years later, when Violet lost her arm, it occurred to her that this was not her first amputation, but her second.

Later, when she came to know how love can slam reason and responsibility to the mat as easily as a heavyweight takes down a bantam, Violet forgave her mother for running off (Yarby Gladstone did have nice clean hands, after all, and an entire set of teeth, or at least all of the ones that showed in a smile), but she never forgave Erlene for *forgetting* about her, for never sending a letter or postcard, for never sending for *her.* Mothers who disappear off the face of the earth leave their children feeling as if they've disappeared too; disappeared from everything they thought was certain and safe and true. Abandonment can be crueler to a child than death; Violet would rather her mama had died because at least a grave would have given her a place to visit, something to touch, something to talk to.

✳

THERE WERE FEW PEOPLE in Mount Crawford, Kentucky, surprised by the young Mrs. Mathers taking a permanent leave of absence; it didn't take any great power of observation to see that Violet's parents were as mismatched as a crow and a canary. Judd Mathers was Erlene's senior by fifteen years and had always looked older than his age; he was not yet forty when his wife left, and yet his long thin face was as creased as a bloodhound's, his black hair leeched to a lusterless gray. He was one of those men hobbled by his inability to exercise his emotions (except for anger), although Violet thought that in his stunted capacity, he really loved his wife. She remembered him smiling at her mama's jokes, watching Erlene with a shy delight when she put the corn bread on the table, crowing, "Ta-da!" or when she hung the clothes out on the line, grabbing his union suit and pretending to waltz with it.

What registered most on the young Mrs. Mathers's face when she looked at her husband was disbelief and impatience, as if she were always asking herself, "*How did I get here?*" and "*How soon can I leave?*" Had she not gone and got herself pregnant, Erlene would have laughed out loud at Judd's marriage proposal, would have swatted it away as if it was a black and pesky fly.

There was a certain flightiness to her mama that, even as a child, Violet recognized. The young (she was only eighteen when Violet was born), trim woman could be in the middle of kneading dough when she'd wipe her hands on the dish towel and dash out of the back door, calling out that she was going to town to see what was playing at the picture show, and would Violet mind punching down the bread when it rose? The little girl longed to chase after her but had learned early on that she was usually included in those things from which Erlene needed to escape. When her mother was in an affectionate mood, she might invite Violet onto her lap, but it wasn't long before the girl would be flung off, as Erlene would be distracted by chores or a sudden need to manicure her nails, to wave-set her hair, or dance to the crystal radio in the boxy little room she called the parlor.

Erlene was full of fun ideas—"Let's pick raspberries and have a picnic on Mount Crawford!" "Let's throw a tea party on the porch!"—and once or twice these ideas blossomed into reality, but most always Violet would be left waiting on the crumbling front steps, her eagerness bright as a balloon and just as sure to deflate. The bulk of memories concerning her mother were those in which Erlene stood her up (indoctrinating Violet early on into the sorry club of wallflowerhood), and yet the little girl believed her mama when she called her her "precious flower," *clung* to those rare terms of endearment, knowing they were proof of her love.

Violet made all sorts of excuses for her, but in her deep heart she knew that mothers who loved their precious flowers didn't leave them to grow up in a musty old house on the edge of town with a father whose personality vacillated between melancholia and meanness; surely Erlene knew how that would make a precious flower wither up and die?

Violet. It didn't take long for everyone to see that the child had been misnamed.

"Gawd Almighty," Uncle Maynard said the first time he saw her, "she's homelier than Tate Seevers!"

(Tate Seevers was the one-eyed World War I vet who lived in a shack outside the junkyard with his half-wolf dog.)

Uncle Clyde nodded. "Yuh, I reckon you'll see prettier faces in a horse barn."

These stories were gleefully told to Violet by her cousin Byron, who seemed to have an endless collection.

"My mama says only people with hexes on 'em got faces like yours."

"I heard your daddy says the only way you're ever gonna get a boyfriend is if he sends you to a school for the blind."

"Sit up, Violet, speak! Good dog."

The Matherses' back porch was the local speakeasy for Judd

and his brothers-in-law, who'd congregate there to drink the corn liquor Uncle Maynard showed some talent at making; but after Erlene left, her brothers never came around. It wasn't shame over their sister's transgressions (Violet doubted they *had* shame, over their transgressions or anyone else's) that kept them away; but their abandonment was double the hurt for her father, who not only lost his wife, but his drinking buddies. Violet didn't miss them at all—they were loud and crude, like most drunks—and she could easily live the rest of her life without her cousin Byron and the two gifts he so conscientiously gave her during each and every visit: the "Indian burns" that cuffed the girl's arms in welts and the constant taunts about her looks.

✳

"WHY DOES EVERYONE think I'm so ugly, Mama?"

A giggle erupted from Erlene's throat; she had an odd sense of what was funny and what wasn't.

"Violet, now put that away," she said, recovering her composure. "It's time for bed."

Erlene's interest in things domestic was minimal, but occasionally she'd bring out her sewing basket (made of willow, it was the sort of crafted object that would be sold years later as folk art for the kind of money its creator, a mountain woman named Gimpy Mary, never saw in her lifetime), and wanting to share something—anything—with her mother, Violet was determined to sew too. Like her father, she was good with her hands; they were quick and deft and seemed able to figure out things with little guidance from her brain.

Jabbing the needle in the handkerchief she was hemming for her father, Violet set it on the upended flour can that was her nightstand.

"And everyone does *not* think you're ugly," said Erlene, bringing the faded patchwork quilt up to her daughter's neck and crimping its edges. "It's just that, well, I suppose it's because you've got a chin that looks like it wants to pick a fight." She smiled, fondling the jaw that would have fit a man's face better than a little girl's. "You'll just have to work on your other attributes."

"What are 'attributes,' Mama?" asked Violet, liking Erlene's hand on her face, even as she disparaged it.

"Well, look at me: I'm pretty, but I don't stop there. I work on things, things like being smart and clever—who can tell a joke as good as your mama?"

"No one," whispered Violet.

"That's right. Plus, I'm a good dancer and have excellent grammar. Those are all attributes, just to name a few."

"Erlene," shouted Judd from the kitchen, "ain't we got more biscuits than these?"

The young woman sighed and got up as if she were an old lady whose bones hurt. She stood at the side of the bed for a moment, the light from the kerosene lamp throbbing like an ache against the wall.

"Don't say 'ain't,' Violet," she said finally. " 'Ain't' is a word that makes you sound like you don't care."

"Okay, Mama," whispered Violet, willing to do anything asked of her. "I won't ever say 'ain't.' "

She didn't either, until her mother left, until Violet realized that every time she disobeyed her absent mother, she felt a tiny jolt of power that let her forget, for a breath, how much she missed her. So she said "ain't" and did all the other things Erlene had told her not to: she chewed her fingernails and burped and didn't brush her hair and slept in her clothes. She became a dirty, tangle-haired, wild-looking thing; the kind of girl the school nurse always suspected as ground zero for lice and impetigo infestations; the kind of girl who found notes like "You stink!" and "Take a bath!" scattered like land mines inside her desk.

As the years passed, Violet became less a stranger to soap and water, but her improved hygiene couldn't deflect attention from her freakish growth surge: by age thirteen she was five feet eleven, and it didn't take Violet long to realize that height does a homely girl no favors.

"Hey, Stretch!"

"Look, a giraffe escaped from the zoo!"

"Hey, Olive Oyl!"

Puberty was not done playing dirty tricks either, deepening Violet's voice like a boy's and inspiring her tormenters to add the name "Froggy" to the many in their arsenal, or to ask why Olive Oyl had a voice like Popeye.

Every inch she grew on the outside, every bass note her voice registered, made her smaller on the inside. There were a few kindhearted children who tried to befriend the odd Mathers girl, but her mother's abandonment, her father's neglect and cruelty, and her own shame had worked like rust on Violet, corroding her ability to accept amity and eating away the belief that she deserved to have friends.

School was her one respite; Lord, to draw maps of places like Burma and Ceylon and write reports on their major exports! (Rice! Rubber! Hemp!) To listen to Miss Mertz recite (in a practiced British accent) "The Raven" with the window shades pulled! To figure out how many apples Farmer Brown harvested if he had an orchard of 350 trees and each tree yielded approximately 3.8 bushels!

She loved each and every subject, as was evidenced by her report card, on which without fail marched a straight row of A's.

Her father was not impressed. "So, you think you're pretty smart, don't you, gal? Think you're smart just like your ma, huh?"

Yes, Daddy, thought Violet, *being smart is what saves me.*

When she was thirteen and stomach cramps had sent her to the outhouse, she had nearly fallen through the hole in the rough board platform after seeing her underpants soaked through with blood.

Running into the house, she found her father at the kitchen table, examining the heating coils of a neighbor's broken toaster.

"Daddy, something's wrong with me!" she said, panic racing through her like an internal tornado. "I'm bleeding to death!"

Her father's long creased face paled, and as Violet sought

comfort in his arms, he set down his screwdriver and with both of his big grease-stained hands pushed her so hard that she would have fallen to the floor had not the edge of the kitchen counter stopped her. Still, the force of the push made her smack the back of her head against the cupboard, and she stood dazed and frozen, her disbelief melting into a puddle of resignation: of course her father would push her away even as she was bleeding to death, *of course.*

He stood up, not making eye contact with his daughter, whose own eyes, she was convinced, would soon be the blank and unseeing ones of a corpse.

"You ain't dyin'," he said. "You go ask Mrs. Mochler what it is you're doin'."

He tore out of the kitchen as if someone had called "Fire!" but as he reached the door he turned to her in one sharp move. "Now don't you . . . don't you be bringing any trouble into this house." He pointed the screwdriver at her as if it were a knife. "Don't you be doing anything like your mother."

Staring at the space he left when he banged through the screen door, Violet gripped the counter edge so tightly that when she finally let go, her fingers were as crabbed as the tines of a rusty old rake.

Mrs. Mochler, a farmwife who lived down the road, would have liked to set the poor girl down and reassure her, but she was in the middle of canning peaches, and the heat and steam and a baby who needed to nurse did a good job of vaporizing her patience.

"Violet dear, you're just changing into a woman is all. That blood'll come every month 'less you're gonna have a baby."

"A *baby*?" said Violet, wondering what on earth blood had to do with a baby.

Stirring the pot of peaches with one hand, Mrs. Mochler used the other to pull at her dress, pasted as it was to her back with sweat.

"I swan, Violet, a big girl like you don't know where babies come from?"

Violet shook her head, bewildered and embarrassed.

"Well, I s'pose then I'm—" began Mrs. Mochler, but her voice was drowned out when the baby in the basket by the sink cried out for her mama's breast, and Hyram, her two-year-old, pushed the box of jar lids off the table, where they clattered on the floor like dissonant cymbals.

"Honestly, Hyram, I swan I'll give you a whoopin'!" she said, and reacting to the threat, the little boy wailed louder than his sister. Violet knew all her questions would be ignored in the calamity of the household, and she slunk out the back door, watching the ground to see if any blood dripped on it.

She stuffed an old sock into her underpants and spent the afternoon at the Carnegie library downtown, and the most important thing she learned there was that she was never going to be in a position of not knowing again.

Understanding exactly what Violet needed from her urgently whispered, "I need to read a book about bleeding!" Miss Louise supplied the girl with a short stack of books from her "reference" library. While she did not believe in censorship, the young and pretty Miss Louise did believe in the immaturity and hooliganism of Mount Crawford's teenage boys and therefore kept the few books she had on human sexuality shelved behind the front desk.

Violet spent the afternoon reading, and learned that her low stomach cramps were a common accompaniment to menstrual periods and sometimes relieved by aspirin and hot-water bottles. She read about estrogen and testosterone, fallopian tubes and menarche, about foreskins and clitorises, sperm and ova, contractions and placentas, about premature ejaculation and orgasm, masturbation and homosexuality, about syphilis and gonorrhea, about frigidity. She pored over the pages like a precursor to Kinsey's copy editor, and when she returned the stack to Miss Louise, Violet felt years older than the thirteen-year-old who had walked in just hours ago.

"Thank you," she said, willing herself not to blush, something the librarian was unable to do herself.

"You're welcome," said Miss Louise, and as her face boiled

in a wash of pink, she said in her most businesslike voice, "Whatever your field of study, Violet, the library can always help you."

Preparing supper that evening—fried hash from the leftover pork shoulder a customer had paid for a recent appliance repair, and greens from the garden—Violet felt nauseated. Supper was twenty minutes of guaranteed misery; the one time she had to sit with her daddy and listen to him berate her or her mother or both, and now today—what was he going to say today? The words and phrases she had learned at the library swirled in her head; how could she even look at him, knowing that he knew about her, about the *onset of her menstrual period,* about *the shedding of her unfertilized eggs*? And how could she look at him when she knew he had had *sexual intercourse* with her own mother? Feeling light-headed, Violet closed her eyes, but when her father tromped into the kitchen, she steeled herself and served his dinner and then her own.

They ate in blessed silence, but just as Violet began to think she was home free, her father scraped up the last of the hash with a heel of bread and asked, "So you saw Mrs. Mochler?"

Violet nodded.

Judd Mathers took a swig of his preferred dinner beverage— corn whiskey (Violet didn't know who his supplier was now that Uncle Maynard wasn't around, but he'd found one)—and after emitting a short burp, his hand lunged outward, smacking his daughter's face.

Violet's hand cupped her burning cheek. "What . . . what was—"

"It don't have to be for nothin'—but in this case, it's to remind you not to be bringin' any babies around here."

A laugh gurgled out of Violet, surprising her father and herself.

"You laughin' at me?"

"No sir," said Violet, but her denial bobbled on laughter and he slapped her again.

He got up quickly, like a hired gangster who had rendered his hit and felt no need to check for breathing. He did offer one last thought, though, on the odd chance that he hadn't made her feel as low as possible.

"Just remember, you ugly mutt, your mother was a slut and they say those things are in the blood."

When the screen door slammed and Violet knew he was out of the house, she began to laugh again. *Those things are in the blood*—did he mean in the *menstrual* blood? Was he making that good of a pun? And when he had warned her not to bring home any babies—was he aware that she couldn't conceive by herself—that she'd need a *boy* to assist her, and was he aware that there was no boy in the county, no boy in the *state,* who would offer that kind of service? She leaned back in her chair, reveling in the laughter that shook her shoulders until it turned, as it often did, into tears.

You ugly mutt.

Sticks and stones may break my bones, but words can never hurt me. As many times (and it must have been thousands) as Violet said this to herself, she couldn't believe anything so asinine, not when she could feel each mean word cutting and bruising and hurting her more than any sharp stick, than any jagged stone, than even her father's fist.

Many times, her face hot from either his hand or his name-calling, Violet wished for his death, but if he would have opened his arms to her, opened his arms just once, there wouldn't have been a watch fast enough to measure the time it took to leap into them. She couldn't remember the last time he had touched her with something other than force, and finally, after having been rebuffed so many times when reaching out for him—honestly, he acted as if she were made of stickers and burrs, and every time she touched him, he was snagged by them—she put her arms down for good.

When the urge to hold another living thing became a necessity, she went to hug the river birch that grew by the creek behind the woodshed, pressing herself against the trunk and running her palms against the fissured, shaggy bark. It became her little joke to call it "Tree Pa," to accept as personal gifts its tiny yellow flowers in the spring, its cones in the summer.

If she could be sure her father wasn't banging around in the shed, she would have run to Tree Pa now, to feel the wind whispering through its leaves, telling her with each *whssh, whssh, whssh,* that it was all right, that she was loved.

Instead, she cleared the dishes, forcing herself, as the words to a popular song urged, to look on the bright side of life; reminding herself that at least she had a home (a mildew-smelling, rotting home that had been in the Mathers family for years) and at least she wasn't living in Tent City; at least she wasn't out panhandling for the spare change nobody had.

Judd Mathers was an excellent mechanic but a bad drinker, and even before the Depression closed down the farm equipment plant, he had drank himself out of a job. He made his living at the kitchen table, repairing appliances, or out in driveways or farmers' fields, bringing the engines of idled cars and tractors back to life, and every Wednesday and Saturday night, he cleaned the Methodist church, of which the family were not members. The Matherses were poor, but poor in those times was like being sunburnt in the summer: everyone suffered to some degree.

Along with her schoolwork, Violet tended the household and the garden, and in her spare time (of which there was plenty; the girl managed her chores with a quick thoroughness) she sewed; designing her own patterns out of newspaper. For fabric, she used tablecloths she bought for pennies at church rummage sales, or she would rip apart and then refashion the worn blouses and dresses she also bought at these sales, usually on bag days. (There was an Episcopal church in the next town over, and Violet made a point to attend their sales, finding the perspiration stains a little less conspicuous and the tears a little more repairable than the old clothes sold at the churches in Mount Crawford.)

The girls at school were too cowed by her status as an untouchable to compliment Violet on her fashion sense, but the teachers did, along with townswomen Violet passed on the street.

"What a smart outfit!" Miss Louise, the librarian, said time and time again, and every time Mrs. Rothman, the dentist's wife, saw her, she'd clutch the girl's arm and opine, "Violet Mathers, I swear you look like you just stepped out of the *Harper's Bazaar.*"

When Violet wasn't cutting, pinning, and stitching, she was drawing, and she was as good a sketcher as she was a seamstress. She filled pages with wardrobes a "woman of means" would wear, signing them "Fashions by Violetta," the name she decided to use when she became a famous designer. She reserved other pages for faces; nearly all her classmates and teachers had been surreptitiously caricatured, and a special section of a Red Chief tablet was devoted to likenesses of her father. Her portraits were not pretty like her designs; she liked to embellish them with scars or leaking wounds; she gave Marjorie Melby an excess of facial hair, while denuding Clint Ganz, the most popular (and meanest) boy in her class. Her father often sported horns, crossed eyes, or jagged pebbly teeth.

The third in her triumvirate of pleasure was reading, which was what Judd found her engaged in the day after school let out. On the porch, letting the sun warm her long legs, Violet was reading *Arrowsmith,* an activity that enraged the man. He couldn't articulate his anger, but if he could, he would want to know why this homely, lazy daughter of his could look so happy when life was nothing but one stinking misery after another. And what right did she have to think she was so superior, enjoying book learning like that? He grabbed the book out of her hands and threw it into the overgrown azalea bushes, telling her it was damn well time that she started bringing in some income, " 'cause I don't want you sitting on your scrawny can all day doin' nothin'!"

"Fine," Violet answered. It wasn't as if she hadn't worked—she watched the Mochler kids and sat with Mrs. Kilroy every Friday night so her daughter and son-in-law could get a reprieve from the old woman, who was sweetly addled and powerfully flatulent; she scoured the streets for returnable bottles and took in sewing—but the idea of a real job appealed to her. She considered counter help at Woolworth's, or selling tickets in the Bijou box office, but even if they had been hiring, Violet was intimidated by the jobs' glamour, deciding that if she was suited for anything, it was factory work.

Marcelline Threads was owned by Eugenia Demming Dodd, daughter of the company's namesake. Much later, people would have referred to her as a "feminist," but back then she was simply known as "crazy," writing editorials in the *Mount Crawford Messenger* about how the world would turn a whole lot easier if women were given their rightful place "*beside* men instead of *behind* them." ("You women won the right to vote," the usual rebuttals went, "what more do you want?")

Miss Eugie (she was Eugenia only on official documents) practiced what she preached, hiring as many women as she did men all through those Depression years; mostly women who were heads of their households, who'd lost their husbands to death or, more often, desertion. Normally Miss Eugie would have readily dismissed a teenage girl over needier candidates, but for a certain item of clothing Violet happened to be wearing.

"Excuse me," she said to the tall gawky girl filling out an application on a bench outside the reception area, "but may I ask you—who did that to my tablecloth?"

Violet looked around helplessly, hoping the stocky, meticulously dressed woman with the chic hat was speaking to someone else, even though they were the only two in the room.

"I . . . I . . ."

The older woman fingered the crocheted collar of Violet's blouse. "If I'd known something like this could have been done with it, I'd never have thrown it out."

And so Violet came to realize that the tablecloth she had remade into a blouse was the same tablecloth that Miss Eugie had donated to the Episcopal church's rummage sale.

"But it was all stained," said the factory owner, squinting over her glasses as she examined the blouse. "With turkey gravy. My girl tried and tried and couldn't get it out."

"Well," said Violet shyly, "I just cut around the dirty parts."

"It's exquisite," said Miss Eugie, shaking her head. "Look how you used the crocheted hem for the collar—absolutely exquisite!"

Pleasure was like a bubble bath, and Violet soaked in it; imagine having something she made be called *exquisite* not once, but twice!

Miss Eugie believed in hiring those who needed helping, but she also believed that talent and ingenuity should be rewarded, and so over a long list of applicants, most of whom had at least two children, Violet was hired.

✸

SHE STARTED WORK on the hottest night of the year, when the smell of perspiration curdled the already stuffy air, when moths banged against the caged light fixtures like convicts in a cell-block riot, when people's tempers were short fuses, lit again and again and again.

"Florence, how we ever gonna make quota if you don't turn that thing up!"

"Polly, I'm workin' feeder and that's all there is to it. Now move!"

"June, if you can't keep track of these spools, I'm telling Lamont, and don't you doubt it!"

Amid the noise of the factory and the hollered threats, the floor supervisor took his new charge over to a tiny little thing (she was nearly a foot shorter than Violet) whose hair was tucked into a kerchief on which was embroidered a picture of Niagara Falls.

"RaeAnn'll show you around tonight," shouted the floor supervisor. "You just do what she says and you'll be fine."

"I don't know about that," Violet thought, but when RaeAnn laughed, the trainee realized she had spoken aloud.

"Sorry," said Violet, "I'm just a little scared is all."

"Don't be," said RaeAnn. "This job's so easy, a monkey could do it."

The two got along like pork and beans, like Laurel and Hardy, like buttons and bows. RaeAnn was cute, in a pudgy, dimply sort of way, and at break time she took Violet's hand and walked her outside.

"I suppose you need a cigarette break," she said, and when Violet shook her head and told her she didn't smoke, RaeAnn said, "Oh, good, me neither! I just thought you did 'cause your voice is so deep!"

Violet felt herself closing up to the insult, but then RaeAnn added, "Sorta like Marlene Dietrich's! Anyway, all the other gals smoke—I tell you, you practically need a gas mask to breathe inside that break room!"

By the end of their shift, when the morning sun had already burned away the dawn, Violet had heard RaeAnn's entire life story. She was nineteen years old, the mother of a two-year-old boy named Silas whose father "lit out the day after I told him he was gonna be a daddy," and lived with her mother, "who, I swan, is just about the fattest woman you'd ever want to see. You'd think these hard times would make her lose a little bit of that weight, but nope; she's still bustin' up the springs in the sofa."

RaeAnn didn't show a keen interest in her new friend's story, which was fine by Violet, who much preferred the listening side of a conversation to the talking side.

Seeing that Violet hadn't brought anything to eat when they stopped (at 3:30 A.M.) for "lunch," RaeAnn unpacked her tin bucket and split everything inside it: corn bread soaked in molasses, cold ham, a slab of apple pie, and a jug of sugared tea.

"Did your mama make this?" Violet asked, her cheeks bulging with the sweet corn bread.

RaeAnn nodded.

"Well, no wonder she's fat. Who could stop eating food this good?"

RaeAnn shared her lunch every night after that.

"Heck, you're only helpin' me keep my figure," she said, waving away Violet's thanks. "You think I wanna look like my mama?"

Violet loved working the graveyard shift, loved feeling productive and capable running the machines, loved eating hush puppies and blueberry buckle as she listened to RaeAnn talk about how smart Silas was or what she should wear on her date with the hardware clerk. Sometimes they sat outside during breaks and sometimes they joined the others in the break room, and Violet didn't care that the smoke made her eyes water because her co-workers accepted her just as RaeAnn had and teased her the same way they teased each other.

"My gosh, June, look at them new shoes of yours. You thinkin' of goin' into nursing?"

"Oh, shush. They might be ugly but they're comfortable."

"I guess when your feet are as wide as a bread box, y'all gotta grab comfort where you can."

" 'Least my feet ain't as long as Violet's! What size shoe do you wear, Violet, a fifteen?"

The tall girl shrugged. "I don't know the size—but I gotta order them through a circus catalog!"

She could crack them up—with them, Violet let out all the smart remarks that came to her instead of swallowing them—and the more she made jokes at her own expense, the more the others defended her: "You're not ugly, Violet—look at your eyes! Man, what I'd give for eyelashes like that!" "You are not flat-chested, Violet, you're just delicately built!" "Would you rather have big old cow teats like mine?" "What's the matter with your chin, honey? It's just got character, that's all." "And don't even start complaining about your voice—it's got out-and-out sex appeal is what it's got; men like when a woman talks deep."

More than living up to her name, Violet, the precious flower, *bloomed*. She was part of an alliance, an all-girl crew wide-awake and telling dirty jokes or commiserating over broken hearts and empty bank accounts while the rest of the world slept. Not only did she have *friends,* she was *popular.* One night on break they even plopped an empty Maxwell House can on her head, crowning her "Miss Marcelline Threads," an honor she was qualified for, they explained, seeing as she was the only one who actually knew how to use the product they manufactured; the only one who knew how to sew.

"You're not just 'Miss Marcelline Threads,' " said Lula, gesturing at Violet's homemade blouse with its box neckline and fabric-covered buttons, "you're Kentucky's own Coco Chanel!"

As everyone raised their soda-pop bottles and coffee cups to cheer the new queen, RaeAnn whispered, "Plus you're so much fun."

Lula and June would play-fight over who got to sit next to her; Polly brought her copies of *The Saturday Evening Post* and *Time* ("Heaven knows," she whispered, "no one else reads around here"), and Violet spent just about every Sunday at RaeAnn's house, playing horsey and catch with Silas and eating her mother's wonderful cooking. Enid *was* huge, and her size made her shy, but it doesn't take long for damaged people to warm to one another, and hours passed as she and Violet laughed and chatted, slapping cards on the table, shouting, "Gin!" or sitting shoulder to shoulder and paging through the Monkey Ward's catalog, picking out the one item on each page they would buy, if they only had money. That summer was the happiest time in Violet's life, until her arm got cut off.

She was convinced some sort of malpractice occurred in that operating room, because while the doctors stitched up the ragged end of her arm (apparently she was "lucky"—there was enough skin remaining to avoid a graft), the Violet she had become that summer got sewn up too. Sewn up with stitches so tight that all the fun, all the laughs, all the friendliness had no chance of slipping out.

When RaeAnn and Polly and Lula came to see her (ignoring Lamont's orders to get back to work, they had kept a vigil in the waiting room), RaeAnn started to cry and Violet told her to get out.

"You think I need you to feel sorry for me?"

"Oh, honey," said Lula, her cool hand on Violet's forehead, "RaeAnn just feels so bad is all. Same as me and Polly. Same as everyone."

"And I don't need your pity either," Violet snapped. "And I sure as hell don't need a bunch of gawkers hanging around my bed."

RaeAnn came back the next day with a grease-splotched bag of Enid's fried doughnuts, and Polly brought a stack of *Look* and *The Saturday Evening Post,* but Violet yelled at them again.

"Can't you get it through your dumb thick skulls that I don't want to see you?"

RaeAnn came back a third time, and when she tried to tell Violet how Silas and Enid had been asking about her, the patient looked her in the eye and said she didn't care about Silas, didn't she know that?

"I don't care about stupid Silas or your tub o' lard mama or you, for that matter, RaeAnn. Don't you know I was only your friend because I liked the free grub?"

RaeAnn's sweet plump face collapsed under the blow of her words, and in that hospital room that smelled of chlorine bleach and overboiled broccoli, Violet lay there and watched it. She was nearly bursting with tears and apologies but waited until RaeAnn ran out of the room before she allowed them to erupt. She cried for a long time—for the friends she'd chased from her life, for her missing arm that was screaming at her to scratch it, to massage it, and for the screaming inside her ears that made no request, just screamed.

✸

BY THE TIME SHE WAS released from the hospital, school had started, and if little mercy had been shown a homely, lantern-jawed, five-foot-eleven skinny girl, none was shown a homely, lantern-jawed, five-foot-eleven skinny girl with one arm.

Wearing a sweater, the cuff of her left sleeve pinned to the armhole seam, she tried to pretend that she wasn't a circus sideshow, but her schoolmates weren't buying it. In the hallways, crowds dispersed at her approach. In class, talk stopped as the amputee made her way to her desk, her face blazing with shame as she fumbled open a book with one hand. Each teacher, with the exception of Miss Mertz, thought it necessary to begin the hour with a public welcome, making claims to Violet's bravery and promises that everyone would gladly pitch in and offer any help needed. Lunch was a humiliation; it hadn't been easy packing it in the privacy of her own kitchen, but unpacking it in front of a watchful audience was more than Violet could bear, and pretending she had forgotten something, she got up and ate outside on the front steps.

In assembly, the football coach gave a rousing speech about the team's chances, and as the students wildly applauded, Dewey Drebach leaned over and whispered, "Come on, Violet, show some school spirit. Clap your stump."

Even that, added to all the stares, all the nudges, and all the comments whispered behind cupped hands, was not enough to make Violet surrender. What made her raise the white flag was all that *and* the ringing in her ears. How could school be her refuge when the teachers' voices had to compete with the high-pitched buzz that came from somewhere deep in her skull?

She wasn't brave enough to leave during the coach's boosterism, but when the bell rang she walked, a frozen smile on her face, up the inclined aisle, through the main hallway, and out the door. She couldn't have ached less than Napoleon leaving France for Elba.

They took her back at Marcelline, but not on the floor. Miss Eugie set her up in the accounting office (Violet replaced old Doris Eames, whose glaucoma had caused her to misread one too many numbers), tallying time cards and remitting invoices. Working the day shift, she never saw RaeAnn or Polly or Lula, and her life closed up like a condemned building. Everything she loved and was good at—her sketching, her clothes designing, her sewing—had been taken from her. Every time she reached for a needle to thread, or a pencil to do a quick drawing, she was shocked anew; the hand she was reaching with didn't exist, and neither would Fashions by Violetta. At least she could still read; every day after work she went to the library, and at the table hidden away in the corner, she read almanacs and encyclopedias, journals and newspapers, amassing information, memorizing facts, collecting data. It was diligent reading, but joyless; she ignored the library's fiction section now, having no desire to be transported by characters who felt things other than anger or hate.

Bitterness grew inside her like a tumor. Her jaw ached from its constant clench, and it was only when she lay down to sleep that it relaxed, its hinges creaking like the shed door. The brief sun that had shone on her before the accident was in permanent eclipse, and Violet lived like a mole, in shadow.

If Judd Mathers didn't know how to be a father before the accident, he sure didn't know how to after. Violet thought she saw tears in his eyes when he first came to the hospital, but that was the extent of his sympathy, his first and only words about her arm being, "You shoulda been more careful—how you gonna work now?"

He still drank his nights away, but the liquor failed to embolden him in the face of Violet's temper, and he quickly learned that if he hollered at his daughter, she only hollered back louder. Meanness had grown like a weed inside her, taller and spikier than his own.

Two birthdays passed and Violet joined the world in not celebrating. She heard RaeAnn married the clerk at the hardware store and that June was promoted to floor supervisor. She offered congratulations to neither.

On her lunch hour one hot, still day in August, she deposited her check and studied the figure the teller wrote in her passbook.

"Chaw," said Violet, "that's a lot of money."

After the teller agreed, an idea, borne of a recently read newspaper item, took root.

"I'd like to withdraw all of it, please."

The teller, a moonfaced girl with a black mole that hunkered like a bug on her eyelid, looked up at her customer, surprised.

"You . . . you want to close the account?"

"Yes," said Violet, nodding her head. "Yes, that's exactly what I want to do."

The bank manager was called over, and when the transaction was completed, Violet went home and, for the last time, laid her hand on her river birch tree.

"I'm leaving, Tree Pa," she said, pressing her cheek against its trunk.

Whssh, whssh, it's all right, whispered its leaves.

She hugged the tree, and in her mind felt her missing left arm against the bark as surely as she felt her right.

Whssh, whssh, it's all right.

"No it's not," Violet whispered back.

In her bedroom, she threw some clothes, her sketchbooks, and her old doll Jellycakes into a frayed carpetbag she had bought at a tag sale.

Her daddy, sitting on the porch smoking his nasty-smelling pipe tobacco, asked her where she thought she was going.

"I don't know," said Violet, walking down the wooden steps. "I just am."

"You ain't coming back, are you?" he asked, and while Violet liked to think there was a trace of sadness in his question, she wasn't about to bet cold cash on it.

Not bothering to turn around, the girl said simply, "Nope."

Two hours later Violet Mathers was on a bus heading west. Her plan was to ride all the way across America to the Golden Gate Bridge, where she would admire the amazing engineering marvel all the newspapers claimed it to be. After her curiosity had been satisfied, Violet would join the man she'd just read about in the newspaper; the man who had chosen to traverse the bridge vertically instead of horizontally, and jump off it. There was no doubt in her mind that had she made it to San Francisco, she would have ended her life. But Violet only got as far as North Dakota, where, to her everlasting surprise, she started an entirely different one.

———

Chapter Two

HAVE YOU EVER HAD REAL CREAM WITH YOUR COFFEE? CREAM *that's fresh off the separator and sits on your spoon fluffy as a cloud? It takes your coffee to a higher plane is what it does—not like these little tubs of "nondairy" creamer. What knot-head decided to package "nondairy" cream anyway, and is it the same knot-head who named it "creamer"? But go ahead—don't not use it on my account. People your age probably don't even notice the chemical aftertaste.*

Other than the library, the only other place Violet visited after her accident was the Bijou Theatre, where she escaped to every Thursday night. Sitting in the soft darkness, she watched Jeanette MacDonald and Nelson Eddy, Myrna Loy and William Powell, Clark Gable and Jean Harlow, fall in and out and then in love again. She wasn't the type to be swept away by the stories—she had no patience for their usual happy endings—nor did she find these movie-star faces without flaw (although Mr. Gable came close to perfection); what Violet enjoyed most about the movies was that they allowed her to look at people without the burden of them looking back at her.

Being reminded of her ugliness by people and mirrors and class pictures (the only time she was ever photographed as a child); having her looks judged so mercilessly made her a severe critic of others', and she studied faces and bodies with a harsh and unforgiving eye. She did not agree, for instance, with the majority who thought Marjorie Melby deserving of "Class Cutie" year after year—could only she see that Miss Hoity-Toity's blond hair couldn't hold a curl, that her ankles were on the thick side, and that her turned-up nose wouldn't have looked out of place rooting around in a slop bucket?

Cora Eldridge, on the other hand, was old, but Violet didn't need to see her sepia-tinted wedding picture to know that she was the most beautiful woman in Mount Crawford. She had a long swanny neck and cheekbones that slashed across her face and a nose as pretty as Loretta Young's. Everytime Violet saw her shopping downtown, dressed up in her kid gloves and Lilly Dache hats, she felt a little zip of surprised pleasure; the same way she felt when hearing Gracie Allen's voice on the radio or when a breeze blew in the fragrance of apple blossoms or cut grass into her moldy-smelling bedroom.

Her daddy was a thin man, but he had beautiful shoulders; a wide span with a bump at each end where the bones knotted together. Mending the ripped shirt seams that Judd's big shoulders busted out of had been a regular chore of hers, and it didn't seem fair (although Violet had resigned herself to the fact that nothing was) that exaggeration in some things made them beautiful and exaggeration in other things (like her chin) made them ugly.

Hilda Breslau with her teeth that overlapped like rotting roof shingles, Marney Joel and her rickety legs and splayed feet, the post-office clerk with pouches under his eyes that looked like vein-filled dumplings—Violet noticed everything, her eyes were always working. It was a kind of sickness, the way she looked at people, like a portrait painter who wanted to capture the worst in her subjects.

The man who got on the bus in Indianapolis, for example, was running away from his wife, his kids, *and* the local authorities who wanted to question him regarding a double homicide. Violet could tell all this by his squinty eyes and jug ears, by the way his weak chin and the back of his head sloped into his clavicle and shoulders without bothering to leave room for a neck.

When he introduced himself as Pastor Ward Peele, she almost laughed out loud at the audacity of his alias, but instead she offered a short nod and a half smile (no sense riling up a murderous maniac) before turning to the window.

"Farm accident?" asked the "pastor."

Violet was surprised at how quickly he noticed her arm; she was wearing long sleeves and sat with her stump pressed close against the window to avoid the attention.

"Factory," she answered, still staring out the window.

"My deacon lost his foot to the diabetes. Still, he insists on carrying the collection plate every Sunday."

Suspicion narrowing her eyes, Violet regarded the "pastor."

"What's the fifth commandment?"

Ward Peele blanched, as if the girl had asked him to fondle her stump. Killing time, he coughed into his fat-fingered hand.

"Why, it's 'Honor thy father and mother that thy days may be long upon the land that the Lord has given thee.'" His shifty eyes narrowed. "Break it, did you? In need of a little confession?" He smiled, scratching the curled edge of his jug ear. "I won't give you a penance—I'm a Presbyterian, not a Catholic—but if it'll ease your heart to talk, I'll be happy to listen."

Chastened, Violet tightened her lips. It wasn't impossible that a criminal could know the fifth commandment, but the way Pastor Peele said it, earnest and teacherly, convinced her that shifty looks be damned, he really was who he said he was.

"No thanks," she said, not wanting any more conversation.

"Well, it's nice to know the Lord's words are in a young woman's head," said the pastor, giving her knee an avuncular pat. "Now if you're sure you're not in need of my ear, I think I'll take this opportunity to get a little shut-eye." He squeezed her fingers before bringing his hand back to his own lap. "We've got squirrels in the parish walls and those critters kept me up half the night." He tamped down his yawn with a fist. "Sounded like the little varmints were holding a square dance is what it sounded like."

He smiled at Violet before he shut his eyes, and she turned to the window and the passing green view. Some might think God himself had put a minister next to a girl who was on her way to her own suicide, but if it was providential, why did she get a man of the cloth (although, Violet had noticed, he wasn't wearing a collar) who only wanted to take a snooze? Not that Violet was looking for spiritual counsel, let alone *salvation;* in her heart of hearts, she knew that no one—not Aimee Semple McPherson or Billy Sunday or the Pope himself—could talk her out of what she had planned.

With a perfunctory "Bless you!" the pastor got out in Fort Wayne, leaving Violet with an empty seat until Chicago, when about a dozen people burst onto the bus like a modern-day James Gang. All they were holding up, however, was their own good spirits; they were a family of robust redheads, on their way to Madison, Wisconsin, for a reunion.

"Ma's family is from there," explained the teenage girl who assumed Violet was as interested in her family as she was. "Pop's from Chicago—he wanted to drive, but Beatrice—that's my sister over there by Ma and Will—she thought it'd be fun to take a bus. Beatrice's going away to college in the fall—Radcliffe, how do you like them apples?—and Ma says we've got to spoil her up a little now."

I could have gone to Radcliffe, thought Violet bitterly, hating Beatrice for being college-bound, and for laughing heartily at the joke her redheaded brother had just told her and their red-headed mother. What would it have been like to sit easily next to one's kin, sharing hair color and a sense of humor? Violet couldn't imagine it.

Her seatmate's prattling continued; her chatter was so constant and steady that it lulled Violet to sleep, and when the entire clan tumbled off the bus in Madison, shouting about who was going to ride with Uncle Butch and who was going to ride with

Uncle Bud, the bus was too quiet, or else the ringing in her ears was too loud.

If she could have anything in the world—a loving family, beauty, her arm back, or the buzzing in her ears stopped—Violet would have chosen the last without an iota of a second's thought. The first few weeks after the accident, when it still shocked her to scratch her right arm only to realize there was no left hand to scratch it with, she begged her doctor (the Marcelline Thread Factory paid for all her medical bills, and Miss Eugenia Demming Dodd herself chose the patient's doctor; he was, after all, the best in the state) to stop the ringing in her ears; didn't he know it was driving her crazy?

"Perhaps it was the severity of the accident that resulted in this manifestation," said the doctor, who put the P in pompous and then capitalized it for good measure.

"It's not a manifestation," said Violet urgently, "it's real—and I want it stopped!"

"The trauma you suffered is to your arm, Miss Mathers. Anything else we must look at as psychosomatic—"

"Psychosomatic?"

"An imagined ailment, one without biological basis."

"Are you saying that this is all in my head? That I'm just *imagining* this ringing?"

The doctor closed the file on his desk—he had all sorts of gestures that let her know his patience with his patient had been met.

"Miss Mathers," he said, "let me assure you that time and time alone will alleviate this so-called 'ringing.' " He smiled as if offering sympathy for the girl's profoundly low I.Q. "Now, I hope you've lost some of your stubbornness regarding your prosthesis?"

The willful patient shook her head; she hadn't lost a damn bit. Asking a girl like Violet to go out in the world like Captain Hook was asking her to bear more than she was honestly able. She'd rather give up the "increased usage" of her left arm than to be pointed at more than she was, to frighten children more than she already did.

She severely disappointed the doctor, in the way that all patients who dared to believe that he might not be God disappointed him: didn't the stubborn little hillbilly know the importance of His Word? But Violet remained adamant; she didn't get a hook, and she didn't get her ears fixed either.

"Mostly it's like bees," she told Miss Eugie, who sat wringing a handkerchief at the girl's bedside. "It sounds strange, but when it first started, I thought a swarm of bees had flown into my ears. Other times it's a higher-pitched, single note—like a really mad bee . . . or a crazy bird . . . or a dentist's drill." Violet fought off the urge to scream by closing her eyes tight. "Imagine that sound way down deep in your ears, inside your head. You know the relief you feel when the drill is turned off? That last spurt of whine and then you think, 'Phew, thank goodness *that's* over.' Only you don't get that relief, because it's never over."

During the first weeks of the ceaseless buzzing, the endless ringing, Violet's breath was shallow and rapid, making her feel claustrophobic whether she was outdoors or in.

"Maybe Dr. Mitchum is right," said Miss Eugie. "Maybe you need to try harder to *think* the sound away."

Violet's eyes were squeezed so tight her whole face looked distorted. "I'm trying," she said. "I'm trying to think the sound away . . . and all the stupid advice I get."

Miss Eugie blanched but she didn't move. She had volunteered at the Veterans Hospital during the Great War (she had more civic-duty plaques than she had wall space) and knew how grievous injury could harm the mind worst of all, and that when its victims lashed out, she was not to take it personally.

Still, she did; she felt tremendous guilt for Violet's injury and for the great potential that was snuffed out (before the accident, she had begun to make inquiries to dressmakers in Lexington and Cincinnati, trying to arrange apprenticeships for Violet), but underneath her pillows of sympathy were hard lumps of impatience.

For heaven's sake, wallowing in self-pity was not going to help matters! If ever there was time to stop feeling sorry for oneself, it was now! And this ear-ringing business: stuff and nonsense!

But Miss Eugie only advised Violet to get some rest, patting her blanketed hip.

"Sure, some rest," agreed Violet, but Miss Eugie didn't hear the sarcasm, only the words, and she smiled and patted Violet's hip again, proud of her bedside manner.

Turning her head, Violet pretended to sleep, even as the high-pitched whine went on and on, like a terrible vengeful hummingbird trapped inside her ear canal.

Over and over, as the weeks passed, she tried to dislodge the noise; she pounded at her ears with her open hand the way she used to after a swim in Cutter's Creek; she shoved her pinkie inside and tried to wiggle the noise out; she sobbed, hoping to out-cry the cry in her head.

"What am I going to do, Tree Pa?" she asked, clinging to the birch tree with her right arm. "How can I make it stop?"

It was a still, sunbaked day and there was no wind to blow through the leaves, allowing them to whisper an answer. Still, thought Violet, her eyes smarting with hot tears, I probably wouldn't be able to hear it over the noise in my head.

After a while she got used to it, but Violet never forgot it was there; it was as if she had a gash over her forehead that never healed, and every day she felt the blood trickle down her face, every day she felt the pain. The ringing in her ears didn't make her crazy in the carry-me-off-in-a-straitjacket way, but it wound her up tight and contributed a generous amount to the despera-tion that made her want to kill herself.

✳

VIOLET MIGHT NOT have been long for this world, but that didn't mean she was averse to exploring it; when the bus pulled under-neath the awning of a small-town depot and the driver turned around in his seat to announce a half-hour lunch or dinner break, she was always one of the first off the bus. She used these times not to eat the egg salad or hamburger sandwiches that were sold in the adjoining cafés, but to stretch her long legs by taking a walk. She liked looking at the local scenery, at the clothes in shop windows, liked the fresh air on her face.

In Winona, Minnesota, she walked along the banks of the Mississippi River, listening to the overlapping layers of birdsong filtering through the bordering trees. The sun was twelve o'clock high, and it was a humid hot that had sweat speckling her upper lip and trickling down her armpits. Still, being off that stuffy bus and moving under her own power, she felt like a colt free of its stable.

"Hey, sugar, where you headed in such a hurry?"

Thinking there was no one around but herself and the birds, Violet's upper body spasmed in surprise.

The man who wanted to know her destination was a hobo crouched under a weeping willow tree.

"Where I'm headed is none of your beeswax," she said, causing the grimy old man to gape at her in a toothless smile.

"None of my beeswax," he said, pushing aside a swag of leaves and stepping onto the path. "That's a good one."

Up close Violet could see he wasn't an old man at all, despite the lack of any discernible teeth. He leered at the young woman like he was a fox and she was a hen, and a flare of fear shot through her.

"Well, real nice talking to you," said Violet, forcing a smile across her face, "but I've got a bus to catch."

Before she realized he was close enough to touch her, his hand clamped on her shoulder.

"Where's a one-armed gal like you going anyway?" he asked, and Violet smelled the dirtiness of a man whose primary residence is a boxcar.

"I . . . I'm going—"

Before she could sputter out her itinerary, the man had included in his grip more of her body than her shoulder, and for a moment Violet felt she might faint, overcome by heat and fear and most especially by the pungency of hobo cologne: a heady blend of body-made odors—perspiration, dirty feet, shit, and urine, spiced with an alcohol accent.

His beard scratched her face as his mouth zeroed in on Violet's, and the bile wasted no time rising in the girl's throat. Pushing or attempting to push him away only made him laugh and tighten his grip.

"Hey, that stump of yours is pretty strong," he said, pressing himself against her so Violet could feel his erection against her pelvis. "Now why don't you just relax so's we can have some fun?"

Rigid with fear, Violet was ready to give him another push when suddenly she grabbed his face in her hands—one hand was on the left side of his face and her half-arm rested against his shoulder—and kissed him like they were lovers who'd looked forward to this riverside tryst for days.

It was the surprise element and it worked; he weakened in that kiss, long enough for Violet to send her knee up between his stained and greasy pant legs and then, as he yelped and hollered, to push him off. Frozen for a moment, Violet watched him stagger backward, and then, obeying her flee instinct, she began to run. The hobo lobbed cusswords but didn't bother to give chase; or at least Violet didn't hear his footsteps, and it wouldn't have mattered if she had; she was a fast runner, and when fear was in the quotient, Jesse Owens himself would have a hard time catching her.

In the bus-station ladies' room, she washed her face and gargled the bum's sour taste out of her mouth. She retched, and after drying her face on the thin gray cotton towel that looped down from the dispenser, Violet Mathers did something she hardly ever did: she looked in the mirror. Surprising herself even further, she did something she never did while looking in a mirror: she smiled. Using her brains and wiles, she had fooled that old dipso and fought him off. A wave of self-appreciation washed over the girl, but like all waves, it was short-lived, and by the time Violet boarded the bus it had ebbed into nothingness. She slumped into her seat, wishing the next stop was the bus's and her last: San Francisco.

✹

THE WIND FLATTENED the dry Dakota prairie grass as the bus rumbled toward the horizon, which was never more visible.

"Gracious, it's flat," Violet said to her seatmate, a barrel-chested man who'd introduced himself as "Norbert Claus, soybean farmer" who was on his way to Boise for his sister's funeral.

He nodded. "It's one of the states you can sleep through and not feel bad about missing the scenery."

Violet had resented Mr. Norbert Claus, soybean farmer, for sitting next to her when there were still vacant seats, but had come to appreciate his occasional commentary. When a screaming toddler had gotten off in Moorhead, he said, "One more mile and I would have gagged that young'n or tossed him out the window," and when he opened up his dinner pail, he said, "I can't offer you dinner at the Ritz, but how's about a piece of fried chicken?"

She helped herself to a wing, and when she licked her fingers, lapping up the last traces of grease, Mr. Claus laughed and said, "That's what I tell the wife: who needs napkins when we got fingers?"

"Well, since I'm short of fingers, I wouldn't mind the napkin," said Violet, and she flushed at the farmer's chuckle, so long had it been that she'd bothered to make someone laugh.

She accepted a drumstick—her favorite part—and wondered if other passengers might assume they were father and daughter. It was an assumption, she realized, she wouldn't mind them making.

The farmer shared his apple too, cutting it in neat wedges with his pocketknife, and then Violet leaned back in her seat and, feeling safe (an unusual state for her), fell asleep. When she woke up, the weather had turned.

The wind had picked up, yanking and pulling at the tassels of the corn like a playground bully. Gray clouds had chased away the white ones, and through the crack of the opened window, Violet could smell the beginnings of rain.

"Storm's comin'," said a man across the aisle as he lit a Chesterfield.

"Praise God," said a voice from the front.

"Amen to that," said Mr. Claus.

"Hey, ain't you gonna give me one?" asked the woman sitting next to the smoking man. She wore a straw beanie and a checkered dress that was so tight across the chest it looked like the left side of her bodice was playing tug-o'-war with the right.

"Just did," said the man, taking the cigarette out of his mouth and passing it to her.

The sky grew darker and a jag of lightning zipped down it, followed by a crack of thunder so loud that the woman in the beanie squealed a little protest and snuggled up to her man.

Seconds later the sky split open and rain came down in sheets. There was a scramble to shut the windows, and everyone looked out them with an awed silence, for it seemed they were no longer passengers on a bus, but in a submarine.

"What a beautiful sight," said Mr. Claus. "Lord, let it be raining like this on my beans."

Lightning and thunder took turns flashing and crashing and suddenly, as the brakes squealed, everyone was pushed forward in their seats and a bang big enough to break through the ringing in Violet's ears sounded, only it wasn't thunder, it was the bus hitting something. Luggage tumbled out of the overhead racks and people tumbled out of their seats and the girl in the straw beanie and tight checkered dress cawed like a crow, "Jim! Jim! Jim!"

Nobody was dead, but the driver did have a nasty cut on his head, an old lady's wrist was bent funny, and people were banged up enough to know they'd be awfully sore in the morning.

"The one tree in North Dakota and we've got to hit it," said Mr. Claus, holding on to his side as he looked out the front window.

"Think you can still drive the bus?" asked Jim of the driver, watching as the third handkerchief held to his forehead turned from white to red.

"If he can't, I reckon one of us can," said Mr. Claus. "That is, if the bus can still be driven."

"Why doesn't someone go out and see what the damage is?" asked the chubby woman.

"It's still raining," said Jim.

"A little water never hurt no one," said Mr. Claus, untying his shoes and taking off his socks. "I'd just as soon be moving as sitting."

"How come you're getting all barefoot?" asked a teenage boy, after he pulled a rubber poncho over his head.

"I got trench foot in the Great War," said the farmer. "Ever since then I just can't stand to get my shoes wet." He looked out the window. "And if I'm going out there, they're gonna get wet."

Violet and the teenage boy took off their shoes too and followed Mr. Claus down the aisle.

"Mama, that gal's only got one arm," said a young girl, pointing.

"Yeah, and you're missing your front teeth," said Mr. Claus. He smiled, but his lesson in manners was imparted nevertheless.

A grayish-yellow sheet of lightning mottled the horizon, and the chubby woman handed the farmer an umbrella.

"You don't have to come with us," said Mr. Claus to Violet.

Violet shrugged. "Like you, I'd rather be moving than not."

Like bugs under a mushroom, the three huddled under the umbrella while the rain beat a frenzied rhythm against it. Even though it was only half past six, it was as dark as midnight.

The front of the bus was mangled around the tree so that the beams of the headlights crossed each other instead of shining parallel. The boy, under the protection of his poncho, ventured a few steps to further inspect the damage.

"This bus ain't going anywhere!" he hollered through the rain.

"You're right about that," said Mr. Claus, looking at the

pleated hood that gaped open. "Radiator's pushed all the way into the engine."

The trio stood there for a moment as if paying respects at a grave site, and then Mr. Claus tapped on the bus door and the young girl with the missing teeth pulled the door handle and let them back in.

"How's he doing?" asked Mr. Claus of the driver, who was now sprawled across the front seat.

"Well, head wounds do tend to bleed a lot," said the chubby woman, who held a balled-up shirt to his forehead. "And this one's no different."

"I'm fine, I'm fine," muttered the driver, feebly waving one arm.

The passengers, clustered in the first few rows, looked at Mr. Claus, and sensing their need for a leader to replace the downed driver, he cleared his throat.

"We'll stay here until the rain lets up," he said, crossing his beefy farmer arms in front of his big farmer chest, "then a couple of us can walk to the nearest town for help."

"What if the rain never does let up?" asked the girl who'd opened the bus door.

"Rain always lets up," said Mr. Claus, "otherwise we'd all have fins and swim instead of ride buses."

It didn't take long for things inside the bus to get festive; having survived a bus crash, the passengers were in a giddy mood, despite, or maybe in addition to, the storm that raged outside.

"Anybody thirsty?" offered Jim, taking a flask out of his jacket pocket.

A woman in the back whose hair was rigged up in a bun so severe that anyone looking at it got a headache piped up, "I'm a Baptist woman and there are Baptist children on this bus!"

"Didn't ask no one what religion they are," said Jim. "Only asked who wanted a drink."

Jim's girlfriend, who'd introduced herself as Opal, "like the semiprecious stone," giggled and took the flask.

"Bombs away," she said, shuddering as she swallowed.

———

The Baptist woman and the children abstained, but no one else turned down the flask as it was passed around (the old lady with the broken wrist taking several robust sips). Because of her father's reliance on alcohol, Violet had vowed she'd never forge one herself, and in fact had never in her life taken a drink. But she was not about to be a party pooper at what was no doubt the last party of her life, and taking a swallow, she quickly realized, as the liquid set fire to her throat, that she hadn't missed out on anything. But the burning changed; stopped being a raw scorching and became a warmth, an ember glowing in her chest, and she thought, Boy oh boy, this feels *good*.

Food was added to the party when the chubby woman announced she had a pie she was bringing to her niece in Dickey.

"This is my blue-ribbon recipe, if you don't mind my bragging," she said, cutting slices with a pocketknife she borrowed from the teenage boy and serving people in their outstretched hands.

"I can see why," said Mr. Claus, who with his thumb steered an errant blueberry off his lip and into his mouth.

"Best pie I've ever tasted," said the driver, whose wound had finally stopped bleeding and who had gotten enough energy from his turn at the flask to sit up halfway in the front seat.

"Well, shoot, I wish I would have brought my brownies," said the chubby woman. "Not to toot my own horn, but I do believe they're even better than my pie."

"Mama, we got them cheese sandwiches," said the daughter of the Baptist woman who didn't look thrilled with the prospect of sharing her rations.

"They were for our supper," she said grudgingly as she divvied them up for the crowd.

Outside, the sky offered nothing but rain and darkness; inside, several flashlights were propped up to offer dim illumination. Mood lighting for a party—and it *was* a party, with laughs and music and even dancing (Jim and Opal swaying in the aisle as the teenage boy blew out "Aura Lee" on a harmonica he pulled out of his back pocket). Violet had to think back to RaeAnn's Sunday night get-togethers to remember when she'd last had so much fun.

When Mr. Claus announced that there were headlights coming toward the bus, everyone felt disappointed; rescue was here, only no one wanted to be rescued.

There was a rapping on the door, and the girl who had appropriated this part of the driver's job as her own, ran and pushed the door handle, and when the rescuer climbed up the bus steps, there was an audible gasp.

"Oh, Lord on high," said the Baptist woman, her hand over her heart, "it's a robbery."

"It's no such thing, ma'am." Violet was sure this was spoken by the blackest man ever to find himself on the North Dakota prairie. He was as shiny black as spit-shined shoes and everyone on the bus stared at him, most with their mouths open.

Of course there were Negroes in Mount Crawford (they even had their own business district on the south side), but Violet had noticed the farther north the bus went, the whiter the population had gotten, and these northerners acted like they were seeing a ghost, or the negative image of one.

"We—that is to say, my associate and I—were just coming up the road and saw the wreck. Anyone badly hurt? We've got a truck and we'll chauffeur anyone hurt—or anyone at all, for that matter—into town. Once we get there we can notify the authorities and enlighten them as to your predicament."

What in the world? thought Violet, who hadn't heard this kind of talk since she'd last seen Basil Rathbone in a Sherlock Holmes picture show. She looked the tall Negro over carefully; he had a broad face, close-cropped hair, and slightly bulging eyes.

"Why should we go with you?" asked the Baptist woman, the tip of her nose reddening as if she'd caught a sudden cold. "How do we know you and your 'associate' won't drive us into the woods and . . . and rob us and beat us . . . or worse!"

"Mama!" scolded her daughter.

The black man smiled, and his teeth couldn't have been whiter if they'd been whitewashed *and* bleached. In contrast to them, the whites of his eyes looked faintly yellow.

"Well, firstly, there aren't any woods around here, and secondly, you don't have to go anywhere with me. And my associate—if this eases your mind—is of the Caucasion persuasion, and our only aim is to help."

"You should take the driver," said Mr. Claus. "Have his head looked at."

"I'll go with him," said the chubby woman, and from the proprietary tone of her voice, it was evident nurse had fallen for patient.

"How many can you fit in your truck?" asked Mr. Claus.

"Eight or so could arrange themselves in the back," said the man. "We've got a tarp you can hold over yourselves but I can't guarantee a dry ride."

It was decided the driver, the chubby woman, Mrs. Baptist and her three children, the old lady with the broken wrist and her grandchild, would go.

"Woo hoo, I'm going for a truck ride!" said the old lady, who had helped herself more than once to Jim's flask.

"If we don't come back for the rest of you, someone else will," said the Negro, tipping his hat.

"What if he *is* a criminal?" asked Opal as they watched the truck's taillights recede into the black night. "What if all those people are being driven away to their deaths?"

"That's right," said the teenage boy. "I don't trust coons far as I can throw 'em."

"You got any better ideas?" said Jim, with a little smile stretching out of the exaggerated points of his upper lip. "Right now I'd trust a monkey if he could get me out of this predicament."

"*Tuh,*" said the teenager. "*Monkey's* right."

"Who's up for a game of gin?" asked Mr. Claus, and a group gathered around the soybean farmer while he dealt out cards on the tabletop their pressed-together knees made.

✸

SOMETIME LATER THE LIGHTS of a police car flashed swoops of red into the bus.

———

"Well, the jig's up," said Mr. Claus, putting down his cards. He gave a pointed look at the teenager. "Maybe that untrustworthy coon will oblige us and let you throw him. I for one would be very interested in seeing how much distance you could cover."

The boy's nostrils flared and his ears reddened dark as bricks, and Violet wondered if Mr. Claus would stick up for her if someone said something bad about her. Happily, she remembered he had.

There was a rap on the bus door and the teenager rushed down the aisle to open it.

"Evening, folks," said a man, the bill of his cap poking out like a duck's from the gathered edge of his poncho hood. "Sheriff Bill Flore here to escort you folks back to town."

"You mean we get to ride in a police car without doing nothing wrong?" asked Opal, grinning and batting her eyelashes as she silently asked, "Aren't I cute?"

The sheriff returned a smile that answered, "You sure are." Out loud he said, "Anybody we can't fit in the squad car is welcome to go in Kjel's pickup." He pronounced the name "Shell."

"Is Kjel the Negro?" asked Jim.

The sheriff laughed. "Nah, Kjel's as white as you or me. Now get your things and let's get going. The tow truck's not far behind."

The rain had lost some of its power but it was still falling as they drove into town, and as Mr. Claus discoursed about drought and crop yields, Violet watched Opal, who sat in the front seat between Jim and the sheriff, pressing her shoulder ever so surreptitiously against the latter's.

Hating to see that sort of thing going on, Violet sent a mental message to Jim: *Get rid of her now!*

Why was it that sex appeal was most often wasted on the treacherous? Violet had known about this injustice for years (in high school, Marjorie Melby trampled the hearts of boys the way Sherman trampled Atlanta), but still, it made her sad that Jim would be betrayed over and over by Opal, his semiprecious stone. Not that Jim struck her as a paragon of virtue, but he was nice enough to include her in the party when passing the flask, and Violet was always obliged to anyone who treated her like a regular person. If she ever had been lucky enough to have a man, Violet would have pledged her faithful heart to him, and thrown in her troth to boot.

She was in a blue mood, all right—even the bees in her ears seemed to be buzzing in a minor key—but instead of her usual dead feeling, this gloom made her feel tender toward herself. There she was, days away from her date with the Pacific Ocean, watching a master flirt do her business, knowing the only person she would ever kiss was a tramp who ambushed her on the banks of the Mississippi. There she was; a girl whose closest physical relationship had been with a birch tree!

Oh, Tree Pa, she thought, and then looking at the older man next to her, she thought, Oh, Mr. Claus! How could she thank the farmer who'd treated her more kindly in eight hours than her own father had in years? What a good daughter she would have been to him; she wouldn't have needed her river birch had she been lucky enough to have Mr. Claus for a daddy.

"Well, here we are," said the sheriff, slowing the car. "Beautiful downtown Pearl, North Dakota."

"I should live here," piped up Miss Jezebel, "being an Opal and all."

What there was to the town was hard to see in the dark and rain, and the displaced bus passengers were hustled into what looked like a small storefront but proved to be the sheriff's office.

"Please use the boot scraper," said the young deputy at the desk, looking at all the muddy shoes. "Sheriff makes me do all the mopping."

"Cyril thinks his job as deputy has far too much housekeeping and far too little crime-busting." Looking around, the sheriff brushed water off his shoulders. "Where is everybody?"

The gangly young man stood up, revealing pant legs that had been outgrown about four inches ago. "Well, the Ralph Peasleys came by and took four of 'em, and the Fred Peasleys took the rest."

"We did have a hotel once," explained the sheriff, "but it burned down in—when was that, Cyril?"

"Nineteen twenty-eight, Sheriff. I remember because we had our senior banquet there just a week earlier. It was sort of our claim to fame; we were the last senior class to eat at the Foxmore. It's a shame too, because they had real good food."

"Nobody could make a pot roast like Winnie at the Foxmore." For a moment the sheriff let himself be lost in a reverie that included mashed potatoes and gravy and a side dish of stewed tomatoes. He shook his head, getting back to business. "Now don't you folks worry. Agnes—she's our phone operator—put out the word that we've got some stranded travelers, and the citizens of Pearl are volunteering to put you all up for the night."

Violet didn't know the details of which bus passenger went home with what Pearl resident, although she did see Jim and Opal pass themselves off as legally wed when a sweet old man said he had enough room for a married couple (Opal blowing a kiss to the blushing sheriff as she traipsed off in her tight checkered dress and straw beanie), and the teenage boy was able to convince the sheriff to let him sleep on the jail cot ("I'm John Dillinger!" he said, firing bullets from his fingertips, his teenage toughness shrinking into a little-boy swagger).

Maybe the bus driver and the chubby woman with the knack for nursing *and* baking were taken in by the Ralph Peasleys, who would witness the couple pledge their undying love to one another at the breakfast table; maybe the Fred Peasleys took the strict Baptist family with plans to teach the mother the Lindy and the kids stud poker. Maybe Mr. Claus (who squeezed Violet's shoulder in a half hug and said, "See you in the funny papers!") shared a home with a fellow farmer who'd invented a new hybrid of wheat or barley that Mr. Claus would test out in his parched and underperforming north forty.

And Violet? Who took in the homely one-armed gal? Only the man who was to become her world, her breath, her reason for being, her light, her hope, her wide-opened and multicolored everything.

It sure made a person believe in bus travel.

———

Chapter Three

MAYBE IT'S BECAUSE OF MY NAME, BUT SOMETIMES WHEN I LOOK *back on my life, I picture a garden. The life of Violet Mathers, landscaped. Through a long stretch it is dark and weedy and full of withered plants that stick you or ones that never got to flower, but keep looking—you might notice a smattering of roses (my mother's touch on my face, her voice), some daisies (the way I felt in school when I won the fourth-grade spelling bee), and look, a whole camellia bush (the first dress I designed and sewed)! And up a little farther, why there's barely room to walk, so lush and bright and dense is the flora.*

And those waxy white blooms scattered throughout my garden? Gardenias, of course, which represent all the times I said yes in my life, even when it might have been easier to say no.

Gardenias are a complicated flower; many find their scent cloying, but I find it intoxicating. So even though my garden's got plenty of roses, lilies, petunias, and pansies; poison ivy, dandelions, and cacti; the scent of gardenias is the pervasive one. I must say I'm proudest of these flowers, my badges of bravery, my choosing yes.

Oh, that? You would have to notice. Those are stinkweed plants. They represent envy.

———

Yes, I know there are a lot of them. But are you telling me if I strolled through your garden there'd be nothing but apple blossoms and orchids?

Violet had sat down at a table with a woman so obese that she had to arrange, like an upholsterer, the folds of her skin to fit in a chair; she had sat down at a table with a man who didn't feel the need to say grace, yet was compelled to say "Your whoring mother" at least once during every meal, and she had sat down at a table with a half-dozen women at three-thirty in the morning and witnessed an argument so volatile that the debater claiming that Coca-Cola douches were a reliable form of contraception threw a fried bologna sandwich at the debater who was convinced they were not. Breaking bread with Enid, her daddy, and—literally—with Lula and June were not typical dining experiences; still, there was no place in Violet's imagination that could have conjured her sitting down at a table with a bug-eyed Negro named after a Texas town and the man who had made her do something she had never done before, which was to fall head-over-heels, howl-at-the-moon, in love.

"How about some more scalloped corn, dear?" asked Mrs. Hedstrom, who bustled around the big farm kitchen exactly the way Violet always pictured a mother should.

"Why thank you," the girl said, her voice a whisper. A blush burned across her face; she'd been having these attacks of reddening heat ever since Mrs. Hedstrom's son had first spoken to her.

"I never did taste corn made in quite this configuration," said Austin, the man who had been the first rescuer to step on the bus. "Excellent, I must say."

He was a loquacious fellow who believed if there was a lag in the conversation, it was his job to fill it.

"I've a sister named Odessa and two brothers: one named Beaumont—now sadly departed—and the other, Dallas," Austin had explained at the beginning of the meal. "Our mother had a fondness for Texas, although I cannot explain that particular partiality." He paused for a moment, carefully pushing peas onto his fork with his knife. "Now you, Violet. Might you have sisters answering to Pansy, Daisy, or Rose?"

Despite her low status in Mount Crawford, at least the coloreds there addressed her as "Miss," and Violet resented the man's familiarity.

She shook her head. "No, I'm an only child."

"There's nothing wrong with a garden with one bloom," said Austin, to which Kjel let loose a peal of laughter.

"Garden with one bloom," he said. "If ever I've heard a man who should be up at the pulpit, it's you, Austin." He shook the salt shaker over his plate. "Isn't that right, Pa?"

Mr. Hedstrom smiled. "The church could always use good speakers. Lord knows I've struggled with my sermons."

"You'd never know it," said Mrs. Hedstrom, brushing her husband's cheek with her fingers. "It'd be hard to find a more faithful flock than yours, Esben."

"Well, I do admit we had a big crowd Sunday, but that's because all the young ladies heard Kjel was back in town."

"They were just trying to collect on all the money I owe 'em," said Kjel, and he and his parents laughed, and Violet was too astonished at what was going on around her to do anything more than stare at her plate.

There she was, eating a late supper in a kitchen with starched curtains and a ceramic cookie jar shaped like an apple, at a table not scabbed over with cigarette burns, but decorated with an embroidered runner anchored in the middle by a vase of zinnias. (The only centerpiece to ever appear on the Matherses' table was a jug of whiskey and an ashtray.) And the food! The fresh peas and the scalloped whatever-it-was corn, and deep pink ham and a lettuce and tomato salad with a vinegary dressing that startled Violet with its tang. Light and fluffy biscuits (disproving Mrs. Mochler's claim that only southerners could make light and fluffy biscuits; she said you could play baseball with the ones northerners liked) with butter churned that morning and jam Mrs. Hedstrom made from gooseberries she got from her sister in

Minnesota. There she was sitting in a kitchen with a pastor who joked about his sermons, with his wife who kissed him openly, and who both welcomed a colored man and a one-armed girl into their homes as if they were visiting royalty.

And then there was their son. He was taller than Violet (a lot of men weren't) and had a face her critical eye could not criticize. A shaft of wheat-colored hair striped with blond dipped over his forehead, and while every feature of his face might not take the blue ribbon in a competition (his nose was too short, his bottom lip too full), together they made up one of those wildly hand-some, slightly boyish faces that made good girls rethink the value of being good and bad girls want to stay that way.

But it's his eyes, thought Violet, I could get lost in those eyes. Sitting across the table from him, she was astonished to see that one was blue and one was green and their difference wasn't slight—the blue eye was *blue* and the green eye was *green*. There was a slight cast to his green eye too, but Violet didn't notice that until she was brave enough to look at his face longer than a quar-ter second.

✳

FOR THE FIRST TIME in her life, Violet Mathers slept in a guest room.

"This is Berit's old room," said Mrs. Hedstrom, turning down the chenille bedspread. "It gets such a nice breeze in here." She smoothed a pillowcase across whose edges were strewn an embroidered chain of daisies. "It's cool now because of the rain—isn't it *wonderful* we finally got some rain?—but still, I think a person always sleeps better when there's a breeze in the room, don't you?"

Violet's head bobbed in a nod.

"Well, you have a good night, dear," said Mrs. Hedstrom, and then further adding astonishment to a night that had been one surprise after another, she squeezed both the girl's upper arms and gave her cheek a kiss.

"Sweet dreams, Violet," she said, crossing the room. "Oh, and remember, when you use the biffy, jiggle the handle after you flush. They called it 'progress' when we got our indoor plumbing, but that bathroom's given us more trouble than Father Brady." She giggled then, and Violet smiled back at her, as if she understood the joke.

It had been almost ten by the time they'd finished off the strawberry shortcake that was their dessert, and when Mrs. Hedstrom had told Violet she'd show her her room, Violet hadn't protested; as much as she didn't want to leave Kjel, the effort she had to make *not* to stare at him, *not* to somehow touch him, had exhausted her. To be polite, she asked to help with the dishes (she could manage washing all right; drying was a little more difficult), but Mrs. Hedstrom had shooed aside the girl's offer, saying the boys would do it; it was late and the womenfolk needed their beauty sleep.

That'd be a mighty long nap for me, Violet thought, certain everyone else was thinking the same thing.

She lay under sheets that smelled of sun and grass, listening to the crickets chirp their percussion over the bees droning in her ears. The black rain-washed sky was speckled with starlight, and a crescent moon balanced itself on top of the barn roof. The nice breeze that her hostess had promised gathered up scent from the rosebushes and blew it through the open window.

Shivering with giddiness, she turned to the doll who lay next to her on the pillow. "So what do you think, Jelly? How in the world did we wind up here?"

The homemade doll's flat face stared up at the ceiling with her button eyes. She had no answer, but then Violet hadn't either; all she knew was that after eating the best meal of her life, she was about to fall asleep in the cleanest, most comfortable bed she'd ever been in, while somewhere nearby was the man she didn't know but already loved.

"Somewhere nearby" proved to be close when Violet heard a soft laugh and a guitar strum. A few notes were picked off the guitar, shortly joined by a sweeping wail of a mouth organ, and then a voice rose up and wandered into the room and Violet couldn't have been more hypnotized if Mesmer himself had ordered her to look into his eyes.

"Good golly," she whispered, squeezing Jelly's rag-filled body to her chest as she scrambled up into a sitting position. "Have you ever heard anything like that in all your life?"

The voice was deep and mournful and yet there was a sense of play underneath it, a sense that after the singer was done crying about the woman who scorned him, he might recall how she'd once passed gas while they were on the dance floor, or how her eyes would cross when she'd pull apart the split ends of her hair, and remembering these things, he'd laugh. It was a voice Violet didn't just want to hear, but wanted to sit in, to wrap around herself like a blanket, and she slunk out of bed and sat to the side of the window, not wanting, as usual, to be seen.

They were on the back porch, the two young men. When Violet's eyes adjusted to the dark, she could see Kjel sitting on the porch railing, see that it was he who was playing the guitar and singing. *Of course,* she thought. Not only was he at the head of the line when they passed out looks, he'd also been first when they were doling out talent. Every day, life seemed to get a big kick out of reminding her how unfair it was, only now her usual sting of resentment was replaced with a sense of awe; there she was in North Dakota being serenaded (what was the harm in dreaming?) by a man who looked like Gary Cooper, only prettier, and sounded like Bing Crosby, only wilder. It was enough to give a gal chills, and it did, and Violet rubbed her stump where the gooseflesh had risen.

When he wasn't playing the harmonica, Austin picked up another guitar and sang in harmony, and Violet listened to them sing and play, realizing when they stopped to go over a passage or sing a different line that they were singing original music. She hadn't recognized any of it and yet it sounded familiar, the way good music will.

After his wife ran off, Judd Mathers had thrown out everything that reminded him of her, except the treadle sewing machine. (He was, after all, a practical man who had Violet doing sewing repairs by the time she was big enough to reach the pedal.) Included in his purge was the crystal radio, which he took pains to chop up with his ax. Deprived at home, Violet sought out music everywhere she could; listening more intently than other young girls to the bluegrass and John Philip Sousa marches that were played in the town-square band shell during "Mount Crawford Days." She went to the movies for many reasons, and music was one of them; she'd see *Flying Down to Rio* or *Top Hat* or *The Little Colonel* as many times as she could, and she'd sing the songs she memorized; loudly and joyfully to the world as she walked the country road to the Mochlers, or softly, to herself in bed, after her father had ignored her or scolded her or smacked her. Even though her deep voice could barely climb two octaves without cracking, it could climb them on key, and she certainly would have sung in the school choir had Mr. Garret, the choir teacher, not positioned her by height, in the back row with boys who, more than singing, enjoyed poking her and mocking her voice by making frog noises.

Violet did sing loudly, happily, at the Sunday-night gatherings at RaeAnn Puffer's house, but after her arm was cut off and she went into exile, the urge to sing, like the urge to do anything joyous, withered away.

When she was transferred off the floor of the thread factory and into the accounting office, Miss Eugie had presented her with a radio.

"Just keep it low enough so it doesn't bother Mr. Pfitzer," she had said, nodding toward the old accountant who sat at his desk fiddling with his suspender buckles or rolling his wiry eyebrow hair between two fingers when he wasn't writing down figures. Since anything said to Mr. Pfitzer was answered with, "What'd you say?" Miss Eugie added, "which means you could turn it up full blast, I reckon."

Violet had heard all kinds of music on that little radio but none like the music she was hearing now.

"Your love's so mean and dirty, it just ain't fair—
Love should be sweet, girl, like a . . . like a big juicy pear—"

Kjel plucked a twang from his guitar and stopped singing. "Nah," he said, "let's try it again."

They played a few bars before Kjel began singing again.

"Your love's so mean and dirty, it just ain't fair—
Love should be sweet, girl, like a—"

"Like a chocolate eclair," Violet whispered.

"Like a . . . nah . . . Love should be sweet, without a care." There was a moment of silence, and then the sound of a hollow bump as Kjel set down his guitar. "Dang it all, why don't we call it a night? I'm getting a headache thinking up all these bad rhymes."

"It would seem," said Austin, "that the muse has abandoned us."

A little flare lit the night and the end of the men's cigarettes, and they smoked for a while in silence.

"Muse, muse, here muse," said Austin, as if calling a dog. "Where are you, girl?"

"Far from here," said Kjel. "And you'd think she could hear how bad we need her." After a moment he added, "Hey, we could always pretend it's Violet."

The tip of Austin's cigarette glowed as he inhaled. "No," he said, his laugh riding out on a trail of smoke, "No, my muse has a voice like an angel—not an archangel. And my muse would win beauty contests. That gal wouldn't."

"Not even a one-armed one, I reckon," said Kjel, and as they laughed, Violet's heart, which had been enjoying a little holiday outside its black pit, plunged right into it again.

"Bastards," she mouthed to the open window. She crept back to bed and held Jelly in a breath-strangling hug, finding no warmth at all under the clean-smelling covers.

A gust of wind teased the curtains but Violet didn't smell the

---

roses in it, or the wet grass; everything that she had fooled herself into thinking was beautiful was ugly again, small and dark and ugly, and she called herself a dozen names, mostly ones that included the word "stupid," scolding herself for believing her world could be anything different.

She didn't sleep well that night; her thoughts an unquiet bedmate, jabbing her awake, and by the time dawn began tiptoeing over the fields in her pale pink skirt, Violet had made the bed (it was important to her that Mrs. Hedstrom knew she had manners, even if her son had none), packed her worn carpetbag, and was stealing out of the house, quiet as the shadow she was.

Not wanting to make noise in the indoor bathroom, Violet used the outhouse, resisting the urge to page through the Sears catalog. She didn't dare use the pump to wash her hands, and so she wiped them in the wet grass and then gave her face a cursory swipe.

She raced across the yard, and by the time she got to the road, her shoes and the top of her trousers were soaked clear through from the dew on the wide lawn. She wondered what her feet would feel like when she plunged into the Pacific, would they feel wetness, or only impact? Would she even be conscious when she hit the water? It consoled her to think of her suicide, to think that there was going to be an ending to this life that sadistically had teased her with a taste of something wonderful, only to snatch it away, leaving her with her usual heaping helping of pain and disappointment.

Remembering that the town and the bus station were east, she began walking toward the sun. The air was chilly, but in it Violet felt purposeful, knowing that her own motion, with help from the rising sun, would soon warm her up. A hawk swooped and glided in a private air show above her, and a bull bellowed from a distance in a pasture; more a hello than a warning.

But so big was her self-loathing that the pleasures of a country morning escaped her: how could she have mooned over Kjel like that, thinking that he was somehow different than any other bastard? How could she think she'd ever be more than a joke, an object of pity to a man like him, when she could never be more than a joke or an object of pity to *herself*?

When she ran out of names to call herself (and the list was long), Violet began counting her steps, with only an occasional editorial comment.

"Ten, eleven . . . sixty-three, sixty-four . . . soon I won't be anymore . . . five hundred seven, five hundred eight . . . death soon will be my fate . . . four thousand twenty-one, four thousand twenty-two . . . with this life I'm finally through."

She was up to nearly six thousand steps and had made more rhymes about death and doom than she could count when she heard the *clop clop clop* of horse hooves behind her. A farmer making his rounds, she assumed, and preparing herself to answer his greeting, she gritted her teeth in a smile.

"Hey, Violet," said Mr. Kjel Hedstrom, pulling back the reins of an old brown workhorse. "Where you headed in such a hurry?"

Surprise leaped up from Violet's stomach to her throat. "Kjel! What . . . what are you doing here?"

He patted the graying mane of the horse. "Old Mo here doesn't get out much, so I thought I'd take her for a little stroll. And you? Where're you off to?"

He smiled, and his smile was just another bonus on his already beautiful face, and Violet's body forgot her mind's directive that she hated him; her knees liquefied, her heart hammered, and all the music in the world struck one glorious note that sang out, "Yes!" even though that wasn't the proper response to his question.

"I'm going to the bus station," she said, far more pragmatic than the world's music.

"It's eight miles to town."

"I reckon I already walked two or three of them."

"Come on, Violet, let me take you back to the house. I know my folks would like to give you a proper good-bye—and besides, there's a stack of pancakes on the table with your name on it."

"I ain't hungry," said Violet, starting to walk.

———

In one quick swoop Kjel dismounted and, leading the old horse by the reins, fell in step with the not-so-happy wanderer. Violet struggled to breathe the air her lungs no longer had room for.

"What happened, Violet? Why are you running off like this?"

Not about to be fooled by this patronizing sincerity, the girl set her mouth in a tight line.

"Violet?"

She had every intention of never opening her mouth again, but words forced their way out of the unlocked trapdoor her mouth proved to be.

"I . . . I heard what you said about me last night."

Kjel's eyebrows crinkled.

"What I said about you?"

Humiliation acted like a fever, and Violet felt the spike of temperature on her face.

"Last night—out on the porch. After you'd quit singing." Her eyes stung with tears. "Your colored friend said I had the voice of an archangel. Then he said I'd never win a beauty contest, and you said, 'Not even a one-armed one.' "

This time it was Kjel's turn to blush, and Violet watched his Adam's apple bob down the length of his throat and then back up again.

"Aw, Violet, I'm sorry you had to hear that." He ran a hand through his sun-streaked hair. "I didn't mean anything by it. I was just making a joke."

"Yeah, you and the rest of the world." She laughed, a bright, tinny laugh. "Violet Mathers—Miss Butt of All Jokes, 1937." She gave an Al Jolson wave with one hand. "Hey, that's a contest I *could* win—Miss Butt of All Jokes! No, wait a second; that's a contest I've been winning all my life."

She had never spoken so freely about herself to anyone, let alone a man like Kjel Hedstrom, but like a convict minutes before facing the firing squad, she felt a panicky urgency to talk, to make a final case for herself.

" 'Hey, Violet, take off your mask. It ain't Halloween.' 'Too bad you didn't buy your face at Drentlaw's Dry Goods—at least they got a return policy.' 'Hey, Violet, wanna play fetch?' "

Her voice rose and lowered as she impersonated the many who had teased her. "And then add a mother who ran off when I was only six, and throw in a daddy who'd just as soon slap me as kiss me, and . . . are you getting the picture yet, Mr. Kjel Hedstrom? Are you getting just the slightest picture of what a barrel of monkeys it's been for Miss Butt of All Jokes?"

Even though Violet was shocked at her outburst, she was pleased that Kjel looked wounded; it gave her a feeling of power that she had made him look that way, that she was able to smite him with one one-zillionth of the hurt that had been hurled at her.

They walked a long piece, the silence broken only by the sounds two humans and a horse make on a dirt road. Anger, embarrassment, and shame boiled inside Violet, transforming into an adrenaline that made her want to bolt, yet stronger than her need to flee was her need to hear Kjel apologize—could she for once get one simple apology?—more than he already had.

"Violet—Violet, are you all right?"

What's he asking me that for? she wondered. Where were his contrite words, his agreement that, yes, things must have been awful tough for her?

She glared at him, and in return, Kjel offered the kind of smile people give when they don't know what else to do.

"It's just that you . . . well, you were going like this." He scrunched his shoulders until they met his ears. "And your face was like this." Squinting his eyes, he pulled his mouth down.

"What else?" Violet snapped. "What else can I do to repel you?"

She couldn't believe it; she knew she was ugly, but it did her no service to see him mimic her ugliness.

"Cripes, no, Violet. It isn't . . . it's just that you looked . . . well, you looked like you were in pain." He reached out and touched her stump, and she gasped as if she'd been electroshocked.

"Sorry," said Kjel, wide-eyed. "I . . . I didn't mean to scare you."

Like a nasty virus, a sudden weariness struck Violet, and energy drained out of her like water out of a broken main.

"I . . ." The simple syllable struggled up her throat. "It's just that . . ."

"What, Violet? It's just that what?"

He stopped walking and the old horse snorted its disapproval.

"Well, I . . . it's just that there are these . . . these bees in my head."

"Bees in your head?"

"Not real bees—I'm not crazy, for Christ sake."

Kjel's voice was soft. "I don't understand what you're saying, Violet."

"I have this ringing in my ears! Sometimes it's like a drill or a bird but most of the time it sounds like a bunch of bees and sometimes it gets so loud I can barely stand it!" Her voice was sharp with impatience. "That's probably why I was making that face, *okay*?"

Kjel stood there looking at her, and because she was afraid to look in his eyes, she stared at the old nag's front leg, bent and posed like a showgirl's.

"Your ears have been ringing?" said Kjel, as if he still wasn't comprehending what she'd told him. "For how long?"

"Since my arm was cut off," she said miserably.

"And when was that?"

At the dinner table, Reverend Hedstrom had gently asked Violet what happened to her arm, but after Violet's brusque reply—"Factory accident"—everyone had been too polite to ask for details.

"Two years ago."

Kjel whistled. "And it never goes away?"

Violet shook her head. "Sometimes I don't notice it as much, but other times I can't notice much else."

She was still staring at the Busby Berkeley horse, but out of the corner of her eye she could see Kjel shaking his head. Violet had never told anyone but the doctor and Miss Eugie about her ears ringing—didn't she have enough against her without people thinking she was crazy too?

"How does it sound?" he asked.

"Huh?"

"The ringing. How does it sound?"

Looking at his face, expecting to see mockery in his eyes, she saw concern instead.

"Well, it changes; sometimes it's higher-pitched and just one note, and sometimes—like now—it's more a swarming sound. Like I said before—like bees."

"How does it sound?"

Violet looked at him, confused. "You . . . you want me to make the sound?"

He nodded. "If you can."

"Like this." She clenched her teeth and from the back of her throat made a high, vibrating sound. Kjel leaned close enough so his ear was inches from her mouth.

"Jesus," he said after a moment. "Doesn't that drive you nuts?"

"That and my whole life in general."

Surprise flicked away the concern on Kjel's face and he laughed, and Violet basked in that laughter like it was a wolf whistle.

Its horn honking, a roadster approached them on the other side of the road, and they looked up to return the passengers' waves.

"Missouri plates," Kjel said, patting the flank of Mo, who was doing an agitated two-step. "I wonder what brings them up here?"

"Not the scenery."

"You are a funny one, Miss Violet Mathers," said Kjel, but the laugh he offered was only three syllables, and when he spoke again his voice was as serious as a mortician's. "What's going to happen to you?"

Starting to shiver, Violet folded, in her fashion, her arms

across her chest. Her lungs, feeling as if they were ready to blow, reached for breath and drew in oxygen, and after she exhaled, she breathed deep again, determined to cap the pain, the huge volcano of pain that rumbled deep inside her. She would allow no one, especially not Kjel Hedstrom, to witness the explosion of Mount Violet.

Staring down the road for a long time, they watched the roadster shimmer and fade into the west.

"What's going to happen to me?" she said finally, lightly, as she brushed aside a tear that had leaked past her resolve. "Well, I'm going to get on the bus to San Francisco, and when I get there, I'm going to the Golden Gate Bridge."

"I'd like to see that bridge," said Kjel.

"Did you know it's 8,981 feet long?" asked Violet. "And ninety feet wide?"

Kjel laughed. "That's a big bridge."

"It's got a two-tone foghorn and they call the color it's painted 'International Orange.' "

"Why, Miss Mathers, you sound like a regular tour guide."

"Well, I've read a lot about it, but I'm not going to the Golden Gate Bridge to sightsee."

"No? Then what are you going to do?"

On a puff of breeze, Violet smelled weeds and cow manure.

"I'm going to be the second person."

"The second person?"

"To jump off of it."

Kjel stared at Violet, who for once stared back.

"No you're not," he said finally, and making a stirrup out of his hands, he said, "Get up on Mo, Violet."

Violet shifted the handles of her carpetbag up onto her right shoulder and stepped into Kjel's palm and was boosted up onto the old horse. Kjel hefted himself up in front of her, and turning Mo around, they headed back to where they'd come from.

Chapter Four

HAVE YOU EVER HAD ANYONE SAVE YOUR LIFE? WAS YOUR BEYOND-*measure gratitude sullied with just a trace of resentment because you knew you could never fully pay that person back? How can you thank some-one for a gift like that? How could I, whose plan only moments before had been to throw that gift away?*

On that old swayback horse, I pressed myself against Kjel's back not because I was bold but because I was scared; scared because now more than anything, I wanted to live. And not just live, but live, *my arms wrapped around this man who loved me enough to rescue me.*

Hey, I can recognize a fantasy just as easily as Walter Mitty's psychi-atrist; still, that a fantasy had the power to make me want to stay alive when nothing else did . . . like I said, it was scary.

And his body heat! Whew! Never in all my years on this blue-and-green-planet have I felt coming from one person the heat that came from Kjel Hedstrom. When Miri was little and fevered, I'd put wet washrags on her to cool her down, but she was never as hot sick as Kjel was hot well. It was the strangest thing. We used to joke about using his back as a grid-dle and frying up some eggs and bacon on it.

The smells of a summer morning in the country, Mo's sure-footed, plodding gait, the heat seeping from Kjel's back into my front; all these things plus knowing beyond anything that I was alive and in love pixilated me, made me so woozy that when we got back to the farmhouse and the knight helped me off the stead, this fair lady nearly fell to the ground in a faint.

Upon seeing her son and the gangly, one-armed girl come through the kitchen door, Leola Hedstrom hid her disappointment behind a bright smile, and getting up from the breakfast table, said, "Oh good, you're just in time for the second batch of pancakes."

She took notice of the carpetbag Violet set under the coat hooks and mentally scolded her son for retrieving the girl—what was it in his nature that always made him rescue the wounded?

While her guileless husband told Violet that before his knee went bad, he too used to like an early morning walk, Leola stood at the cook stove, glad her back was to everyone because she could hold up her fake cheery smile for only so long.

✸

IN THE FALL OF 1918 the influenza virus had swirled its way into the Hedstrom family. They were four days from boarding the ship that was to take them to Africa, where the Reverend and Mrs. Hedstrom had accepted a two-year post at the mission school in Tanzania.

After leaving their parish in Minneapolis, they had spent three days in New York City being dazed and dazzled by the hustle and bustle, by the way they had to tip their heads back to see the tops of the Woolworth or the Flatiron buildings, by feeling like they were wading in a river when they walked in a crowd of people down Fifth Avenue and that if they let go of each other's hand, they'd be swooped up by the current and thrown miles uptown.

Their hosts were Mr. and Mrs. Minnick, an elderly couple who demonstrated their belief in the righteous goals of the

Lutheran Church by donating liberally to their worldwide mission relief as well as opening the doors of their three-storied brownstone to any number of sewing circles (it thrilled the church women to think that their quilts were warming potential converts in the wilds of Africa, China, and India), planning committees, seminary students, and most especially, to mission families themselves.

That one day these welcoming doors should admit a seminarian from Poughkeepsie who, upon seeing Kjel and Berit in the foyer, motioned them over and pulled a nickel from behind the left ear of each ("an' he let us keep it!" the thrilled children told their older brother Nils, who promptly ordered them to hand over the coins for safekeeping), and that the next day these same doors would be marked with a pink QUARANTINED sign and shuttered against all company except a grim-faced woman in a white geometric hat, was a puzzle to Kjel, who didn't understand why everyone had taken to bed, leaving him and Berit to slide down the swooping walnut banister or to play kickball in the long hallways, or to do any of the loud and naughty things they did to attract adult attention.

Their ship set sail on schedule, but the idealistic young minister and his family did not, mourning as they were the deaths of Mr. and Mrs. Minnick and, most deeply, the Hedstrom's youngest child, eight-month-old Lena.

Reverend Hedstrom would have gone on to Africa, believing not only that the dark continent needed the light he had to share, but also believing that a drastic change of scenery might be the best tonic in helping them deal with their loss, but then his wife, his lovely, lively helpmate for whose presence in his life he thanked God every day, began having a rough time.

Those were the words he used when setting down his blond, wide-eyed children and explaining to them why they wouldn't be taking the big ship across the ocean, why they wouldn't be teaching less fortunate children about Jesus' love, why instead they'd be taking the train to North Dakota and staying with

Grandma Hedstrom for a while, because Mother was having a *rough time.*

His wife's mental breakdown would shake the reverend to his core, and to his great regret, he showed his fear to his children. It was fear as palpable as that first winter on the farm—cold, icy, and sunless—and in its shadow Nils began stuttering and Berit began wetting the bed. Kjel, at four years old, showed no outward signs of distress, and in fact gave comfort more than he sought it; knowing exactly when to crawl on his father's lap and give him a reassuring hug, or when to go to his sister's bedroom just before she cried out in the night.

One frost-coated morning Kjel tiptoed into the room his mother seemed incapable of leaving. She was where she always was, lying on her side on the iron-framed bed, facing the window that looked out over the pasture.

"Mama?" he whispered, because he knew anything above a whisper was too loud. When his mother didn't acknowledge him, he crept across the room, holding the present he had for her behind his back.

Standing before her, he whispered again.

"Mama?"

Her eyes were open but that didn't mean she saw him; her gaze seemed both far away and locked inward. Kjel looked at the square of bright, unfaded wallpaper that had been protected for years by a mirror. A few days earlier the mirror had inexplicitly crashed to the floor, and the noise of it had been the only thing to get a rise out of his mother, her surprised yelp being the first sound she'd made in months.

Looking at the vivid purple lilacs that were surrounded by a wall full of faded, lavender ones, Kjel felt hopeful. The un-touched vibrant square of color reminded him of the way his mother used to be. He inched closer to her bed.

"Mama, Baby Lena told me you needed a present."

His mother's eyes flickered and fixed on him and he drew back in fear.

"She . . . she," he began, answering to the demand in those penetrating eyes, "she said she will always be your baby but she's God's baby now, and you . . . you need to be with your other children."

The little boy's knees wobbled and he wondered if he was about to be struck down by his mother or God for telling such a big whopping lie. He did sense his baby sister around him, and he did talk to her, whispering about how high the hayloft was and how one day he was going to climb the ladder all the way to the top; whispering about the cat who'd just had kittens in the barn, and asking was she with Grandpa in Heaven? But when the baby answered him, it was in his own voice, so he was never sure if it was really Lena or his own wishes he was hearing.

He waited for a moment, his heart like a fist trying to bang through his chest wall, and he bit his lip until he tasted the red salt of blood. But when he didn't collapse under God's wrath or his mother's stare (now less penetrating than beseeching), he brought forward the teddy bear the German bakery owner in town had given him.

"This is for you, Mama. It's not a real baby but it's something to hug."

His mother didn't lift her head off the pillow, didn't move her fingers, which were gnarled together like old vines under her chin, but Kjel saw her nostrils flare and her eyes fill and he watched as one tear moved at a slant across her cheek, and when it hit the pillow, he was sure he could hear it, a soft yet heavy *ppuh*.

✱

IT WAS SUCH A STRUGGLE for Leola Hedstrom to be a good Christian. Everyone who knew her would insist that she was the kindest, most bighearted woman they knew, and Lord knows (literally) she tried, but a day didn't go by without her battling between doing the right thing and doing what it was she wanted to do.

She held herself responsible for her husband's loss of faith.

He had stopped preaching to take care of her, and when she got better (getting out of bed two days after Kjel gave her his teddy bear) he claimed that he seemed better suited to ministering to the land than to people, and worked his widowed mother's farm for ten years before going back to the church. She loved having him just acres away, loved bringing lunch to him in the field, and especially loved those warm spring days when passion overtook them and they'd sink to the newly plowed earth, Esben pushing up the thin cotton of her dress and Leola in turn clawing at the metal fasteners of his overalls.

Afterward, they'd lie still in each other's arms until their breathing quieted, tenderly kissing an eyebrow, a cheek, and when duty was finally remembered, they'd scramble to their feet, brushing dirt and seeds off each other's backsides.

"Spring planting" was their code for sex outside their bedroom, and when Esben's mother moved off the farm and into town, they spring-planted year-round and all over the place—in the hayloft, on the tractor, and once on the front porch during a thunderstorm.

As much as Leola Hedstrom enjoyed their lovemaking, she was embarrassed over her sex drive; especially once Esben returned to the ministry and she got to know the church women well. She sometimes thought the Esther Circle met not only to figure out how to aid the needy, but to complain about the sexual demands of their husbands.

"Leonard wants his way with me every Saturday night! Can you imagine—*every Saturday night!*"

"Well, that's nothing—Haldor wanted to do it on the davenport once!"

"No! What'd you tell him?"

"I told him what any sane woman would tell him; I said, 'Haldor, like we tell the kids—that davenport's for company only!' "

Leola didn't see sex itself as sinful (if it was bad, why would God make it so *fun?*); where sin came in was in the *frequency.* Gluttony in anything was sinful, and Leola feared her need for

Esben's body sometimes crossed the line separating propriety and lasciviousness.

But it wasn't only that she was a too-avid student of carnal knowledge (admittedly, things had slowed down as they aged, but her grades for effort and enthusiasm would still put her on the honor roll) that made Leola think of herself as un-Christian, it was in her stinginess of spirit, her tendency to hold tight to the gifts she was given and to not want to share them.

Maybe it was the loss of her baby that had made her so ferocious about her surviving children, wanting everything for them and doing whatever she could to ensure they got it. She couldn't count the sleepless nights she spent, worrying over Berit's cough, Nils's 4-H project, Kjel's math test, ad infinitum.

It made her sick with jealousy when Mae Chelmers was announced valedictorian over her eldest son (she knew that Mae had been crafty enough to use her looks and wiles to boost her grades—no one was brighter than her Nils), and when Rita Warnig didn't invite Berit to her eleventh birthday party, Leola forced herself to serve refreshments (even though it wasn't her circle's turn) at the Men's Bible Discussion just so she wouldn't be tempted to crash the birthday party and pop little Rita right in her mean little snoot.

She could barely watch any athletic competitions her children were in, so bothered was she if a teammate made more baskets than Berit, or hit a home run after Nils had only doubled.

And Kjel! More than anyone, her youngest son made her aware of how selfish and insular her love was; Kjel befriended everyone and everything. As a boy, his bedroom looked like a veterinarian's recovery room, filled with birds with broken wings and runts of every litter. In school and church he was easily the most popular boy and yet brought home the class outcasts time and time again, forcing Leola to pretend that, no, Ben Jacobson *didn't* smell, or to take Ruby Anderson aside and gently tell her that she didn't have to sneak those extra cookies; why, Leola would be happy to wrap some up for her to take home. Kjel invited in the whole world, which in Christian principle Leola knew to be right; still, she would have preferred to shut the door far more times than she opened it.

Esben never believed his wife when she confessed her failings to him: "Actions speak louder than words, Leola, and yours are always marked by love and concern." A Christian was supposed to serve God in thought, word, and deed, and yet Esben believed his Maker was probably amused by a reverend's occasional contemplations about certain female parishioners in their underwear ('Why thank you, my son, I *did* give Matilda Imholte a beautiful body") or an infrequently muttered "Damn it!" whereas no doubt disgust was His reaction when He saw one of His flock cheat or steal, or turn his back on another. It didn't matter if Leola wanted to sit by the fire and read the new *Ladies' Home Journal* instead of directing a church choir that included a bald soprano (Gerta Peasley had some ailment that had taken all her hair) as well as a robust but tone-deaf baritone; Leola would pile on her winter clothes and steer the fussy Packard through the snow and get to practice, where she'd be so cheerful and enthusiastic that everyone thought that in the singing department, they were second only to angels. Esben was convinced that because she did things she didn't want to do and did them *joyfully,* her Christian heart was beyond reproof, whereas Leola was of the mind that if the thoughts were rotten, everything that sprung from them had to be tainted too. She remembered the great swarm of grasshoppers that descended upon Pearl's farmland several years back, the moving, horrible whirring cloud that blackened the sky, and how Roger Himmler's wife went crazy, how a doctor and Esben had been called to their farm to administer to the shrieking woman who stood by the pump, apologizing to God and her husband for unleashing all her evil thoughts.

"Mrs. Himmler," Esben had shouted from the front seat of his car, a shelter he and the doctor were loath to leave until the swarm passed, "they're awful and they're ugly, but they're only grasshoppers!"

The wild-eyed Mrs. Himmler, who could barely be seen through the curtain of insects, laughed an ungodly laugh and waved her hands.

"No, they are my thoughts, Pastor! They are every single evil thought I've had in my entire evil life!"

After Esben came home and told her that story, Leola excused herself to the toilet, where she threw up until she spasmed. She understood all too well the fear of one's thoughts, and she prayed to God that she'd never again walk those few extra steps sweet Mrs. Himmler had, into madness.

✻

KJEL HAD FOLLOWED HIS SIBLINGS to the University of North Dakota in Grand Forks, but whereas Nils was always fond of math (he was now a bank examiner in California) and Berit played "school" for hours on end as a child (she taught first grade in Bismarck for a year before retiring to marry Lloyd Glattie, the school's principal), Kjel had no idea what he wanted to study, let alone major in, and after completing his second semester, he wired his parents that he was: DONE WITH SCHOOL STOP HITTING THE ROAD STOP WILL WRITE.

Leola had been beside herself—"*Hit* the road—what does that mean? You don't suppose he'll be hopping freight trains, do you?"—but Reverend Hedstrom wasn't surprised. Even though his youngest child was calm by nature, he was also restless, always the first one up in the morning, always the one to ask, "What's next?"

Weekly postcards followed, with short messages from Wyoming, "Ever had chiggers?—I have!"; from Utah, "Ever float in a salt lake—I did!"; postcards from small towns in the West and Midwest, and with each one's arrival, Leola would retrieve the map out of the junk drawer and try to imagine her son in the orange square that was Wyoming, or in mint-green Iowa, a state that looked to Leola like a profile of W. C. Fields.

After five months of travel that brought him farther and farther east, the Hedstroms received a letter whose first line blithely asked, "Guess who's putting on greasepaint and memorizing lines?"

"Acting," said Esben. "Did Kjel ever tell you he was interested in acting?"

"Well, he was always in the Christmas pageant."

"Leola, every child in the church was in the Christmas pageant."

"Read me the letter again," said Leola, "while I get out the map."

The reverend shook the piece of paper and cleared his throat. He enjoyed reading aloud, and knowing this, Leola had him read all the children's letters, as well as mail from other relatives and friends. He read a large section of the biweekly *Pearl Gazette* aloud too, making his wife laugh when he imitated garrulous Ivy Patterson's voice while reading her "Goin's On" column, or by reading in a monotone the price of sorghum or flax listed in the farm report.

" *'Dear Folks,'* "
began Esben as Leola spread the map out on the oilcloth.
" *'Guess who's putting on greasepaint and memorizing lines?'* " The couple locked eyes for a moment before the reverend continued. " *'I know it's just about the last thing you thought I'd be doing but it sure beats standing in a breadline!'* "

Leola grimaced; Kjel never offered much information as to how he supported his travels, and Leola preferred to think that he could always find day work, that he was never hungry, that no one ever mistook him for a tramp.

"So this is what happened. I'd been in New York City for less than two hours and was sitting in this diner on Eighth Avenue and I asked the guy next to me if I could look at the want ads

when he was done with his paper and he asked me what kind of work I was looking for and I said anything that pays and he said he worked for the Federal Theater Project and he was going to the theater for a 'read-through' of his play and did I want to come along and so thinking 'Why not?' I said, 'Sure!' and one thing led to another and now I'm being paid by the government to play the part of this teenager named Tad who goes against his old man's wishes and becomes a union scab. We 'open' in three weeks and I'm with a swell bunch of people who don't just want to get onstage for vanity purposes, but to say something. At least that's what they tell me—over and over, ha ha. I'm not making much money, but that's a lot more than I was and I'm meeting some real nice people. Even the communists who want to save the world are decent in their hepped-up way.

Anyway, don't worry about me, I'm having the time of my life—you can't turn your head without finding something new to do or see in this city—and I even learned which side of the stage 'stage right' is on. Ha! Your ever lovin' son,

Kjel
P.S. Don't worry.
P.P.S. I sure could go for a piece of your rhubarb pie about now, Ma."

And nothing more would make Leola happier than to run out to her pie plant patch and break off a few stalks of rhubarb. She used to scold Kjel for cramming her pie (or her chocolate layer cake, or her toffee bars) into his mouth—how she missed that enthusiasm now, how she'd give anything to see Kjel's bulging cheeks and hear his garbled, "Gee, Mom, this is *good!*"

She looked at the map of New York, and remembering how bad things had gone for her there, said a quick prayer that Kjel be fine.

"An actor," she said finally, shaking her head.

"Do you suppose we should send him flowers on his opening night?" said Esben, and they laughed together, as they had learned to do whenever their children threw them for a loop.

★

BECAUSE HE WAS the youngest member of the troupe, most of the older members—and especially the women—wanted to take Kjel under their wings, and Kay Burns, an actress with curly black hair whose Bronx accent occasionally pierced through the high society one she had affected, took it upon herself to see that the basic needs of this hot-blooded farm boy were taken care of, particularly his sexual needs.

In Grand Forks, Kjel and Shyla Larson, an English major and trumpet player in the marching band, had lost their virginity together in the social studies section of the college library (Shyla crying on his shoulder afterward and asking him if they'd ever see each other again. "Well, sure, Shyla," Kjel had said, stroking her hair. "We've got physics class tomorrow"). But their couplings (far more infrequent than either would like, as Kjel worked late at the library only two nights a week) had in no way prepared him for the likes of Kay Burns, who at the moment of orgasm liked to holler out favorite passages from her days as a page at the Catskill Shakespearean Festival.

"We few, we happy few!"

"Lord what fools these mortals be!"

"I love you now, but not, till now, so much!"

Not that Kjel minded these gasped minimonologues; he found them, as he found everything about Kay Burns, fascinating, although when she screamed, "We shall not go down!" he thought it an entreaty to stop what he had thought she *loved*.

"I'm sorry, Kay," he whispered earnestly, "I just don't understand what it is you want."

She found this misunderstanding hilarious and would have rolled off the narrow Murphy bed laughing had not Kjel grabbed her by a meaty arm.

"Act Two, Scene Four," she reminded the startled farm boy. "When I'm trying to convince the other wives to support the union."

After rehearsals in New York, the company took *We've Got Rights!* on tour. Kjel loved the travel as much as the performances; he would never join those who chorused "they only came alive" when acting. (Kay had often mouthed this, as well as the statement that "only theater has the power to engage me," which surprised Kjel, who thought she certainly seemed engaged when they were in bed together.)

Although he was the only untrained actor in the troupe, he had what couldn't be taught: a charisma that garnered him love notes and offers of free lodging from audience members (most always young, single women, although invitations from men were not unheard of). Kay Burns was tickled by his effortless appeal.

"You've got the audience in the palm of your hand the moment you walk onstage, Kjel. Poor Don could recite Romeo's last soliloquy and there wouldn't be a *wet* eye in the house."

Don Creighton had the lead as the strike organizer, and although he often claimed that stage actors and Hollywood actors were two different breeds—the former artists and the latter cattle—in his secret heart he thought of himself as a matinee idol, in particular a John Barrymore–type matinee idol, not that an audience member was ever remotely reminded of Mr. Barrymore when seeing Mr. Creighton's acting, or his profile.

In his two scenes with Kjel, he noticed a change in the audience—they seemed stirred-up and more alive—and Don was vain enough to think it was because of him. ("How commanding I am! Look how I show this young pup who the lead dog is!")

To the other members of the company whose sanity hadn't been eroded by ego, it was obvious Kjel Hedstrom had it: star quality.

"I don't know what you're doing," said Tom Tripp, the stage manager, "but you're doing something."

Kjel made a dismissive sound, a short *baah*. The group was

taking up several tables at an Italian restaurant in Albany named Manny's.

"It's true," said Caroline Duckworth, who had performed in vaudeville as the child singer, Baby Ducks. "You remind me of this sword swallower I used to know. Even Sophie Tucker hated to follow him because he always got such a huge ovation."

"Oh, Eddie LeRoi," said Dirk Selwyn, the lighting director. "I saw him once at the Palace—he was great! Whatever happened to him?"

Caroline shook her head. "He took sick and left the circuit—I heard a railroad heiress took care of him until he died."

"What'd he die of?" asked the lighting director.

"I can't be sure," said Caroline, her voice sly, "but I believe it was complications of a sore throat."

The backstage and offstage life were the most fun for Kjel; he enjoyed the camaraderie of his fellow actors and crew, writing his parents that "a more fun bunch I've never met."

They were more impassioned than other people, telling better stories and laughing louder at them, fighting harder over politics. (One would think they were all FDR fans, considering the program he implemented had put them to work, but Don Creighton thought the country was going to the socialists, and Rusty Brenner, the antiwoman props master, thought the president might as well hand over the reins to Mrs. Roosevelt, "who's running the whole damn country anyways.")

"So, Kjel," said Kay Burns, blotting her full mouth with a white napkin, "you're not going to run off with a rich railroad heiress like Eddie LeRoi did, are you?"

Kjel scratched his earlobe. "Depends how rich."

"That's telling her," said Don, punching his arm a little harder than necessary.

"And I'm telling *you,* if an heiress doesn't grab this fellow, then Hollywood will," said Caroline. She leaned across the table, cupping Kjel's chin in her dainty, liver-spotted hand. "Oh, my lamb, if I were a couple years younger, wouldn't I give Kay some competition!"

———

"In your dreams, old woman," said Kay, swatting Caroline's hand away, which caused the older woman to swat back, which resulted in a mock catfight, which resulted in one or two meatballs and some chunks of bread being thrown, which resulted in Manny, the restaurant owner, and Kjel both thinking, *Actors,* although behind Kjel's thought was affection and behind Manny's was disgust.

When the company finished its tour (attracting nearly full houses at each theater they played), everyone went back to New York to begin rehearsals on a new play about space travel written by a woman who sincerely believed that one day man would walk on the moon.

"How could they?" Rusty asked the playwright. "How could people ever walk on the moon when they haven't figured out yet how to walk on Uranus?"

✳

"YOU SHOULD READ for the lead," said Kay. "You'd be so much better than Don Creighton."

They were walking to a theater in Harlem to see a Federal Theater Project production of *Macbeth.*

"Maybe," said Kjel.

"Honey, what's wrong?"

Kjel's shoulders bunched in a shrug. Although technically he and Kay were sharing an umbrella, Kay had nine-tenths of it shielding her from the rain while the remaining scalloped edge occasionally nicked Kjel's temple. It was a good thing he was wearing a hat; not only did it keep his head dry, but it softened each spiky jab.

"I really can't see myself as a leading man, Kay."

The actress stopped in the street so suddenly that a man walking behind them had to swerve to avoid running into her.

"Jeez, lady," he muttered, passing them.

"It doesn't matter if you can't see yourself as a leading man, Kjel; the rest of the world sure can."

The wind had picked up and was now directing the rain at a stinging slant. With one hand, Kjel held his upturned collar together, with the other he took Kay's arm.

"Come on," he said. "We don't want to be late."

It was a night at the theater Kjel never forgot, for two reasons: it was the first time he had ever seen an all-Negro cast onstage and it was the night he met Austin Sykes.

Kjel had almost taken a rain check on the evening's entertainment, not being a particular fan of the great bard. Some of the blame could be focused on Mrs. Nyman, who began her eighth-grade English class by selecting a volunteer reader (although there was nothing volunteer about it) to read a portion of Shakespeare, selected at random by Mrs. Nyman herself.

The recitations were almost always stumbled through, the words mispronounced, the diction flat as the North Dakota prairie seen through the windows out of which the bored students gazed. Should the class get too restless, Mrs. Nyman would patrol the aisles, slapping her ruler across the shoulder or knuckles of each student, further conditioning them to equate Shakespeare with pain.

Matts Knutsen, the butcher's son (a boy with all the brawn of an ox but only a portion of the brain) had the unfortunate task of reading Hamlet's "To be or not to be" soliloquy. To the class, this was great comedy, the boy's face reddening by degrees while inflecting, "To be? Or not to be?" the way he might ask a housewife which cut of meat she preferred.

To stifle the laughter, Mrs. Nyman strode down each aisle, democratically doling out a ruler-smack to everyone.

But this Shakespeare! So wild, colorful, and lively; so painful and human and real that Kjel, like Kay and the rest of the audience, sat forward, not wanting to miss anything that was happening on the island of Haiti, where this wild *Macbeth* was taking place.

When Malcolm intoned his last lines and the curtain dropped, a resounding bell of silence tolled, and then the crowd was collectively yanked up to its feet, beating their hands together and shouting, "Bravo! Bravo!"

In the lobby, the audience looked euphoric, as if it had just been baptized in something holy and wasn't it thrilling to be part of this select and enlightened group?

"The acting was so earthy; so 'in the moment.' "

"The direction was so bold, and yet so subtle at the same time."

"Did you notice how the lighting set so much of the emotional tone?"

When a group of people heading off for a drink invited Kay and Kjel to join them, Kjel declined.

"But you go ahead, Kay," he said. "I'd just as soon head home."

"You sure, hon?" said Kay, and when he assured her, she kissed him before looping her arm through that of an actress with whom she had acted in *Awake and Sing!* "Well, then, let's go find a place where the wine flows and the peanuts are free!"

Stepping out of the theater, his hands bunched in his pockets, Kjel breathed in the night air of Manhattan, smelling the big-city perfume of cigarettes, pushcart hot dogs and sauerkraut, hair tonic and sweat, newsprint and shoe polish, bus exhaust and sewer. Passing two young, elegantly dressed women, he tipped his hat, and their soignée, out-on-the-town looks were abandoned as they nudged each other, giggling like sorority sisters at a mixer.

Kjel hadn't packed the monogrammed Bible he'd been given for confirmation, and since leaving home had been inside a church only once (a Congregationalist one in Iowa City, and only because it had been hosting a free ice cream social). As a preacher's son, he performed many duties (regular church and Luther League attendance, devotions read around the table, acolyte service), but one thing he never had to fake was a sense of gratitude. He woke to each day with a special prayer, and like a two-year-old, he was always ready and expecting to be astonished and delighted by what the day might bring.

The play, for instance—his travels had widened his world, but it was still an overwhelmingly white one, and to see so many black people onstage, hearing their voices and watching them move, was . . . thrilling. It made him feel more a part of the planet, and conversely, less, and he wanted nothing more than to walk into the city night, letting that feeling settle on him and trying to figure out what it meant.

"Hey, Smiley! Got a smoke?"

Not surprised at the address—it wasn't the first time a stranger had called him "Smiley"—Kjel patted his coat pockets.

"Sorry."

The man nodded as if he were sorry too, and was about to turn away in search of other prospects when Kjel reached out, touching his coat sleeve.

"Hey, weren't you in *Macbeth*?"

Nodding, the man beamed, a smile filling half his face.

"A soldier. With the commanding line: 'Hail, King of Scotland!' Still, I can't deny the thrill in being in a production of this magnitude." He sighed. "Although truth be told, it may well be my last venture as a thespian; in a perfect world my filthy lucre would be earned as a musician."

Wondering if the man's lack of lines onstage made him feel a sudden need for extra verbiage, Kjel asked, "What do you play?"

"The piano, but for portability one can't beat the guitar."

"I play a little guitar myself."

"Mine's a regular-sized one," said the Negro, and then with a laugh, he clapped the white man on the back. "And at this very moment, I'm on my way to join a consort of mine to create a little Bohemian Rhapsody of our own. Care to come along?"

Kjel shrugged. "Sure."

Chapter Five

WHAT ARE YOUR THOUGHTS ON NATURE VS. NURTURE? DO YOU *believe that we come out of the chute with our personalities already in place, or do you believe that our upbringing is the bigger determiner of our natures?*

My tent is staked in the first camp—I know I was born with a good sense of humor (I don't believe it arises as a defense mechanism; if it did, all criminals would be funny) and a mean streak. But, if my mother had stuck around and my dad thought I was his greatest achievement, they would have applauded the humor and tempered the mean streak, so they wouldn't have bled so much into each other. They would have built up my assets and tamped down my liabilities. That's where the importance of nurturing comes in; the already sculpted personality is not recast, but re-fined. Loving, caring families can sand and polish, but they can't chip away at a lawn ornament and turn it into Michaelangelo's David. Or vice versa.

Want another analogy? Regarding personality, I am convinced that at birth the cake is already baked. Nurture is the nuts or frosting, but if you're a spice cake you're a spice cake, and nothing is going to change you into an angel food.

When he was eleven years old, Kjel had been given seven-and-a-half guitar lessons by Maynard Eclesson. The music teacher and owner of Garden State Feed had just shown his pupil a tricky chord progression when he suddenly slumped over his Martin guitar, his fingertips grazing the worn oak floors of his feed store office.

For a moment student thought teacher was making yet another editorial comment on his playing (Mr. Eclesson tended toward the flamboyant gesture, giving his students standing ovations when it was clear they had practiced and pretending to cry when it was clear they had not) and apologized twice for his clumsy fret-work before realizing that something more lethal than a missed note had felled the elderly instructor.

Mr. Eclesson had two grown sons who ably took over the feed store (and in fact had been waiting for the opportunity), but neither had any desire to inherit their father's four guitar students, and so Kjel was out of a teacher, as well as the twenty-five cents for the half lesson he was still owed.

But the basics Mr. Eclesson had provided were enough for the talented young guitarist to expand upon, and by the eighth grade Kjel was the first-chair (albeit only) guitarist in Pearl High's orchestra, as well as providing occasional accompaniment for his mother's choir members. (It was only occasional because there were still those in the congregation who were of the mind that any instrumental accompaniment besides organ or piano was sacrilegious.)

Early Saturday mornings, the boy tuned in to *Howie's Round-Up*, broadcast out of Fargo, and played along to the eclectic musicians (Glen Miller, the Delmore Brothers, Howlin' Wolf) Howie liked to round up. Kjel was almost sixteen when Howie bid his listeners farewell, announcing he was taking a job in Jacksonville, Florida.

"It's been fun," he said in his smooth radio voice, "but one more of these winters and I'd be broadcasting out of the loony bin."

Howie's Round-Up was replaced with *Pete and Judy,* a show hosted by a folksy married couple who were fond of knock-knock jokes and reading recipes and inspirational poems which featured stanzas like, "Keep your head high/for we'll get through hard times by and by." The show attracted a large listenership, of which Kjel was not a part.

★

THERE WAS ENOUGH MONEY in the Sykes household for music lessons, but no need; as the sons of Mokey Sykes, Austin and Dallas learned how to play guitar from the many musicians who performed at their father's club, which offered "the best chops—pork and musical—in all of Missouri."

From the time the Sykes boys were old enough to bus dishes without breaking them, they spent their weekends working in the club. Beaumont didn't last long; he was a sickly boy plagued by respiratory problems that the club's smoke-filled air aggravated, and their sister Odessa was banned from Mokey's by their mother, who did not believe a young lady's place was in a rib joint. Austin and Dallas felt sorry for their siblings, who not only missed out on the dollar-bill tips folded and tucked into their pockets by the big spenders, but most important, missed out on all the music, especially what was played after hours.

This was the boys' favorite time; while cleaning up stacks of sauce-smeared dishes and silverware, while sneaking any Coca-Cola remaining in glasses (Coke that had been fortified by the whiskey customers poured from flasks they kept hidden in their coat pockets), while wiping down tables and sweeping the floor, the boys listened as Pee Wee Wiley or Injee Hanks or Slippery Zeke Caroll retuned their guitars and began their extended jam sessions, singing about how their babies left them or how low-down they could get before being buried underground.

Their father had warned them not to get in the musicians' way, and they started out listening from the kitchen, perched on cabbage crates (Mokey's coleslaw was nearly as revered as the ribs). But as they got braver, they began sitting at tables to the side of the stage, to finally sitting on the stage itself, watching intently the hands of the musicians work their magic on guitar strings and piano keyboards.

It was Injee Hanks, a toothless guitarist from Biloxi who first told his employer, "Mokey, why don't you procure these boys their own axes so they ain't salivatin' after mine!" (Not only was Injee instrumental in Austin's guitar training, but in opening up the boy's ears to the musicality of language.)

"Why, these boys got guitars Christmas before last," said Mokey. "They gettin' good enough so the cats don't even howl no more."

"You bring those guitars tomorrow night," said the old guitarist, "and show Injee what you got."

Austin had a nervous stomach so severe that he was in the toilet more than he was on the floor, and when the club closed and Injee invited him and his brother to the stage, he couldn't tell what was knocking harder—his knees or his heart. But when he lifted his guitar out of its case with the reverence a painter opens a new set of paints, or a newly licensed doctor his black bag, his heart chugged to a steady rhythm, his kneecaps stopped shaking, and a rightness filled him; a reassurance that "Here I am, and it's okay."

If memories were precious stones, the first night Austin and Dallas played with the great Injee Hanks was a diamond, a diamond so shining and incandescent that glints of its light remained undimmed through the passage of years and all that comes with that passage.

The man was patient yet challenging, showing them chords they didn't know and then calling them out faster and faster, watching their fingers. The boys played a simple accompaniment to Injee's lead, but when Dallas suddenly went off on a riff of his own, the old man tipped back his head in a toothless laugh, revealing a span of blue-gray gums.

While Kjel, several states north, was playing along with musicians on *Howie's Round-Up,* the Sykes brothers were jamming with the finest blues musicians on the circuit. Austin sat on the piano bench next to M'Lynn "Princess" Donnelly whenever she played after hours, and would go home and practice over and over the things he'd watch her fingers do.

When Austin was fourteen and Dallas fifteen, their idyllic lives were shattered by a robber who did the same thing to their father's skull.

Mokey Sykes had come across the intruder when coming through the kitchen one morning, his arms filled with a bushel basket of potatoes. The intruder reacted poorly to being surprised, striking Mokey with the tire iron he'd used to force open the back door. Mokey staggered and the potatoes thudded to the floor in a steady rain and the intruder struck again, a blow that sprayed blood in a red arc over the kitchen sinks. He struck again and again until Mokey lay unmoving on the floor, and then before racing out the door, he riffled his hands in the dead man's pocket until he found his wallet.

No one was ever caught (no surprise to the patrons of Mokey's, who considered police harassers more than protectors), and the bereaved Mrs. Sykes put her brother in charge of the club, whose great disorganization and bad temper ran it to the ground a mere eight months later.

Grief struck everybody who knew Mokey, and while Austin was dazed by it, Dallas was knocked clear out of one world and into another. Fueled by anger and fear, he got on a road that led to juvenile hall and after that, jail.

"I was saved by my music," Austin told Kjel at the end of one of the late-night conversations that always seemed to follow their jam sessions, "and by my need to *help* rather than hurt our poor mother, and certainly by books—what a comfort it is to read about someone whose problems outweigh your own by *tons*—and of course—and most important—by the knowledge to go Dallas's route was to go an old and tired one." Taking a breath, Austin shook his head. "But the music—Dallas was more talented than I; he could get notes out of his guitar you didn't even know were there—why wasn't that big enough to save him?"

Kjel shook his head; he had no answer. As sad as the story was, what struck Kjel was Austin's claim that Dallas was the more musically talented brother. More talented than Austin, the freest, most innovative guitarist Kjel had ever played with? Admittedly, he hadn't played with that many people, but he had heard plenty of guitarists, and as a listener he was astonished at the flights of fancy Austin Sykes's fingers took.

✵

WITH REGARDS TO THEIR MUSIC, the two men made no plans except when to schedule their next jam session; it was only one evening, while eating supper at the automat (like an art patron, Kjel strolled slowly by the display of windows, studying what was inside; if anyone wanted a symbol of the modern age, it was the automat), that Austin announced his brother was being released from prison and that he was going to Chicago to "see what I can do to help him stay out."

"How are you going to do that?" asked Kjel.

Austin peeled off the top triangle of bread and inspected the egg salad underneath it. "Well, I think the only thing that can save Dallas right now is music. So I'm desirous of getting a band started with him."

"I wouldn't mind playing in that band."

"A white boy like you? Playing with the Sykes brothers?" Austin laughed as he salted the pallid mound of egg salad.

"Why not?" said Kjel lightly, even as there was no levity in his green and blue eyes.

As if gargling, Austin pushed his mouth back and forth across his face and then, giving up the pretense of thinking it over, he said, "Would you be willing to change your name to Houston?"

✵

"YOU CAN'T BE SERIOUS," said Kay Burns, who was still angry at him for not trying out for the lead in *Future Space*. "You're willing to throw away what could be a *big* career here to traipse off to Podunkville and God knows what?"

"God better know what," Kjel said, smiling, "because I sure don't."

Kay felt a thickness in her throat; she hated that the theater was not enough to hold Kjel, but more so, that *she* was not enough. But as a woman who didn't believe sentiment should get in the way of practicality, she was not about to waste time sniffling, not with Kjel lying naked beside her.

"Then show me what you do know," she said, reaching for him.

✳

AFTER THE PANCAKE BREAKFAST, when the men had adjourned to the backyard to work on the pickup truck, Leola had taken the opportunity to get to know Violet a little better. Her motives weren't purely friendly ones; Leola hoped to find something out—anything!—that would help her in her mission to keep Violet from going along with her son.

Setting up the creaky ironing board, she asked Violet to keep her company while she did her least favorite chore.

"Could you sprinkle?" she asked, indicating with a nod of her head the basket of clean clothes, and before Violet answered, she handed the girl a 7 Up bottle outfitted with a perforated cap.

Sitting on the kitchen chair, Violet took a shirt out of the basket, set it on the table, and shook water over it. Aware of Mrs. Hedstrom's eyes on her, she tried to execute the task with a brisk efficiency, wanting to impress upon her hostess that while she might be a cripple, she wasn't a *cripple*.

Thankfully for Violet, Mrs. Hedstrom had turned the radio on—"I never miss *Chub Johnson*"—and so for a good fifteen minutes she was not called upon to converse; her only job while sprinkling clothes was to listen to Chub and his wife Slim and laugh along with Mrs. Hedstrom and the studio audience at their jokes. Just as she had fantasized about Mr. Claus the soybean farmer being her father, Violet allowed herself a little daydream: she was sitting in this cozy kitchen, morning sunshine sparkling through the southern windows, doing chores with her mother. *What will we do next?* Violet wondered as she directed a light sprinkle of water on a shirtsleeve. *Roll out the biscuits? Wax the floor? Beat the rugs?* Maybe they'd polish some of the old silver and Mrs. Hedstrom would remind her that one day all of it would be hers.

As the radio audience laughed over Chub's whining about his lukewarm coffee, Violet was about to hand the dampened shirt to Mrs. Hedstrom when instead she held on to it, examining the blind stitches of the yoke.

"Chaw," she said, trying to see the stitches better by squinting, "did you make this shirt?"

Hanging a newly pressed shirt on a kitchen cabinet pull, Mrs. Hedstrom nodded.

"I make all the boys—well, the *men*—their shirts. I just sent Nils three new white ones—he never wears sleeve protectors at the bank and gets ink all over his cuffs." Smiling, she rolled her eyes as if thinking, The scoundrel!

"You're such a good sewer!" said Violet. "I can't even see where you've tacked on the facing, and the way you finish your seams!"

A smile bloomed on the older woman's face. "Why, thank you, Violet—they're French seams, and you're the first person to ever notice them."

"Doesn't . . . doesn't your daughter sew?"

Leola waved her hands before arranging a shirtsleeve on the tapered end of the ironing board. "Sad to say, it would take some effort for Berit to sew on a button. Nowadays she only wears store-bought—maybe because I made all her clothes when she was a girl.

"Do you," she said, as the iron hissed, making contact with the damp cloth, "do you sew?"

Violet nodded, and her nostrils flared as tears made the quick, surprise appearance tears are so good at.

"I . . . well, I used to."

Mrs. Hedstrom stared at the girl for a moment, then realized she was holding the iron in midair, and set it on its metal plate. "My land," she said, moving toward Violet. "Don't tell me you made your blouse."

The girl nodded. "And the pants too."

She had made her first pair of trousers when she worked at Marcelline Threads; it was so much easier working when you didn't have to worry about a skirt, and she rued, now that she had decided to live, that she'd packed only one pair. She had made the trousers out of a gray gabardine that matched one of the stripes in her blue-and-gray plaid shirt.

"It's beautiful!" said Leola, squatting in front of Violet and examining her shirt the way her son looked at bank ledgers. "Well, the whole outfit is—I myself have never worn a pair of pants in my life—but, oh my, look at those pockets. I tried to make inverted pockets on a jacket once and had to rip up the whole thing."

Leola was ashamed of herself—what had she been seeing when she looked at Violet? Knowing the answer shamed her more: she hadn't seen anything but a flawed and needy girl.

"Covered buttons," she said, taking inventory as she looked Violet up and down. "Topstitching—my goodness, did you use a ruler with that topstitching? And the plaid's matched perfectly at every seam . . ." She shook her head, like a county-fair judge asked to rank World's Fair–quality work. "Do you have more?" she asked, standing up. "I'd love to see anything else you've made."

Violet was quick to stand up, even though her legs felt wobbly. It was funny, instead of shoring her up, each compliment made Violet feel crumpled-up inside, reminding her of how much she missed her arm and hand, and all it could do.

After fetching the carpetbag she had left by the coatrack, Violet followed Mrs. Hedstrom into the front room.

"Sit here," said Leola, patting the fancy sofa hardly anyone ever sat on.

"I didn't pack much," said Violet, feeling a blush begin in her hair roots and spread down her face. "I . . . I was going to

90

send for my things when I got settled." In her nervousness, she fumbled with the latch.

"Here, let me help you," said Mrs. Hedstrom, opening the bag.

Violet sat quietly for a moment, willing her breath and heart to slow down. Leola watched the girl, as interested as an audience member the moment the curtain goes up.

"This," Violet said finally, pulling out her best dress, the dress she'd planned to wear when she jumped off the bridge. "This was the last thing I ever sewed."

She and RaeAnn had made plans to go on a double date—RaeAnn's hardware clerk had a cousin coming to town—and Violet had made herself a dress for the occasion. Her arm was amputated two days before the cousin arrived, and the dress had never been worn.

"Oh, my," said Leola. She took the dress and draped it over the back of the sofa. "Violet, it is just beautiful."

It was too. The dress was a dainty yellow color, and over the bodice was a white eyelet bolero. The buttons of the jacket were tiny white satin rosebuds.

"Oh, Violet," said Mrs. Hedstrom. "I've got to get this pattern. A dress like this would make Berit forget all about store-bought."

"There is no pattern," said Violet quietly.

"No pattern," said Mrs. Hedstrom, and it took her a moment to realize what the girl was saying. "You . . . you designed this yourself?"

Violet nodded and again blinked back the hot spurt of tears ready to flood her eyes.

"I never use . . . used a store-bought pattern. Never really saw the need." She reached in the carpetbag for her sketchbook and handed it to Mrs. Hedstrom.

" 'Fashions by Violetta,' " read Leola, opening the book, and with each page she turned, she issued an "Oh, my!" or a "Gracious me!" or a simple gasp.

Violet pressed her lips together; Mrs. Hedstrom was the first person since Miss Eugie to see Fashions by Violetta, and shyness, fear, embarrassment, and delight were working their way through the girl's system, causing her to blush, flush, and tap her right foot against the floor in a pace worthy of a drummer trying to pep up contestants in a dance marathon.

After she finished looking at the book, Mrs. Hedstrom sat quietly for a moment.

"I had no idea how talented you were," she said finally, her voice a whisper.

"I wish I had more to show you," said Violet, taking out the other handmade clothes she'd packed. "I wish you could see what I left behind—for fun, I used to make blouses out of embroidered tablecloths, and once I made a bathrobe out of a chenille bedspread!" How proud she'd been of that bathrobe; she'd even padded the shoulders, and everytime she wore it she felt like Joan Crawford ordering her maid around.

"I was pretty fast too—I only worked at Marcelline Threads for two months but I managed to sew something for each of my co-workers—June's skirt was my favorite; I made it out of a pair of curtains! And once—once I cut down an old Confederate soldier's dress coat I'd found at a tag sale and made it into a jacket—I only wore it once, though, because my history teacher said it was blasphemous, but my English teacher said it wasn't the coat that was blasphemous, but the war!"

Violet was crying now, hard. Pushing aside the bag, Leola put her arms around the girl and did what Tree Pa could never do, what no one had done for years: held her tight.

Chapter Six

OH, LOOK, THE TRUCKER'S LEAVING. I DON'T KNOW WHY HE *doesn't just sit this rainstorm out—but I suppose he's got miles to go before he sleeps. Doesn't look too happy about it, though.*

Hey, is that a five-dollar bill he just tucked underneath his plate? He's tipping the waitress who believes in "partial service with no smile" five bucks? I'll bet he was raised by a mama who had to wait tables to pay the bills; somehow he knows the importance, the balm of a big tip. He sure didn't give any clues to his kindness by that mean old face of his, did he? Hasn't he figured out that frowns and scowls trap the anger inside? Really, serenity is not possible when the muscles of your face are scrunched up like a fist. Come on, try it—frown as hard as you can, with your whole face, and then think of the person you love most in the world. Concentrate on that big love, on the first time you met, on a trip you took together . . . see? See how your face is relaxing? How your mouth is turning up? People shouldn't slap on fake smiles—I hate fake smiles—but I'm not doing anyone a disservice by offering this simple prescription, this physiological apple a day: if you're not truly mad at something, unbunch those frown muscles. Even if you have every right to be mad, unbunch 'em anyways. Everything is always worse when your face is all screwed up.

"All right, baby, that's it, that's it!"

These were the words that signaled Violet's life was to make another seismic shift, and they were shouted by Kjel as he leaned out the truck cab window, shaking his fist in victory as the engine roared to life.

"Are you sure you want to go with them?" Leola asked Violet as the two women packed a box of provisions. When Kjel had brought back the girl who'd run off and they all sat down at the breakfast table, Leola had been stunned at Kjel's announcement that Violet was going to be traveling with the two men for a bit, and from the look on Violet's face, Leola could tell the girl was stunned too.

"Violet's in between jobs," Kjel had said blithely, pouring syrup on his pancakes, "so I thought it'd be fun to show her parts of the country she's never seen."

Austin, his mouth agape, stared at Kjel, and Leola saw that this news was news to him too.

"Ah," said the reverend, "fancy-free youth. Don't you envy it, Leola?"

"I certainly do," agreed Leola cheerfully, a response that was the exact opposite of what she was thinking, which was: Kjel, have you gone absolutely *crazy*?

Now that two days had passed and she'd gotten to know Violet better, Leola's aversion to her son's plan had softened; although she still wanted to protect Kjel from the difficult entanglements that were sure to arise with Austin and Violet in tow, she now wanted to protect Violet too.

"I could contact my brother," said Mrs. Hedstrom, wrapping a meat sandwich in waxed paper. "He owns an insurance agency up in Minot and maybe he could find some work for you to do. Or we could ask around Pearl; Juanita Henks is about to deliver her baby, and I'll bet they'd like someone to replace her at the five-and-dime."

The sense of feeling wanted made Violet light-headed, and she gripped the edge of the countertop to steady herself.

"I . . . thank you," she said, "but I . . ."

"Oh, you don't have to explain," said Leola, knowing how shabby the allure of insurance agency work or five-and-dime cashiering was when compared to a road trip with her son. "I just . . . I just want you to be careful. It's just so . . . unconventional, what you're doing, and I worry that you're going to get hurt."

"I don't worry about getting hurt," said Violet softly. "I'm pretty used to it."

Leola hugged Violet then, and hugging her back, Violet nearly laughed: how different it was—how warm and soft and yielding—to hug a person instead of a tree.

When they got back to the business of sandwich making, Violet said, "Don't worry about me. I may look like a delicate flower"—here the five-foot-eleven lantern-jawed girl with half a left arm batted her eyes and offered a smile—"but inside, inside I'm tough as nails."

✳

LIGHT FROM THE CAMPFIRE flicked shadows against the stone bluff that rose behind the trio, and after a stuttering flap of wings, an owl settled itself in the high branches of a spindly tree and let out a "Hooo!"

Not *who*, thought Violet, trying to find the bird in the sparse dark canopy of leaves. *What*. What am I doing here?

The usual edginess she felt because of the bees in her ears was tripled by her circumstances, and since they had left the farm that morning, she felt as if her muscles were coiled springs about to defy the boundaries of skin and jump out of it. Seated in the cab with Kjel, she nodded as he pointed out local landmarks ("That's Pearl's oldest homestead, built by a beer maker named Heidecker in 1817") and made whatever small talk she was capable of, which was not much. She didn't feel subdued by her self-consciousness as much as she felt strangled by it; but as hard as she tried, she couldn't untie the heavy scarf wrapped and pulled tight around her neck. She thought relief might only be found by swinging open the cab door and jumping out, but it seemed the purse Leola had given her ("Pockets are for boys, Violet—a girl needs a purse") was a block of ice on her lap, and her hand clutching it was frozen.

As silence filled the cab like a suffocating gas, Violet almost wished for the bluster of Austin, but when they drove, the Negro sat in the bed of the truck, stretched out and shaded by the brim of his felt hat, paging through his dictionary, admiring the view or snoozing, and in general looking as relaxed and limpid as Violet was not.

There was an entirely different mood that night, by the campfire; Kjel and Austin had taken out their guitars, and the conversation—of which Violet had little part in—was exuberant and dealt mainly with their music.

"So we started to play," Kjel explained. "And after about the third song, I thought, something's going on here!"

"It was as if we were brothers born to the same musical mother and sired by the same soulful sound!"

Violet rolled her eyes, a reaction she had to almost everything Austin said, but one she usually stifled. Sitting in the darkness, she was giving her eyes a calisthenic workout. She was dead tired and wanted to go to bed, but not knowing where bed was and too shy to ask, she waited for the two men to call it a night and take her cues from them. But it seemed they never would call it a night; after the fire had been built and supper made (desperate to prove her worthiness, Violet seized the cook's position, made easy by the boxes of food she had helped Mrs. Hedstrom pack), they began playing music and Violet settled back, happy at first because nothing was demanded of her but to listen, tired and angry hours later.

"How 'bout 'School's Over,' " said Kjel.

"Is that what we're calling it?" asked Austin, and at Kjel's nod, he added, "in G, then."

He plucked a chord, and Kjel answered back with a run of fingers up the fret board, and Violet, squelching a jaw-cracking yawn, thought, *Not another one, please.*

It had not escaped her mind that had the bus not broken down and had she continued her westward journey, she would have been dead by now, assuming second thoughts or a rescuer hadn't intruded on her plans to leap off the Golden Gate Bridge. It was doubtful *anything* could escape her mind at the moment, so jam-packed was it with questions, worries, and most of all, exhaustion.

Why, after all, had Kjel asked her along? How long would she stay with them? Where were they going? How could she love him so deeply when she didn't even know him, and more so, when she knew love was something he would never reciprocate? She mourned the fact that she wasn't dead—how easy everything would have been!—and yet she couldn't look at Kjel without rejoicing in that same fact. Playing his guitar now, his eyes closed, his head moving in rhythm: how beautiful he was! She didn't care how silly or stupid it was—she was sick in love with him—even as she knew the only thing he could feel for her was pity. Pride, Violet's lifeboat in the harsh waters of hostility and rejection, had capsized, and she happily, willingly, kicked it away. For so long she didn't want to do anything for anybody, and now there was someone for whom she'd do *anything*. And yet . . . and yet of course it was all craziness.

"School's over/It's finally done/So take off your shoes and/ let's have some fun."

The campfire snapped and Violet smiled, imagining it was her feet Kjel wanted unshod. Propping her carpetbag against a rock, she had made a backrest, and leaning back against it now, she closed her eyes and the honey of Kjel's voice poured over her.

"Where's she going to sleep?" Austin asked Kjel when the campfire was nothing more than a faint glow under the rubble of black wood.

"There, I guess," said Kjel, putting his guitar in its case. "I mean, why wake her up? She looks pretty comfortable."

"For the first time all day," said Austin with a snort.

"You're telling me," said Kjel, taking a pouch of tobacco and rolling papers out of his pocket. "Man, it was painful in that truck. I couldn't get two sentences out of her."

———

Austin shook his head. "I'm not a man who gets a lot of joy out of saying 'I told you so,' but didn't I tell you so? Didn't I say that bringing her along was not going to be an amenable situation for anyone?"

Kjel sealed the cigarette paper with his tongue. Handing the cigarette to Austin, he agreed that, yes, Austin had said just that. "But it's not as if traveling with you is exactly an amenable situation for me."

"Fuckin' white honky."

Kjel laughed. "And what exactly is an 'amenable situation' anyway? Something that benefits someone, or something that's easy? Playing music with you—yeah, that benefits me, but walking down the street with you in a strange town?" Kjel shook his head. "Not only does it not benefit me, it might even hurt me."

"I hate to tell you, brother, but you ain't seen nothing yet." Austin lit his cigarette and, exhaling, pointed it in Violet's direction. "So what's the benefit—or the easy part—of bringing Miss Personality along with us?"

Kjel stared at the cigarette he was rolling for himself. "Well, I haven't figured out what the benefit might be for us—but I know what it is for her." He licked the paper shut and lit the expertly rolled cylinder. "She was all alone, Austin, and now she's not. As for the easy part of this 'amenable situation,' well, at least she can cook."

Austin snorted again. "She unwrapped some sandwiches. She handed us apples. That's cooking?"

"I'm giving her the benefit of the doubt," said Kjel. "Now shut yer yap so I can get some sleep."

✹

THE LATE-AUGUST DAYS were full of humidity, but it hadn't rained since they left Pearl, and the heat hung in waves over the road, and the waves barged through the open windows like the ocean at high tide. Violet, arm crooked, hung out of the open window, getting slight relief from the wind on her face and even more re-lief from conversational responsibility. Kjel's efforts at discourse had been valiant, but her muteness coupled with the heat had worn him down; Violet was running a boycott on conversation, and he was tired of trying to cross her picket line.

Meals were tense; Violet busying herself with food prepara-tion, eating as she assembled their sandwiches or fried their eggs so that when she handed them their plates, she had an excuse not to sit with them and break bread. She didn't request her own bathroom breaks, but took them whenever Kjel or Austin needed to, never making eye contact as she scurried into a filling station restroom or into a clump of roadside bushes. Once, they stopped at a café for coffee, but the discomfort was so intense that they hurried out before finishing one cup, especially after Austin, in response to the waitress mumbling she'd served Austin only be-cause Kjel looked like a nice enough person, said, "And it's your misfortune that I'm the one who tips!" Violet, by her eyes, had hoped to telegraph her opinion that, yes, she didn't believe the Negro should be joining them either, but the waitress was obliv-ious to Violet's signals, staring instead at her stump, then at Kjel, and back to her again, as if she couldn't believe the two belonged in the same room together, let alone next to each other at a counter.

"Too bad she can't get a job in the staring business," said Austin as they left the café. "She certainly has a bigger talent for it than she does waitressing."

With the relative cooling at night, the men's spirits improved and they invited Violet to join their jams in whatever capacity she saw fit ("Can you sing, Violet?" "How about playing some per-cussion?"), but once they found their campsite, Violet would take her bedroll and stake out her place to sleep in the most private, out-of-the-way spot she could find. It was only then, with their music, that the tensions of the day dissipated for Kjel and Austin, and they played deep into the night, stopping only for cigarettes and whispered conversations.

"Jesus Christ, how long must we endure this?"

Kjel stared at the fire for a long moment before asking, "Did He answer you?"

"Who?"

"Jesus Christ."

"I forget sometimes, Kjel, how funny you are." Austin took a long drag of his cigarette. "Come on, man. I know I'm not the only one who believes our Miss Mathers is somewhat of a burden, a load, an incubus, an onus, excess cargo, a spoiler, a—"

"I get your point," said Kjel. Taking a candy bar out of his pocket and unwrapping it.

"Kjel, I thought we agreed we'd only spend money on the essentials."

"Chocolate is an essential," said Kjel, breaking off a small piece of the Hershey bar and handing it to his friend. "And I didn't spend any money on it—it sort of found its way into my pocket at that café."

Austin chuckled. "Lord have mercy—a light-fingered preacher's son."

"So what do you suggest we do?" asked Kjel when the diversion of the chocolate bar was gone. "Pack up and leave her here?"

Austin began to stand. "You get the bedrolls, I'll grab the coffeepot."

"Sit down," said Kjel, lighting a cigarette. "We're not leaving her and you know it. At least not tonight." He took a deep drag. "And who knows—she can't be having much fun—maybe she'll ask us to drop her off at the nearest bus station."

Austin clasped his hands in front of his chest. "Are you listening, God?"

Chapter Seven

EVEN THOUGH I WAS NOT CONSIDERED A "CATCH," I HAD MY *standards, and no one had ever risen to meet them the way Kjel Hedstrom had. Being in his presence, breathing air he might have exhaled moments earlier, watching him push his wheat-and-straw colored hair out of his eyes; well, it made everything—even the awkwardness and misery of the first few days—tolerable. I had never had a first love before; as an adolescent, I was less attracted to the opposite sex than afraid of it, plus none of those Mount Crawford boys came close to what I wanted in a man, which was everything. (Why accept dribs and drabs—why not hold out for everything?)*

When I woke up after our first night of camping, I was lying on the ground, trying to count how many stones and pebbles were pressing into my back. The night was still lingering, diffused by gray but still reluctant to leave, despite the slivered crescent of sun that edged over the eastern horizon. The air smelled green and dewy, and I was debating whether to stay wrapped in the warmth of my bedroll or get up and empty my bladder when three words broke the silence of these predawn thoughts.

"Oh my stars," said Kjel, his voice low.

I waited to hear more, for example, "There's a bear in the bushes," or "My nose is bleeding," but no words followed, and a minute later Kjel was out of his bedroll and headed toward the bushes I now looked at with longing.

I don't know what happened the next morning because I slept later than everyone, but the morning after that I heard Kjel wake up and offer the same words.

I was too shy to ask what he meant, and so I fantasized: what inspired these words of awe and reverence was me lying close by.

It's funny what a tonic a good fantasy can be; this one was like swigging down a glass full of vitamins and minerals, and set me up to face the day; not to seize it, necessarily, but to at least get through it.

On the fourth day of travel, Violet awoke feeling as if she'd been on the losing side of a saloon brawl. Sore from her neck to her feet, she sat up, and pushing aside the blanket someone had put over her, she rubbed her cramped left wrist.

"Good morning," said a pleasant voice. "Might I inquire as to what you're doing?"

Austin was tending the fire, smiling at Violet as if they were the best of friends.

"Nothing," she said, putting her right hand in her lap.

"Forgive my observance, but it looked to me as if you might be trying to soothe a phantom pain. The local storekeeper in my boyhood neighborhood was the unfortunate recipient of an arm amputation, and he often said he felt the weather change in the arm that was no longer there. It also on occasion drove him wild with itching."

Her outrage and embarrassment showed on her crimson face and she looked everywhere but his eyes, hoping to see Kjel and/or a place where she could piddle.

She didn't see the former but a proper distance up the creek was a clump of bushes, and she hurried off to it without explanation.

"The local storekeeper in my boyhood neighborhood was the unfortunate recipient of an arm amputation," she muttered softly, her voice a nasal singsong. The gall of that man—not only did he speak like he was some high-toned so-and-so, but he spoke of things that were none of his g.d. business and never would be. She had once heard a man running for mayor of Mount Crawford tell a crowd gathered at the town square that "if you educate a nigger, you're just asking for trouble," and with regards to Austin Sykes, his point was well taken.

Life had taught Violet a general dislike of people, and her animosity was not aimed at one particular race; still, in gathering reasons not to like him, it was easy to add "color" to her list, and she found that his color underscored all her other reasons. She would have disliked his show-offy way of speaking and his over-familiarity in anyone; that he was colored made these personality defects worse. She would resent anyone who was a rival for Kjel's attention, but the fact that he was a black man pushed her dislike into hatred.

Ruefully thinking of the clean, beautiful bathroom in the Hedstrom house (how had Mrs. Hedstrom made it smell like lavender?), Violet yanked down a cluster of leaves as she crouched over what she hoped was not poison ivy. Holding her skirt in a manner that gave her the most privacy, she did her business, and as she wiped herself with the leaves she wondered idly if there was a type of leaf with a particularly strong absorbancy.

She washed her face and hands in the creek, and as she brushed her teeth with her finger she looked up and down the bank, not expecting to see anything special, particularly not the sight of Kjel Hedstrom sitting up in an elm tree.

What on earth is he doing? she wondered, scoutin' for Injuns? Surveying the lay of the land? Picking apples? (In which case he was literally up the *wrong* tree.)

Deciding not to disturb him in *whatever* he was doing, Violet turned around, but she hadn't taken three steps before hearing " 'Morning, Violet!"

Her body tensed as if she'd just stepped under a cold shower, but she turned around as if she were pleasantly surprised to hear

Kjel's greeting. She made a good show of looking along the creek, and it wasn't until Kjel laughed that she allowed herself to look upward.

"Kjel," she said, her voice bright with surprise, "what are you doing up there?"

"It looked like the best place to watch the sunrise. You want to come up?"

Flushing, Violet raised her stump. "I can't."

Kjel's smile was sheepish. "Well . . . it's already risen anyway. The sun, that is." He swung down from the branch he was on to a lower one, to a lower one again, and then he jumped to the ground, and even though he landed on his feet, he brushed at the knees of his denim jeans.

"Sorry," he said, nodding at her stump.

Violet shook her head spastically and shrugged her shoulders; her silent answer for, "That's all right."

"Austin up?" asked Kjel as the two began walking back to their campsite, Violet silently screaming with self-consciousness.

"I guess so."

A chipmunk raced across the path and was swallowed by weeds.

"So what's for breakfast?" asked Kjel.

"Well, I could make some eggs and fry up that slab of ham—"

"Hey, Violet, stop a minute."

Violet stopped in her tracks; if he asked her to do the fandango, she would have shaken her hips and shouted, "Ay yi yi!"

"Here, help me tie this."

"What?" said Violet, watching as Kjel pulled a bandanna from his back pocket.

"I can't tie it with one hand—here, hold onto this end. Were you left- or right-handed?"

Unconsciously, Violet cupped her stump with her hand, trying to protect it from view. "Left. Although when I went to school the teachers made me use my right hand."

"Well, I'm right-handed, so that's the hand I'll tie up."

Violet stood dumbly, holding out a corner of the cloth that

Kjel had wrapped around his right forearm and under his upper arm. At his request, she helped him tie the bandanna at his wrist so that his elbow was bent and his hand level with his shoulder.

"There," he said, waving his improvised stump. "I don't know why I didn't try this long ago."

The air was pushed out of Violet as if she'd been punched, and within seconds she gave into her impulse to run.

"So now we're having a race?" said Kjel, smiling as he caught up to her.

Violet ran faster, brushing aside the overgrown chokecherry branches that butted out onto the path.

Austin, making coffee over the fire, looked up in surprise as Violet raced into the campsite with Kjel directly behind her.

"Lord Almighty, where's the fire?" he asked, jumping up and scanning the environs for the bear or wolf or conflagration that was giving chase.

No one stopped to illuminate him as to where or what the fire was.

"Kjel!" said Austin, joining the chase. "What's going on? Why's your arm tied up like that?"

Kjel didn't answer, lunging at Violet as she slowed to grab her scruffy carpetbag.

"Let go of me!" the girl screamed, twisting her body to loosen his grip.

"I will, Violet," said Kjel, holding onto her good arm with his good arm, "as soon as you tell me, A, what's the matter and, B, where are you going?"

Violet's eyes glittered as she stared at Kjel, and except for her bright red cheeks, she was pale as an invalid. Austin could see her pulse throbbing in her thin neck.

"Let go of me and I'll tell you," she said, and because that sounded like a fair bargain to Kjel, he did, giving Violet the opportunity to break the agreement and race off into the woods. Or try to race off; she might have gotten a head start but Kjel wasn't about to let her take advantage of it; his leap covered a good four feet and he again grabbed her by the arm.

Now Austin saw the fury in her glittery eyes—he'd seen the same look in his brother's eyes whenever he faced off against someone he thought had done him wrong—and he tensed, expecting Violet to haul off and hit Kjel. As puzzled and shocked as he was about the unfolding drama, he was also excited, the way any bystander is who comes across a fight.

On top of the hot fire the coffee percolator began to burble. "Now what is transpiring here?" asked Austin, looking back at the coffee and making the decision to try to end whatever it was that was transpiring, so he could pour himself a cup.

In Kjel's hold, Violet was squirming furiously but was not succeeding at freeing herself.

"Nothing," she said, a sneer twisting her features. "Nothing but another joke. A little more humor—in case you haven't had enough—at my expense."

"A joke?" said Kjel, letting go of her arm. "Violet, I'm not trying to be funny—I'm trying to understand you!"

"So you tie up your arm like that?" she said, spitting out her words more than speaking them. "*That's* how you're going to understand me?"

Austin watched as Violet and Kjel stared at each other, saw the expression on the girl's face change from furious contempt to furious disbelief to plain disbelief.

Kjel's guileless expression did not change at all.

"Why?" said Violet finally, defeat in her voice. "Why do you want to 'understand' me?"

"Violet," said Kjel, his voice gentle as a lullaby, "let's all sit by the fire and have a cup of coffee, okay?"

"I want to know why you want to understand me!"

"I know you do, Violet, but can't we have some coffee while we talk about it?"

"I second the motion," said Austin, whose morning really didn't start until he had his caffeine.

They were in Iowa now, in a campsite surrounded by a half circle of oak trees that, with the help of a good breeze or industrious squirrels, sprinkled the ground with acorns. As they gathered their enameled tin cups and watched as Austin poured them coffee, the oak above them lobbed down a dozen acorns, one of which pinged against the edge of Kjel's cup, making him splash coffee on his hand.

"Ow," he said, setting down the cup and bringing his thumb to his mouth. "That's the second one—last night one beaned me on the head. I was dreaming about a baseball game too—the Yankees were playing themselves, how do you like that?—when bam! Beaned me right on the head!"

He rubbed his forehead and Austin laughed, a tense and nervous laugh.

There was a tree stump near the fire and Kjel and Austin had dragged a log next to it. Violet took the stump, and when Kjel sat next to Austin on the log, he nearly fell off it.

"Geez, Violet, even sitting is hard, isn't it?" he said, righting himself. "A person's whole balance is thrown off."

His arm was still tied up in its bandanna sling, and Violet's jaw muscles bulged as she clamped her teeth tight, surveying the landscape again for available escape routes.

Kjel sipped at his coffee and set his cup on the dirt in front of him. "Violet, don't get that look in your eye—you're not going anywhere. We're going to sit here and get everything out in the open."

Shaking her head, Violet scoffed.

"Now what's that supposed to mean?" asked Kjel.

"We're going to sit here and get everything out in the open," said Violet, mocking the earnestness of Kjel's voice. "What's 'everything'? My life story? How it feels to be one-armed and ugly, with a beehive in my ears?"

"A beehive in her ears?" said Austin, looking helplessly at Kjel.

Violet's smile was as malicious as her voice. "Oh, didn't he tell you about that? That I'm crazy and have—"

"No, Violet," said Kjel, his voice even. "I didn't tell Austin about that. I didn't tell him about anything. I figured whatever you told me was in confidence—but hell, that's the trouble, you haven't told me anything since I picked you up on my horse. Four days we've been traveling, and every day you sit there like a bump on a log, and trying to have a normal conversation with you is like trying to have a normal conversation with somebody deaf and dumb!"

"I listen," said Violet defensively. "I talk."

"One- or two-word sentences," said Kjel. " 'Yes,' 'no,' 'I don't know.' "

"That's three," Austin pointed out helpfully.

It was true and Violet knew it, Kjel had virtually given up trying to make conversation with his passenger, so unresponsive had she been. Sitting in the cab with Kjel had been torturous; trying to figure out how to act, how to *be* with this man she loved so much that it actually pained her heart, had made her less on pins and needles than on blades and pitchfork tines; lost in her need to make a good impression, she gave up being herself, knowing that was the last person Kjel Hedstrom would be interested in.

"And what do you mean," continued Austin, "by a 'beehive in your ears'?"

Violet stared at the ground.

"She," began Kjel, "she . . . well, there's always this ringing in her ears."

"What do you mean by 'always.' "

Violet looked up. "What do you think he means? *Always.* My ears are *always* ringing. Day and night, night and day. A noise like bees in my head, twenty-four hours a day."

"Even now?" asked Austin.

"Twenty-four hours a day."

"So you see," said Kjel, "things are hard for Violet."

"Hard?" said Austin. "She doesn't know hard."

Violet yelped out a laugh. "I don't know *hard*?"

Wearing a half smile, Austin shook his head. "Forget about a little ringing in your ears—you try bouncing along in the back of a truck because it might *disturb* people seeing a nigger sitting in the cab of a truck with a white woman. And boy oh boy, ah jes cain't wait for it to rain; yes suh, so's I can sit back there all wrapped up inna tarp!"

Violet shrugged. "I didn't ask you to sit in the back of the truck."

"Nobody had to!" said Austin, and his slightly bulging eyes looked as if they'd migrated farther out of their sockets. "Don't you think I know how to act? Don't you think I always have to figure out what's going to be easiest for everybody? Don't you think that might be just a little bit *hard*? Well, let me tell you, people: I'm sick of it!"

With this admonition, he flung his coffee to the ground as if it had somehow betrayed him too.

"Jeez, Austin," said Kjel, who was prepared to hear Violet spout off, but not his friend.

"Shit! You tie up your arm like that to see what it's like to understand *her*." Austin spat out the last word. "I don't see you blackening your skin to see what it's like to be me! I'd wager any amount of money that it's a whole lot harder to be me in the world than her!"

"Chaw!" Violet said.

"*Chaw!* What kind of expression is 'chaw'?"

"It's something we say back home, all right?" Violet's face was red. "And let me tell you—even if I did have my whole arm, it'd still be twice as hard to be me than you! A man—even a black man trying to talk like he's a duke or something—I've seen that dictionary you read in the back of the truck!—has it a hundred times easier than any woman!"

"Oh, now it's a hundred times, huh? That's quite a jump from twice as hard! And why shouldn't I work on my vocabulary? *Chaw!* What's the matter with a man trying to better his speech?"

"Better his speech," mimicked Violet. "The *matter,* the matter is that you sound so . . . so ridiculous. It . . . it *displeases* me to hear you wax *un*poetically, so *un*eloquently."

"What I'd really like to wax is your mouth shut."

"Try it and you're a dead man."

"Hey, hey," said Kjel, finally breaking in. "No hitting, no kicking. This is a clean fight."

"This isn't any kind of a fight," said Austin. "This isn't any kind of anything. Let's just load up the truck and get going."

"We're not going anywhere until we clear the air," said Kjel. "Until we're all friends here."

Taking a step toward him, Austin pointed his finger at Kjel's face.

"Let me tell you something, *friend*. You don't always get to say what I get to do."

He picked his tin cup off the ground and tossed it up into the air. When it came down, he snatched it and then threw it up again, and kept playing his ferocious game of catch until he reached the truck.

Chapter Eight

IMAGINE THE TENSION THAT WAS PART OF THE AIR BEFORE OUR
*little set-to and then imagine the tension that was the air after Austin
walked off.*

"Honestly, Violet, you should go apologize to him."

"Apologize for what?" I asked in my best sneer-filled voice.

*Kjel avoided my eyes as he took the percolator off the grate and
dumped the coffee on the fire.*

"You really hate him that much?"

"For your information, I hate just about everybody."

*Kjel's face sort of caved in then, which made a part of me raise a ban-
ner of triumph—I had won something, and it didn't matter how small
and ugly it was.*

"Meanness doesn't have a whole lot of rewards, Violet."

"Yeah, well neither does this conversation."

*Both of them told me later that they wouldn't have gone after me had
I decided to run off right then; but my stubborn streak had solidified into
steel, and now there was no way I was going to make it easy for anyone,
let alone myself.*

Even though he had humiliated me by tying up his arm, by his

---

clumsy attempts at peacekeeping, I was still madly, irrationally, crazy in love with Kjel, and the knowledge that I might sicken him mattered little. I needed to punish him for making me feel things I'd never felt before, and so instead of disappearing into the figurative sunset, I silently, sullenly helped him take down camp.

Kjel gave a whistle when we were all loaded up, and I was disappointed but not surprised when Austin emerged from the woods. Of course he wouldn't leave—he had less guts than I did.

I got into the truck, but in my mind I was a witch, standing before a big black pot, stirring its hissing, steaming hate and flinging ladlefuls at him.

Kjel started up the truck and we rattled out onto the road, and I kept tending to that pot of hate, letting it simmer and then lobbing spoonfuls at Austin. It simmered for over two hours, until we stopped for gas, and then circumstances arose that tipped the pot over, tipped it over and smashed it so that I could never tend to that particular hate, would never want to tend to that particular hate in that way again.

Every time they drove over a bump, Austin thought bones would break, either in his hand, which clenched the side of the truck so hard his knuckles looked pale blue against his skin, or his jaw, which was clamped shut. He had a gift for seeing the bright side of things, but at the present moment the shadow of his anger obliterated any light, any brightness.

"Uneloquent," he muttered to himself, for of all the things Violet said to him, this he remembered most. Just because he was in love with words, just because he could hear the music in them, did that mean he was trying to "talk like a fancy white man"? It was his vanity—his way with words—and it pained him to think Violet had not been impressed by them. It pained him even more that what Violet thought should be of any concern at all to him; what did he care what a mean, amputated giantess thought of his language?

The truck rocked over a rut in the road, and as Austin banged against the side of the truck, he thought of the sheer delight that would be his if Violet would slam against her door, hard enough so that she spilled out of it and onto the road, where her mean ugly head would crack open like an egg.

In the front seat, Kjel wasn't entertaining fantasies about Violet's demise; although he wasn't entertaining thoughts about her long life either.

> *There once was a ship named Violet*
> *Who no one dared to pilot*
> *She'd steer into rocks*
> *And crash into docks—*

And that's why I write song lyrics and not limericks, thought Kjel as he tried to figure out how to work "file it" or "style it" into the last line; better to occupy his mind with a poorly rhymed limerick than to worry about his circumstances.

What am I going to do, Lord? he asked, once he realized he had gone through every possible word that rhymed with Violet. He didn't expect an answer; his father had schooled him in prayer ("Just keep asking, son, because even if it seems like a one-sided conversation, God's listening"), and it was a comfort to put the question to someone/thing bigger than himself.

He looked to the line of pines on each side of the road, looked at their heavy, spiky greenness and put his question out to them: Trees, what should I do? To the blue unknowable span of sky he asked: So what do you think, sky? Shifting gears as the truck climbed a slight incline, he addressed them: Gears, how 'bout a little guidance? Tires, steering wheel, engine, carburetor, fan belt, camshaft; all these parts that fit together, that worked together: *What should I do?*

But the pines were silent, the sky wide open but mute, and the machinery of the truck went quietly about its business, offering no secrets in its spins, its whirs, its humming.

Kjel didn't even try to converse with Violet; he was tired of her, sick of her silence, but now more sick of whatever she might say. It had been a mistake to bring her, but now what? How to rectify the mistake? How to get her out of the truck, out of his life, without making bigger mistakes?

Tell me, crow, he thought, watching as the black bird swooped across the road, what should I do? But the crow offered not even a sullen, testy caw.

✳

AUSTIN STOOD OUTSIDE THE TRUCK, looking at a map, when an old Model T rattled into the filling station lot and two red-faced men tumbled out of the passenger-side door and loped crookedly toward a copse of sumac that signaled the start of the woods. The rust-riddled car lurched forward to a gas tank and its driver killed the engine.

"You lost?" he asked Austin.

"Don't think so," said Austin, offering a polite smile.

"Them's Dakota plates," said the man, jutting his chin at the truck's license. His face matched the others in ruddiness and it was spotted with acne scars and carbuncles. He jutted his chin at the truck's license and in a liquor breath that curdled the air, asked, "What's a nigger doin' with Dakota plates?"

"It's my employer's car," said Austin evenly, folding up the map. He got back into the truck, silently bidding Kjel and Violet to hurry up.

The men had let Violet have first dibs on the restroom and relieved themselves in the woods, but when Austin had returned to the vehicle, Kjel had taken a little walk to stretch his legs. Sometimes these little walks lasted ten minutes, sometimes a half hour, and as Austin looked at his watch, he sincerely hoped it would be the former.

The station owner ran out to the Model T.

"Whew!" he said to the driver, "A little early in the day to be into the hooch, wouldn't you say, Pops?"

"Just fill the tank," snarled the man, and spit out a stream of tarry tobacco juice onto the cement.

Holding a peace offering of tiger lilies, Kjel was just emerging from the woods when he saw two tall men outside the restroom, one boosted up, his foot in the other man's laced hands, peeking through the transom window above the door.

"Turn around, baby," said the Peeping Tom, as his brother implored him to get down and let him have a peek. "Let me see them boobies."

At the sink, Violet froze. She had her blouse and bra off and was washing her armpits; a filling station restroom was a luxury of which she made full use. She was working her way down, having already scrubbed her face and neck (she was always surprised how travel dirtied a neck). Now, looking at the mirror to see a pair of eyes looking through the slatted window, Violet scrambled to get back into her bra and then her blouse, buttoning it up without drying herself off.

"Hey, she ain't got an arm," reported the Peeping Tom.

"And you have no manners," said Kjel, standing behind the men.

"Huh?" The man who was acting as ladder dropped his hands and his brother stumbled to the ground.

"What'd you say, pretty boy?" asked the Peeping Tom, picking himself up.

At the smell of cheap liquor, Kjel's scalp prickled but his voice remained light. "Why don't you just get on your way."

"Get on our way where?"

The door squeaked open and Violet peered out, her eyes wide.

"Violet, go get in the truck," said Kjel.

"See, I told you she was one-armed!" said the Peeping Tom, pointing at Violet's stump.

It was the wrong day to pick on Violet, and a flare of anger rose higher than her one of fear.

"Yeah, well at least I ain't no drunk and ugly carbuncully spy-boys."

"Whoa—nice voice, Froggy," said one of the brothers.

"And who said you ain't ugly?" asked the other, and because

he hated an uppity woman, especially an *ugly* uppity woman (whose breasts he'd been gypped out of seeing), he pushed her, hard.

"Oof," said Violet, the air rushing out of her as her back struck the doorjamb.

"Ugghh," said the man who'd pushed Violet, as Kjel's fist slammed into his stomach.

"Hey!" said the Peeping Tom, jumping on Kjel, and suddenly fists, feet, arms, and elbows were flying as the red-faced brothers squared off against the man and the one-armed woman.

Violet tried to shake off the man who squeezed her stump with one hand and grabbed her hair with the other.

"Oww!" she cried as he yanked her head back.

"Dirty bitch!" he cried as she kicked his shin.

The bees in Violet's ears were a distant buzz, so loud did the sounds of fighting—heavy breathing, cries, smacks, and thuds—fill them. Adrenaline pumped through her, working as both an analgesic, numbing the pain she felt every time her assailant struck her, and as an amphetamine, giving her the strength and speed to strike back.

When her head was yanked back, her hair feeling as if it were being pried out by the roots, the numbness faded and she cried out, grabbing the man's hair in retaliation.

The man pulled Violet's hand off his hair and pinned it behind her back, and with his other hand he reached into his boot. Violet saw a flash of light but it was blocked out by the battering ram that was Austin.

As Austin tackled her assailant, Kjel landed a solid punch to the midsection of the other one, and he sank to his knees, gasping.

A spurt of blood from someone's nose splattered red drops on a rock by the restroom door.

I'm bleeding, thought Austin, stopping the flow from his nose by holding a finger horizontally underneath it.

"Hey!" shouted the father, swaying a short distance away. "What're you doin' to my boys?"

"Getting them off my property!" said the station owner, who had jogged into the fray. He nudged one of the brothers with the toe of his shoe. "Now get up and be on your way before I call the sheriff!" To Kjel, he said, "And you all best be on your way too."

"More than happy to," said Kjel, and taking Violet's arm, they race-walked past the father, who shook his fist at them.

Austin, close behind them, suddenly stopped.

"I'll be right with you," he said, squatting by the side of the rusty Model T.

"Austin," said Kjel—as the red-faced men lobbed taunts of "nigger," "nigger lover," and "one-armed freak," at them—"now is *not* the time to tie your shoe."

"Okay, okay," said Austin, standing up and wiping his palms. He was ready to jump into the back of the truck when it occurred to him to get in one final dig at their drunk aggressors. He followed Violet into the front seat. Startled, she nonetheless moved to the middle, and after Austin slammed the door shut, he threw them a kiss, like a county-fair beauty contestant riding a parade-day float.

"Well, if that doesn't make them want to come after us, I don't know what will," said Kjel, firing up the engine.

"Let them come," said Austin. Dabbing at his still-bleeding nose, he began to laugh.

Flooring the engine as he turned onto the road, Kjel said, "You won't be laughing if they catch up to us."

"That's just it," said Austin, examining his blood-spotted handkerchief. "They won't. It'll take them a while to change their tire."

"You did something to their tire?" asked Violet, wide-eyed.

"Why, yes I did, Violet." His swollen lip parted as he chuckled. "I stabbed it to death."

"You stabbed it to death?" repeated Violet.

"Well, when I realized I had their knife, I knew I had to return it. I just didn't think it would behoove us if I returned it directly to them."

"So you stabbed their front tire," said Kjel, laughing.

Bunching the handkerchief under his nose, Austin wiped away the last of the blood.

"All the way to the rim."

"To the rim," said Violet, and their laughter bounced around the cab as the truck hurtled down the road.

✳

"WELL, VIOLET, NOW you match your name," said Kjel as they sat by the fire that night assessing their wounds.

The left side of the young woman's face bore a purple reminder of when her cheek made solid and brutish contact with her assailant's knobby fist, and her stump, in random patterns from her elbow to her shoulder, was the same color.

"He wouldn't let it go," said Violet, rubbing her bruised upper arm. "He was like a monkey on a vine."

"I wonder how long it took them to fix their tire," said Kjel, and he and Violet laughed, again, at the idea of those poor drunks' vengeance delayed by a flat tire.

"I just hope we don't meet their acquaintance again at a later date," said Austin, making another security check with his eyes, his earlier tire-stabbing bravado long since having faded, replaced by his usual caution. His face had suffered most in the melee; his nose was swollen and his lip split, and for the hundredth time he stretched and then curled the fingers of his right hand. Having seen the effects of fistfights on his brother and his brother's opponents, he went out of his way to avoid them. He expected the places where he'd been hit to hurt, but what surprised him was how sore his hands were from hitting. Sore, but as far as he could tell, nothing was broken. He looked toward the darkened, tree-lined road. "There are other people in the world I'd definitely rather run into."

Kjel reached for his guitar and played a diminished G chord. "Austin, you worry too much."

"Worry, my friend, keeps me on guard, and being on guard is a practical position for a man in my racial situation."

Austin cradled his guitar on his lap and played the same chord and Violet thought, Here it comes. But in her acknowledgment of what the night held, there was not her usual resentment, but excitement; for once she didn't feel as if their music was a wall of notes and tones that said, "Keep out." Tonight she felt for the first time that it wasn't Kjel and Austin vs. Violet; tonight she thought she was part of a team. It was a mangy and bruised, ragtag, in-need-of-a-bath team, but it had been a long time since Violet had felt part of anything, and as she shifted her aching body against the dirt that was her chair and the tree that was her backrest, she decided to announce her membership in it.

"Lord, Lord, Lord," she sang as Kjel and Austin began playing their guitars, "I ain't never felt so good when I'm feeling so bad."

The whites of both men's eyes showed more than usual but they didn't let their surprise seize and strangle the moment. They kept playing and Violet kept singing.

"Yeah, I got smacked, I got hit—

"Got pulled and pummeled till I felt like shit—"

The men hooted.

"But after kicking all those carbuncully asses, I bet it ain't easy for them to sit."

Kjel answered Violet's words with notes that sounded like a taunt, *Wuh, wuh, wuh,* and Austin embellished those notes, ending his riff with the tune, "Shave and a haircut/six bits."

They broke the moment of "What just happened here?" silence with more hoots and laughter, and Violet couldn't help herself—she looked up, searching among the stars for the vapor that had just been released, that potion of hate that had evaporated and floated up into the dark summer sky.

"Violet, you can sing!" said Kjel with the same exuberance he might have announced her taking flight. "You sound like Marlene Dietrich with a case of the blues!"

"Not only can she sing, she can curse like a—" For once words abandoned Austin. "Like a fuckin' sailor!"

"Carbuncully asses!" said Kjel, dabbing at the tears in his eyes. "Did you ever hear of such a thing?"

———

"Well, if they have them on their faces, I just assumed—"

"You just assumed their asses were carbuncled too?" Austin leaned back, his hand resting on his chest above his guitar. "Oh, Violet, you're priceless."

The campfire was small and near to extinguishing itself but it offered up a snap, and Violet was so intoxicated by the day's events that it was easy to convince herself that even the fire was in agreement.

She sang along with two songs she had learned from the past night's concerts, but when they started improvising again, urging Violet's participation, she declined, choosing instead to sit back and listen. As exhilarated as she was, she was bushed; they had traveled less than sixty miles today, and yet Violet felt she had crossed several borders.

How was it that she had sung about and discussed carbuncled hindquarters with two men, one whom she was in love with and one who was a Negro? How was it that the Negro said she was priceless and she hadn't slapped his face and told him to watch his sassy mouth?

Closing her eyes, she saw in the theater of her mind the looks on the drunk men's faces when she came out of the filling-station restroom; saw the red whiskers of her assailant and felt their bushiness when she grabbed a handful and pulled. It was so quick, that fight; so violent that even in its brutal certainty there was something surreal about it. The shock of her father striking her without warning had never softened, but it was far less shocking than being in the middle of a fight, throwing punches and dodging them, pulling hair and having hers pulled, kicking and stomping whatever could be kicked and stomped. It was like being in the middle of a cyclone, only the wind wasn't the enemy; two bad-skinned brothers and their bad-skinned father were. Time had passed in slow motion and, conversely, in a blur, but what blazed in her mind was the picture of the knife that one of the brothers drew out of his boot, and how the sun reflected off the blade like a tiny burst of flame, and how that burst of flame was meant to burn her, and how Austin's hand had caught that flame as it moved in an arc toward her, extinguishing it as he tackled the man and wrenched it out of his hand.

He had screamed, the man with the knife, screaming so loud that Violet couldn't hear the small crunching snap that was his wrist bone breaking.

"I never expected them to take it that far," Austin had said in the truck. "I never thought that miserable drunken inebriate would try and *stab* somebody."

Kjel shook his head. "I never saw it coming. I'm sure glad you did."

So that was the thing, thought Violet, her eyes closing as the heaviness of sleep pressed down upon her. The Negro saved my life.

If it had happened when she still wanted to kill herself, she would have regarded his saving her as pointless meddling, but now that she wanted to live, she had to acknowledge that he was on her side, and his goal—to save her life—was her own.

There's one less person in the world to hate, thought Violet, but still skeptical of any lightness of heart, she added, *for now.*

Chapter Nine

I WAS LUCKY—IN THE FRESHNESS OF MY YOUTH, I GOT TO LIVE *in the freshness of America's youth. Okay, not in its "natives-roaming-bison-filled prairies" youth, not even its "settlers-kicking-those-natives-off-their-land" youth, but in its "untrammeled-by-industry" youth. That's not to say we didn't have automobiles and plants and factories churning out goods and their residual poisons, but the percentage was so much smaller compared to landmass and population. Just think of the places of your life—your town, your city, your childhood home. How much of what you remember as a kid is still there, unchanged? A half? A quarter? Anything?*

How much open space have you seen, been in the middle of? Out on the Dakota plains you could see the horizon in all directions, the only man-made interruption being the occasional silver silo or Burma Shave billboard. In Minnesota we were surrounded by trees and water—lakes whose shorelines were free of docks, vacation homes, and boats with names like Lucy-Fer and Atta Boy; creeks and rivers whose clear water allowed you to see your toes when you were standing waist-deep.

And the quality of light—of course the days were brighter, since the sun didn't have to sift through so many pollutants—and the night, for the same reason, was darker. A darkness all dressed up in billions of diamonds—I didn't know why Kjel waited until morning to praise the stars—I could barely shut my eyes to the glory that was those night skies.

Even though we had slept outside every night, we didn't have to make reservations at a campsite—we could pull off the road almost anywhere and find a nice sheltered place to build a fire and lay out our bedrolls. Nowadays you might drive along what looks to be the edge of a forest, but most likely that's all it is—the edge of a forest and nothing more, the trees giving way to a freeway going the opposite direction, or to farmland, or most likely to a new development of condominiums or outlet malls. But back then those roadside trees were only the edges flanking acres and acres of forest, and the smell in the air was so green—pine sap and wild crab apples, underbrush, mud, and wood. Have you ever pressed your face against a tree and inhaled? (Remember, I knew the smell of Tree Pa better than my own dad.) Bark is a subtle smell: woody, and of the dirt, and also a little oily, like hair that needs a shampoo. It comforts me that tree bark still smells the same; it makes me think the world isn't as out of control as it often seems to be.

My stiff knees make it harder to camp now, but I still get out in the wilds a couple of times a year. 'Course camping out is not what it used to be—what is?—it's harder and harder to get away from the modern world, but trust me, the effort is worthwhile. The modern world takes a person away from their essence (has anyone really ever had an epiphany while shopping?); the natural world helps fortify that acquaintance.

Let the elements be in charge—because in the end, they are. Sniff tree bark, sleep on a mattress of leaves, let your radio be the crickets and hoot owls, and your alarm clock the rising sun.

There are still those sacred outdoor spaces, so I say—get off your fanny and honor them! Being in open spaces is a tonic for just about everything. Unless, of course, you're agoraphobic.

Another check had to be marked on the side of life's unfairness when it came to Violet's menstrual periods. They were heavy-flowing and cramp-filled, and when the morning sun nudged her awake she knew the deep ache low in her belly was not from the previous day's fistfight; that the pain and the stickiness between her legs were signs that her least favorite part of the month was upon her.

"Damn it all to hell!" she whispered, chastising herself for not anticipating its arrival. Since the filling-station fight, she had slept close to the men, for safety, but usually on the other side of the fire for privacy. Grateful that they weren't at the campsite now, she whispered frantic cusswords, trying to figure out how to get the bloodstains out of her pajama bottoms (she never slept in her clothes, so as not to wrinkle them more than necessary) as well as her bedroll. Their campsite was nowhere near water, as far as she could see.

She dug in her carpetbag for her supply of rags, and after folding several into a thick layer, pinned the makeshift pad to a clean pair of underpants.

"If we pass any dollar hotels today," she said later, as they had their breakfast coffee around the campfire, "do you think we could check in?"

"I second the motion," said Austin. "I'd certainly like to spruce up a bit before we make our grand Chicago entrance."

"Yeah, I guess it's about time we all got a real shower," said Kjel, and nodding at Violet he added, "especially you."

The bees in Violet's head hummed in a complex chord as she wished for mercy from the Earth, wished it would crack open and swallow her up.

Kjel laughed. "Oh, Violet, you should see your face. I'm sorry—I didn't mean to insult you. It's just so obvious that you're on the rag."

Heat flamed Violet's face, but it was Austin who sputtered, choking on the coffee he had just sipped.

"Lord have mercy! Did you just say what I think you said?"

"I didn't mean anything by it," said Kjel. "Sorry, Violet, I didn't mean to embarrass you—it's just that . . . well, I have a sister. I know about these things."

"I have a sister too but that doesn't give me license to use vulgar slang for a subject that shouldn't be discussed in mixed

124

company!" Austin jabbed the air with his coffee cup, causing him to yelp after a splash of coffee landed on his hand.

"Vulgar slang," said Kjel. "Austin, I swear, you're worse than some of the old church ladies at Pearl Lutheran." He took the pot off the fire, and emptying the last of the coffee into his and Austin's cups, said to Violet, "I'm not going to refill yours because coffee's not good for cramps."

"Lord, does this man never learn?" implored Austin, looking to the sky.

Ignoring him, Kjel asked Violet if they were bad, and when she looked at the ground and gave a short nod, he said, "I thought so. You really do look peaked, Violet. Same as Kay. She used to run me ragged refilling the hot-water bottle."

"I thought your sister's name was Berit," said Violet.

Kjel laughed. "Berit is my sister. Kay was a friend of mine. Like most women, she had periods too."

"Oh," said Violet, and in her heart she felt a stab of jealousy for this Kay person, this woman with whom Kjel had been intimate enough to heat her hot-water bottles.

"Can we just pack up?" said Austin, flinging the last remains of his coffee into the fire. "Can we just pack up and change the conversation—or how about let's have none at all while we're doing it?"

Kjel stood up and stretched. "I don't know what's the matter with you. It's a natural part of life, you know."

"So are bowel movements! So are nocturnal emissions! Does that mean they should be topics of conversation?"

"Why not?" asked Kjel, shrugging. "In fact, just yesterday I had to—"

With hoots and boos, Violet and Austin drowned out the rest of his sentence, and as they packed up the truck they made sure that everything else Kjel tried to say was vigorously shushed.

"Austin, maybe we—"

"Shhhh!"

"Are we—"

"Shush!"

"When are—"

"Quiet!"

✦

THAT EVENING, WHEN THEIR MOODS were as bright as the flames that danced in the campfire, Austin said, "The word of the day is *excellent*."

"What are you talking about, man?" asked Kjel, poking at the fire with a stick.

"You have your own ritual, your words to greet the day; now I'm going to have my own ritual. My own personal word of the day. And what comes to mind as I look back over the past daylight hours is *excellent*."

"You read the dictionary like it's your own personal Bible and all you can come up with is *excellent*?"

"Yes," agreed Violet, "I would have thought your word of the day would have at least five syllables in it."

"You wound me," said Austin, shaking his head. "I don't choose words for their length or density, I choose words to correctly describe what it is I want to say."

Kjel twirled the stick in the ashes, raising sparks. "So what you want to say is that today was excellent?"

"Exactly."

Pushing his lip out, Kjel thought for a moment.

"Violet, would you say the word of the day is *excellent*?"

Violet stroked her chin in exaggerated thought. "Yes. Even more so if we would have found a hotel, but yes, I believe I would."

"Then there you have it. The word of the day is *excellent*."

"Hey, this is my ritual, remember? I don't need a consensus. If my word of the day is *excellent*, it's *excellent*, whether you two agree or not."

"Okay, okay, you don't have to get all bent out of shape about it."

———

"Yeah," said Violet. "Then you'll have to change the word of the day to something like *malleable.*"

"*Moldable,*" offered Kjel.

"*Pliant.*"

"*Excellent!*" said Austin, his voice rising in agitation. "The word of the day is *excellent!*"

Chapter Ten

EVEN THOUGH MY POSITION ON ORGANIZED RELIGION IS REORGanize it, *I realize you don't have to be a firebrand Christian to see the worth of those Ten Commandments but if I were in charge, I'd give Jesus' advice to "love your neighbor as yourself" official commandment status. Just think about that for a minute. Why are most of us unable to follow this deceptively simple directive, because we hardly love ourselves. If we all worked on that first—acknowledging the gift that each one of us is—and then acknowledged the gift that everyone else is, well, try to imagine that world! Every ocean would be the Sea of Tranquility, and Eden would be restored to its original concept and would no longer be just another name for a strip-club star. It would be a commandment that if followed would cancel the need for the ten others: Love your neighbor as yourself.*

Oh sure, you might think that bit of philosophy is as deep as a wading pool, but the most obvious things, by virtue of their obviousness, are sometimes the hardest to learn; when Austin became my friend, his differentness, his darkness, became inconsequential to that which was really him—his personality, his character, his essence.

I'm not saying my great iceberg of hate melted just like that; for a long while it was hard enough to consider Austin as my equal, let alone his brother. I did think Dallas was handsome, for a black man; he didn't have Austin's lanky but barrel-chested goofiness, his protuberant eyes, or his wide spread of a nose. No, Dallas had a fine face, and his upper body proportions were of those who'd put some time in shoveling rock on a chain gang. He was certainly polite when Austin introduced us, tipping his hat and offering a "Very nice to meet you, miss." But in his slow smile, I saw the corner of his mouth turn up in a sneer, and when he looked me in the eye, my impulse was to cover my private parts, which suddenly felt exposed.

You no-good, sly, and sneaky bastard, I thought, you don't fool me.

Later, Austin and I would laugh about the prejudicial conclusions my first impression jumped to, but it was world-weary laughter, because in my last impression of Dallas, there'd be so much remaining of my first.

The first jam session the three men played was one that ended with Kjel whooping and Austin hollering.

"What'd I tell you, what'd I tell you?" Austin asked.

Kjel couldn't seem to stop shaking his head. "You said he could play, but I never guessed he could play like *that!*"

With his guitar cradled in his lap, Dallas lit a cigarette, his attention focused on the smoke rings he languidly sent up toward the moon. Pleading exhaustion, Violet huddled on the bedroll she laid out beneath a spruce tree, hiding herself behind the sweeping curtain of green the lower branches offered. Her body pulsed in jittery shivers, but she knew it was more from her own uneasiness than the cool night air. Why, just as things were beginning to get comfortable, did Dallas have to join them?

Austin had asked himself the same question earlier that day in Chicago, when the apartment door opened to a woman whose loose robe gaped open to reveal a lobe of breast dotted with red.

Good heavens, he thought, *those are bite marks!*

Austin stammered for a moment, furiously looking everywhere but at the woman's bruised breast and hard face until he finally stated his business.

"Dallas!" She hollered his name the way a mother who's sick of mothering calls to her brattiest child. "Dallas, some bug-eyed nigger wants to see your sorry ass!"

"Stop screaming, woman," said a voice, "'less you want me to give you somethin' to scream about."

Austin forced himself to remain at the paint-blistered door, breathing in the smells of hallway urine, rancid cooking oil, and mold, his heart lurching around his chest like a drunk looking for an exit.

I could run out, he thought, *out of this flea trap and back to the truck, and tell Kjel and Violet that I couldn't find him.*

"Austin?" shouted Dallas, and although the sharp sound of his voice gave Austin no clue as to whether his brother was happy to see him, the massive, bone-crunching hug did. "Brother of mine!" Dallas said, squeezing him the way a child squeezes a long-lost doll, "Austin Jefferson, it's you in the flesh."

Austin looked around the dingy room he'd been pulled into as he patted his brother's hard-muscled shoulder, and finally, when the flow of oxygen had resumed to his lungs, he said, "Yes, Dallas Washington, it is I in the flesh."

"Dallas, Austin, Jefferson, Washington," said the robe-wearing woman out of the side of her mouth. "Couldn't your mama thinka no original names her ownself?"

She continued her mumbled commentary as she watched Dallas throw his clothes into a cardboard suitcase, and did not seem upset at his imminent departure.

"Good, leave, I'm glad. I got plenty of men who beat down that door to get to me."

"Sure, Floraday, that's how it's gonna be," answered Dallas, throwing a wink at his brother. "I'll bet my brother Austin passed 'least a dozen coming up."

"At least," said Austin, offering a hopeful smile, but his charm was lost on the woman.

"Shut your mouth," she said, pulling the ties of her robe tight around her loose waist. "Shut your mouth and get the hell out of my house."

———

Austin was only happy to oblige, as was Dallas, from the sound of his delighted laughter.

"Ha! She told you, Austin!" he said as they walked down the dark, dank hallway. "You shoulda seen that look on your face! I ain't seen you that afraid since Grandma Lovey used to take us out back with the switch."

As they walked down the crumbly apartment stoop and toward the truck, Austin reminded his brother, "They're white, but they're cool."

"White but cool," muttered Dallas, with the same puzzlement someone might say "hot but cold" or "happy but sad."

PROVING ITS REPUTATION FOR FICKLENESS, Fate reached down and tickled the motley crew when, forty miles outside of Chicago, they happened to pass the few tents and rides that constituted a county fair.

"Cotton candy," said Kjel, reading a roadside sign. "Pulled taffy and caramel apples!"

Violet smiled at the awe in Kjel's voice; he said "pulled taffy" and "caramel apples" the way a pirate might announce "the lost treasure of Atlantis!"

She'd never met anyone with a sweet tooth like Kjel's—the only thing that ever gave him cause to complain was when there was no sugar left, when his ration of Baby Ruths or Bit-O-Honeys or Snaps ran out and he was left with a few hours of unsweetened consciousness.

"We're going to stop in for a minute and get ourselves a treat," he said after parking the truck in a rutted lot. "You guys want to come along?"

Austin nodded at his brother, who was stretched out in the truck bed, asleep. "He always fell asleep on car rides, bus rides— our mother said she'd barely get him in the stroller before he'd embrace the arms of Morpheus." Austin smiled at his brother. "But I thought he'd probably outgrown it."

"Do you want me to get you anything?" asked Kjel.

"I wouldn't be adverse to a Coca-Cola," said Austin. He lowered his hat over his eyes and, with his arms folded over his chest, leaned back in the truck bed, hoping to join his brother in a little shut-eye.

Passing a barker who promised "Everyone wins a prize!" Violet followed Kjel as he race-walked toward a refreshment kiosk.

Opening his mouth as wide as it could be opened, Kjel bit into a caramel apple.

"Oh, man, this is good." With his tongue, he flicked up a string of caramel off his lip and back into its rightful place inside his mouth. "You want one, Violet? Or how about some cotton candy?"

"I wouldn't mind that," said Violet. She dared herself to meet the eyes of two young women who whispered to each other as they stared at the handsome fellow with the one-armed gal.

"Well, then, m'lady, it's on to the next delight," said Kjel, and thrilling her, took her right arm, tucking it into his crooked elbow.

The girls' eyes grew wider and their whispers more frantic, and Violet blushed with pleasure that they might think that she and Kjel were a couple.

After two bites, Violet handed Kjel the paper cone topped with dissolving, sticky pink fluff, the back of her jaw tingling from the sweetness. She wanted to take his arm again, but he didn't offer it, and Violet wasn't about to claim it without an invitation.

"Now what about that pulled taffy?" asked Kjel, looking around the booths. "I don't see any pulled taffy."

"See the Bearded Lady!" cried a barker. "Just two bits gets you in to see the Bearded Lady and the World's Tiniest Man!"

"Hey, let's—" But Kjel was quick to drop his eyebrows, tempering the excitement on his face when he saw Violet's; it was as if she had just swallowed a piece of trout that was more bone than fish.

"So where's that gol-danged taffy?" asked Kjel, turning away from the freak show. Relief surged through Violet; it had been her fear that if she had gone inside the freak-show tent, they would have tried to recruit her to join the bill, or at the very least given her a membership discount.

A late-afternoon breeze flapped the canvas awnings of tents; they were into September now, and despite the placement of the equinox, it was a September that identified itself more with autumn than summer; although the temperature still managed to push up to seventy degrees in the daytime, it liked to take a careening, twenty-temperature dip in the night. Already, hours before sunset, a chill had descended. Violet was glad she had put on her sweater; a piece of apparel she put on less for keeping warm than for hiding her stump.

A trio of teenage girls, noticing Kjel, stopped cheering on a boy who'd spent all but a nickel of his fair money trying to smash a couple of plates with a softball (he'd stolen seventy-five cents from his grandma's cookie jar to supplement the dollar she'd given him for hauling firewood and was certain that it was guilt that made his hands sweaty and threw his aim off).

"Look at *him*," said the prettiest of the three. "Where'd he come from?"

"Who cares where he came from," said the boldest, "let's see where he's going," and just as the boy succeeded in shattering three plates in a row, he turned to find his audience disappearing in the crowd.

"I'll take the Betty Boop doll," he said, and after the carny got it down with a pole, he grabbed it and chased after the three girls. He'd be hanged if he was going to spend so much purloined money trying to impress them and then have them think he hadn't even been able to win a prize.

In front of a small stage, a heavy man in a fedora and a sweat-soaked glen-plaid suit paced, kicking aside a red-striped box of popcorn.

"When's the show start?" asked Kjel, nodding at the sandwich board that read, DOO CRESS AND HIS FABULOUS CROONERS.

"*Ptah,*" said the man, spittle flying. "You tell me. Forty minutes late and counting."

"We drove all the way down from Joliet," said a woman in a shiny brown dress. "We love Doo Cress."

"Well, the wife does," offered her husband, rolling his eyes under the brim of his gray felt hat.

"What are you going to do if they don't show?" asked Kjel.

"Make sure I never book 'em again," snarled the heavy man, mopping his face with a wad of handkerchief.

Kjel looked at the small group of loyal Doo Cress fans who stood clumped by the stage, still hoping that he and his Fabulous Crooners would appear and sing "Good night Irene" in that wonderfully melodic way of theirs. Then, looking past them toward the parking lot, he saw his truck and, more so, the glimmer of a great idea. Violet saw it too; saw his ocean-green and sky-blue eyes light up, and the grin that raced across his face.

"Well, sir," said Kjel, trying to rein in his smile to appear more businesslike, "it just so happens I have a band, and seeing as—"

"Get lost," said the man, with a wave of his ring-studded hand. "I'm not interested in your band, I'm interested in where in Hades Doo Cress and His Fabulous Crooners are!"

"A bird in the hand is worth two in the bush," said an old woman whose head tilted forward, as if weighed down under her coil of coronet braids.

"Yeah," said the boldest of the three girls who'd followed Kjel. "Why don't you give him a chance?"

"I think you'd be pleasantly surprised," said Kjel to the woman in the shiny brown dress, knowing that to win her over would go a long way in winning over the man in charge.

"Well," said the woman, with a giggle so uncharacteristic her husband stared at her, "I've been a fan of Doo Cress for years, but I'm always willing to give new things a chance."

Her husband hardened his stare; his wife was the sort who, for all the twenty-eight years of their marriage, did the wash on Wednesdays (and always with Duz, her brand of choice), the ironing on Thursdays, and the grocery shopping on Fridays; the sort who repainted rooms the exact same color; the sort who had two shiny brown dresses for special occasions and two unshiny beige ones for everyday.

"In fact, I was just saying to my husband Vernon, 'Vern, if variety is the spice of life, then ours must be the zestiest!'"

Vernon's jaw dropped so fast he almost unmoored his lower bridge. His wife had said no such thing but had given him the line he'd use that evening when joining her in their marital bed. A spurt of laughter gurgled in his throat.

Sticking his bottom lip out, the man in the fedora and fancy jewelry looked at his watch, at the crowd, and finally at Kjel.

"I can't pay you, you know."

Kjel shrugged. "The opportunity will be payment enough." He held out his arms at the gathering of people. "Don't any of you move—please. I'll be right back with my band."

He was gone in a shot, and Violet was left to field the stares that now bombarded her. Tucking her big chin into her chest, she pretended a newfound fascination with the second button of her shirt and didn't look up again until she heard, over the frenzied bees in her ear, "Hey, you. They any good?"

Violet nodded her head, slowly lifting it until her eyes met the questioner's.

"Yes," she said, consciously raising the timbre of her voice so it wouldn't scare him away. "He—the band—was a big hit in Chicago." For once she was glad her voice was so deep; it seemed to offer better bolster to her lies.

"Chicago?" snarled the fedora man. "Where'd they play in Chicago?"

"Oh, all over," said Violet, the lies blossoming in her mouth as easily as orchids bloom in Hawaii. "They had an especially long engagement at The Painted Cat."

"Is that right?" said Mr. Fedora as Violet screamed to herself, *The Painted Cat? Couldn't I have thought of a better name than that?*

"Is he your brother?" asked the bold teenager, unable to accept that a girl like Violet could be with a guy like Kjel without being related to him.

"Uh . . . no," she said. "No, I . . . take care of the band. I run things."

Mr. Fedora's eyes narrowed. "You the manager?"

"Yes," said Violet. "Yes, that's right. I'm the manager." *And did I neglect to tell you I'm also Greta Garbo's stand-in?*

"How'd you ever get a job like that?" asked the pretty teenager, impressed.

Violet managed a casual shrug of her shoulders.

"Well, after the . . . after the accident . . . you see, my daddy raises horses—Arabians, mostly back in Kentucky—and I got thrown off a bridge by a high-strung filly—she shared a bloodline with Man O' War, by the way . . . anyway, I was in a coma for a week and the doctors said I was lucky to have only lost my arm. My parents were devastated, naturally, and didn't want me to go back to school—I was a sophomore at Radcliffe . . . in Massachussets? Well, my parents mean well, but their overprotectiveness was driving me crazy, and when Kjel"—she nodded in the direction he'd run off in—"he's an old friend of the family, and had gotten this band up as sort of a lark, and he said, 'Well, since you've got such a head for business, why not come along on this little road tour—'"

When Violet finally stopped to take a breath, the shyest of the trio of teenage girls was moved to speak. "Of all the luck."

"Yes," said Violet, tossing back her straight black hair. "It's been quite an experience."

The bold teenager remembered her boldness. "Does he . . . does that 'Kjel' fellow have a girlfriend?"

Violet smiled. "I'm just the band's manager. I let the president of his fan club give out that sort of information."

There was a shift in the crowd then, a sort of chemical reaction in the air that caused the molecules to swirl, the atoms to pulse, and a tall widower on his third date with his lady friend—the nurse at his daughter's school—pointed and said, "Here he comes, and look who he's bringing with him!"

With his guitar slung across his back, Kjel ran through the crowd, Austin and Dallas directly behind him.

"Them boys's colored!" protested a man who'd just gotten done judging pies and whose bad mood was a direct result of tasting a disproportionate amount of soggy and uninspired crusts.

The three musicians jumped on the stage as more people shouted their observations in various degrees of disapproval, and as Mr. Fedora began bleating about never agreeing to have any mixed musicians up there onstage, Kjel wheeled his arm around in a circle, dragging his hand, hard, over the strings in a C chord. Several of the voices quieted.

Dallas answered back with a running riff, and another protester shut his mouth.

Austin took up the guitar riff and embellished it on his mouth organ, and then a song was launched. Violet was so nervous (certain that if a riot didn't break out, surely a few fistfights would), and her ears so full of buzzing bees and her own lies, that it took her a while to realize that no one in the crowd was shouting, no one was talking; everyone was listening.

"Say, baby, don't you worry—
I ain't goin' anywhere, I ain't in any hurry—"

Kjel's voice was cajoling, and echoed by the teasing wail of Austin's harmonica.

"Come on, honey, shut that door—
Whaddya mean, you don't love me anymore?"

The music drew in more people; a couple who passed back and forth the wax-paper wrapper holding the pulled taffy Kjel had been looking for, farmers' children giddy from an afternoon free of chores and collecting ribbons for their 4-H projects, and clots of young people, for whom the county fair ranked high on their social calendar. The teenagers listened to the music with their shoulders swaying and their heads bobbing until finally the need to move overrode their awkwardness and restraint and they began to dance.

As the crowd grew, shivers thrummed through Violet. The woman in the shiny brown dress stared at Kjel the way a nun stares at the pope, and the three teenage girls all had their hands clasped under their chins, participants in a communal, celebratory prayer. Mr. Fedora's bottom lip was still thrust out, but Violet could see him discreetly tapping his fingers against his thigh.

Every time Kjel took a few steps or swiveled his hips (something Violet had never seen him do during the campsite jamborees), the female members of the audience responded audibly, with either gasps or cheers or by clapping. When he danced across the stage, moving as if his hip joints had been lubricated in oil, the bold teenager staggered, feigning a faint. The men were watching Kjel closely too, some in the same excited way as the women, others in the way earnest students do a favorite teacher, and still others looked angry or scared.

Good heavens, thought Violet. *I don't remember any of this going on when the Blue Holler Boys played in Mount Crawford's town square.*

After the first song, the crowd seemed unsure in their applause—this was a kind of band they hadn't seen before—and after Kjel announced the name of the second song, the band plunged in. The applause grew exponentially, so by the end of the fourth song, Kjel felt confident enough to banter a little with the crowd.

"So how do we compare to Doo Cress?" he hollered to the woman in the shiny brown dress.

"Doo who?" she hollered back.

After the sixth song and what seemed like a duel between guitars, Kjel, his brow slick with sweat, said, "And that's our band, ladies and gentlemen—thanks for listening to us!"

But the audience would have none of this farewell speech—they clapped and hooted and howled until Kjel, laughing, looked at Austin, who mouthed, "You're My Gem."

This was a ballad Violet had heard several times, but never like this; with Dallas playing the E string of his guitar so it sounded like a cry; with Kjel singing so plaintively about the girl who'd been his diamond, his emerald, and his ruby; with Austin adding a harmony that made the chorus seem even lonelier; with grown men and women tearing up. The boy who'd won the Betty Boop doll with stolen money decided then and there that he was going to give the prize to his grandmother, with his apologies and an offer to paint the barn; the widower thought he might wander down to Pearson's Jewelers tomorrow during lunch break and look at rings a school nurse might like; and the three teenage girls all thought, to some degree, how beautiful and terrible love was and how they'd just lie down and die if anyone ever wrote a song comparing them to a gemstone.

When the song was over, everyone stood mutely for a moment before detonating into wild applause.

The musicians played until the sun behind them was swallowed into a red sea and they were soaked in sweat.

"That's gonna have to do it," said Kjel, breathless. "We're all played out."

It seemed to Violet that the crowd had grown to include everyone at the fair—even the merry-go-round operator had abandoned his post to come and listen—and their applause rose up in the rural night sky like a flock of migrating geese.

Both women and men swarmed the edge of the stage so that when Kjel stepped off it they could touch him, pat his back, and some even spoke to the brothers, saying, "That's quite a mean guitar you play!" or "What do you call that music you were playing?"

"I haven't seen Imogene this happy since she got her Amana range," said Vernon, the husband of the woman in the shiny brown dress. "Here. You give this to the band with my compliments."

He pressed two dollars into Violet's hand.

After thanking him, an idea formulated in Violet's head.

"May I borrow your hat for a minute?"

"Be my guest," said Vernon. "I expect Immy's going to be the last one to leave anyways."

Violet held out the gray felt hat as she walked among the fairgoers, and over and over was surprised how cheerfully they took their hard-earned nickels, quarters, and dollars out of their purses and pockets and dropped them into the hat.

"Where can I see them next?" asked the pretty teenage girl, putting in a quarter.

"Well," said Violet, "why don't you just write your name and address down and we'll let you know where our next appearance is."

"Why, I'd love to." Turning to her friend, she said in a frantic voice, "Evelyn, please tell me you have some paper in your purse!"

Others left their names and addresses, assuring Violet that even if they couldn't make it to the band's next appearance, they'd certainly tell their friends, and when the crowd finally dispersed, Violet was left with a hat filled to the brim with pieces of paper, both white and green.

"I'll trade you," said Vernon. "My hat for this bag."

"Deal," said Violet, dumping the money and addresses into a paper bag Vernon had gotten from the caramel-apple vendor.

Vernon sat the hat on his balding head, angling it with what he hoped was a certain jauntiness.

"Now, if I can just pry my wife away from that singer of yours," he said, thumbing his hat brim. "It's been a pleasure meeting you, miss, and best of luck in all your endeavors."

"Thank you," said Violet, and because kind words were still something she never expected, her eyes brimmed with tears. She watched the man approach his wife, watched the woman in the shiny brown dress fling her arms around Kjel, and then watched the man cup his wife's elbow with his hand and gently lead her away. She was glad that Imogene leaned into Vernon, resting her head on his shoulders; it was as if they both knew that while they didn't have everything, they had each other, and that was enough.

Chapter Eleven

THAT APPEARANCE AT THE FAIRGROUND WAS THE MATCH THAT LIT *two fires: one under the band and one under me. I have looked back on that day in my life more times than I can count, and never, never has the memory failed to tickle me. And touch me, because even after relaying to the boys all the tall tales I'd primed the crowd with, they didn't scold me for the lies, but applauded me for them.*

"That's just what we need," said Kjel. "A booking agent with a little imagination."

We were standing at the back of the truck, on whose tailgate I had arranged five piles of money. There were equal shares of fifteen dollars for everyone, plus eleven dollars and forty-two cents that I'd decided would go in our "General Fund."

"And look here," I said, reading one of the seventeen pieces of paper that had been stuffed in Vernon's hat.

" 'My cousin has a roadhouse outside Urbana, just south a here. Tell him I sent you and that I think you'd do great business for him. Sincerely, Marshall Arendt, mortician.' "

"Oh, I saw that guy," said Austin. "He was a real stiff."

When no one responded, he added, "I'm actually surprised he likes 'live' music!"

As Dallas rolled his eyes, Kjel asked, "Any more referrals in there, Violet?"

Shaking my head, I read a few notes I'd collected.

" 'Are you married? Even if you are—call me! Hennie Lingbloom at Sherman Hills 0-9651.'

" 'To the lead singer—you are the greatest! I couldn't believe when I saw you up close and one of your eyes is blue and the other is green! I loved that song about being "your gem"! I'd love to be! Deeply, Wilma Davis of Kankakee (if you're ever in town, drop in!)' "

I thought I was tricky, but Kjel saw me put the next one in my pocket.

"What's that one say?"

"Oh, just a bunch of—"

"Come on, Violet," he said, reaching his hand into my pocket.

Have I told you about Kjel's body heat? When his hand dipped into my pocket, I could feel the heat through the gabardine of my trousers. His hand in my pocket, an intimate gesture that had me secretly screaming for smelling salts, and for the second or two that his fingertips grazed my hip bone I thought, I am completely satisfied, and, I want more.

" 'So what if them—' " Kjel began before a frown lowered his forehead and his voice trailed off.

"Go ahead," said Dallas, his voice a challenge. "They can't say nothin' that I ain't already heard."

He held out his long-fingered hand like an elocution teacher waiting for the gum he knows a student has tucked inside his mouth.

Kjel dropped the slightly crumpled piece of paper into his palm.

" 'So what if them apes can play guitars and mouth organs—it don't mean I want to watch apes play guitars and mouth organs. So you apes—get your black asses out of my county.' "

I saw the nervous flicker in Austin's eyes, and like a little pink sentry, the tip of his tongue moved from one side of his mouth to the other and back again.

"Maybe we'd better pack up."

Dallas stared at the note in his hand. "Black asses," he said. "This is what this ape's black ass'll do to your stinkin' county."

Bending his knees, he stuck out his rear end and mimed wiping it with the note.

There was a moment when a pall of surprised discomfort dropped over us, but I flung it off by laughing.

Emboldened by my response, Dallas hopped and shimmied in what I can only describe as an elaborate dance of ass-wiping/arm-flailing/chest-beating. Kjel grabbed his guitar and Austin began tapping out a beat on the edge of the truck, and Dallas—his lips stretched into an O—let out a string of apeworthy "Ooh-ooh-oohs." Pushing out his behind, he began singing.

"Wiping up your county with my big black ass."

The song went on and on and included rhymes like "How's your county like this bounty?" and "I won't take no sass about my big black ass," until Kjel had to set his guitar down, he was laughing so hard. We all were—even Dallas—consumed by mirth, and when we were too weak to laugh anymore, I said, "So, are we going to open the next show with that song, or is that our encore?" and Dallas turned his head, which he was resting on the lip of the truck, and said, "You decide, you're the manager."

So you see, Dallas could be a lot of fun; he had a gift for mimicry that I'd never seen before and have not seen since. (You should have heard him singing "On the Good Ship Lollipop"—if you shut your eyes, you'd swear America's Sweetheart was sitting beside you. Imagine that, a grown man being able to do a dead-on Shirley Temple impersonation!)

In all my good memories of him, like this one, he's made me laugh until I nearly lost continence; the trouble is that the other memories, the bad ones, take up so much more room in my head. Put in Realtor's terms: the good memories comprise a city block, the bad ones the whole city.

Violet's lies continued, but never had she felt more truthful. At Ivar's Place, she sat in the back booth with the roadhouse's namesake, negotiating the terms under which the band would play.

"How about a free supper *and* we pass the hat?" asked Violet.

"That's what we did at Sonny's."

"Sonny's?" asked Ivar, staring at her from under a bushy hedge of eyebrows.

"A club in Minneapolis," said Violet, not batting one of her long eyelashes.

"Never heard of it."

Violet shrugged, implying his ignorance wasn't her problem.

"All right," said Ivar finally. As a courtesy to his cousin Marshall, who had gone to all the trouble of placing a long-distance telephone call (his own wife claimed the mortician's fingers were stained copper from pinching pennies) to rave about this trio of musicians he'd seen at some county fair, Ivar had agreed to let the band audition.

The club owner had been operating his nightspot from the time flappers rolled down their stockings and Lindied and Charlestoned up and down the dance floor, and after hearing the band play one song, he didn't need to look at his daughter, who was stacking glasses behind the bar, to know that these fellas would *draw*. Oh, he might hear a few complaints from the Hess brothers or Tink Tarlow, but at six feet and 290 pounds, Ivar was as good a bouncer as he was a club owner, and he prided himself equally on the fine music he brought to his club as well as his ability to toss out anyone who did not agree with him. He hired Treetop Adams for a whole weekend and there'd been no trouble at all, especially not after he hurled Isaiah Hess out the door after he'd heckled the legendary blues musician by calling him "a damn black bastard."

True, he'd never had a mixed band on his stage, let alone a band on a Thursday night, but along with an allegiance to good music, good food, and good women, Ivar Copenhaver strongly believed there was always a first time for everything. And he liked dealing with this no-nonsense young woman (gad, she couldn't be older than his own daughter, who, he reminded himself, he'd better keep an eagle eye on with regard to the blond singer); she was direct in a way few women were, looking at him straight on, with no google eyes, no simpering little laughs or fooling with her hair. Ivar had fallen too many times for women who used their wiles like sharp-eyed trappers, and a conversation with this Miss Mathers was like breathfuls of fresh and windswept air.

He nodded toward her arm. "So how'd that happen?"

For the first time in her life, Violet didn't blush at the question.

"A threading machine bit it off."

Ivar Copenhaver exhaled a great puff of air. "Jesus."

Violet smiled. "You should have seen what I did to the machine."

The club owner's shoulders rose once, in acknowledgment of the young woman's joke.

"So it's agreed, then," he said, "supper and all proceeds that come from the hat."

Violet offered her right hand and they shook on the deal.

"With the possibility of renegotiating after tonight."

"I've already got a band coming in tomorrow night."

Sliding out of the booth, Violet shrugged. "You still might want to renegotiate."

AFTER THEIR AUDITION, the band members had come to the booth, eager to hear what the club owner had to say, but Violet had shooed them away.

"Fellas, Mr. Copenhaver and I are going to hammer out a few details; why don't y'all play a game of pool?"

Nodding their heads, they backed away, as acquiescent as schoolboys warned by the headmaster. Now, after her discussion with the club owner, the swarm of bees in Violet's ears were in a frenzy of buzzing, but for once it wasn't noise that pushed her to the edge of sanity; instead it seemed accompaniment to the way her whole body felt—brave, gutsy, and thrumming with excitement.

"He's going to let you play tonight—we'll pass the hat at the end of the set *and* we get free supper."

"That's *it*?" said Kjel, and for a moment this new Violet, this modern, hard-edged, full of brass *band manager,* for crying out loud, felt herself folding up, shriveling into the old Violet—what had she been *thinking*? But then Kjel's smile split open, spilling its megatons of sunshine, and Austin laughed, and sending the eight ball into the corner pocket, said, "Superlative effort, Violet, *superlative.*"

"So what do you call yourselves anyway?" asked Ivar moments before stepping out onstage to introduce the band.

I should have thought of this already, Violet scolded herself. *I've got to stay on top of things.*

Dallas looked at Austin, who looked at Kjel, who looked at Violet, and desperately wanting to please him, to have an answer to pierce the mute fog that had descended, she blew a loud whistle in her brain, calling for something, *anything,* to respond.

"The Pearltones," she said quickly.

"The Pearltones," said Ivar Copenhaver. Nodding, he walked out to the stage.

"Is that all right?" asked Violet as Kjel grabbed her. "Because we can—"

Kjel kissed her hard, on the mouth, and when he pulled away his eyes—his Atlantic Ocean eye and his Caribbean eye—were shining. "It's perfect."

Austin nodded. "An homage to both a hometown and a certain mellowness of tone that if I do say so myself—" But his oration was interrupted when the club owner introduced the band.

"Ladies and gentlemen, I give you the Pearltones!"

There were a dozen people sitting at the bar and tables when the band started, but thanks to Millie Schuyler, who because of her position at Shear Magic was privy to most things that went on around town, there were fifty-seven by the time the band sang their final song.

"Gladys," she had shouted over the wall phone, "call Charlotte Frey's house and tell her to bring everyone over to Ivar's Place, *pronto.*"

"What's that?" asked Gladys, who thought it professional to ask twice for instructions.

"You heard me," said Millie, who'd wave-set the operator's hair that very morning. "Charlotte's hosting the Ladies Auxiliary tonight. And while you're at it, call Boyd Cunningham and Junior Winner down at the shop. Tell them Ivar's Place, *now.*"

Gladys did as she was told, and because the Auxiliary meeting was lagging (they had already gone through old business, applauding themselves for their successful Ice-Cream Social and the careful tending of the Main Street flower boxes, as well as new business, voting once again to fund the Halloween hayride and the Main Street Christmas wreaths), the ladies were ready to break up early. When Charlotte got the call from Gladys, they were braced for the apple cake Corrine Bly was serving. (Corrine had *always* baked as if there were a Depression going on, skimping on the more expensive ingredients like butter and sugar over those less costly, like flour and baking soda. The results were always a bland, dry concoction that gave those who ate it a thirst that lasted the entire evening.)

"Ladies," said Charlotte after hanging up the telephone. "Millie says it's our duty as city ambassadors to hightail it over to Ivar's Place and welcome this new combo that's playing there."

What Millie had really said was, "Charlotte, if Errol Flynn and this musician fellow were to ask me out at the same time, I'd have to give Errol my regrets."

Charlotte, whose fiancé had gotten a job in Milwaukee and, as an added bonus, a girlfriend he married two weeks after their meeting in a beer hall, was always interested in new men, especially ones whose looks came so highly recommended. Her fiancé had been plain verging on homely, and Charlotte, realizing that homeliness was no guarantee of loyalty, vowed that her next man was going to be a handsome one.

"I'll have to call Lester," said Effie Young, who sought her husband's permission on practically all matters (including when to use the ladies' room, thought most of her fellow Auxiliary members).

"Tell him to meet you there," said Charlotte, grabbing her new pretty hat off a hook by the door. "Tell him to bring all the guys at the Stardust."

147

Most of the husbands of the assembled women bowled down at Stardust Lanes on Auxiliary night, and the timing of the call was good, in that they were nearly done with their second game and on their way to Ivar's for a quick beer anyway.

"So I'll see you down there," said Lester to his wife. "But I don't want you drinking on a weeknight."

"Yes, honey," said Effie, who didn't drink on weekends let alone weeknights, at least not publicly.

Just as Ivar had thought, several members of the audience made their displeasure known when the band first came out. Sighing, he sidled over to Tink Tarlow, who'd shouted out, "Hey, it's a bunch of jigaboos!" and clamped his big hand around Tink's shoulder, squeezing as if it were a lemon whose every drop of juice it was imperative Ivar get.

"One more word and you're out of here," he said amicably into Tarlow's ear, and then turning to the other hecklers, he said, "That goes for all of you."

It was almost an unnecessary warning; the band had ripped into its first song, and as ready as the thugs had been to throw the black men off the stage, their curiosity was stronger than their need to riot. Six-foot-six Elwin Sather, who was a sidekick in the brawls his pal Tink liked to instigate, had nevertheless a sensitive ear with regards to music (his grandmother had insisted he take violin lessons until his growth spurt in the ninth grade gave him leverage to say "No more!"), and he realized immediately he was hearing something new and something special.

Squinting his ratlike eyes, Tink watched Ivar amble to the bar, and in a low voice said, "If he thinks I'm gonna—" but was silenced by a "Shhh!" from several directions, including his friend Elwin.

The audience wouldn't let the Pearltones off the stage when Kjel announced they were taking a break.

"We've got to," he said. "Look at this." He wiped his forehead with his hand and shook the droplets into the air. "It's full of sweat. I've got a miniature salt lake here."

"I'd like to swim in that lake," whispered Millie to Charlotte.

"I'd like to skinny-dip in it," whispered Charlotte back.

"Ten minutes," Kjel said, laughing, as the crowd booed. "Ten minutes to get something to drink and we'll be back."

In the small space that constituted "backstage," Violet told them, "Y'all wait here—I'll go get your water."

"Water?" said Kjel. "Who said anything about water? I want a beer."

Like a traffic cop, Violet held up her hand.

"You can have a beer when the show's over. Right now I'll get you water, while *you wait here.*"

"*Boss-ee,*" said Kjel, with a laugh. "Okay, I'll drink water. But why do we have to wait here?"

"Keeps up the mystique."

"Mystique?"

"She's right," said Austin, nodding, "but more than mystique, I'd worry about safety. If you step off that stage, Kjel, those women'll maul you."

Kjel lifted his arms to the ceiling. "Let 'em at me!"

When the hydrated Pearltones returned to the stage, Kjel winked at Dallas and nodded at Austin, and after playing a D, E, and E flat, he screamed, "*E-yow!*" and began singing.

> *"Ready to be yours, if only for a day,*
> *Ready to be yours, in every single way,*
> *Ready to beg, ready to crawl,*
> *Baby, baby, baby, I'm ready for it all!"*

Millie brought her hands to her chest, wondering if her rib cage was strong enough to hold in her rioting heart. Charlotte felt a fluttering in her lower belly, the same sort of feeling she got when she saw her fiancé take his shirt off. (His face wasn't anything to write home about, but his abdominal muscles were worth at least a postcard.) The reactions of the other Auxiliary ladies were variations of the same, and everyone felt that the temperature in the room had gone up.

Watching the band from her backstage perch, Violet didn't

need to see the faces of the audience members to know that Kjel was having the same effect he had at the carnival, the same effect he had on her: he was *mesmerizing*. In every leg wiggle, in every leap, twist, pelvic jut, and shoulder shimmy, there was an invitation, and every woman present wanted to RSVP *yes*. With each note his warm-honey voice sang, the women present begged: *pour it on me*. With every fancy guitar lick, the men thought: *I want to do that*. With all that Kjel offered, and with the fast and fancy guitar and harmonica work of the brothers, Ivar Copenhaver thought, *This is one of the most extraordinary group of musicians I have ever heard*. Considering he had featured hundreds of bands and solo performers over the years, this was no mild praise. His next thought was one of relief: it would be easy to cancel the band he had scheduled for the weekend. They weren't local boys, but close to, living in Champaign and filling in for him whenever needed. All he needed to do was promise them a couple extra bucks for their next engagement, plus the assurance that he'd throw another after-hours party featuring Millie Schuyler and selected friends (most townspeople were aware of the Ladies Auxiliary's civic accomplishments; what few knew were that some of its younger, single members showed quite an interest in music and, in particular, musicians).

All totaled, the band played for three hours, and when the three men, as wet as if they'd performed outside in a rain shower, staggered off the stage, the audience, who'd been on their feet for most of the show, shouted and whistled and pounded their hands together as if they were punishing them.

Violet, showing yet again her innate skills at management, handed each man a bar towel from a pile stacked in the storeroom down the hall, and each man held it to their faces so that for a moment they looked like mourners at a funeral. Unlike mourners at a funeral, however, when they took the towels away, their faces shone with glee and their words tumbled out on top of one another's.

"Man, you guys were on fire!"

"Dallas, you were playing so fast on 'Don't Need Nothin',' I thought your guitar was going to explode!"

"Did you ever hear 'She's Gone Now' sound so good?"

"And when you put in that chord change! That was brilliance, man!"

Ivar Copenhaver waded through the laughter and bonhomie of the backstage and after patting each man on the back and congratulating them for "the best show I've ever seen, *ever*," he said it would be his honor to invite them back for the weekend.

"But let's negotiate later," he said to Violet as she opened her mouth. "I want to buy you all a drink and let you meet some of your fans." He laughed, and because his laugh was like a sneeze, he held his forefinger under his nose. "It's gonna be crazy."

Things happened at Ivar's Place that night that never happened before. Elwin Sather, who assumed he hated niggers as much as his friend Tink (who had left early on, letting everyone know he was not about to waste his time watching "a bunch of coons onstage"), wound up standing at the end of the bar with Austin, discussing music (although truth be told, it was more a lecture, with Austin the professor and Elwin the student). The big man's circle of friends talked about whose panties they'd like to get into, or whose ass needed kicking, or who that mutt-ugly Eleanor Roosevelt thought she was anyway, and Elwin found it fascinating to listen as the black man expounded on music: "Is George Gershwin more closely tied to Mendelssohn or Joplin?" "Will opera be able to embrace the modern—why not a guitar-playing *Barber of Seville*?" "Ultimately, does passion ace technique?"

Elwin Sather, whose fantasies of going to college were especially strong when he began his workday (he was on the day shift at the rendering plant), craved knowledge, and that his teacher was a bug-eyed colored fellow was—now that Tink was gone—of no consequence.

Dallas had moved away from Austin once he started yapping—he had his limit as to how much of his brother's jive he could take—and was joined shortly by Ivar Copenhaver, who insisted that for the band, all drinks were on the house. That was an announcement that warmed Dallas to the big white man, and after his second whiskey he became, in his fashion, downright talkative.

"Well, see," said Dallas, in answer to Ivar's question about his musical history, "our daddy had a little joint in St. Louis—they bragged on the barbecue but went wild for the music, and Austin and me—"

"Wait a second," said the club owner. "You're not talking about Mokey Sykes's place, are you?"

"Damn straight, I am. Mokey Sykes was our old man."

"Mokey Sykes," said Ivar, swiping his hand over his bristly face as he looked beyond the bottles across the bar and into the past. "Good God, he was a legend! Only the best played Mokey's!"

Dallas had spent many years building a barricade around his heart, preventing deep emotion from getting close, but there was something about this man's voice, his respectfulness, that seeped through the cracks of the barricade, and for a moment Dallas was awash in sadness. He emptied his whiskey glass; liquor always helped him ease the pain of memory.

"One night," said Dallas, his voice soft, "we had Jebby Hayes and Delta Pitts and Miss Sheba Mae."

"Miss Sheba Mae," said Ivar, and there was something like pain in his voice. "I saw her in Chicago once, and I swear to God, I thought I was listening to velvet—velvet that had been liquefied and poured."

For a moment Dallas let himself go back to the club, let himself smell the barbecue, the spilled beer, and the perfume on sweaty skin, let himself hear the way Jebby Hayes giggled like a girl everytime his fingers danced on the keyboard in a complicated riff, let himself hear Miss Sheba Mae bring tears to every eyeball in the house as she sang of the man who stole her heart, her ring-studded hands splayed against the big swell of her belly.

"She was something," said Dallas, his eyes still shut. "She could sing all night—her voice never got tired. Of course," he added, opening his eyes and chuckling, "she always did have that jar close by. My daddy gave her a flask—even had her initials engraved on it—but she said drinking gin out of a jelly jar improved its flavor." He regarded his own empty glass, and the club owner signaled his bartender for another.

"When did you and your brother learn to play?" asked Ivar.

"When we were kids. Nine . . . ten. But you know where I got really good?" He didn't allow the man to answer. "In the hole. I'd be sweepin' the kitchen, usin' the broomstick as my fret board. In my bunk, I'd lay on my side and stick my hand under the mattress—if you could call it that—and around the bed frame and play on that. For three years my hands were always moving, making music that only my ears could hear."

"You play beautifully," said Ivar soberly.

Dallas took the refilled glass the heavy young woman had placed before him and slid off the bar stool. The time had expired on his friendliness.

"Yeah," he said with a bitter laugh. "They should send all musicians to the pen. Make 'em play air all day. Builds technique—and backbone."

He raised his glass to Ivar in a salute, but his smile was turned down at the edges, and suddenly he stood up, slapped the edge of the bar, and walked out in a way that invited no inquiries as to where he was going.

Austin nodded at his brother, discomfited, as he always was, by the knowledge that Dallas-on-the-loose more likely spelled trouble than not, but he was still high on the music he'd played and the goodwill it had engendered in the all-white crowd and was not about to chase after his brother, who was not the type who appreciated being chased anyway. Besides, his new friend at the bar had already complimented him twice—once on his vocabulary ("Man, you know a lot of big words!") and once on the breadth of his musical knowledge ("Man, you know a lot about music!")—and compliments were a balm to Austin's fragile ego, especially compliments given by a man whose skin was twenty shades lighter than his own.

Kjel was enjoying the attentions of every woman in Ivar's Place, with the exception of Lindy Grossflekker, who would have cast an approving eye at the handsome musician had she not been blinded by glaucoma. Of course, even if she had her sight, she was usually too pickled to notice much of anything but the glass of hard cider in front of her. Occasionally a new customer complained of the blind old lady slumped and mumbling at the end of the bar, but Ivar quickly let these new customers know that he'd sooner give them the boot than Mrs. Grossflekker. She had, after all, been Ivar's and most of the townspeople's first-grade teacher, and if she now found solace in the bottle instead of teaching the ABCs to a bunch of brats, who in Hades were they to complain?

Of the Auxiliary women, Millie was pressed to Kjel's left side and Charlotte to his right, and the other members leaned toward him as if he were the sun and they were sunflowers. Lester Young, not liking the look on his wife Effie's face when she watched the gyrating, shaking man onstage, had long ago taken her home, with the whispered promise of a whupping. There were other women present who were not affiliated with the Ladies Auxiliary, but no one could say they didn't share the same welcoming goals; Beryl Beasley, a nurse who'd wandered into Ivar's after her swing shift, and Patty Wilkerson, who had come in to drink away the bad news that she was pregnant again, had both been trying to depose Millie and Charlotte of their privileged positions next to Kjel ("She's on him like a leech," Beryl noted of Millie), but their jostling and false alarms ("There's a telephone call for you, Charlotte") were all for naught; indeed, Millie and Charlotte *were* on Kjel like leeches.

Intoxicated less from the free-flowing liquor than he was from the close proximity of all these women, Kjel felt nearly cross-eyed taking in all their pretty faces, their pretty necks and shoulders, their pretty, pretty breasts. And their perfume! Lavender and rose waters, Jungle Gardenia, Tabu, and talcum powder, and underneath that, the musky tang of a woman that thankfully hadn't been covered up by all the canned and bottled scents. Kjel knew he wasn't in Heaven, but he knew he was close.

"So where are you staying tonight?" whispered Millie in the ear she wanted to outline with her tongue. "I've got a real comfy couch and an even comfier bed."

"Hmm," said Kjel, smiling the smile all the women considered a personal gift. "I'm not really all that tired."

"All the better," said Millie, and catching the gist of this conversation, Charlotte pressed her lips against Kjel's other ear and said, "If you're looking for someone to stay up with, I'm your gal."

Then one of the sunflowers who believed a way to a man's heart was through his stomach said she had a chocolate cream pie at home she'd love Kjel to try, and another sunflower who believed men liked women with a little intelligence asked Kjel if he'd read Dos Passos's *USA,* and then Ivar's daughter lumbered over from the bar with another beer on the house, and believing that a musician likes nothing more than to talk about music, said as she served his drink, "Your guitar playing reminds me a lot of Ramon Henderson's."

"Thank you," said Kjel to all the women, to all their offers and all their compliments, but such was his earnestness that each woman thought he was only thanking her.

The bar was a long L, and at the short end, Violet sat, nursing a cream soda. She had listened to the old blind woman scold her dead husband ("Why'd you leave me, Otto? You said you were going to get better!"); had tried to listen to the conversation between Dallas and the club owner, and watched Dallas skulk out of the bar; she had heard snippets of Austin's oration and watched the wide-eyed reaction of the man to whom he was orating; she had watched a group of men retreat to the poolroom when it became obvious that the blond fella was not going to be sharing any of the women's attention with them.

It had been a bad day for her ears, the buzzing intermittently rising up past the noise in the bar in notes so loud and sharp it seemed her eardrums might burst. Her panic found purchase in her heart—*thumpety thump thump*—but with slow deep breaths she pushed down her fear, reminding herself that the buzzing would soften, that it always did. Once calmed, she'd ignore the buzzing whine and use her ears to learn about the people among whom she sat.

It was Violet's nature to want to know what was going on; the fewer surprises in her surroundings, the safer she felt. Like a good watchdog, she had learned long ago to keep her eyes and ears open, and if need be, to adjust her actions to the prevailing mood. And tonight's prevailing mood—excitement, energy, and the euphoria people feel upon being in on something special— was *her* prevailing mood. The other women in the bar might be scrambling for Kjel's attention, but there was no need for Violet to do the same. She had, after all, already been *kissed* by him. *Kissed* as in *his mouth had touched hers,* and in comparison the cream soda she sipped was flat and sour.

Chapter Twelve

KJEL WAS LOOPED WHEN HE LEFT THE BAR; LOOPED WITH LIQUOR *and around the arms of the two women who flanked him. He peeled his arm away from one of them long enough to wave at me, and I waved gamely back. The bees were a loud and angry hive in my ears, but the voice that screamed inside my head was louder: "You stupid idiot!"*

I watched as the loopy trio pushed open the door and stumbled out into the black rectangle of night, and then I sat there on the bar stool as my heart shattered and its pieces fell, taking their place next to the cigarette butts and sawdust and beer puddles on the floor. See, the thing is, Kjel had kissed me and I thought it meant something. I had been hanging all night on the wild and improbable hope that that kiss meant something, that it was only the beginning of all things beautiful between us, and now my humiliation was nearly equal to my hurt. Stupid! Stupid! Stupid! I screamed, and the bees went bzzzz bzzzz bzzzz.

These were the sleeping arrangements for the Pearltones and their manager: Austin and Dallas stayed at the club owner's house ("It's a pretty good town," said Ivar, "but still, I'd feel safer if you'd stay with me") and I stayed at his daughter Jean's. Kjel didn't need the Copen-

haver's hospitality when so many townswomen were willing to offer up their own.

It was 2:00 A.M. by the time we got to Jean's apartment, but I was nowhere near sleepy and happily accepted her offer of tea.

"Jeez," she said as the kettle began whistling. "Can you believe those women throwing themselves at him? I hope they all get the clap."

I don't know what was so funny about the look I gave her but it tickled Jean and she laughed.

"It's just so unfair," she said, pouring our tea. There were magazines laid out on the table like place mats, and she set the pot on a Hollywood Confidential and my teacup on a Photoplay. "Millie always goes home with the good-looking musicians. Although she's never gone home with anyone half as good-looking as . . . as . . . how do you say his name again?"

" 'Shell.' As in 'seashell.' But it's spelled K-j-e-l." I felt proud, like a schoolgirl who did all her homework.

"K-j-e-l," said Jean. "Is that Czech? Polish?"

"Norwegian," I said, going for the extra credit.

"I don't know what the point of letters are if you're not going to pronounce them," said Jean.

Sipping our tea, we sat in silence for a while, pondering those silent k's and j's and the man who was behind those unpronounced sounds.

"You have such pretty things," I said finally, noticing that the gold rim of the cup matched the gold rim of the teapot lid.

"They were my mother's. When she died, I got all the china—and my mother loved china." She dipped her spoon in the gold-rimmed sugar bowl. "My dad tried to buy her jewelry, but she always said, 'Bone china, Ivar. All I want is bone china.' " She stirred her tea, the spoon clanging against the cup. "Me, I'd have taken the jewelry. And speaking of diamonds," she said, switching back to our original conversational track. "Is there anyone on earth as good-looking as Kjel?"

"On earth? I doubt it."

From each end of the small dinette table, we sighed. I barely knew Jean, but anyone could see we were in the same boat—the ugly-girl boat that has no chance of sailing in the pretty-girl regatta.

"So how long have you been in love with him?"

I was about to scold her for her presumptuousness, but then asked myself who I was trying to kid.

"Since the minute I saw him."

The heavy features of Jean's face sagged. "Me too."

"And the thing of it is," I said, "he had kissed me tonight. Right before the show."

"No," Jean whispered.

I nodded. "I see now it was nothing—he was just excited about the show, about me coming up with the band's name, but still . . . I thought it meant everything."

"Oh my gosh, on the lips?"

I nodded.

"Now you can't ever wash your mouth!"

"Hmm," I said, considering this. "Can I brush my teeth?"

"Brush your teeth?" said Jean with a scoff. "Not only can you not brush your teeth, you can't eat or drink. Violet, you've got his germs on your mouth!"

"But if I don't eat or drink . . . well, eventually I'll die."

Jean rolled her eyes. "Love demands some sacrifice, Violet."

We laughed then; that whole weekend we spent together was one big gabfest/laugh riot. The big news in town was of course the Pearltones— Ivar's Place was packed with people on Friday and Saturday nights—but the big news inside that apartment full of movie magazines and fancy china was the friendship Jean and I formed. I had loved my girlfriends at Marcelline Threads, but my rapport with Jean was so quick and so deep that after an hour's worth of talking, I felt I'd known her all my life. Every day I was adding reasons to the Why I'm Glad I Didn't Kill Myself list, and now Jean's name was on it.

It's funny, the family heirlooms we pass down to kids—bone china, jewelry, cash, real estate—but we can't bequeath them the really important things, like friends. The really important things they have to find themselves. Still, it would have meant a lot to me to be reminded of my mother every time I poured a pot of tea.

"Violet, might I borrow your scrapbook to peruse the latest journalistic rave?" asked Austin.

———

"It's in my bag," said Violet in the high English accent she fell into when responding to Austin's particularly stilted word-play. It didn't seem to offend him; sometimes they held entire conversations pronouncing each and every word like British roy-alty.

Austin pulled out the chair across from her and sat down at the nicked wooden table.

The librarian glanced at them and smiled; she'd been a suf-fragette, and was heartened by examples of a new world order, where men and women, black and white, crippled and whole, came together.

All the best things happen in a library, she reminded herself once again, before getting back to tabulating the fines of a habitually delinquent customer.

INTERRACIAL TRIO FILLS CLUB TO THE RAFTERS!
FANS ARE COLOR–BLIND WHEN IT COMES TO THE PEARLTONES!
A BLACK & WHITE TREAT AND IT AIN'T A SUNDAE!

The Pearltones were like a fire blazing through the cold mid-western winter, and music reviewers were breathless in reporting on the conflagration. While Violet cut out and pasted every one of their headlines, every ad, every inch of press, it was Austin who read them over and over.

His guitar playing had been described by one reviewer as "bluesy, yearning, excitable, and poetic—and that's just in one song." Another said, "The Pearltones are the band of the fu-ture—but I'm sure glad I got to hear them in the present." Still another declared, "Those of us in Hap's Roundhouse know that we won't hear a group like the Pearltones in a long, long time."

Taking the scrapbook out of Violet's carpetbag, he prepared himself for the thrill of seeing his name in print, but after turn-ing the first page, it was obvious he had the wrong book.

"Violet," he whispered, "did you draw these?"

Seeing her Fashions by Violetta spread out in front of him, Violet flushed down to the roots of her hair.

———

"Yes," she said, reaching across the table to claim her sketchbook.

Austin held on to it. "Violet, these are really good."

"Shh!" admonished the librarian, but with a smile. She was all for big ideas being discussed, but in a quiet voice.

"Here's the scrapbook," said Violet, hoping for a trade, but Austin continued looking at her drawings, his forehead scrunched so that a wavy W formed above his nose between his eyebrows.

The at-home relaxation Violet felt whenever she was in a library (it was where she escaped to whenever she had free time in a new town) evaporated. The bees in her ears began buzzing louder and anxiety dropped like a weight in her stomach. She stared at the book she was reading, but the R–S *Encyclopedia Britannica*'s words were lost in a blur of curves and lines. Despite Mrs. Hedstrom's complimentary reaction to her sketches, Violet had not shown them to anyone else; they were too painful a reminder of the loss of her arm, of what she used to do.

Austin studied each page for so long that the anxiety in Violet's stomach rose, filling her chest and her throat with what felt like a suffocating gas. She wanted to get the key to the ladies' room from the librarian and lock herself in, but the seat of her chair and her own seat seemed to have formed an adhesion she could not unglue.

"Good heavenly days," said Austin finally, looking up at her. "You'll have to draw me sometime, Violet. Draw me dressed up like Cary Grant—or the Aga Khan!"

The bees were singing in a high-pitched frenzy.

"I drew with my left hand." Violet's words hissed like droplets of water on a hot grate. "As you may have noticed, I don't have a left hand anymore."

"Can't you draw with your right?" asked Austin. His question was so guileless, so childlike, that it blew out Violet's anger, leaving only her sadness.

"I haven't tried."

"Well, you should," said Austin. "I'll bet your right hand

LORNA LANDVIK

could figure out a way to channel the power that was in your left. And even if your skill isn't immediate—shouldn't you keep practicing until it is? Goodness gracious, Violet, it's a sin to—"

"Shh!" reminded the librarian.

Austin leaned toward Violet as he lowered his voice. "It's a sin to ignore a God-given talent, and I'm sure the talent is there, even if the hand isn't."

A flame of Violet's anger returned. "Oh, really?" she said, gathering up her things. "What about your talent? If you lost your left arm, do you think your right arm could make up the difference?"

She rushed out of the library, and Austin, grabbing his jacket off the back of the chair, followed after her.

"Is everything all right?" asked the librarian, who thought the dignity and sacredness of a library demanded a quiet and orderly exit from its patrons.

"Everything?" said Austin. "I hardly think I'm an authority on *everything*."

Catching up to Violet on the snow-dusted sidewalk, Austin apologized.

"I didn't mean to offend you."

"You didn't offend me," said Violet crisply, as if she cared so little of Austin's opinion that she was deaf to all of them, including insults.

"And with regards to your analogy," said Austin, who had a hard time giving up an argument, "I couldn't play guitar with just one hand because the design of the instrument requires two. But you don't need two hands to draw."

"You need the hand that was good at it!" said Violet, stopping suddenly on the sidewalk. "You can't just automatically transfer what your left hand could do to your right hand—it doesn't work that way!"

Austin saw the sparkle of tears in Violet's eyes, and he shoved his hands in his pockets, stifling the impulse to reach out and blot them with his finger. They stood there for a moment, staring at each other until a man on his way to the post office stopped and asked Violet if this boy was bothering her.

"No!" said Violet sharply, and the man frowned and doffed his hat as if to say he didn't believe her but if she didn't want his help that was all right with him.

Austin's skin was smooth and whole, but inside he felt he'd been cut. It wasn't a deep, gaping wound, but a sharp quick slice, and he felt that if his psyche had form and shape, it would be covered with the slashes of thousands of scars, from thousands of slurs and invectives. Even as each fresh cut, each "boy" and "nigger" stung, he had learned to anesthetize it by ignoring it, and so, matching Violet's long strides, he asked, "What were you planning to do with those drawings?"

"They were my designs," said Violet. "Some I sewed up, some I was going to sew up."

"You sewed too?"

Violet's voice was soft. "Austin, you wouldn't believe how I sewed."

At the corner by the soda fountain, they split up, Violet turning left toward the motel, and Austin to the right, toward the tavern where he was certain his brother could be found. In the middle of the block he turned around, watching Violet march down the street like a majorette, certain of her destination and not about to let anyone stop her from getting there.

Thanks to Ivar Copenhaver's good word, a club owner in Champaign hired them for a whole week, and upon his recommendation, they were given two weekends at the High Hat in Decatur and then a week at the Riverside Theatre in Peoria. One sold-out engagement led to another, and Kjel happily reported in letters to his parents, "It feels like I'm living a dream, but don't wake me up!"

Elwin Sather, the young music aficionado who'd first heard them at Ivar's Place, had quit his job at the rendering plant to travel with the band, bringing with him three important things: his conviction that the music they played was going to change the world, his willingness to serve as roadie and all-around errand boy, and his panel truck. His aforementioned view and willingness to work were appreciated, but more than anything, his panel truck was his ticket in. Two vehicles made for easier travel, and when the weather warmed up again, would make for easier camping; although thanks to Violet's negotiations, it looked as if camping might be a thing of the past. Unlike Ivar Copenhaver, most club owners were not willing to open up their homes and those of their daughters' to the band, but were willing to reimburse lodging as part of their payment.

The Pearltones lead singer had scant use for these motel rooms and auto parks, fending off a slew of please-come-home-with-me invitations after every show. There was always one lucky young woman whose invitation Kjel didn't fend off; as he confided to Austin, "It wouldn't be neighborly to refuse *all* hospitality."

It didn't surprise Violet on the rare occasions that they performed to an integrated audience that Dallas left in the arms of a woman; what astounded her was the white women who sometimes slipped off with him.

"That's disgusting," Violet said one night to Elwin Sather as the band was clearing out of a club.

"What is?" asked the huge man in his placid, friendly way.

"That," said Violet, jutting her long chin toward Elwin's panel truck, into whose interior Dallas was guiding a giggling platinum blonde. "You let them use your truck for *that*?"

"For what, Violet?" asked Elwin innocently. Because he was a little intimidated by her—by her voice, her height, her stump (it jarred him every time he saw that incomplete arm, nearly made him dizzy), and most of all, the force of her personality— he sometimes didn't listen to her carefully, his mind already working on what his response might be to whatever it was she said.

"Oh, *that*. Well, Kjel said he wouldn't be needing it—"

"Never mind about that," said Violet, her cheeks hot. "I just don't want anyone to get in trouble. Miscegenation is illegal in most states, you know."

"Right," said Elwin, and after a long, awkward moment, excused himself and went back into the club.

During their performances, Violet was all business, and no one would have guessed how she suffered watching Kjel leave with his latest conquest (although judging by some of the pushier females, she wasn't sure who was the conqueror and who was the conquered). Surreptitiously watching the couple exit, she'd imagine what it must feel like with Kjel's arm around her waist, imagined the words whispered into her ear and the words she'd whisper back. Even as it pained Violet seeing him with these women, what really galled her was when he didn't choose the prettiest girl in the room; she hated when he snubbed the woman earning that title for someone a tad mousy, or a little chubby, or with wild hair. If Kjel was going to betray her, he might as well betray her with a genuine knockout—when he chose a plain Jane, it somehow demeaned her even more.

✳

SPRAWLED ACROSS THE SCRATCHY blanket whose middle stripe read HOYT'S MOTEL, Violet was reading one of the books Austin had lent her. In whatever town they were in, his antennae led him to the used bookstore willing to take a trade, or to the church rummage sale offering a bag of books for a quarter. Violet used the libraries to indulge in her almanac and encyclopedia perusal, but as she was never in a town long enough to apply for a library card, she was beholden to Austin and his particular tastes when it came to outside reading.

Now, in the light of the fading wintry afternoon, she was reading a pulp mystery, surprised at how quickly she turned each page, eager to find out just what the philandering Spaniard with the flashing black eyes planned to do with the beautiful young Greek woman who had discovered him on the shores of the Aegean Sea, draping seaweed over the body of his dead wife. Just as the Greek girl had screamed, just as the Spaniard leveled one of his toxic smiles at her and assured her that "*Non, señorita, non,* this is not what it seems," there was a knock on the door.

"Who is it?" Violet said, darkening her naturally deep voice enough so that if the person at the door had been a stranger, that person might think twice with regards to knocking again. But the person at the door was not intimidated, giving the door a little kick to emphasize his desire to gain admittance.

"Violet, let me in!"

Good gracious, thought Violet, her heart thumping, *it's Kjel!* Suddenly the beautiful Greek girl had nothing on her—she was about to be ravaged by the philandering singer with the dual-colored eyes!

"Hey!" said Kjel, stumbling backward as Violet flung open the door.

The fresh cold air slapped back the sense Violet had momentarily taken leave of, and she realized that while Kjel wanted something, it most certainly wasn't her.

"Kjel!" she said, flustered. "What are you doing here?"

"Are you busy?" he asked.

Stifling her urge to shout, "Never too busy for you!," Violet offered a simple and quiet, "Not really."

"Then get your coat and your sketchbook," said Kjel, "and come with me."

"My sketchbook?"

"Yeah, the one you showed Austin the other day. Come on, hurry up. Time's wasting."

Shrugging into her coat, she grabbed her carpetbag and followed Kjel to the truck.

"Remember, we've got to be at the club at six," Violet said, calming her excitement at being sought out by Kjel by remembering her role as manager.

"Good show last night, don't you think?" he asked as they bounded over a bumpy road that led out of town.

Violet nodded. "They all are, Kjel. You're not capable of putting on a bad show."

"You're spoiling me, Vi," said Kjel. "I'm getting so used to your praise that the first time you criticize me, I'm going to have to fire you."

"Hmm," said Violet, not knowing what to say.

"So you still think we can afford that bass?" asked Kjel.

"We've got enough in the G.F. to afford a whole section of basses."

Violet split their payments in three parts: two-thirds went into the G.F.—the General Fund—which covered operating and living expenses, as well as rainy-day savings. The other third was divided into payments, with Elwin getting half of what each member of the Pearltones and Violet got. ("Heck," said Elwin, tearing up when Violet handed him his envelope of money, "I'd do this for free!")

The band had just purchased a stand-up bass at the town's music store. The owner (who had attended three Pearltones shows and planned on attending the remaining two) had given them a deep discount, but still, it wasn't a trifling amount.

Austin and Dallas had spent hours since taking their turn on it, and while their proficiency lagged miles behind what they displayed on guitar, everyone agreed that soon the upright would make an appearance in the show.

"Of course our signature is three guitars," Austin explained to Violet, "but there are some songs that are crying out for the anchor of a heavier beat."

"At first I thought it was Austin's fingers," said Kjel as they drove past a farm in whose yard a woman was struggling to take down the wash that hung frozen on the clothesline. "Each one is at least an inch longer than mine."

Violet watched as the farm wife seemed to break the arms of a white shirt she was trying to fold.

"But Dallas's hands are smaller than mine! And man, his fingers can beat mine in a race anytime!" There was no sense of envy in Kjel's voice, only wonder.

Looking backward, not wanting to miss the washerwoman's wrestling match with a frozen union suit, Violet said, "You're just as good a guitar player as they are."

"They're the ones who make me better than I am. Take last night; I swear, playing with those guys was like a religious experience."

"How do you mean?" asked Violet, curious.

Kjel's eyes were fixed on the frozen landscape for a moment. "This friend of my dad's came to visit once—they had gone to seminary together and he told us about his trip to the Boundary Waters—between Minnesota and Canada—and he said he never felt closer to God than when he was rowing his canoe in the quiet morning waters. In fact, he said God was in his canoe!" Kjel laughed. "I was just a kid—maybe seven or eight—and I remember thinking, 'God's too big to fit in a canoe!' But nights like last night; well, I feel God's in my guitar, in all of our guitars."

"So *that's* where He is," said Violet.

"We'll have to save your conversion for another time," said Kjel as he turned off the road. "Because for now . . . we're here."

The dirt drive they pulled into was rutted with holes, and the truck bounced as it drove over a particularly deep one.

Disappointment thudded through Violet when, at the door of the gray-shingled house, she saw Kjel's current "girlfriend."

Walking toward the house, Violet wished she were back on the Greek Islands with the dastardly Spaniard; a fictitious villain had to be better company than the real-life rival who reached out for Kjel, giving him a kiss after he bounded up the wooden steps.

"I'm so glad you could come," she said to Violet, who noticed that her smile was rather gummy and her nose was on the thin and pointy side. "I'm Ginny, by the way, and let me take your coat."

After she hung it in the hall closet, she faced Violet with a smile. "My goodness, look at those eyelashes!"

Violet smiled thinly, taking in the one regular compliment about her appearance she could count on.

Ginny searched and found another topic of conversation. "They said on the radio we might get five inches of snow tonight!"

"*Five inches!*" said Violet, mocking the young woman's

chirpiness. She was feeling prickly and ready to let all sorts of smart remarks fly—but surprise muted her words.

"Hey, Violet," said Austin, sitting on a couch with a young white woman.

"Oh," said Violet, trying to keep her voice light, "it's a party."

"No," said Kjel, grabbing Violet as if she was Ginger Rogers and dancing her across the room. "The party's *after* the show."

Violet joked away her feelings (mostly mortification, but a small part of her was thrilled to be in Kjel's arms, no matter if he were teasing her or not) by curtsying to her partner when he released her.

"Please, Violet, sit down," said Ginny, gesturing toward an easy chair upholstered in a tropical fabric. "Can I get you anything to drink?"

"Oh, I don't know," said Violet, eyeing the fabric's explosion of palm trees as she sat down. "How about a pineapple daiquiri?"

"I do have some coffee on," said Ginny.

"Then coffee it is!" Violet's voice was as bright and shrill as a tin bell.

As Kjel followed Ginny into the kitchen, Violet turned toward Austin and the woman on the couch, who offered a smile as gummy as her sister's.

"I'm Dottie," she said, and carefully avoided looking at Violet's stump. "Can you believe the to-do these guys have caused? My gracious, we haven't seen this kind of excitement since Calvin Coolidge spoke to the Masons!"

"Everywhere we go," said Violet with a sigh, "we're always second billing to Calvin Coolidge."

Dottie laughed, nudging Austin in the ribs. "You guys are right. She *is* funny."

Austin's long fingers fanned in a shrug. "Funny is but a mere sliver of all that is our Miss Mathers."

Violet sniggered, and Austin looked pained that she doubted his sincerity.

"I can't wait to see your drawings," said Dottie. "He's been going on and on about them like you're some kind of, I don't know, *genius!*"

"Yes," said Ginny, emerging from the kitchen with a tray. "We can't wait to see your drawings!"

The phrase "shooting daggers" came to mind when Austin caught the look Violet lunged at him.

"I'll get your bag, Violet," said Kjel at the same time Ginny handed her a cup and saucer.

"Cream? Sugar?"

Violet shook her head, and with her eyes still aimed at Austin, said, "I take it black."

Sipping her coffee, straining to project nonchalance, Violet watched as the foursome, squeezed together on the couch, paged through her sketchbook.

Their expressions of admiration were occasionally interrupted by words like "Goodness gracious" or "Look at this one," and when Dottie turned the last page, they sat for a moment, the way a congregation sits after hearing a potent sermon, taking it all in.

"So," said Kjel, pulling his hands out in front of him and cracking his knuckles. "Why don't we show Violet what you ladies have got for her?"

Suddenly everyone on the couch rose in a flurry, Ginny and Dottie giggling together, as they had countless times in their lives as sisters.

Ginny pushed Kjel and Dottie pushed Austin—neither man was moving fast enough for them—and Kjel said, "What are you trying to do, knock me down?" and Austin said, "Watch your hands, woman!"

Watching them disappear behind the corner, Violet felt the old shroud of wallflowerhood descend upon her. *Sure, they said they were getting something for me, but they're probably tired of the fifth wheel in the house and are figuring out how to sneak out.*

She sipped her coffee and told herself to calm down, no one was sneaking out.

Bzzzzzzzzzzzzz. Well, at least her bees hadn't deserted her.

Cuckoo! Cuckoo!

Startled, Violet turned to see a tiny, jaunty bird pop out of the door of an ornate chalet.

Cuckoo!

"Speak of the devil," said Kjel, and the group came back into the room.

They were like a conga line, Austin in the front, Kjel taking up the rear. When they were positioned in front of Violet, they broke away in a choreographed move, gesturing toward Kjel, who held what looked like a bulky suitcase.

Their voices were a two-note chorus: "Ta-da!"

Violet looked at their faces, smeared with big smiles all, and then looked at the case that Kjel set on the coffee table. She was flustered by their behavior so it took her a moment to determine what it was.

"A sewing machine?"

Ginny smiled. "A Singer Featherweight. It was my husband's first Christmas present to me."

Violet was taken further aback than she already was. "You're married?"

"Not anymore; my husband died last year."

"I'm sorry."

Ginny shook her head. "Don't be. Wes was—"

"A two-timing so-and-so with an extra dash of *so*," said Dottie. "I can't say as I was glad when I heard he got killed, but I can't say I was sad either."

"How—"

Dottie waved her hand. "Car accident. Drunk as a skunk, and he killed the little floozy who was with him too."

Silence pressed down for a long moment.

"Well," said Violet finally, "he sure did give you a nice sewing machine."

"He sold them for a living," said Dottie with a scoff. "In fact he'd just sold one to his little floozy passenger. I'll bet that was one purchase agreement she wished she'd never signed."

"Dottie," scolded her sister. Her hand pushed at the waves

on the side of her head as she smiled apologetically at Violet. "Anyway, I'm not much of a sewer—in fact I'm no sewer at all, and Dottie only wears store-bought—"

"I work at Heinlen's Department Store, in Novelties—"

"—and I thought, 'Well, it's not as if I'm keeping this around for sentimental reasons—' "

"And so," finished Dottie, "when Kjel and Austin told us about you—they think you're really something, by the way—we thought we'd give it to you."

There was little difference between the movement of Violet's mouth and a beached carp's. Why would these giggling sisters whom she didn't even know want to give her a sewing machine? She was moved in one direction by their generosity and in another by their thoughtlessness. Couldn't they see that she couldn't sew anymore? Couldn't they see why she'd stopped?

Austin lifted the lid off, revealing the machine.

"Now I know you say you can't sew anymore," he said, his voice gentle, "but why don't you just try? Take a crack at it, Violet, and if it's too hard, we'll try to figure out a way to make it easier."

Fighting tears, all Violet could think of to say was, "Why?"

Kjel twisted his mouth and scratched his jaw. "Because you should have it, Violet, plain and simple."

✳

THEY SAID GOOD-BYE to the sisters two days later. Sometimes Kjel's "girlfriends" made a scene before the band left town, clinging to him and sobbing that he couldn't leave, what would they do without him, didn't he know how much they loved him?

Watching these farewells, Violet whispered invectives to herself ("Flabby whore!" "Beady-eyed trollop!") but Kjel was always gentle, dousing their frantic little fires with calm, soft words, peeling their hands away from him like a kindly doctor delicately removing stitches; didn't they know he was going to make sure this hurt as little as possible?

Ginny, however, was dry-eyed and businesslike, offering only her hand to Kjel and then laughing when he pulled her to him by the ends of her muffler.

"Boy, is she gonna miss him," Dottie said, crossing her arms as she leaned against the truck by the open passenger window, watching them kiss. "Good men aren't the easiest to find around here—especially good men that look like *him*."

Violet gave her a look that let her know she wasn't telling her anything she didn't already know.

Dottie laughed. "So how's the sewing machine working for you?"

Violet admitted she hadn't taken it out of the case yet.

"But I've looked at it a lot." Then in a gesture so uncharacteristic she could hardly believe it was her hand reaching out, Violet gave the woman's arm a feeble squeeze. "I can't thank you enough for it."

Dottie leaned into the passenger window, returning the puny embrace with as tight a hug as she could offer in her bulky wool coat.

"If you ever have time, make me a dress," she said. "Like that one in your book, with the flouncy sleeves."

"I'll get right to it."

"I'd wear it to my wedding," said Dottie, "if there is ever such a thing." As a second thought occurred to her, she tapped Violet's shoulder. "Wait a second, being seen in a dress like that would probably *inspire* my wedding."

When the good-byes were finally over and Kjel's truck followed Elwin's out of the pitted dirt driveway, Dottie yelled, "You ditch those boys, Violet, and head out to Hollywood! I can just see Paulette Goddard and Norma Shearer wearing Fashions by Violetta!"

When the caravan got to the road, Dottie cupped her gloved hands around her mouth and added, "And don't forget to send me my dress!"

Violet waved at the two sisters until she couldn't see them anymore, and it wasn't until Kjel asked her to roll up the window because the snow was getting in that she felt the cold.

———

Chapter Thirteen

ON NEW YEAR'S DAY, WHEN THE PEARLTONES WERE SLEEPING OFF *its wild welcome of 1938 (right before the countdown, the band played a sped-up version of "Auld Lang Syne," while Kjel, acting as a square-dance caller, urged everyone to "swing yer partners, kiss 'em hard"), I was seated in front of my Featherweight, trying to find the courage to thread the needle. I knew it wouldn't be that hard; I was more proficient with my right hand than I let on, having been forced to use it in school; what made me feel clammy under the armpits and slightly out of breath was the knowledge that it wouldn't be easy.*

My preamputated life had been hard; hard enough that I didn't so much take the easy things for granted as revel in their easiness. I was so proud of my hands and what they could do; they were good, true scouts taking me where other parts of my body couldn't. Never timid, never wavering, they were always certain they were up to whatever task was facing them. My hands were so quick, so assured, that I didn't want to denigrate their memory by forcing the one remaining to plod along. I felt, as odd as this seems, that my right mourned the loss of its mate more than my conscious self did; sometimes it would flap across my lap and up to my breast pocket, the way your hand will when it's searching for lost keys or a pack of cigarettes. I've heard that it's the lack of symmetry that disturbs people when they see someone who's lost a limb, but I think it's their innate understanding that an amputee's body is in deep sorrow, grieving for its lost partner.

When we got to the next town, Kjel took me to the fabric department of the Woolworth's, pulling me over to the fancy voiles and tulles.

"Kjel, I want to make a skirt, not a wedding gown."

I paid $2.78 for a yard and a half of sturdy blue chambray, a packet of pins, blue thread, and two navy buttons, and when the clerk (from her openmouthed, wide-eyed look, I knew the question screaming in her head was, "What is he doing with her?") handed me the package, I hesitated for a moment, the way someone does on the high dive. But I took that package; I jumped.

Back in my little rented room that smelled of menthol, I realized I was frozen on that high dive again, and this time I might back down the ladder. Not only was I afraid to thread the machine, I was afraid of the thread itself, the feel of it, remembering when I tried to free the clotted machine and that stunned instant when I felt it bite my arm off.

The radiator hissed out stale heat, and I sat there. Outside, snow flew, as if trying to impress the new year by its industriousness, and resenting its motion, I got up to pull the shade. At that moment, Austin walked by the window, and seeing me start, he smiled and mouthed the word "Sorry" and then "What're you doing?" I pointed to my sewing machine, but he shook his head before pressing his face to the glass, his hand cupped on the side of his head to see in better. I don't know what propelled me to the door, but propelled I was, opening it and inviting him in.

Wary, he looked to his left and to his right before entering. The auto parks and motels we stayed at now that it was so cold were either cabins or low-slung, one-story buildings with each room having its own entrance, and even though "Whites Only" signs weren't posted yet, we knew we weren't going to run across any "Negroes Welcome" signs either. Either Kjel or I rented out the rooms (paying cash in advance oils the squeakiest of wheels), and usually the motel clerk was not aware that included in our party were two colored men; the Sykes brothers waiting for their key and room number in the shelter of the panel truck.

For Austin to enter my room in broad daylight was an occurrence that would have inflamed many motel owners and/or guests, and I pushed the door shut, the way you do when you don't want a draft to get in.

"So what's transpiring in the tailor's shop?" asked Austin, immediately going to the sewing machine.

"Nothing. I can't start."

Austin sat at the rickety desk and inspected the machine, turning the wheel, lifting up the presser foot, and jumping back when the needle darted up and down after he stepped on the treadle.

"Careful," I said with a laugh. "It's plugged in."

"It just about sewed up my finger!" Getting up, he gestured toward the empty chair. "Show me how it's done, Violet."

I sat down but my head was shaking, expressing its disapproval.

"I'm afraid. I'm afraid to even touch the thread."

"Well, sure you are, Violet. Anyone would be."

I sat there.

"You think Harriet Tubman wasn't afraid the first time she led someone to freedom? You think Sojourner Truth wasn't afraid the first time she preached?"

"Okay, okay," I said, laughing.

"You think Victoria Woodhull wasn't afraid the first day she went campaigning for the presidency? You think Amelia Earhart—"

"Jeez, Austin—did you just read a 'great women in history' book or something?"

Sheepish, Austin nodded. "Actually, I did. In the last town we were in . . . and I believe the book even had that title."

I couldn't help but laugh.

"Of course they had nothing about the Misses Tubman and Truth in their pages. Those references come from a different source."

"Well, I appreciate all your references. But I hardly think threading a sewing machine puts me in the same sphere of courage."

"Don't talk to me about spheres of courage, Violet. Not one of those women had to go back to her work after she lost an arm."

Austin didn't touch me, but it felt like he had patted me on the back with a steady hand, and those blame tears of mine flashed up, mocking once again the tough cookie it was important everyone think I was.

"Is it in here?" asked Austin, reaching for the Woolworth bag next to the machine.

I nodded, a geyser of adrenaline fuel coursing through my body. If a match had been struck, I would have combusted.

Austin took out the spool of blue thread and handed it to me.

"It's okay, Violet." His simple words and the certainty of his voice made me tear up again, and I shut my eyes until I was composed. I don't know how long that took, but when I opened them, the thread was still in Austin's open hand, and with a ragged breath I took it, pulling the single thread out of the nick at the edge of the spool, unwinding several inches.

Austin got to his haunches and, squatting beside me, watched carefully as I threaded the bobbin and then the machine. He watched me but didn't move when I got up to get the pieces of fabric I had cut out and pinned together earlier and left on the bed. He watched, and didn't move, when I lifted up the presser-foot lever and lined up the fabric underneath it. It was slippery, and I felt my face darken as I struggled to put it back.

"Violet." His voice was soft, still steady. "Violet, don't be afraid to use your stump to hold it down."

I didn't need a mirror to know my face was the color of a colicky baby's trying to pass a gas bubble. Still, I put my stump down on the left side of the presser foot, turned the wheel so the needle pricked into the fabric, and stepped on the treadle, guiding the fabric with my right hand and my stump, until the entire seam was sewn. Neither of us spoke as I turned the fabric around and sewed the other side seam.

"Oh my," said Austin as I turned the fabric right side out and held it up. "You just sewed yourself a skirt."

"Well, I have to put in a facing—I'm not going to sew a waistband right now—I want to keep it simple—although the buttonhole for the side tab might be a problem. And then of course I've got to hem it."

Austin patted the bicep of my stump, and it was the first time someone had touched it that I didn't recoil. "It's not a whole arm, but there's still a lot you can do with it." Looking out the window at the still-furious snow, he sighed and said, "Well, I guess it's time to shuffle off to Buffalo." He dug out the hat he had folded into his jacket pocket. "And . . . and Happy New Year, Violet. It seems yours is off to an auspicious start."

"Happy New Year to you too," I said, and if I had been a braver woman, I would have given him one of the long and bracing hugs I used to give my old Tree Pa.

Violet told Elwin he was in charge of "Costume Maintenance," which meant he laundered the band members' clothing. He diligently performed his duties, but even so, there were some nights when Kjel's shirt was stained or wrinkled or when all three wore different clashing colors or patterns. Violet knew their fans couldn't have cared less if the band had worn flour sacks, but she thought a little professionalism would not hurt the freewheeling Pearltones.

"I've decided," Violet told them in the early spring, "that the Pearltones should wear matching jackets. And this is what I'm thinking of."

Looking at the fabric Violet held up, Dallas shook his head. "I ain't wearin' no pink jacket. Nope. Uh-uh."

"It's pearl pink, which is hardly pink at all. And this gray material is for the lapels and collars. They're perfect colors for the band."

"There're black pearls too," said Dallas. "Why don't you make us black jackets?"

"Because these colors are perfect," said Violet tightly. "When people think of pearls, they think of pale pink or pale gray."

"I think of white," offered Elwin. "Or more off-white, I guess. My great-aunt Melvina had a pearl necklace and those pearls were off-white, or even kind of yellowish, now that I think about it."

"Thank you for that recollection," said Violet, tighter still. "But off-white or 'yellowish' is not a good stage color, and neither is black."

"So you're saying me and Austin shouldn't be onstage?"

"No," said Violet, and if her voice got any tighter it would have snapped in two. "What I'm saying is that flashy colors look better onstage."

"There ain't no flashier color than black," said Dallas. "And *I* ain't wearin' nothin' pink."

Violet enlisted Elwin's help (he dared not question anything Violet asked of him) in measuring each man (even if she had two hands, she wouldn't have been able to handle the intimacy of wrapping a tape measure around Kjel's pectorals, Austin's shoulders, or Dallas's waist), and she worked on the jackets in her rented rooms.

After she made her skirt (the hem was crooked and the waistline gapped, but Kjel and Austin raved about it like naked cavemen seeing one of their own model a mastodon skin), she practiced putting in sleeves a dozen times until she was able to make one without a single pucker; she practiced making collars whose points matched; she practiced making pleats and gathers; she practiced—and was almost done in by—sewing in zippers. Since her fine hand-stitching was no longer possible, she practiced hemming by machine and finishing buttonholes by machine. Her spending money, which she almost always saved, now went toward fabric, and in her spare time she made patterns from local newspapers, cut material, and sewed. Everything settled down when she sewed; the bees' buzz was muted by the drone of the Featherweight's motor, and her mind pushed aside its usual hundred-a-minute thoughts and concentrated on what she was seeing and touching in front of her. Sometimes she sang or hummed a Pearltones' song, or one from her childhood, or one she'd heard on the radio, but if someone had asked her what she was singing, she'd have looked up and said, "I didn't know I was."

She made one pattern for the men's jackets, making her alterations for each (Elwin didn't tell Violet how mercilessly he'd been teased taking the men's measurements) as she cut out the fabric, and when she presented the finished products, Kjel said, "Oh man, Violet," and Austin said, "Violet, I never dreamed you could make something like this, which just goes to show you how limiting dreams can be." Taking his jacket, Dallas said nothing.

Pride was like a yeast, puffing Violet up as she watched the Pearltones onstage, wearing jackets she had designed and sewed, but her buoyed state was not long-lasting. She saw quickly how impractical her costumes were; Kjel especially sweated great circles of sweat, and as he dashed around the stage, Violet watched in dismay as his pale-pink jacket darkened under his armpits and between his shoulder blades.

"From now on," she told them after the show, "you'll wear the jackets when you walk onstage and when you walk offstage. In between you'll have to take them off."

"Man, but you're bossy," said Kjel. "Isn't she bossy, boys?"

"Bossy ain't the word," muttered Dallas.

"And what do you propose we have on when we take off the jackets?" asked Austin.

"Gray T-shirts," said Violet, thinking on her feet. "They'll be easy to wash and cheap to buy."

"T-shirts," said Austin, who felt he expressed himself with as much care sartorially as he did with his speech. "We're a band of musicians, Violet—not ditchdiggers!"

"Well, you work up a sweat like they do," said Violet, and looking at Kjel, she added, "especially you. Now give me your jackets—I'll clean them up tonight, Elwin—and tomorrow night we'll try it with the T-shirts."

Violet had watched a few shows from backstage, but she preferred seeing the band as the audience saw them and now stood in the back of the roadhouse they had been hired to play for three nights. It was packed with people, and just as many had been turned away.

"I thought I was gonna have a riot on my hands," said the nervous owner, swabbing his bald head with a red bandanna. "Couple a girls out there were crying like there was no tomorrow, but I told 'em my place can only hold so many and so many is already too many!" He mopped his forehead, looking around at the crowd. "Let's just pray there ain't a fire 'cause who could run for cover if there was?"

When it came time to introduce the band, he tucked his

damp bandanna in his back pocket and bounded up the stage as if he had tucked aside his worries too.

"Ladies and gentlemen—if you haven't heard them, you've heard about them! Let's give a warm Galesburg welcome to the Pearltones!"

The three musicians strode out in their pale-pink and gray-accented jackets, and a cheer went up from the crowd. When they took off their jackets and handed them to a blushing and smiling Elwin, they cheered louder.

"Holy cow," said a young woman to her friend, "pass me the smelling salts."

Violet watched the show from the back, from the middle, the front, and the side, pushing herself through the crowd that had stood during the first song and forgotten to sit down since. There were several familiar faces who greeted Violet—the band had attracted fans who sought them out in other towns after seeing them once, and in fact a core group of them had banded together, following them from show to show and sometimes even advising them as to a club they knew of in another town that would be amenable to booking them. Their apparent leader, a woman named Birdie Howe, had told Violet they referred to themselves as "Clamshells" and their mission was to attend every show and be the first on the bandwagon ("pun intended") that was going to change the world.

"Change the world?" Kjel said when Violet repeated Birdie's words to him. "Tell her that's a job for Roosevelt, Churchill, and Stalin."

Along with the Clamshells, the audience was comprised of teary-eyed young women and young men whose faces wore a look of longing and a wish that they could do what was being done onstage.

"What do you think of their jackets?" Violet asked two schoolteachers who'd seen the band in Kewanee and had come back for second helpings.

"I think they're swell," said the one who'd left on her desk a pile of ungraded tests on the Louisiana Purchase.

"But I like them even better in those tight little T-shirts," said the other, a woman named Alice who was questioning her calling to be a teacher. ("I used to think that educating our youth was the most important thing I could do," she confessed to her friend, "but that was before I saw the Pearltones.") "They really show off their . . . assets!"

They leaned into each other and giggled, acting like the seventh-graders they taught.

After three encores (the fewest, they had learned, that audiences would settle for), Elwin, blush and smile intact, walked out again with the men's jackets, and when they put them on and took their final bow, it seemed to the club owner that the applause would knock the walls down.

"Violet," said Austin afterward, "of your many talents, your genius for show business may be your most impressive."

"Aren't we lucky to have her?" asked Kjel, pulling Violet to him and lifting her up in a hug.

Don't put me down! Violet silently pleaded, and when he did, she negotiated, *Just hold me a little while longer.* But then Elwin handed him a beer and Kjel was ready to wade through the throng of women that awaited him outside.

Chapter Fourteen

IN THE WHIRLWIND THAT WAS THE PEARLTONES ON TOUR IN *Illinois, it is astonishing to think I was only eighteen years old. Eighteen years old and looking a grizzled roadhouse owner (who wore a holster, no less!) in his bloodshot eyes and telling him that sorry, the deal he offered wasn't good enough; eighteen years old and acting as the band's manager and accountant and costume designer! Eighteen years old and setting rules for three musicians and a roadie and then letting them hear about it if they disobeyed!*

Of course, everyone was older back then; in those days you saw ten-year-old boys driving combines or breaking up the earth behind a team of mules; nine-year-old girls toting baby sisters on their hips as they comparison shopped at the grocery store. "Acting your age" as an eighteen-year-old meant acting like an adult; we weren't coddled and didn't have the luxury of stretching our adolescence into our thirties, as seems to be the trend now.

I think of those months in Illinois as our golden age. One sold-out engagement effortlessly followed another; the band was working on music and had a new song to perform every couple of days; and most important, everyone was getting along.

We were now a band of brothers plus one sister; all formality and stiff manners were trampled when the door of propriety came crashing down once and for all when I pushed through the open door of the dressing room during intermission.

"And did you by chance get a look at the cantaloupes on that redhead in the front row?" Austin was saying, his back to me. "What man wouldn't want to smother his face in those and squeeze them till the juice ran dry?"

My dry cough as well as his bandmates' all-out grins alerted him to my presence, and looking mortified, he turned around to apologize.

Wearing my best I'm-so-wounded face, I stared at him for a long while.

"Austin, I'm ashamed of you," I said finally. "If you didn't spend so much time leering at those cantaloupes, you might have noticed the watermelons on the gal behind her."

Kjel, Elwin, and even Dallas hooted with laughter.

"Violet, please excuse me," said Austin with a little bow. "To say that I am embarrassed is to minimize what I'm feeling."

"Well, save your embarrassment for after the show," I said, looking at my watch. "Your public—and it's filled with casabas and muskmelons just waiting 'to be squeezed dry'—awaits you."

Do you have close friends of the opposite sex? If so, you know how ribald you can get, how some regression takes place. From that night on, if a dirty joke was being told in the dressing room, the men didn't go silent upon my entrance, but recapped it for my benefit before getting to the punch line. Conversations were no longer censored, and rather than being offended, I felt honored.

"Fellas, show a little respect!" one theater owner said at a rehearsal that was getting sort of bawdy. "There's a lady present!"

I quickly looked over both my shoulders and asked, "Where?"

Laughing, Kjel draped his arm around me and explained, "She's no lady, she's our Violet."

"Our Violet." Out of all the names I'd been called, imagine how that one made me feel.

Lending to my sense of camaraderie and the general sense of bonhomie was the world itself, covered as it was in the soft colors spring is so possessive about. Trees had bud their new green leaves, the light purple foam of lilacs lathered up banks of shrubs, and looking up at the tender blue sky, well, it was easy to understand the concept of Heaven.

How can a person not wax romantic about spring; wherever there's promise, there's romance. Anything was possible that sweet, soft spring, and for once I was on the invitation list.

"All right," said Kjel, "fifty cents say you can't make it from there."

"I'll take that bet," said Elwin, and stepping back, he closed one eye and aimed.

"Pay up!" cackled Austin.

On a fishing trip on a sweet day in May, Elwin had revealed a secret talent: he was a master with his rod and reel. Whether or not his talent transferred to catching fish had yet to be tested, but he had cast off and hit every target offered him.

From under a canopy of crab-apple blossoms, Violet alternately watched him land his sinker in any number of containers (a bucket, a tin can, Kjel's hat) while reading a detective novel Austin had loaned her.

When target practice was over and they decided to move into real water and fish for real fish, Kjel urged Dallas to join them, but he had appropriated a camp chair and was not moving, playing his guitar instead.

"Come on, Dallas, Violet's only got one arm. What's your excuse?"

"Hey," said Violet, looking up from her book, "even if I had two arms, I wouldn't use them fishing. What a waste of time."

"Amen to that," said Dallas, striking a discordant chord. "All fishin' is, is taking a nap with a pole in your hands."

"You've just described how you go to sleep every night," said Austin.

"Except my pole's a lot bigger than that skinny little rod you got in your hands," said Dallas.

"Hey, I think I got something!" shouted Elwin, mercifully interrupting the scatologia, and as he reeled in his catch, Dallas matched the movement of the rod with his guitar playing; strumming three dramatic chords over and over when the rod curled, and playing a light little ditty when it straightened itself out. When Elwin finally pulled a thrashing perch out of the water, Dallas played the first bars of Beethoven's Eighth Symphony.

"Hey, Violet," said Kjel, "why don't you and Dallas build a fire so we can eat these up?"

"These?" said Violet. "There's been only *one* fish caught."

"How about a little *faith?*"

"Two or three fish would inspire faith," said Violet. "One doesn't."

She and Dallas did set to collecting wood, however, and when the fire they built was a serviceable roar, the fish count was four.

"Now I see the light," said Violet, watching as Elwin gutted the fish with his pocketknife and placed it in the pan he'd gotten out of his truck.

"Violet, if you have any butter," said Austin, watching the thin trails of smoke rise from the pan, "I'll marry you."

Violet thought hard as to what was in the provisions box and how long ago she had stocked it. "Well, for sure there's no butter, but there should be some Crisco left."

Kjel raced to Elwin's panel truck, and when he came back he handed Elwin a can of Crisco and three potatoes, and gave Dallas a jar of pickles and two apples.

"Bread-and-butter pickles," said Austin. "Don't we have any dill?"

"Oh, sure, you'll marry Violet for some butter," said Kjel, raising his voice to a falsetto. "I come bearing gifts and you give me nothing but scorn."

"Bread-and-butter pickles deserve scorn," said Austin. "Pickles are supposed to be dill."

As Elwin served up lunch on the speckled tin plates, Violet asked, "Elwin, do you always cook like this?"

Bracing himself for criticism, Elwin asked, "Like what?"

"Well, who would have thought to slice up those apples and

cook them up with the potatoes and the fish?" Violet speared food on her fork and held it up. "It's just so unusual . . . but so good."

A smile spread slowly across Elwin's face. "Thanks. I do like to cook."

Kjel reached over and speared a piece of Violet's fish off her plate.

"Hey!" she said, not wanting to give up any of her food to the marauder that was often Kjel around a campfire. "But how'd you think to cook up the apples too?"

Elwin shrugged his beefy round shoulders. "Well, they were there."

"We've all had the lesson 'waste not want not' emblazoned in our brains during these hard times," said Austin, "but I would daresay many of us are not so creative with it."

"Well, thanks," said Elwin. "I guess."

A jam session followed lunch, and in the middle of playing "You're My Gem" (a song audiences always demanded for an encore), Kjel set down his guitar and offered his hand to Violet.

"Dance with me." He grabbed her hand and pulled her off the camp chair. "Somebody handle the vocals so I can concentrate on my lovely dance partner, okay?"

The brothers were happy to oblige; Austin took the melody Kjel usually sang and Dallas added harmony. Violet, woozy from self-consciousness, stared past the ledge of Kjel's shoulders and to the ground, trying hard not to faint, not to trip, not to do any of the dozens of stupid things she was capable of. She didn't know where to put her stump, didn't want to touch Kjel with it, but he grabbed it with his hand.

"Jeez, Violet, I thought you were through with all that nonsense. Just rest it against my arm and forget about it."

Air caught in Violet's throat but she yelled at herself to relax, to breathe.

"Next to you, the Hope diamond's just glass,
Next to you, all gold's just brass,

*I could pick the Du Pont's safe, the Rockefellers' too—
There'd be nothing in there that could compare to you."*

The Sykes brothers' voices were a rich, seamless blend, and Violet shut her eyes. It was a good impulse; shutting down the sense that aided and abetted self-consciousness calmed her. The spring day was mild, and Violet, cocooned in the arms of a dance partner who gave off heat like a furnace, found her own body temperature was elevated. The bees were astir in her head, but not to a frenzied degree, and she found that she was in fact relaxing. She stopped counting steps under her breath and let her feet follow Kjel's, the music a tonic and a guide.

*"Like a ruby you glimmer, like a sapphire you shine,
But the biggest treasure is that you're mine."*

Suddenly, a reedy, slightly off-key female voice jumped into the chorus and the Sykeses' fingers froze on their fret boards. Kjel whirled around, and Violet, still in his arms, whirled too.

"I love that song," said a slim, young woman dressed in shorts and a sailor top.

"We saw your shows at the Carlyle," explained the man with her, whose mustache looked painted on with a fine-pointed brush. He too was slim and young. "We're certainly fans."

" 'Course, whoever thought we'd meet the Pearltones out at Beecher Lake! I'm Isalee by the way." The nautically dressed woman walked toward Kjel and Violet, arm extended.

"And I'm LaMar." The man offered his hand first to Elwin, then to the brothers. "And we're tickled to be in your company! Tickled that you might find Beecher Lake as conductive to your artistry as we do!"

Violet saw a flash in Austin's eyes; the eager professor ready to correct a student who's erred in the teacher's field of expertise.

"And how," he said, "is Beecher Lake *conducive* to your particular artistry? And also, might I ask what *is* your particular artistry?"

The thin mustache stretched as the thin man smiled. "Isalee and LaMar?" He waited a moment for recognition, for a bobbing of heads or a breathy "No kidding!" but when no recognition came, LaMar smiled, bemused; he didn't fault people who didn't recognize them, only felt sorry for them. "Isalee and LaMar *the adagio dancers*? We won honorable mention at the Midwest Invitational!"

"And we came in nineteenth in the Nationals," said Isalee. "Which is pretty good on account of there were forty-five couples competing."

LaMar's smile was pained. "Most expected us to be in the top ten, but I was suffering from a pulled groin."

"Ouch," said Kjel.

"Exactly," said LaMar with a nod.

"But I was the one who was dropped," said Isalee.

LaMar held his arms out, appealing to the others. "You try to hold someone over your head with a pulled groin."

"It wouldn't occur to me," admitted Austin.

"So you . . . you practice out here?" said Kjel.

"When the weather permits," LaMar replied. "When it doesn't, you can find us in our home studio—"

"It's my aunt's dance school. It's called 'Bal-Ay'!" said Isalee, "although she doesn't spell it the way the French do. We get to use the room for free on account of she's my aunt and all."

"But as I said earlier," said LaMar, gesturing to the lake, to the blossoming crab-apple trees, "we enjoy the open spaces of nature, finding a pastoral atmosphere aids our art."

"And this is certainly *pastoral*," said Austin.

Elwin, who had been staring at the couple with open-mouthed fascination, broke out of his trance to ask the couple if they'd mind showing them a little of their act.

"That is if it ain't too much trouble."

LaMar and Isalee exchanged a look that said it was no trouble at all.

"If the minstrels wouldn't mind minstreling," said LaMar.

"Minstrel," muttered Dallas.

Austin picked up his guitar, and directing his question to the dancers, he asked, "Any particular song or type of song?"

"At the Nationals we danced to 'Cheek to Cheek,' " said Isalee.

"So did a half-dozen other couples," said LaMar. "I personally think that's why we didn't score as well as anticipated."

"That and you dropping me," said Isalee.

"Well, Irving Berlin's not in our usual repertoire, but we can sure give it a shot, right boys?" Kjel strummed a chord on his guitar.

Austin set down his guitar and took his harmonica out of his pocket. He played an introduction, and Dallas and Kjel jumped in.

Violet sat down on her camp chair and Elwin leaned against a tree, waiting for the show to start, but the couple didn't move.

"Could you give us a count?" asked LaMar. "We're not sure where to come in."

"Sure," said Kjel. "A nice four count. And a one, two, three, four."

As Austin played the first lines of the melody, LaMar and Isalee joined hands, executed some fancy footwork, several dips, and suddenly the slim young woman in shorts was lifted above the slim young man's head and he twirled while she held her arms out and pointed her toes.

"Oh my," said Elwin.

Violet thought they looked more like two gymnasts who'd decided to move together, and in fact they rarely danced cheek to cheek; mostly their faces were inches or even feet away from each other's. She did gasp a few times, as did Elwin, when Isalee was flung into the air and it was questionable whether she was going to get caught. But LaMar's groin appeared to be in fine fettle and he didn't drop her once, although his footing wasn't always the surest when she landed in his arms. Near the end of the song he asked—through deep breaths—the musicians to "speed it up because we're almost done."

He flipped Isalee over his head as the Pearltones frantically played, and she slid down his back, both landing on the ground in full splits. LaMar's legs then spread, but he was not able to get as close to the ground as his partner. Still, he offered a gap-toothed smile, happy with the performance, and both he and Isalee held their arms up to the sky for a final "Ta–da!"

Their audience and accompaniment applauded soundly as the dancers got to their feet, brushing a few twigs and pebbles off their legs.

"One of the pitfalls of dancing outside," said LaMar.

"We try to stay away from bramble patches," said Isalee, and as she smiled at Elwin, he lit up like the White House switch-board after a Fireside Chat.

"Mind if we sit down for a spell?" asked LaMar, still breathing heavily.

"Be our guest," said Kjel, offering one of the camp chairs.

"So, we couldn't help notice you two dancing," said LaMar, sitting down and fanning his face with a monogrammed hand-kerchief he took out of his vest pocket. "I don't imagine it's the easiest thing to do when you're crippled."

Violet flushed and looked out at the lake.

"Violet's not crippled," said Kjel. "She just lost her arm is all. In an adagio accident."

Violet spasmed as if she'd been shocked, and then, thrilled at Kjel's outlandish lie (as outlandish as any she had told), she added, "Yes. My partner and I liked to practice outside too. In farm-yards, usually. Those were special times—until he threw me in front of a thresher."

"No," said LaMar, his dark eyes wide.

"No," laughed Isalee. "They're kidding you LaMar, can't you see that?"

LaMar scratched under the collar of his shirt. "Of course I can see that, Isalee. What do you take me for—blind?"

"But really," said Kjel, slapping the dancer on the back, "is it *hard* to dance the way you do?"

"Well," said the mustachioed man, brightening. "Some say

not only do we have to be exceptional dancers, we have to be exceptional acrobats."

"I can do a flip," said Kjel.

"Dallas can do it *backward*," said Austin. "Flip, that is."

"That's all well and good," said LaMar, "but it takes more than being able to do flips—back, front, or *sideways*."

"Could you teach me something?" asked Kjel.

"Sorry," said LaMar. "I couldn't risk an injury to my partner. Capezio shoes is sponsoring a contest next month in Chicago and we're hoping to get at least in the top five."

"Well how about if I use Violet as my partner?" asked Kjel.

Violet was not the only one who looked at him as if he were crazy.

"But she's only got one arm!" said Isalee.

"Actually, she's got an arm and a half. And don't sell that half arm short."

"Well," said Isalee, embarrassed that she'd pointed out the tall woman's disability, "she certainly has the legs of a dancer. Thin, but shapely."

"That's right," said Kjel, cocking his head to look at Violet. "She does have a nice set of stems, doesn't she?"

Violet felt as giddy and befuddled as if she'd spent the morning adding whiskey to her coffee. There she was, sitting in a clearing by a lake, having just watched a slightly fumbly adagio dance exhibition, having been volunteered as a teaching partner of Kjel's and having her legs scrutinized and complimented.

She felt that same crazy, zippy flame ignite the dry grass of reason; felt herself asking the question she had asked more and more: Why not?

Standing up, she brushed the wrinkles from her skirt (thankfully, the stiff chambray could do its part in keeping her covered), and then with a salute said, "Violet Mathers, reporting for duty, sir."

"All right," said LaMar, standing. "But we won't take any responsibility if anyone gets hurt."

Kjel nodded somberly. "Got that, Violet? If you get hurt, it's not their fault."

Violet chuckled. "Don't worry about me. You're the one who's going to be doing the heavy lifting."

"Well then, let's get started," said LaMar, clapping his hands. "We'll start with a simple lift."

As Isalee arranged herself in front of LaMar, Dallas beat a drumroll on his guitar with his fingers.

"See how we've both got our knees bent?" he said of himself and his partner who stood facing him. "Then I put my arms around her waist and . . . lift!"

With a little bounce, Isalee was lifted into the air and LaMar straightened his arms, lifting her until she was parallel to the ground, her toes pointed, her arms out. After a few moments he brought her back down to the ground.

"Your turn," he said, and watching as Violet stood in front of Kjel, he remarked, "Good gracious, you're tall."

"Thank you," said Violet in a high tone.

"Violet, be careful," said Austin, watching as Kjel put his hands on her waist.

"All right, now, bend your knees," said LaMar. "And, Violet, kind of jump into the lift, all right?"

"On the count of three, okay?" said Kjel, his face just inches from hers. Violet nodded, smelling roses, tasting chocolate, hearing bells. "One . . . two . . . three."

They both bent their knees deeper, and as Violet jumped, Kjel lifted. She was airbound, but not for long, Kjel bringing her down to earth in quick progression.

"Jeez, Violet, how much *do* you weigh?"

"I don't believe it's her weight," said LaMar. "I believe it's her height. She's a long one to lift."

"I'll bet I could do it," said Elwin.

The day had held too many surprises for Violet to be flummoxed by this one; of course big shy Elwin wanted a chance to hurl her in the air.

"Let me try one more time," said Kjel, and again Dallas beat out his drumroll and they faced each other, knees bent, and after a three count Violet jumped in his lift and he hoisted her upward. She got above his head, but just as she was ready to strike the pose Isalee had, Kjel's arms bent and he sent her southward.

They were both seized by laughter after her feet hit the ground, and they gave in to it for a moment, half crouched and holding their stomachs.

"Okay, Elwin," said Violet when she had collected herself, "let's see if you've got what Kjel doesn't."

"That hurts, Violet," said Kjel. "To my core."

She repeated the same position with Elwin. Usually he avoided eye contact with her but now his gaze was steady.

"Ready?"

Violet nodded, and three seconds later she was above Elwin's head. She pointed her toes and stretched out her arm and stump.

Kjel whistled low. "Look at that form, that grace!"

As LaMar had done in their dance exhibition, Elwin slowly turned around in a full circle, and all the while Violet remained horizontal, as rigid as a statue.

Austin began playing "Waltzing Matilda" on the harmonica.

" 'Waltzing Matilda'?" said Kjel, picking up his guitar. "They're not waltzing."

Austin lifted the harmonica away from his mouth. "It's a dance song, isn't it?"

"I'm bringing you down now, Violet," said Elwin, and he lowered her to the ground as lightly as a breeze sends an autumn leaf to earth.

"You're a natural!" said LaMar, frantically clapping. "We usually don't see fellows of your size on the dance floor, but apparently that's our loss!"

"Can I have a turn?" asked Isalee.

Elwin colored and smiled, and Violet wouldn't have been surprised to see him paw at the ground with his foot and say, "Aw, shucks."

The Pearltones reprised "Cheek to Cheek" in a bluesier fashion, and LaMar held his arms out to Violet and said, "May I?"

"No lifting, though," said Violet, and LaMar assured her that her feet would remain firmly on the ground.

LaMar pretended that the stump she rested against his bicep didn't bother him, and after a while it didn't and he began to get a little bolder, deviating from their simple box step to do a fancy fox-trot or samba. She was not the most graceful woman he'd ever held in his arms, but he'd danced with worse, and a partner's big easy smile went a long way in apologizing for any clumsiness. Violet's smile was huge.

When the song was over, he was planning on dancing with her again, but as Kjel and Dallas began to play "The Johnstown Rag," Austin cut in.

Violet danced once with him and again with Elwin before Isalee grabbed her arm, asking her to accompany her to the "powder room."

"I swear, I have a bladder the size of a pea!" Isalee said as she squatted behind a grouping of honey locust trees. She gave a little moan of relief as she began to piddle, and after a few moments giggled and said, "I've never danced with a colored man!"

"Me neither," said Violet, staring through the trees toward the lake.

"I did dance with a Cuban once. He was dark, but not like these fellas." The young woman stood, pulling up her navy blue shorts. "But say, they're pretty good. Especially the good-looking one."

"Kjel?"

Isalee laughed. "Not the good-looking white one—the good-looking colored one. The shorter one with the nice build."

"Dallas?"

"Yeah, Dallas." Isalee giggled. "And boy oh boy, would my dad kill me if he saw me dancing with him! Lucky for me, my dad's in Cleveland!"

As the women returned to the grass dance floor, the Pearltones began to play "Ain't She Sweet," and Elwin, quickly tossing his cigarette aside, claimed Isalee as his partner. Dallas set down his guitar and raced LaMar toward Violet, LaMar winning. Dallas feigned great disappointment, until Kjel gallantly stepped up and took him in his arms.

Kjel tried to lift Dallas up, straining audibly while Dallas, in a falsetto voice whined, "Are you calling me heavy?" After ingloriously being dropped, Dallas lifted Kjel off the ground and over his shoulders and begun spinning in tight circles until Kjel claimed he was going to throw up. Dallas literally shrugged him off, and Kjel met the ground on all fours, quickly somersaulting away from his partner.

The wrestling match/adagio dance exhibition continued as both men showed off their prospective flips and Austin blew puffs of laughter through his harmonica, until he had to stop playing altogether. Finally, when both men had showed off (over and over) their talent at back and front flips, Elwin, who was peeved at losing precious dance time with Isalee, asked the Pearltones if they'd mind playing "Ain't She Sweet" again.

The sun made its slow glide across the sky, and the music and dancing went on, sometimes to the accompaniment of all of the Pearltones, and when two musicians danced, to the lone accompaniment of one. In a single afternoon, on grass littered with pink crab-apple petals, Violet danced with five different partners, five more than she had ever danced with in her life.

Look at me! she thought more than once as Kjel dipped her backward or Austin twirled her. *I'm the belle of the ball!*

Chapter Fifteen

BZZZZZZZZZZZZZZZZZZZZZZZZZZZZZZZZZZZZZZZZZZZZZZZZZZZZ
ZZZZZZZZZZZZZZZZZZZZZZZZZZZZZZZZZZZZZZZZZZZZZZZZZZZZZ
ZZZZZZZZZZZZZZZZZZZZZZZZZZZZZZZZZZZZZZZZZZZZZZZZZZZZZ
ZZZZZZZZZZZZZZZZZZZZZZZZZZZZZZZZZZZZZZZZZZZZZZZZZZZZZ
ZZZZZZZZZZZZZZZZZZZZZZZZZZZZZZZZ.BZZZZZZZZZZZZZZZZZ
ZZZZZZZZZZZZZZZZZZZZZZZZZZZZZZZZZZZZZZZZZZZZZZZZZZZZZ
ZZZZZZZZZZZZZZZZZZZZZZZZZZZZZZZZZZZZZZZZZZZZZZZZZZZZZ
ZZZZZZZZZZZZZZZZZZZZZZZZZZZZZZZZZZZZZZZZZZZZZZZZZZZZZ
ZZZZZZZZZZZZZZZZZZZZZZZZZZZZZZZZZZZZZZZZZZZZZZZZZZZZZ
ZZZZZZZZZZZZZZZZZZZZZ . . .

Well, you get the idea. Imagine that sound so deep in your ear canal that it's in your brain, that it's as integral a sound in your body as the beating of your heart. I didn't know until decades later that it had a name—tinnitus—and that I wasn't the only one afflicted with it. For the longest time I thought it was a special curse all my own; that I alone had been singled out to suffer. Sometimes late at night the buzzing wouldn't let me go to sleep, and there were still instances when I thought I'd truly be driven insane, but those months were so happy, with so many moments *of* bliss, *for crying out loud, that it almost seemed a fair trade: unrelenting, maddening noise in my ears for being with Kjel and the Pearltones.*

It's not hard to figure out that clichés got to be clichés because of the general truths they impart; still, the one I've always hated is, "All good things must come to an end." My question is, why? Why does life have to obey the laws of gravity? Why does happiness always have to have a flip side? Why did that enchanted spring of 1938 have to dry up and fester into summer?

Of course you don't get to be my age without learning that "Why?" is the million-dollar question—the who-what-where-when-and-how questions reporters try to answer are a piece of cake compared to the why. If you're able to explain the why, you're able to explain everything, and when's the last time you were that smart?

"My boys!" said Mrs. Sykes when Dallas and Austin entered her bedroom. "My boys are home!"

Odessa, from her chair next to the bed, watched as her brothers embraced their mother and muttered, "It's about time."

"Dessa!" said Austin, turning from his mother to hug her. "How've you been, girl?"

Before she spoke, he sensed the answer; her body was thin and brittle and uninterested in returning his embrace.

"Tired is what I am. While you two gallivant all over the place, I'm the one taking care of Mama—I'm the one hauling her off to the doctors, making her take medicine she doesn't want to take, taking care of her every need, including the ones that happen in the toilet, if you catch my particular drift, and if you think that's a picnic, then I say, 'Well, you're more than welcome to pack your basket, spread out your blanket, and join us!' "

"Dessa," scolded Austin, nodding toward his mother.

"She doesn't know what we're saying!" said Odessa. "And even if she did, she's forgotten it already!"

"Mama," said Dallas, sitting on the side of her bed, his long-fingered hands forming a dome over her tiny gnarled ones. "Mama, how've you been?"

"How do you think she's—"

"Shhh!" said Dallas, glaring at his sister. "I didn't ask you, Dessa, I asked Mama."

"I'm fine, Dallas, real fine," said the shrunken woman, smiling at the attention. "Now you go tell your father to crank up the Ford 'cause I'm fixing to go for a ride in the country."

Dallas's eyes met his brother's.

"Mama, Daddy's not here," said Austin, moving his sister's knees as he sat on the other side of the bed. "Daddy died years ago, remember?"

"Austin, I'm surprised at you," said his mother with a giggle. "Dallas is the big tease, not you."

"Mama, I'm not teasing."

"Odessa, get your brother, Beaumont. If there's a party going on, Beaumont ought to be here."

"*Mama,*" said Austin, his voice tortured. "Mama, Beaumont died in 1928, remember?"

"Why are you saying these things? I don't like you saying those things!" Mrs. Sykes's eyes darted around the room and then, with increasing panic, at the faces of her children. "Mokey!" she screamed, her voice raspy. "Mokey, help! *Help!*"

"It's all right, Mama," said Odessa, pushing Austin aside so she could sit closer to her mother. "It's all right." She patted her mother's tightly braided gray hair, "Dessa's here, Mama."

The brothers watched as the alarm in their mother's eyes shifted into bewilderment.

"Mokey likes his greens fried in lard but I like the taste of butter." She smiled at the pronouncement, but her pleasure was short-lived and her creased face wrinkled even more as she bawled out, "Mokey—faster, faster! We've got to get out of here!"

"All right, you boys get out of here," said Odessa. "You're just riling her up."

Dallas placed his hand on his mother's shoulder. "Mama."

"Mokey—they're killing me!"

"Enough!" hissed Odessa. "Wait for me in the parlor!"

Kjel had been waiting outside in the truck, the plan being

that after Austin and Dallas had their joyful, private reunion with their mother, Kjel would join them for lunch.

"I loved your mother's cooking," Austin had said, "and I know you'll love mine."

Now, seeing how upset his friend was, Kjel said, "What happened in there?"

Feeling tears well up, Austin frowned, dabbing under his eyes with his curled index fingers. "Kjel, it's like . . . it's like I lost my mama. She's still here, but she's gone."

Kjel reached across the front seat and squeezed Austin's shoulder. They sat that way, with Kjel's hand on Austin's shoulder, for a long time, regarding the view of the neighborhood where the Sykes brothers had grown up, until Austin sighed and said he was getting hungry.

"We were so excited about eating our mama's home cooking—I was so excited about *you* getting to taste my mama's cooking—I'd been hoping she'd make us all a pulled-pork sandwich, and Dallas said he'd been dreaming about her buttermilk pancakes—but Odessa said the day she let Mama in the kitchen was the day the house would burn down." He shook his head and brought his index fingers to his eyes again. "Then she said she hoped we weren't expecting *her* to fix us something, ' 'cause in case you haven't noticed, I got more important things than feeding two gallivanting brothers who don't care a thing about their own sick mama.' " The fingers failed at their job and tears inched down his face. "She's been forgetful for a while, but Dessa never let on she had . . . *deteriorated* . . . to this point." He reached in his pocket for his handkerchief and blew his nose. "And so are the trials and tribulations in the House of Sykes." He took a long look at his house before turning to Kjel. "I wonder if Violet and Elwin are at that rib joint I recommended?"

"That's what they were planning."

"Are you hungry?"

"Starved."

"Then let's go get us some barbecue."

✸

DALLAS STAYED AFTER Austin had left, arguing with his sister about her neglect in letting them know about their mother.

"Let you know? How'm I supposed to get in touch with brothers who are gallivanting all over the place?"

"Stop saying 'gallivanting,' " said Dallas crossly.

Odessa's intake of breath sounded like a little snort. "At least when you were in prison I knew where to write."

"Twice," said Dallas. "In all those years you wrote me twice."

Odessa's jawbones bulged as she clenched her teeth. Dallas was shocked at how mean and hard-looking she'd become; she was only twenty-seven—two years older than him—and she looked like a forty-year-old spinster.

"I don't remember the postman getting a hernia hauling all the letters you wrote," she said. "Besides, I—and Mama—were embarrassed to write to you. Embarrassed that a Sykes wound up in the hoosegow."

Dallas held his hands together, fighting the temptation to slap his sister. "Mama wrote me once a week."

"Well, she was embarrassed, I can tell you that. Almost as embarrassed as she was hurt. She cried every time she sealed the envelope."

"And how would you know that, you bitch?"

"Because she's barely out of my sight! And don't call me your common ugly names, Dallas. I won't put up with it in my house."

"This isn't your house—it's Mama's house!"

"I've got a legal paper that says it's mine!" Odessa's eyes blazed. "I've stayed here when everybody else left, and I at least deserve this house!"

"Take the house," said Dallas, grabbing his hat off the hall chair. "Lord knows you don't have anything else."

✸

———

LORNA LANDVIK

THERE WAS A HAPPIER St. Louis homecoming for the Sykes brothers at Whistlin' Pete's.

Except for Violet and the Clamshells, who were still coming to all the Pearltones' performances, the audience was all black, and they were on their feet from the time the three Pearltones ran onto the stage in their pearl-toned jackets, shouting "Hey, Austin!" or "Dallas!" and remained on their feet until the musicians left the stage at intermission.

In the dressing room (which was big enough to dress in, but barely), Violet watched as the owner of the club (who wasn't named Pete, and hadn't whistled, at least that Violet had heard) performed an elaborate handshake with Austin and Dallas that ended with claps on the shoulder.

"Man, how your daddy woulda been thrilled! You boys are smokin'!" He pushed Kjel's shoulder, foregoing the handshake, and every time the big man moved, the air was stirred up with the smell of perspiration and rose water. "And you! Where'd a pretty white boy like you learn to keep up with Mokey Sykes's boys?" He laughed heartily, and after slapping Kjel on the back again, lit up the biggest cigar Violet had ever seen. "Well, I best get outta your way so's you boys can catch your breath. But don't take too long a break—I don't want no riot on my hands." He left the room, blue smoke trailing after his big guttural laugh.

Violet watched the second half of the show from the back of the club, her eyes more on the crowd than on the band.

Why, there's more flash and sparkle in here than in Haugen's jewelry store, she thought, surveying an audience more dressed up than any previous one. One man wore a purple suit and another a gold sharkskin that shimmered when he moved. A tall woman with a red flower in her hair was swaying to the music; a difficult feat, Violet imagined, considering the tightness of her red sequined dress. She saw a yellow dress that dipped low in the back, and a sapphire blue one with a scalloped hem. She recorded all the broad-brimmed hats and the dresses and the suits, the cut and drapery of them, the fabric and color, in her designer's mind. As she watched people, she was being watched, drawing stares for her color and for her arm, but she felt less threatened by them than an object of curiosity. One man asked her, "You with the band?" and when Violet nodded and said, "I'm their manager," he said, "Well then, let me buy you a drink."

Shaking her head, Violet flushed. "I never drink on the job."

"Wise philosophy," said the man, tapping the brim of his fedora.

After he returned to his table, Violet saw his friends turn to look at her and she flushed again; this time out of importance, knowing that they knew she was *with the band*.

The drinks flowed after the show. Dallas and Austin were surrounded by old school friends, old friends of their father's, and new friends. Kjel had a group pressed against him too, and as usual, the majority was female. Elwin was seated next to Violet at the bar, but locked in a conversation with a young man whose black hair shimmered with brilliantine; occasionally Violet heard snatches of it: "But Count Basie isn't—" and "Until radio starts playing—" and "That ballad in the second set—"

"Miss Mathers," said Garland, the owner, smiling as if he were addressing Lena Horne herself. "Isn't it about time you switched to something with a little more zippity-do-dah?"

Violet regarded her glass and shook her head. "I . . . I guess I don't drink much."

"I'd guess there's no guess about it," said Garland, his wide body sinking onto the stool next to hers. In the instant before he sat down, he flipped out the back vent of his suit coat and a waft of his sweat-tinged cologne rose up in the air.

"Jimmy, the usual," he said to the bartender, who poured his boss a glass of wine.

"I'm the only one I know who's partial to the grape," said the club owner after taking a long sip. "A two-month tour of Italy—the happiest days of my life, by the way—is what whet my whistle."

"Whet *Pete's* whistle," said Violet, but if Garland got the joke, he made no indication of it, focusing his attention instead on the wineglass in his hand. "You ever been abroad, Miss Mathers?"

Violet shook her head.

"I was with the Yancy Kent band. Trumpet player. We toured France and Italy right before the Crash, and let me tell you, we could learn a lot of things about a lot of things from them Europeans." His big booming voice had quieted to a near whisper, yet even in all the noise of the club, it was easy to hear him. "Did you know, Miss Mathers, that most married men there have a mistress?"

Violet's swallow of root beer was like a baseball going down her throat. Again she shook her head.

"And when the husbands are out with their mistresses, you know what the wives do?"

Violet's head continued its east-to-west motion as Garland scuttled closer to her.

"They step out with the American musicians is what they do. Don't care what color they are—they just care that they know what to do with their hands."

His two fingers climbed up the side seam of her dress. He dragged them under the swell of her breast, and through the droning in her ears and her silent assurances that he hadn't meant to touch her like that, Violet heard his low, throaty laugh.

"Now I know you ain't Italian, and I ain't a musician no more—I split my lip in 'thirty-four—but that shouldn't have no here nor there on what we could do together."

He leaned into her, his big fleshy hand dropping to her lap.

"So what do you say, you got some sugar for Garland?" His fingers palpitated her thigh, and his breath, a hot amalgam of cigar and wine and spearmint gum, blasted Violet's cheek. "I like my women lean like you—the sleeker the racehorse the better the ride—and I got to admit, I find that stumpy arm of yours sort of . . . sexy."

When the hand on her thigh inched upward and when she felt his lips on her neck, Violet was plunged into a paralysis of fear and disgust.

Move! she silently pleaded with him or with herself. *Move!*

"Gar, my man!"

Through the thrumming tenseness of every muscle in her body, through the droning of the bees, through the man's low mocking laughter, Violet heard her rescue.

"Garland, now you get your hands back in your lap and settle yourself—didn't Miss Violet tell you all about her beau back in Kentucky, the professional boxer with a mean left hook?" Austin's words broke through Violet's paralysis, and when she turned to look at him, she saw that the light and jovial tone of his voice was not reflected in his eyes.

"Professional boxer," said the big man, playfully slapping Violet's thigh. "I'll bet there's no beau, let alone a beau with a left hook." He finished the wine remaining in his glass. "Still, nobody got to tell Garland Weathers twice that they ain't interested." He held out his hammy hand palm side up. "They's plenty of women in here who is." With a low heh-heh-heh, he slid off the stool and sauntered off to find them.

"You want to get some air?" asked Austin, and as Violet nodded, he added, "A girl like you can't afford to get any paler—you don't have enough skin color as it is."

Outside, they passed a knot of people who offered their compliments and invitations—"That's some guitar you play, man!" "Care for a little toot of the happy weed?" "How come I ain't heard the Pearltones on the radio?"—and it took Austin several minutes before he could extract himself from their shoulder claps and handshakes.

"Thank you, ladies and gentlemen, I appreciate your kind words, but at the moment I must tend to our manager, who has suddenly been besieged by a slight case of nausea."

"Gal does look a little peaked," offered a woman whose bosom strained against its satin confines. To her friends, she added, " 'Course with them it's hard to tell."

"Let 'em pass, let 'em pass," said a tall man in a checkered suit. "Nobody needs an audience when they puke . . . right, Reynald?"

It didn't take long to walk away from the laughter and lights of the club into a darkness softened only by starlight, and the emotion Violet had been holding back burst through the dam and she cried so hard Austin was afraid for a moment she might choke.

"It's all right, Violet," he said, taking her by the arm.

"No, it isn't! His—His hands were all over me—like they had every right to be!"

"I know, I know." Shaking his head, Austin patted her hand. "I'm sorry to say there are men out there like that, Violet, that think they have a right to do whatever they want, whether they ask for it or not."

They walked along the road, in the dark, the crickets chirping their percussion.

"The worse thing," Violet said finally, "is I acted like such a dumb cluck. What was the matter with me? I'm not the type to sit there and take it. Why didn't I tell that fat old man to get his stinking hands off me?"

"The fact that he's signing our check might have something to do with it," said Austin.

Violet nodded. "Well, that makes me feel even worse. Like I was somehow bought off." She sniffed, and when Austin passed her his handkerchief, she blew into it with a gusto that made both of them laugh.

"Uh, why don't you hold on to that for a while."

"Thanks," said Violet, pocketing the soggy piece of cloth. "And thanks for rescuing me. I'm embarrassed that I even needed to be rescued, but thanks anyway."

"Thank Kjel. He's the one who alerted me to your predicament."

Violet's heart was suddenly an adagio dancer, turning a little flip. "He did?"

"As much as I'd like to claim all the chivalry; well, it was he who saw what the lecherous Mr. Garland was doing."

"But he sent you over?"

Austin sighed, hearing the hurt in her voice. "Violet, he couldn't have gone over. I mean to say, it wouldn't have gone over well, if he'd gone over." He paused, embarrassed by his clumsy words. "It's just that . . . well, Violet, in that particular situation, it wouldn't be seemly for a white man to scold a black man for his roving hands."

Violet nodded, but even in agreement, she didn't feel any better.

"It's not fair," she said quietly. "Once . . . once a hobo grabbed me while I was taking a walk and tried to . . . well, I fought back before he did anything really nasty. But at least I fought him. With Mr. Weathers, I felt like a sitting duck." She looked at Austin, an urgency in her eyes. "Isn't that funny how we can be sitting ducks just by daring to be in this world?"

Crimping his mouth up, Austin nodded.

"And now . . . now how am I supposed to do business with this . . . this—"

"Violet, don't worry. We won't let you be alone with him for a minute. Not a single minute."

"Thanks, Austin."

Austin pulled her closer to him, but just as little firebombs of panic began to explode in Violet, she realized he was only pivoting her so she wouldn't fall in the ditch as they turned around.

"We'd better get back," he said. "They'll be wondering where we are."

"Yes," said Violet, and even though Austin hadn't intended the sentence to be a balm, it was.

✹

THAT NIGHT, DALLAS got so drunk that at the following night's performance his sweat smelled of whiskey. He got drunk again that night too and tried to get in a fight with the club bouncer.

"Why you tryin' to hit me, man?" asked the former boxer, sidestepping a wild punch. "I'm a fan, man. I'm a fan."

When he staggered into his mother's house the morning after his third night of drinking, Austin called him into the dining room where he and Odessa were trying to have a civil conversation over a cup of coffee.

"Ahhhh, coffee," said Dallas, lurching toward a chair. He sat down heavily, bumping the table leg, causing the cups to shiver in their saucers.

"You're drunk," said Odessa, her lips tight.

"Not so much as I was a few hours ago," said Dallas pleasantly.

"Prison . . . drunkenness . . . what else are we going to see from you?"

Dallas raised his eyebrows, which seemed weighted. "Austin, what's the word?"

"Beg your pardon?" said Austin, hoping his civility might be an example to his siblings.

"The word for when you kill your sister . . ."

Austin couldn't help himself. "Uh, that'd be sorocide."

Dallas aimed a smile at Odessa. "Then that's what's next."

"I'm not going to stand for this," said Odessa. "I want you two out of here by this afternoon."

"Dessa," pleaded Austin.

There was a clatter of china as Dallas reached across the table, upending the sugar bowl.

"Watch my dishes!" snapped Odessa.

"These are Mama's dishes!" said Dallas, and with a sweep of his arm, he sent them to the floor.

The hard woman Odessa had become broke too, and in its cracked wide space was a bereft, wailing girl.

"Dessa," said Austin, reaching toward his sister as she got down on the floor, picking up slices of teacups and saucers.

"Daddy bought this for Mama for their fifth anniversary!" she said in between sobs. "It was to make up for the fact that they couldn't afford any when they first got married!" Her last words rose in a high keen of anguish, and the thought passed Austin's mind that there better not be any crystal close by or surely that would shatter too.

"Dallas, how could you—" he began, and for a moment he saw the sorrow and shame in his brother's face before it was arranged into a sneer.

———

✴

THEY HAD A WEEKLONG record-breaking engagement at Whistlin'
Pete's, and Garland Weathers asked Violet (Elwin always managed
to appear at her side whenever she had business to discuss with
the club owner) if they'd like an extension with a ten percent pay
hike, but when Violet proposed the deal to the band, it was declined. Dallas wasn't around to render his vote.

"I know this is your hometown and all," said Kjel, "but it
just doesn't—"

"You don't have to convince me," said Austin, raising his
hand. "The longer we stay here, the worse Dallas is going to get."

"The Clamshells'll be upset," said Elwin. "They've been eating supper every night at the club, and Birdie says she's never
eaten better food, and that includes the food in Paris, France."

"Well, then," said Kjel, "we can hardly interrupt the fine
dining of our fans."

"Guess we'll have to stay here till they get served a bad
meal," said Austin.

He hated the idea of leaving his mother, but the only help
Odessa was accepting from him was the dollar kind, reminding
him daily, hourly, that it was "more work for me having you
around than having you gone."

His mother recognized him only half the time anyway, and
often not as the grown man he was.

"Austin, baby, go down to Jepson's and buy me a bag of that
horehound candy I like so well," she might say, referring to a store
that had been closed for over a decade. "Austin, you take a bath
when your brother Beaumont's done—you've got Sunday school
tomorrow." He learned not to correct his mother; it only riled her
when he told her the president was Franklin Roosevelt and not
Teddy, or that he was in fact twenty-four years old and not seven.

And Dallas; Dallas was running with his old crowd, barely
making it to the shows, barely speaking to his brother during intermission or afterward, barely putting any effort into anything
that didn't have to do with drinking, carousing, or irresponsibility.

———

"Dallas, I need to talk to you about your behavior," said Violet, waiting for him outside the dressing room as he arrived late—again—and wearing dark glasses, a paltry disguise over the mottled puffy bruise surrounding his eye and spreading down his cheek.

Dallas's laugh was more an assault than an expression of amusement.

"We don't need to talk about nothin'," he said, trying to step around her.

Violet's heart pounded as she stood her ground. "We can't tolerate your tardiness, your bad attitude—"

This time Dallas's laugh was like spittle aimed at her.

"Yeah, well there's a lot about you, Stumpy, that I can't tolerate."

He stared at Violet, and although more than anything she wanted to run away, she stared back.

She almost buckled with relief when Elwin came around the corner.

"Hey, Dallas. You better get in there, they're looking for you."

"All right," said Dallas, his smile pure charm. "Just chattin' with my gal Vi."

After the men went into the dressing room, Violet stood leaning against the wall for a long time, until she was sure that her knees hadn't in fact turned to jelly.

✼

IT WAS ONLY THAT HE was too drunk to resist that Dallas allowed his brother and Elwin to escort him out of his lady friend's apartment.

"Dallas, I don't want you to go!" cried the woman, whose slip straps hung like epaulets from her shoulders.

"I'm only goin' for a little spin, Onie," he slurred.

"I ain't Onie," the girlfriend slurred back. "I'm Jevetta!"

"Joanie, O-vetta," said Dallas, looking at Austin and Elwin. "How'm I 'sposed to keep them straight?"

When Austin and Elwin set him down on the thin narrow mattress inside the panel truck, Dallas asked, "We're leavin'?"

"Yes, it's time to bid adieu to St. Louis," said Austin, unfolding a blanket and draping it over his brother.

"But, Austin," said Dallas, and his voice lost all belligerence, all bravado. "I didn't say good-bye to Mama." A moment later it was back. "Aw, who the fuck cares."

Chapter Sixteen

REMEMBER ALL THOSE BIRTHDAYS OF MINE THAT PASSED WITH NO *fanfare? For years I had antibirthdays: no presents, no cards, no chorused version of "Happy Birthday," no cake with candles all lit and promising a granted wish to that special person who could blow out all flickering spears of flame. Well, when I turned nineteen years old, I got the kind of party that does what a birthday party should do: let the honoree know that her birth and subsequent presence here on earth is something to celebrate. Talk about a radical concept.*

But since then, since that long-ago party on a July day swarming with flies and so much more, I have made it a point to greet each new year of mine—and of those I love—with fanfare up the ying-yang.

I never ever have made that trite and vain mistake of being ashamed of a birthday, ergo my age; sure, I'd like the bone mass and flexibility of my youth, but would I want to slice a decade or two off my age? Not on your life—I'm an old bag and I look it; that's who I am.

Take a look at this newspaper (don't you find it neighborly when people leave their magazines and papers behind?)—see this actress here? How's she supposed to act with that face? How many times do you suppose she's been lifted, ironed, and sandblasted? Did her plastic surgeon warn her that along with some initial soreness and swelling, her face most certainly would undergo a permanent erasure of personality? Did he tell her that every day would be Halloween for her, because she'd never be able to take off that eerie placid mask?

I tell you, I fear the democratization of plastic surgery, when it's so cheap that everyone—the butcher, the baker, and the candlestick maker— goes under the knife and winds up looking like these tightly pulled, slightly surprised–looking society and celebrity aliens from Planet Botox.

Old age is no picnic—wait a second; it is, only it has more ants. Although a case could be made that my youth was awfully bug-ridden as well. When I was young, I could have bottled up my self-loathing and filled a mile of train cars with it. Now that I'm old, I can't think of anyone I'd rather be than me. And even though the words "pretty" and "Violet Mathers" would never be described as synonyms, I know that I'm a knockout. That's what we need now: surgeons who can slice away the self-consciousness, the fear, the loneliness, and inject a little hope instead. A little love. Or a doctor who implants only high spirits, penchants for practical jokes, or the ability to cha-cha even to a dirge beat.

Anyway . . . birthdays. When's yours? Will you be celebrating like it's a national holiday? And if not, why not?

The Pearltones were performing an afternoon concert in a band-shell in Cape Girardeau when Kjel called Violet to the stage and led the entire audience in singing "Happy Birthday" to her. In her rare homecoming queen/debutante/bride happiness, as she beamed, staring at the painted wooden floor as the wall of song surrounded her, she felt a pinch of sadness in that her rag-doll Jelly wasn't with her. Through all of her lonely and uncelebrated birthdays, Jelly had been her constant companion, and she thought of her old friend lying in the dark at the bottom of her carpetbag, limp and friendless. Her parents flickered across her mind too (it was funny that she could stand there with her near-to-bursting grin while these shadows flickered across her mind), and she wondered, Does my daddy remember it's my birthday? Does my mama ever wonder who I turned out to be?

When the song ended, the audience applauded, stomping

their feet and whistling, and Violet jerked in an awkward simulation of a bow and had just decided to exit stage left when Kjel grabbed her by her shoulders.

"And now how 'bout we hear a little song from the birthday girl?"

The crowd cheered, but Violet understood they would have cheered for anything Kjel said.

"Kjel, I—"

"Come on, Violet, it's your birthday. You gotta sing." He nudged her toward the microphone and mouthed words at Austin and Dallas before counting, "One, two, one two three four."

The band launched into the introduction of "All Night Cattin'," which was always a crowd favorite.

Until I start singing it, Violet thought, but seeing no means of escape, she stood squarely in front of the microphone, desperately trying to remember the first word. She heard the chord change— her cue—and the word magically jumped out of her mouth, and the next one and the next, and she realized she was singing. Out of tune, she noticed, bringing her voice up a quarter notch, and by the time she got to the refrain, she couldn't help herself, she added a little sway to her hips as she wagged her finger at the crowd.

"Now if you wanted comp'ny, why'd you learn to knit?
If you want me home to untangle yarn, you're gonna have to wait a bit,
Friday night ain't for makin' sweaters, baby, ain't for makin' mittens,
Friday night is for cats like me to go and find some kittens."

Kjel joined her in the second verse, and the audience, who'd been politely listening to the deep-voiced one-armed girl, clapped and hooted their approval.

When they finished the song, they held hands as they took a bow, and then Kjel bundled her up in his arms and gave her a big kiss and she left the stage knowing her feet were touching the ground even though she couldn't feel it, thinking that for a birthday celebration, a standing ovation, and a kiss on the lips sure beat a kick in the pants.

✦

THE FIRE GAVE OFF a pungent pine smell from the bough Kjel placed in it.

"Scented flames," he said in a French accent. "For ze birthday girl, we spare no expense."

"Pine expensive these days?" said Violet.

"There's a Depression going on, in case you hadn't noticed. Everything's expensive!" Kjel sat next to her on the ground, cracked his knuckles, and then patted his shirt pocket for a cigarette.

From the other side of the campfire and without being asked, Elwin threw him one.

"Violet, whatever we're paying Elwin," Kjel said, lighting the cigarette, "give him a raise."

"Elwin, as of now you're making a nickel a day," said Violet.

"Oh, I couldn't," said the big man. "Waiting on all of you hand and foot is enough payment."

Violet laughed. It was her birthday and everything tickled her, including Elwin's making a rare joke.

After they had enjoyed a bakery birthday cake ("They wrote up the 'Happy Birthday, Violet' special," Elwin pointed out) and coffee, Kjel presented her with a present.

"Ta-da," he said, taking her hand and placing a small box in her palm.

"Oh, is it gift time already?" asked Austin, and getting up from his canvas camp chair, he said, "Now don't open anything, Violet, until I get back."

A gust of wind blew the smoke from the campfire in her direction, giving her a good excuse for the tears in her eyes. She studied the present in her hand; it was wrapped in the funny papers and encircled with twine.

"I should have had it gift-wrapped," said Kjel.

Violet shook her head, inspecting the predominant cartoon panel. "No," she said softly. "No, it's beautiful. I . . . I love the Katzenjammer Kids."

Another rush of wind blew through the campsite, this one sending sparks out along with the smoke.

"Jeez," said Kjel. "Look at that."

A great bank of clouds was rolling in from the west, darkening what moments ago had been a clear blue sky.

They had driven for several hours after their bandshell concert, pulling off the road at supper time to build a fire and eat. The day had steamed in a humid heat, but it didn't matter to Violet that the talcum powder under her arms had long ago failed its job; it didn't matter that red bumps rose on her right arm from the mosquitoes she couldn't swat away quickly enough with her stump; it didn't matter that they might get a little rain: it was still a perfect birthday.

"You'd better open these quick," said Austin as he set down a large package—this one wrapped with a real ribbon—next to her. "We may have to take cover any minute."

"That's from me and Austin," said Elwin, nodding at the package.

"And Dallas," said Austin quickly. He looked around the campsite. "Which begs the question: where is he?"

Kjel and Violet offered shrugs as Elwin turned to look in all directions. Lately, he saw Dallas more than anyone because, for some reason, he didn't irritate Dallas the way everyone else did, and in fact the musician gave Elwin the occasional lesson on the stand-up bass. ("Grandma," Elwin wrote home, "those years on the violin are finally paying off.")

It wasn't uncommon for Dallas to eat and run—he rarely socialized with them anymore, whether they were at a campsite or in motels—but still, it was a birthday party, and Austin thought his brother might have the good manners to stay around for that.

"Come on, Violet," said Kjel. "Open them up."

If a camera had been documenting Violet opening her birthday presents, the photographs would have shown a dark-haired young woman wearing a red sailor blouse (she had liked the one Isalee wore so much, she made one of her own, and Elwin, who still confessed his dream of meeting up with the adagio dancer again, never forgot to compliment her on it), a lanky young woman holding down the packages with her stump while her right hand carefully pushed aside bows and undid paper seams and corners, a young woman whose expressions ran the short gamut between happiness and joy.

"Oh, Austin, oh, Elwin—thank you!" said Violet, unwrapping a box of pastels lying on top of a leather-bound book.

"It's a sketchbook," explained Elwin. "And see what it says on the front?"

Violet gasped as she pushed aside the pastels to read the hand-tooled words: "Fashions by Violetta."

"Compliments of a leather worker in Bloomington," said Austin. "Do you like it?"

It didn't matter that Violet was too choked up to speak; the wind would have whistled away her response anyway. Instead she nodded furiously.

"Okay, time to open mine," said Kjel. "And hurry up."

Kjel's present was a chain bracelet, with two charms already attached.

"See," he said, helping her fasten it around her wrist. "That's a pearl, of course—although not a real one—and that's a musical note. The Pearltones, get it? So you'll always remember us."

"I wouldn't need a bracelet to remember you," she said, but the wind again snatched her words, and then it snatched the gift wrapping, the ribbon, and Elwin's coffee cup, flinging them all into the darkening evening.

"Ow!" said Violet as a smattering of sparks hit her legs.

"Okay," said Kjel, throwing a pot of water on the fire that was leaning eastward. "Everybody grab something and let's get in the truck!"

Violet felt electricity in the air and her own surge of excitement—ever since the thunderstorm that had derailed her bus in North Dakota, she had been a fan of intemperate weather.

"Come on, *move!*"

Violet laughed and would have scolded Kjel for his teasing but suddenly the wind grabbed hold of her skirt, tossing it up past her waist.

"Oh my," she said, blushing as she wrestled it down, but no one was paying attention to the peep show the wind had offered.

Austin was watching the saplings planted alongside the road. Pelted by the wind, they reminded him of the front-row sopranos in the choir of his boyhood church and the way they would sway and toss their heads when moved by the spirit. Elwin was looking at the sky and marveling how something usually so blue could be so green, and Kjel was gathering up the dishes, his hair and shirttail flapping.

Violet fought the wind for a camp chair, finally winning with Austin's help.

"That's everything!" said Kjel, and his voice sounded far away. "Let's all get in Elwin's truck!"

Against a ferocious wind, they staggered toward the truck as if they'd been drinking moonshine all afternoon. To Violet, the air smelled like the thread factory when one of the machines had been running too long and they had to unplug it before the motor burned out.

"Oh my stars," said Kjel, and even though he was shouting, Violet barely heard his voice. "Look!" He pointed to a smeary black cone zigzagging in from the northwest.

"Twister!" said Elwin, in a high note one rarely heard coming out of a big man. He struggled against the wind to open the panel door, and he and the others didn't so much step inside as were pushed.

They all crouched by the window in the back as hail began to hammer the roof of the truck.

"Anyone see Dallas?" Austin asked, and like Elwin's, his voice strained toward an unused octave.

They saw plenty and it was all swirling in the air—clouds of dirt, hail, small leafy branches, a hubcap.

"I'm sure he's hunkered down somewhere," said Violet, hoping that Dallas at least had the sense to do that. She wasn't scared for him as much as she was angry at him. Why did he always have to separate himself from them? Why couldn't he have tolerated their company for just one lousy birthday supper?

"Shoot, we forgot the coffeepot," said Kjel, watching it bang to the ground before the wind picked it up again.

"Good God," Elwin whispered. "It's coming closer."

The whirling triangle was outlined in a blurry smudge of dirt; to Violet it looked like an eggbeater run amok, churning up whatever got in its way and throwing it up into its vortex. They heard a train, a frightening sound considering they were nowhere near train tracks.

"What'll we do, Kjel?" asked Elwin.

"Get down. Get down and cover your heads."

As they positioned themselves on the floor of the panel truck, the train seemed to switch to another track and they were plunged into a silence as deep and still as that found on the bottom of a lake.

"Hold on," said Kjel, and he put one arm around Violet and one around Austin, and suddenly the train was back, was screeching on rusty tracks, and part of it clipped the truck, making it bounce—hard—before spinning it around.

The bees in Violet's ears were an angry hive, trying to compete with the sound of the train, and the thumping of the truck, and the great cracking noise of a tree coming down.

"Lord have mercy," said Austin. "Lord, Lord, *Lord* have mercy."

The truck spun the other way, and then, with a teeth-rattling bang, one end was lifted up and dropped to the ground. The train continued its screaming passage, but the panel truck was no longer on the tracks in front of it.

They lay there holding one another, tense and afraid, like kindergartners whose sinister teacher is deciding whether to let them up from an overlong nap time.

The train sped farther and farther away from them, and when it seemed its powerful locomotive was not going to turn back and roll over them, Kjel said, "Okay, Elwin, you can let go now."

Sitting up amid a pile of camp chairs, tin dishes, fishing rods, and an upended box of provisions, they all laughed, including Elwin, who had found one of Kjel's hands when the twister had overtaken them and hadn't let go.

"Jeez," said Kjel, wincing as he bent and unbent his fingers, "You've got quite a grip there, Elwin."

"Sorry," said Elwin, and to the others, giddy with relief, this one word was one of the funniest they ever heard. Elwin joined in, and all of them would have been happy to spend the rest of the evening laughing, but Austin reminded them of the business at hand.

"We've got to find Dallas," he said soberly.

What ninth-grade girls were capable of on baking days often inspired Violet's home-ec teacher to claim her classroom looked "like it's been hit by a cyclone," but Violet had never seen what the world looks like when indeed it was hit by a cyclone. Trees were in various stages of disrepair; far across the road a basswood had been pulled up by the roots, and the elm tree whose shade they had sought during supper was broken in half, its great green branches decapitated from its jagged trunk.

"We're lucky it fell the way it did," said Kjel.

"Dallas?" shouted Austin, stepping around a rock that had traveled farther in the last five minutes than it had in the last five centuries.

"Dallas!" shouted Kjel, and Violet and Elwin joined the posse, calling Dallas's name as they spread out in different directions.

The row of roadside saplings stood trembling in the last vestiges of wind.

They're all right! marveled Austin. It heartened him; if those lithe and emotional sopranos could remain standing, surely Dallas had withstood the storm too.

Guilt fixed itself across his shoulders like a yoke; as much as he tried to be a good brother, he knew he didn't try hard enough. It was just that Dallas was so bull-headed, so truculent, so unwilling to see that the path on which he was headed led to nowhere any sane person wanted to go!

"You worry about yourself, Austin, and I'll worry about my own self," Dallas had said a few days ago, interrupting one of Austin's concerned lectures.

"But you're drinking way too much and it won't be long be-fore—"

"I can handle myself, Austin."

"That might be your most sincere thought, but the reality is—"

Dallas reached over and clamped his brother's lips shut with his fingers.

"I mean it," he said, with a small, mirthless smile, "if you don't shut your mouth when I ask you to, I'll shut it for you."

Oh, Dallas, thought Austin, *let me find you safe and sound and you can shut my mouth all you like.*

Elwin walked along the road; they had passed a tavern a few miles back and it was a distinct possibility that Dallas had decided to spend the early evening hours lubricating himself with liquor. This worried Elwin almost as much as the thought of Dallas get-ting caught outside in the storm; a colored man walking into a bar and ordering up a beer held the possibility of as much chaos as any passing twister.

"Dallas!" he called. "Dalll–ussss!"

After the group had eaten the fried-egg sandwiches that comprised Violet's birthday supper, Dallas had asked him if he wanted to take a walk, but Elwin, thinking it rude to leave the celebration (and he did want a piece of the cake—he *loved* bak-ery cake), had declined. And so he, like Austin, was burdened with guilt, knowing he should have gone with Dallas, if not to dissuade him from getting in a bar fight, then to drag him back to camp at the first sign of the weather turning.

"Sorry your birthday had to end like this," said Kjel as he and Violet followed a path into the woods.

Violet shrugged. "It's not over yet. Besides, it's the best birthday I ever had."

Kjel smiled at her. The path was almost too narrow for them to walk abreast, but they did, and the occasional hip bumps and body contact were just fine with Violet.

"I can't think of my best birthday," he said. "They've all been swell."

By its self-satisfaction, this comment would have bothered Violet had anyone else said it, but Kjel's sincerity was so genuine that she had to smile and think, *Of course they've all been swell!*

"I remember when I was six I got a kaleidoscope," he said. "Man, I thought that was the be-all, end-all; turning the world into all those cut-up prisms of color." He whistled. "Then the next year I got Mo. She was born the night before, and my mother put a bow on her head and led me to the barn blindfolded. The whole family was in the stable and they all shouted, 'Happy Birthday!' and Ma took off the blindfold and there she was, my own little pony, standing on her little spindly legs. Then her mother—a big black mare named Netty—turned to give me a dirty look and started eating the ribbon off Mo's head."

Imagine that, thought Violet, *a pony for your birthday.*

"But the best present," said Kjel as Violet thought, *There's more?,* "was when Pa cut a hole in the roof for me."

"What?"

"We used to camp as a family—sometimes all that meant was setting up the tent by the barn, but other times we'd drive to the Badlands or into Minnesota. One night we went to sleep and the sky was overcast. I woke up before dawn and the clouds had cleared and there was nothing but a sky full of stars. Pa says he heard me say, 'Oh my stars,' like I was in love or something."

"And you still say it," said Violet. "It's like your morning prayer."

Kjel's voice was soft. "That's just what my pa said. He said it's one of the best prayers he ever heard." He rubbed his arms. "Man, it feels like the temperature dropped about ten degrees." Feeling the chill in the air, Violet nodded.

———

"So on my ninth birthday I wake up to this noise, and there's my pa and Lem Iglehard, the best carpenter in Pearl, up there on the roof, cutting a hole in it! A regular skylight."

Kjel shook his head, smiling at Violet, who shook her head back, unable to imagine a father loving her so much he'd cut a hole in the roof for her. Then cupping his mouth, he cried, "Dallas! Dallas, come out, come out, wherever you are!"

The twister and the big dark clouds that had surrounded it like bodyguards had vanished in the east, leaving the air rain-swept and cleaned. The sun was beginning to set and it was a lovely summer evening, if one ignored the destruction the storm had wrought. The mosquitoes had regrouped, and as Violet slapped her stump, she wondered why the cyclone couldn't have wrapped them up and spit them out miles away.

"Dallas?" she called, and where the others sounded as if they were calling a big dog—a German shepherd or a Doberman—Violet's sounded as if she were summoning a Chihuahua. Her hunch, like Elwin's, was that Dallas was holed up in the bar they had passed, and it perturbed her that she was wasting valuable time—valuable *birthday* time—stepping over tree limbs to find him. Kjel too often disappeared from a campsite, but only in the mornings or late evenings, when his company wouldn't be missed, and Violet understood that his adventures were always about finding something, whereas Dallas's were most certainly about losing himself.

Kjel called out his name again and was about to tell Violet about a present he'd received from his best friend Homer Kissler on the occasion of his fifteenth birthday when a faint sound, like a sheep bleating came from within the forest.

"Did you hear that?" Kjel whispered, holding his arm in front of Violet to bar any further movement.

Violet nodded. "Dallas?" she called again, and the sheep's bleat got louder and shaped itself into syllables.

"Here! Over here!"

Kjel and Violet ran toward the direction of his response, pushing aside the drapery of leaves from a thick grouping of trees.

When Violet spotted him, it looked as if he were casually re-clining, leaning back on crooked elbows. But there was nothing casual about the look on his face; his lips were stretched back, showing all of his clenched teeth back to his molars, and his skin was streaky with sweat.

He was pinned under the trunk of a felled jack pine.

"Austin!" he cried. "Where's Austin?"

"He's out looking for you," said Kjel, bending down next to him. "What—"

"My foot," said Dallas. "I can't get my foot out from under this goddamned tree."

Kjel encircled his arms around the green boughs and lifted. Nothing moved. He tried again, grunting with effort.

"Violet, you're going to have to help," he said. "We only need to lift it up a little bit."

Violet knew her one-armed effort wasn't going to be worth much, but if Kjel asked for her help, her help is what she was going to give.

The smell of pine was strong as she pushed her hand through the branches until she felt the sticky, tarry trunk.

"All right, now. On the count of three," said Kjel, position-ing himself. "One, two, three!"

Despite their strain, the tree didn't move.

"God, oh God," muttered Dallas.

Kjel wiped his hands on his knees and counted off again. Still the tree didn't budge. Finally, on the third try, the grimace on their faces matching Dallas's, they pulled and pulled and the tree trunk rose a few inches, enough for Dallas to slide his foot back.

"It's free!" he yelled, and feeling as if her shoulder had been pulled out its socket, Violet let go of the tree trunk.

"Oh, my," she said, feeling dizzy.

"You're Queen of the Amazons," said Kjel, draping an arm around her and squeezing. "I couldn't have done it without you." He turned to Dallas, who was trying to stand up, but failing.

"I can't put any weight on my ankle," he said. "It must be broken."

"Well," said Kjel, "a tree *did* fall on it, after all." He looked at Violet. "Think you can help me lift him up?"

"Well, I am the Amazon queen, aren't I?"

Hunching down, she and Kjel flanked Dallas, who put his arms around their shoulders. They stood up together, and when Dallas was upright on one leg, Kjel said, "Violet, help him stand there for a second." Moving so he was facing Dallas, he bent at the knees and said, "Okay, Dallas, hop on."

"I can walk," said Dallas, his voice steely.

"I hate to tell you, pal, but you can't. Now come on, the meter's running."

Dallas leaned forward, and with a grunt, Kjel hefted him up and over his shoulder like a sack of potatoes. He staggered before getting his balance, but once he did, he walked steadily and with sure-footedness back through the woods toward their camp. Violet followed behind them and although she couldn't see Dallas's face, she could see the anger in his clenched and unclenching fists.

The tavern keeper directed Kjel, Austin, and Dallas to a doctor who, after demanding cash up front, set Dallas's ankle in a cast.

"Now there's this little heel here so he can walk on it," he said, directing his comments to Kjel, as if he was the patient's parent. "But I'd advise him not to use it for a while. Where's he going to be in six weeks?"

"I don't know," said Dallas, leaning forward in an attempt to make eye contact with the doctor, "wherever the wind blows."

"Wherever the wind blows," muttered the doctor, and then louder, to Kjel, he said, "Looks to me as if your friend should stay away from where the wind blows, considering what it did to him today." The doctor took his pipe off its holder on his desk and lit it. "Well," he said gruffly as the fragrant tobacco filled the room. "Tell your friend wherever that *wind* takes him, in six weeks he should find a doctor to take the cast off."

It was almost eleven o'clock when the men got back from the doctor's and Kjel and Austin joined Violet and Elwin by the fire they had built.

"How's Dallas?" asked Elwin. "Was his ankle broken?"

Austin nodded. "He's sleeping in the truck now. Kjel was able to talk the doctor into giving him a little bit of codeine to ease his pain." The fire crackled, and wound-up from all the events of the day, Austin started.

"Say," said Kjel, "I don't suppose there's any of that birthday cake left?"

"It probably got blown clear into another county," said Elwin sadly. "Too bad—that was a *good* cake."

"Aw, I'm too bushed to eat anyway," said Kjel, and seeing the pile of bedrolls Elwin had brought from the truck, he laid his out. Everyone followed suit, and too tired to look for privacy, and not necessarily wanting it, Violet unrolled hers close to the men's.

They all lay in silence, listening to the night sounds and the cracks and pops of the fire. Violet was almost asleep when she heard Kjel's voice.

"Hey, Austin, it's Violet's birthday and you didn't even tell us what the word of the day was!"

There was a long pause as Austin mulled over the question. The fire made a sound like a rattlesnake's warning, and Violet shifted, feeling a stone under her hip.

"I would have to say," said Austin, his voice low, "on the occasion of Violet's birthday and all that transpired on it, the word of the day would have to be . . . *quixotic.*"

Chapter Seventeen

I KNOW THE MALE EGO IS A FRAGILE THING; PUT DALLAS'S UP *against a hummingbird's egg, and do I need to tell you which one would shatter first?*

Dallas hadn't exactly liked Kjel before, but he really started hating him the night Kjel rescued him. It wasn't hard for me to understand this; after all, I had kept a furnace of hate and jealousy burning in my belly for years.

Just look at the two men: both were pied pipers of sex appeal, although the line of women following Kjel was always longer than Dallas's; both had big musical talents, but Kjel was the front man and it was his voice more than the fanciest of fret work that wrapped people in the gift package that was the Pearltones' music. And then, of course, Kjel was white, and every day in some way, Dallas was supposed to apologize that he was not.

The bad mood that had been simmering in Dallas since St. Louis began to boil. It's hard to explain, but sometimes onstage he played as if he was taunting Kjel; right before a solo refrain, he might play discordant notes that threw Kjel off, or he'd take a line Kjel had just sung and imitate it on his guitar, in a high, mocking whine. Most of the audience was too entranced by Kjel to notice this subtle musical mutiny, but the most devoted fans noticed.

"What's going on?" asked Clark, one of the Clamshells.

I made up an excuse, blaming his broken ankle.

Dallas no longer joined Kjel and Austin in their songwriting sessions, and he barely spoke to any of us, with the exception of Elwin. This arrangement suited me just fine; the less I had to speak to Dallas, the better.

In Caruthersville, after their first show in Tennessee, he got in a fight with the boyfriend of a girl he wanted to take back to his room, knocking the guy out cold with one of his crutches. The only reason he wasn't hauled off to jail is because the sheriff had seen the show the night before.

Added to the tension that Dallas's bad behavior brought on was the direction we were traveling. One gig led to another thirty miles south, which led to another ten miles east and ten miles south, until suddenly we were in Memphis.

To be asked by Selma French to play on her weekly radio program, *Chez Frenchie's,* was not just a feather in a musician's cap—it was a plume, a peacock's plume. The radio hostess (who became French, in all respects, when she married her late husband, Monte) was regarded by the many musicians who filled the clubs and theaters of Memphis as *the* tastemaker of the entire South—if she liked your music, you were *good.*

Violet saw her sitting in the roadhouse watching the band—a small woman smoking a cigarette out of a foot-long holder—and knew by the way people huddled around her that she was someone important.

She came backstage after the show, her eyes smudged with black kohl, her lips smeared with red lipstick, her cheeks blotchy with rouge. She looked like an old clown who'd gotten caught in a rain shower, but apparently she saw something different when she looked in the mirror.

"Hello, darling, Selma French," she said, extending a small hand studded with bloodred nails. "I enjoyed your set immensely. *Très, très, très beaucoup.*"

"Mrs. French has a radio program," said the club owner, hopping around like his shoes were on fire. "For 'connoisseurs of good music'—that's her slogan, and everybody who's *anybody* listens to it."

"What if you're not anybody?" said Kjel. "Can you still pick up your program?"

"You bet you can," said the woman, letting go of Austin's hand to shake Kjel's. She squinted, and a web of wrinkles flecked with mascara appeared. "But you're not just anybody. *Mon dieu!* I must say I'm very *very* impressed with your music."

"Thank you, ma'am," said Kjel, bowing. "I and my colleagues thank you."

"Why don't we let your colleagues thank me themselves," said the woman, extending her hand to Dallas. "And please, no 'ma'am.' Call me Frenchie."

Holding Dallas's hand in both of hers, the woman stared at him until even Dallas was uncomfortable.

"Uh, excuse me, *Frenchie,*" he said, extracting his hand, "I uh . . . got some friends out front I need to see."

"I think it's time you cultivate some friends like me," she said, and her smile was as full of invitation as a young woman's.

"Uh, thanks," said Dallas, and Violet could hardly contain herself; here was Mr. Big Shot Tough Guy, the man who answered to no one (or if he did, with plenty of profanities), squirming with nervousness. "Nice to meet you," he said before bolting out of the room.

"Is it something I said?" said Frenchie, holding her hands up like a mannequin modeling rings. Then she laughed, letting everyone know they didn't have to make any excuses.

She turned to Violet and took a thin silver card case out of her clutch bag. "Mel tells me you're their manager—lucky girl." She handed Violet a card. "I'd like to have them on my show—this Saturday night at seven?"

"Well," said Violet looking at the club owner, "we have a show on Sat—"

"My house band can take the first show," said Mel, still hopping. "You come on by when you're done. Believe me, your audience won't be going *anywhere*."

✳

"YOU KNOW WHAT I love best about your music?" said Frenchie after the Pearltones had played a set in her studio. She laughed, and it was a warm and lovely laugh and Violet could imagine all the men within listening range sitting close to their radios, wishing they'd been the one to get that sound out of her. "*Excusez-moi*—I just realized I can't think of one thing. It's many things— it's your energy, your sense of rhythm, your newness, and your musicality, *certainement*. Truthfully, I cannot think of any category you fit into, and yet you certainly fit in! For you listeners out there, two of the Pearltones are blood brothers, and one can hear that absolute assurance and that sense of fun between people who've played together all their lives—but we hear it from you too Kjel—'Shell'—that's what they name their kids up North— and you're hardly related to the Sykes brothers!"

"Well, there are musical ties as strong as blood ties," said Kjel.

Austin chuckled. "Yes, if Kjel needed a transfusion, I'd offer him an inverted G chord and a diminished seventh—"

"And I'd probably survive!"

The guests at *Chez Frenchie's* stayed on for the full three hours, and when she was signing off, she said, "Ladies and gentlemen, you know I've been bringing you the best, most exciting music for the past thirteen years, and tonight it was my distinct pleasure to bring you the best of the best, and as for excitement— *mon dieu!*—my heart's just now finding a regular rhythm. *Merci beaucoup* to the Pearltones for swinging this studio upside down, and *merci beaucoup* to you, my listeners, for coming along on this *voyage fantastique*. Until next time, *je suis votre Frenchie. Au revoir, mes amis.*"

After the radio show, the Pearltones gave a show the standing-room-only audience would talk about for the rest of their lives.

"I'm telling you, son, this Frank Sinatra's got nothin' on this fella I saw back in 'thirty-eight. Name was Shell or Chell, something like that."

"Come here, dear, and give your grandma a kiss. Let me see that hairdo of yours up close—you've got it all combed up like that Elvis fella, don't you? *Elvis.* Did I ever tell you about this outfit I saw once called the Pearltones? Their lead singer, why, he could sing and dance circles around your Elvis."

"I try to stay open-minded when it comes to the kids' music. Those Beatles aren't bad—although I'd march each and every one of 'em into the barber's if I could—but they're nothing, *nothing* compared to this band I heard down in Memphis. The Pearlettes or something like that . . . man, they were good."

The fight that broke out afterward did minimal damage to both the club and its participants, the breakage count being three chairs, four teeth, and one nose. It was started by a group of men Violet recognized immediately as trouble. As the band sang, they stood off to the side, nudging one another and pointing to Dallas or Austin, spitting brown streams of tobacco onto the club floor.

Elwin had started clearing off the stage, and as the audience screamed and begged for just one more song, one of the men hurled a bottle. It broke when it made contact with Elwin's head, and the big man tipped forward as if tripped. He righted himself before he fell, and touching the top of his balding head, felt blood.

The hushed crowd watched as Kjel and Austin ran onto the stage.

Facing the audience, Kjel asked, "Who did this?"

Dozens of fingers pointed in the direction of the perpetrator, and the hush was broken by just as many people shouting "He did!"

Austin tried to get Elwin to sit down so he could administer to his cut, but Elwin brushed him aside. He had not been in all those beer-hall brawls with Tink to take lightly something like a thrown bottle. He joined Kjel at the lip of the stage to get a better look at the man who'd given him a headache he could feel into his jaw.

It was easy to identify the culprits when they rushed onto the stage. Audience reactions to this ranged from screaming, fleeing, cheering on, and joining in.

Dallas hobbled out on his crutches and began to use one as a weapon, swinging it side to side like a lariat.

Five minutes later, owing to the fact their station was only a mile and a half down the road, the police were in the club, blowing their whistles and hefting their billy clubs.

A reporter for the *Memphis Journal* happened to be at the show, and his story about "a band of brothers, in all senses of the word, and those who would rather have the black man back on the plantation than on a stage," caused an onslaught of letters to the editor.

To the Editor:

I say if you're going to bring in a mixed band playing wild music, then you have to let the chips fall where they may. It's time people remember their places and that black and white mix about as good as oil and vinegar. Any trouble that band has it's bringing on its ownself.

Clinton Peterborough
Smyrna

To the Editor:

I would like to personally apologize to the Pearltones for the brawl that occurred at their recent show—a show I am proud to say I was in attendance. These are musicians, people! Two black men and one white man playing music together—where's the crime? I suggest people not only open their ears to the wonderful music this group plays, but open their hearts too, because it's a new world, people!

Evanda Wheaton
Memphis

To the Editor:

A recent letter writer asks us to open our hearts to a new world; let me just say to this misguided person that it is not a new world I support! We can treat our inferiors humanely but we need not treat them equally! If God thought this way He would have made us the same color in the first place! Nothing good can come from fraternization between the races, nothing but mulattoes and other sins against nature. If I was twenty years younger, I would have been there throwing a few punches myself!

Otis R. Deets
Memphis

To the Editor:

I recently heard a band called the Western Wind at the same establishment that hosted the recent free-for-all. The Western Wind was an all-white band and the lead singer had a voice like a hurt coyote. I'm not kidding—I think his yodels did some damage to my eardrums. Their guitarist didn't believe in tuning his instrument, which might have made his three chords a mite more tolerable to listen to, and the drummer had mastered a 4/4 beat and he wasn't going to stray from it. No fight broke out that night, although it should have. For my money, a band can be black, white, pink, or purple, as long as they can play music. I was lucky enough to see the Pearltones, and believe me, they can.

J. R. Melvany
Murfreesboro

"I can't believe they're still writing about this," said Frenchie, folding the newspaper she had been reading and setting it down on her vanity. "*Sacré bleu,* what you'd pay to get this kind of publicity!"

———

"*Sacré bleu* to you too," said Dallas, reclining on Frenchie's satin bedspread, finishing the cup of strong coffee his hostess served every morning. "Now whyn't you come on over here and translate that for me?"

"*Avec plaisir,*" said Frenchie, twirling the end of her robe tie as she walked toward him.

Since Frenchie's interview with the band, Dallas Sykes had been staying with the venerable radio hostess, a situation that baffled yet relieved the other band members.

"She's got to be at least twenty years older than Dallas!" Austin said as he and the others enjoyed a fried-chicken dinner prepared by Mel Baggs's wife and brought to the club several hours before the show.

Violet wiped the grease off her mouth with a red checkered napkin.

"Twenty!" she said. "I'd say thirty, at least. Maybe thirty-five."

"Hey, she's keeping him off the streets," said Kjel. He surveyed the bounty of food spread out on the rickety card table before dragging a cob of corn across a block of butter. "Man, this reminds me of home."

Austin had taken Dallas aside and asked, "Say, what's the story with you and this Francophile?"

Austin saw his brother struggle not to smile.

"She appreciates me," he said, "and I'm enjoying the appreciation."

"But she's so—"

Dallas held up his hand. "It ain't for you to say she's *too* anything. Why don't you worry about your own sorry love life, instead of always stickin' your nose in mine?"

The truth was, Dallas couldn't explain *what* he was doing going to bed with Selma French either. It didn't exactly embarrass him—he was too confident in his ability to attract women to worry that he was slipping—but it wasn't something he wanted to advertise either. Selma French was old, and her saggy body was a sexual geography unfamiliar to Dallas, but he found himself feeling something alien, something he hadn't felt with all his other women: tenderness. His libido, usually at high tide, was now calm and still; he didn't want to pound himself into this woman as much as he wanted to touch her shoulder, to push back a strand of her dyed black hair, to kiss the rim of her ear and then whisper into it, "You are belle."

Maybe there's something in Memphis water, he thought one morning, standing at her basin, lathering his face with her fancy soap shaped like a seashell. *Maybe my ankle got infected and the poison's gone up to my mind. Maybe . . .* But his excuses faltered under the weight of his feelings.

She had come to the show after interviewing him, the night the fight broke out, and after the police broke it up she followed Elwin, who was helping Dallas out the back entrance.

She asked if they minded giving her a ride home and when they pulled up in front of her house—a brick bungalow on the west side of town—she asked Elwin and Dallas if they'd like to come in for a drink.

Wide-eyed as a country boy getting asked into a bordello, Elwin declined, stammering about errands he had to run the following day, but Dallas, after a moment's hesitation, said, "A drink sounds just fine."

Inside Frenchie's red parlor room, he put his broken ankle up on a tufted velvet ottoman and watched as she made martinis in real martini glasses. When she asked, "Olive or onion?" Dallas smiled, thinking, *Sure beats drinking beer out of a jelly jar.*

"I want to tell you, Dallas," she said, curling her feet under her on the burgundy velvet couch, "I'm honored to be in your presence. I've heard more guitarists, more harmonica players, more stand-up bassists, than I can count, and you, sir, are in a rarefied stratum of genius."

Dallas had never heard the word "stratum," but he sure recognized the word "genius," and as he took a big swig of the martini, he knew the buzz of pleasure he felt was due more to the compliment than the liquor.

"Really, Dallas, I watched your fingers"—to his surprise, she

took one of his hands and began looking at it the way an archae-
ologist looks at a shard of bone—"and it was as if I was watching
Rapunzel—if Rapunzel had been un homme, of course—spinning gold." Under her heavy rouge, she blushed. "I know that
sounds silly—"

"No, no," said Dallas, letting his hand stay in hers. "It's not
silly at all . . . it's nice. Thank you."

He couldn't remember the last time he'd thanked anyone—
maybe Violet when she handed him his weekly pay—but there
was nothing perfunctory or sarcastic about this thank-you; it was
a pure expression of gratitude, gratitude that she had recognized
something special about him.

"I know that Kjel—such an odd name, don't you think?—
gets a lot of attention, and he is quite good—as is your brother,
certainly, but believe me, the way you make your guitar
talk . . . well, it's as if I was listening into the most intricate, the
most interwoven, the most layered conversation I'd ever heard in
my life!"

Dallas's vision blurred, and when he realized its cause was
tears, he quickly blinked them away. *What the hell?*

Their conversation lasted through the night—Dallas remi-
niscing about his father ("Mokey Sykes!" crowed Frenchie. "I
can't tell you how many of my musicians have mentioned Mokey
Sykes!"), of his stint in prison ("My first cellmate—guy named
Trey—was doin' *four years* for stealing a bottle of milk for his girlfriend's baby, for Christ sake"), of his last encounter with his
mother and sister, and when the sun began coloring the eastern
edge of the sky, Dallas yawned a big jaw-cracker and claimed,
"I'm beat."

"Then I've got just the place for you," said the older woman,
and taking him by the hand, she led him into her bedroom,
painted the same deep red as the parlor.

He climbed into her bed and she tucked him in as if he were
a child, and when he awoke at noon, he was curled around her
body. Panic flit through him like an electroshock when he realized it was her *naked* body, but after counting to ten once, twice,

and then again a third time, he relaxed into her body and fell back asleep.

They both woke up an hour later, and when she kissed him, he tasted the remnants of alcohol and cigarettes in her foul morning breath, but it didn't stop him from kissing her back.

Now they had been together for five days, and in her makeup-smeared, loose-fleshed company, Dallas felt, for the first time in a long time, that he belonged somewhere.

✱

"CAN YOU BELIEVE we're doing this?" Kjel asked Austin.

Words for once failing him, Austin shook his head. How many times had he and Kjel fantasized about this, about being in a real live recording studio and making a record?

"I'm sure glad you asked me for a cigarette way back when," said Kjel.

His lips clamped, Austin nodded.

"Don't get your hopes up," was one of the few pieces of advice Violet's father had given her, but watching the band from the sound engineer's booth, Violet thought, *Why not, Daddy? That's where hopes are supposed to be—up. They're like balloons, and you hold on to their strings and they lift you up too.*

As the men tuned their instruments to one another's, Violet felt a thrilling certainty, knowing that she was not supposed to be an alienated young woman working in the accounts office of a thread factory, or a suicide victim. Nor was she supposed to be a shopgirl in Paris, or a midwife in China, or a fisherman in Tahiti. She was exactly what she was supposed to be—the Pearltones manager; exactly where she was supposed to be—in the studio of Red Sky records; and exactly with whom—Kjel!—she was supposed to be.

Then Frenchie asked her a question and the moment was lost.

"Don't you think Dallas should sing the lead vocals on 'Wishin'?"

Violet shrugged. "I think the harmony they have down is pretty good the way it is."

"Yes, but I think Dallas could offer more of a *perspective*. One hears in his voice that he's lived a little more than Kjel."

One hears what one wants to hear, thought Violet, but instead she said, "I think they've pretty much settled on the vocals."

Frenchie raised one penciled eyebrow at Violet before fishing around in her bag for a cigarette, and then the engineer turned on the microphone and asked, "Ready, boys?"

✳

A WEEK LATER, ordinary and extraordinary things occurred. Violet got her period and the attendant cramps, and Elwin picked up a letter from his grandmother at General Delivery informing him that his cousin Peg had triplets and hadn't stopped crying since their birth four days ago. Kjel paid for one Moon Pie while pocketing two Mars bars and a roll of Necco wafers, and Austin sat feeding nickels into a phone booth, pleading with his sister to give him a little more information about their mother than, "Well, how do you think she's doing?" Meanwhile, Frenchie's doctor sawed off Dallas's cast.

For Dallas, being unencumbered of his plaster cast was certainly not an ordinary event, nor was Frenchie's request to keep the cast.

"You want that old stinky thing?" he asked, embarrassed.

"This stinky thing," said Frenchie, "held your beautiful foot for six long weeks. Would that I could ever be so lucky."

"She's a romantic," said her doctor. Not only was Frenchie his only white patient, she was also the one into whose wild exploits he enjoyed the occasional vicarious dip.

Besides the freeing of Dallas's ankle on that day in late August, two extraordinary things occurred: the Pearltones' record came out, and radio-station phone lines were jammed with callers asking that the record be played again; and a cross was burned on Frenchie's front lawn.

Everyone had been invited to Frenchie's after the show to celebrate the good news about the record, and as the two trucks approached her house, Violet leaned forward in the front seat and said, "Look, Kjel, there's something on fire up there."

They all stood on the lawn for a while, watching the wind sprinkle sparks in the air.

It looks like confetti, thought Violet, *electrified confetti.*

Kjel broke their trance when he grabbed a blanket from the truck bed and began beating the flames with it. Elwin quickly joined him, using his jacket to fight the fire, and when the cross fell to the ground, the men stomped on the remaining flames as if they were partners in an angry, ugly dance.

"Well," said Frenchie. "So much for the wienie roast."

Over the small woman's head, Austin and his brother exchanged looks.

"We'll call the police," said Austin. "Then we'll notify the papers—we're getting so much publicity in the *Journal* that I'm sure they'll do a story about this, and with all that publicity, surely a witness will identify the perpetrators—"

Frenchie laughed, surprising everyone.

"The perpetrators were all dressed up in costumes, Austin. Like Halloween ghosts—except with pointed hats. For the life of me, I don't know where they came up with those pointed hats."

She laughed again.

"*Écoutez moi,* if those bastards think they're scaring me, they've got another thought coming—not that they can hold two thoughts in their pointed little heads." She laughed louder, and then suddenly, like a car making a surprise U-turn, she was crying. As Dallas walked her into her house, Austin stood watching them, wishing his hands could do more than ball up in his pockets—wishing they could wield a knife, a gun, wishing he could bring them together around someone's sheet-protected neck.

Chapter Eighteen

LET ME TELL YOU A LITTLE BIT ABOUT DEVOTION. I STILL DON'T *know what their communications methods were, but somehow the Clamshells knew our itinerary even when it changed suddenly and could be counted on to be at our shows, mouthing the words to every single song. Part of me thought they were a little nutty, but then I thought if I hadn't been lucky enough to be a part of the Pearltones, I'd probably follow them around too.*

The Clamshells became great friends and camped out together. Birdie Howe, who was an heiress and sort of the ringleader, didn't throw around her money, but if there was a Clamshell whose funds had run low, she didn't mind floating that person for a while.

"Hey," she told me after a show one night, "if the shoe were on the other foot—and I'm glad it's not, because I get my shoes custom-made— I'd hope someone would do the same for me."

Kjel and Austin and Dallas were flattered by their mobile fan club, although Dallas groused that there were no black Clamshells.

"And these white Clamshells don't want no black pearl climbin' into 'em either."

As much as the Clamshells loved the band, there was a tacit agreement that the Pearltones—particularly Kjel—were off limits.

"If a Clamshell slept with Kjel," Birdie confessed, "why, we'd probably have to kill her."

Hey, I could go for some pie about now, how about you? A nice big slab of blueberry pie à la mode, still warm from the oven so that a moat of melted ice cream forms around the bowl. Doesn't that sound good? The only weight problem I've ever had is holding on to it—even when I was carrying Miri, I only gained eighteen pounds, and not for lack of trying. I'm not complaining, although I wouldn't have minded a few curves here and there.

What do you think—should we risk that old piece of lemon meringue that's sitting there sweating away in the pie case? Nah, I'll bet the crust is as soggy as cereal—let's see if they've got any dessert on the menu. Hmm, a hot fudge sundae? Caramel? Oh look, tapioca. I wonder if it's the large pearl kind—probably not, that's pretty hard to find these days.

Once, it was somewhere in Missouri, the Clamshells came to our campsite with a bag of apple fritters.

"We're not staying long," said Birdie, "we just wanted to bring a token of our esteem for last night's show."

"Best version of 'A Miracle Like You,' I ever heard," said Clark.

"The gal at the bakery saw your show too," said Alice. "When she heard we knew you, she gave us these—free!"

"Anyway, enjoy!" said Birdie, herding them away.

That was the Clamshells. It wasn't enough to be disciples of the Pearltones, they had to come bearing apple fritters too.

"I ain't goin,' " Dallas told the band when they came by to pick him up.

"Of course he is," said Frenchie, and her smile revealed a smear of lipstick on her front teeth. She cupped one side of Dallas's face with her manicured hand. "Of course you are, *mon cher.*"

Austin looked up and down the street; he was not comfortable standing in front of Frenchie's house, broad daylight or no.

"Dallas, come on, man, it's time to go."

"Dallas, honey, we talked about this, remember?" Frenchie's voice was as soft and tender as a mother's to her child. Tucking her hand in the crook of his arm, she ushered him toward the unkempt forsythia bushes by the front steps. "You've *got* to go. Your music is too important not to go."

"But, Frenchie, I told you: I love you!"

"And I love you, *mon amour.*"

"Then you'd want me to be with you!"

"For now, Dallas, you need to be with your music. Now go."

She kissed him hard, and when it appeared Dallas wouldn't let go, she untangled herself from his embrace and gave him a little push. "I mean it, Dallas. Go. *Allez! Allez!*"

The others, who'd been sneaking glances at the couple and straining to hear what they said, pretended to be deep in conversation with one another when Dallas came stomping toward them.

Austin's reflex when he saw his brother's face was to reach his hand out, but Dallas, his face clenched in pain and anger, slapped it away. He flung the door of the panel truck open, the metal screeching when he pulled it shut behind him.

"Take care of him," said Frenchie, and with a jaunty little wave, she turned and trudged up her front steps, using the iron railing like a towrope.

✴

"HE'S HEARTBROKEN, THAT'S WHAT he is," said Elwin, who was playing checkers with Ivar Copenhaver's daughter. Violet was thrilled to have the company of her good friend; Jean wasn't a full-time Clamshell, but had managed an occasional visit with the band when her father gave her time off. "He thinks he threw away his one true love."

"*True love?*" Violet, who was sketching Jean's portrait, made a sound as if she were spitting. "Elwin's idea of true love is throwing a little adagio dancer up into the sky."

Elwin's face darkened. "I am not in love with Isalee, Violet."

"I was just teasing you, Elwin," said Violet. "And sure, Dallas and Frenchie might have had fun together, but it wasn't love. How can a twenty-five-year-old man love a sixty-year-old woman?"

The wide span of Elwin's forehead furrowed as he studied the checkerboard. He was still mad at Violet for speaking so blithely of the most beautiful woman he'd ever met. "All's I'm saying," he said, "is Dallas *loves* her. And besides, Frenchie's not sixty, she's forty-nine. King me."

"Says who?"

"What do you mean, 'Says who?' Says me. I jumped over one of Jean's men and I'm on her side of the board now so she has to king me."

Violet smirked. "What I meant was, who says she's only forty-nine?"

"Well, that's what she told Dallas. Why would she lie?"

Violet erased Jean's eye, which she had gotten all wrong. "She'd lie because she knows sixty is way too old for anybody but an octogenarian!" In truth, Violet didn't know how old Frenchie was, but even *if* she was only forty-nine, she believed she was still too old for Dallas.

"Would you think Dallas was too old for Frenchie if he was forty-nine and she was in her twenties?" Jean asked.

Violet glared at her friend; hadn't she ever heard the word "solidarity"? Jean glared back; she thought that love was open to anybody—for her own sake, she had to believe that. Elwin glared at the checkerboard; how could Violet—a woman!—be so heartless? Love was love—whatever the age! The game ended in silence, and still miffed at Jean, Violet penciled in a faint mustache above her friend's lip.

✴

Tension grew as they traveled farther south. They had to make an effort to segregate themselves as much as possible; they rode in separate vehicles and stayed in separate motels and auto parks. Summer was fading into a mild fall, but they didn't camp anymore, afraid of uninvited company with more than a handout on their minds.

In a little town between Memphis and Little Rock, a sheriff's deputy on horseback planted himself outside Bizzie's, an all-black club in which they were playing a one-night engagement.

Kjel greeted him as the band brought in their instruments. "How ya doing?"

When the man didn't answer, Kjel directed the question at the horse.

"How are *you* doing?" he asked, rubbing its velvet muzzle.

"He's doing fine," said the deputy, yanking the horse's head up with the reins. "Let's just hope you are."

"Well," Kjel said, his voice friendly. "We should be. I mean with you as security, and all."

The deputy leaned down until his face was close to Kjel's. "Who says I'm *your* security?"

When Violet told Bizzie of the exchange, the club owner said, "You can bet he's not out there for us either."

Violet shivered. "Then who's he protecting?"

"Let's just say he doesn't want his friends in their white clothes to get dirty."

If the KKK showed up that night, the Pearltones didn't know about it; they played a raucous set that had people dancing in the aisles and in their seats, and when Kjel pulled a young woman onstage and jitterbugged with her, the crowd roared their approval.

Violet wondered if there was someone in the audience who wasn't sharing the glee that is inspired by watching good-looking people dancing well to good fast music; surely someone did not like the fact that a white man was dancing with a colored girl; surely that someone would convince someone else to share his disapproval. Violet cased the crowd, but amid the shouting and clapping and whistling, she couldn't spot any brewing dissent.

Later, on the drive to the auto park, she asked Kjel why he supposed there hadn't been any trouble.

"What do you mean?"

"When you danced with that girl. I mean, the tighter you held her, the louder they cheered."

"It reminded me of dancing with Isalee," said Elwin as he stared out the windshield at the black starry night.

Kjel looked at his friend. "You still carrying a torch for that little adagio dancer?"

"A torch that'll never be lit," said Elwin with a sigh.

His words were like a wisp of old perfume, inspiring melancholic memories in all three of them. Kjel remembered how Kay Burns rinsed her frizzy hair in vinegar one night, hearing it would help settle the curls down. Then they went to see a show, and Kjel's eyes watered so much from the tang of her hair, he could hardly see what was happening onstage.

Violet thought of a night in the thread factory when it was so hot that Polly stripped down to her underwear and started dancing the hula.

"What the Sam Hill do you think you're doing?" asked Lamont, the foreman.

"Feeling the cooling trade winds of the Pacific on my skin," she said, her eyes closed as she swayed back and forth, her hands waving as if underwater.

"You're going to feel more than that on your skin if you don't get back to work," said Lamont, and even though his voice was gruff, his face was beet red, and the rest of the crew laughed so hard they had a hard time making quota.

Elwin was thinking of Isalee and how light she felt in his arms and how once when he was setting her back on the ground, her breasts brushed against his face and she had laughed and said, "I guess we'll have to work on that move."

Their individual reveries ended when the truck barreled over a pothole and Violet's shoulder smacked up against Kjel's.

"Ouch," she said.

"Sorry," said Kjel. "It's so dark I can hardly see a thing." He shifted in his seat, leaning forward to better see the road ahead. "Now, about what you were saying earlier."

Violet stared into the moonless night. "About why there wasn't any trouble?"

Kjel nodded. "It's because no one wanted to spoil the fun."

"Well, gee, that's insightful," said Violet. "Well, let me tell you, the farther south we go, the less people are going to see the 'fun' in this, and—"

Kjel's laugh cut her off. "Violet, you've got to admit, it was quite a party in there."

"But your shows always are."

Kjel reached for her hand, and bringing it to his mouth, kissed it. "Violet, for your constant support, I will always love you."

A happy little bird fluttered in Violet's chest.

"But you know some shows are better than others. I think this was one of our best, and the audience felt it and we felt it and everybody was just celebrating."

"That's right," said Elwin. "And who wants to get in the way of a good party?"

"No one we want to know," said Kjel, and he took a pack of cigarettes out of his pocket and passed them to Elwin. "Light me one, will you?"

"Those guys in Memphis did," said Violet. "It was just as good a show—just as much of a party that night—and they still wanted to fight."

A match scratched and a tiny blade of flame shone in the truck. Elwin lit two cigarettes and passed one to Kjel. Both men inhaled and exhaled at the same time, and finding that simple piece of choreography funny, they laughed.

"Well," said Kjel finally, "I think the people tonight knew I wasn't trying to take anything away from them."

"And what were you trying to take away from those punks in Memphis?"

"Elwin, was that our turnoff? I'm telling you, I can't see a blame thing."

"Henderson Road," said Elwin. "That's what we're looking for."

"So, come on, Kjel," said Violet, "what did those guys in Memphis think you were taking away?"

Violet could feel his shrug in the dark.

"Their lives as they know it, I guess."

✷

AFTER THEIR SECOND SHOW in Little Rock, a tall man whose tailored suit Violet could tell cost a lot of money approached her backstage.

"I'm told you're the band's manager," he said, tipping the brim of his fedora.

"That's right," said Violet, "how can I help you?"

"Mind if we take a seat and have a little chat?"

"Not at all. Follow me." As the man walked behind her, she pretended he was noticing how well-cut her own clothing was, her pretty legs, her good posture. But she knew his eyes were fixed on her stump, and as she led him into the empty green room (the band members were already out mingling with their fans), the assured young businesswoman had been chased away, leaving the young girl who inspired pity.

"How'd you lose your arm?" he asked after he sat down on the sofa Violet gestured toward.

Don't mince words, she thought, and her anger was like a whistle, calling back her errant confidence.

"I thought it was business with the band you were interested in."

Her words couldn't have been crisper if they'd been ironed, and Violet was pleased to see the sophisticated man flush.

"Well, it's just that—" He took off his hat as if it had suddenly gotten hot. "You see, my sister Catherine lost her arm too, and so I was . . . I was just curious."

"How?" said Violet, because now she was curious too. "How did your sister lose her arm?"

"A boating accident. She was thirteen years old and—I'm sorry, it was rude of me to bring it up."

"I was sixteen," said Violet, and with no prompting other than the concern in his eyes, she told him the whole story.

"And on your birthday," said the man, shaking his head. "What a shame."

"Yeah, and when they wrapped it up for me, they didn't even put a bow on it."

The man and Violet stared at each other wide-eyed in the seconds before they burst out laughing.

"I can't believe I said that."

"Well," said the man, "it was funny."

They smiled at each other and he half stood as he reached out to shake her hand. "Lawrence Zeller, by the way."

"Violet Mathers. Now what can I do for you, Mr. Zeller?"

When the question was answered, it turned out Mr. Zeller was not so much interested in what Violet could do for him as what he could do for the band. He was a vice president for DeLite Records and he wanted to sign the Pearltones to a contract.

"They made a record in Memphis," Violet said. "On Red Sky Records? It's gotten some radio play."

"A paperboy's got bigger distribution than Red Sky Records. I'm not talking about *some* radio play, Miss Mathers. I'm talking about every American with a radio knowing who this band is. I'm talking about a big tour, I'm talking about the King Reynolds variety show, I'm talking about Hollywood."

Violet bit her bottom lip. "And you think the Pearltones could do all this? A lot of people think it's wrong that they're even on the same stage together."

"Miss Mathers, 'a lot of people' are wrong," said Lawrence Zeller, narrowing his eyes. "Listen, I'd like to invite you and the band to come over and meet a friend of mine tomorrow, say around noon?"

"I don't know," said Violet. "They like to sleep in after a show."

"Maybe they could be persuaded if they knew my friend's name," said Mr. Zeller.

"Oh, really?" said Violet, put off by his bemused confidence. "And who might your friend be?"

"Phinnaeus O'Reilly."

✸

THE SMALL, WIRY MAN, draped in a blue bathrobe, sat on a rattan chair on a tiled patio area surrounding, wonder of wonders, an indoor pool.

"I've heard a lot about you," he told the Pearltones. "My housekeeper saw your show last night and she said about the same thing as Larry"—he nodded at the record producer—"*unbelievable.*"

"I just got back yesterday from our overseas tour, and man oh man, does that transatlantic travel knock a person upside down. I hit the sack at four and didn't get up until nine this morning."

In the humid pool room, the Pearltones nodded and gaped and fidgeted, acting as if they were facing a god, which all of them believed they were. Finally, Kjel found the wherewithal to speak.

"Mr. O'Reilly, I can't begin to tell you how much your music has meant to me."

"My sentiments as well," said Austin, and Dallas nodded his agreement.

"I can't wait to tell my grandmother," said Elwin. "You're her all-time favorite."

The thin, freckled man laughed. "Ah, compliments are a balm, aren't they? Now, I've done all my laps but that water feels awfully good—anybody care to join me in the pool? We've got extra trunks galore—my band likes swimming here, and their wives and girlfriends, so you, miss, would be covered too." He laughed again, a snuffly little wheeze. "In both senses."

Violet of course declined, or was going to; she had swum with the band in lakes and swimming holes but always in a halter and shorts outfit she'd made out of a jersey fabric, and she doubted that the bathing suits available would offer the same modesty. But she had never swum in an indoor pool—with a musical legend, no less—and so surprising herself, she said, "Sounds like fun."

Phinnaeus O'Reilly rang a bell, and a butler appeared and escorted Violet to a changing room where, out of seven suits arranged neatly in drawers, she chose a high-necked black maillot. She had stripped down and was ready to step into it when she changed her mind and put on a red suit with a lower neckline instead. Covering herself with a robe that hung on the door hook, she breathed deeply and told herself, "Here goes nothing."

The men were already in the pool when Violet arrived, and knowing the longer she kept her robe on, the harder it would be to take it off, she shrugged the terry-cloth robe off as nonchalantly as Esther Williams and jumped into the pool.

There is no place adults regress into children more than water; Violet was splashed on and in turn splashed; she shrieked when whoever was "it" got close enough to tag her; on top of Kjel's shoulders, she shouted taunts as she tried to wrestle off Austin, who sat on Dallas's. She got dunked and dunked others and applauded at Elwin's explosive cannonball dives and inhaled water up her nose when she laughed.

"Can you believe it?" Kjel said, treading water near her. "We're in Phinnaeus O'Reilly's swimming pool!"

Known as the "Irish Cowboy," Phinnaeus O'Reilly was a western singing star, but he had quit the movie business several years before, revealing to Hedda Hopper in an exclusive interview that "when all the fun's gone out of something, I reckon it's time a body gets going too." Retreating to the countryside outside his hometown of Little Rock, he built a mansion and a new band, Phinnaeus O'Reilly and the Boys of the New Frontier. The band, which blended cowboy and gospel music, had one hit record after another and spent over half the year on the road. They were as popular abroad as they were stateside, and in fact, American tourists visiting France often came home telling friends and relatives about the little boys who'd sing Phinnaeus O'Reilly songs in the streets for spare francs.

"Violet," said Dallas when the two found themselves on the same side in a volleyball game, "you know that Phinnaeus O'Reilly song, 'Señorita Suzanna'? People used to pay me cigarettes in the pen to sing it to them."

Violet and the Pearltones would have happily spent hours more in the pool but no one was going to disagree with their host when he suggested "we dry ourselves off and get some chow."

Lunch was served in a dining room decorated with photographs from Mr. O'Reilly's days in Hollywood.

"Paulette Goddard!" said Violet, looking at a picture of the brunette movie star sitting behind Phinnaeus on his horse, Tristan. "And oh my goodness, there you are with Carole Lombard!"

"*The Wild Wyomian,*" said Austin. "I loved that movie."

"Me too," said Lawrence Zeller. "Never in my wildest dreams did I imagine I'd be signing the star of it to a record deal."

"Life's an enchantment," said Phinnaeus, and after that benediction, beat his two index fingers on the polished walnut table and said, "Any of you boys in the mood for a little jam?"

He didn't have to ask twice, and everyone followed Phinnaeus into his music room.

"Help yourself to whatever you want to play," said the Irish Cowboy, nodding at half a dozen guitars on stands, a standing bass, a piano, a marimba, drums, and a collection of percussion instruments. The Pearltones moved through the small jungle of instruments like shoppers searching for the best deal, and after they had made their selections, Phinnaeus grabbed a guitar and offered the musicians their favorite invitation: "Let's play!"

Violet, Elwin, and Lawrence Zeller headed toward a leather couch across the room.

"Oh my," said Violet, sliding into the record producer, unable to gain purchase as she sat down on the slippery leather.

"You don't have to move on my account," said Mr. Zeller as Violet grabbed Elwin's arm to straighten up.

Thankfully, the music began, saving Violet, who was rattled by the comment—was he flirting with her?—the need to respond.

The Irish Cowboy yipped with pleasure as the Pearltones,

who'd been accompanying him as he played his hit, "Over the Range," began to improvise, speeding up the chorus and filling it with notes that looped around one another before unwinding into an echo of the melody.

Mr. Zeller sighed. "To err is human, to play music like that, divine."

"You said it," said Elwin, staring at the musicians with longing in his eyes.

After "Over the Range," Phinnaeus O'Reilly cackled his delight before launching into another one of his hits.

"Hey, Elwin," said Kjel when the song was over, "come on over and give us a hand with the bass."

The big man looked as if he had been struck by lightning.

"Go on," said Violet, nudging him.

"I can't play with Phinnaeus O'Reilly," said the neophyte bassist.

"If you don't, you'll regret it all your life," said Mr. Zeller. "Now, go."

Elwin rose and walked toward the musicians as if he were in a trance, and with his hands out in supplication, he said, "Mr. O'Reilly, I'm just learning how to play and—"

"I don't need excuses," said the wiry old musician, "I just need someone to give us a good backbeat."

"We'll start with a Pearltones' song you know," said Kjel, and then, to Phinnaeus, he added, "Do you mind?"

"Yippee ki yay," said the kindly cowboy singer. "Let's hit it."

Elwin provided nothing more than a few steady chords and a steady beat, but that was enough for the musicians, and his face gradually lost its grim concentration, his smile slowly growing until it looked as if its goal was to stretch ear to ear.

"Well, I think this might just be the happiest day of his life," said Violet.

Lawrence Zeller responded by stretching his arm across the top of the couch and saying, "I find you very attractive, Violet."

She waited for his smile, and when that failed to materialize, the punch line, and when it was clear he wasn't teasing, Violet forced a smile of her own (her mouth was so dry that her upper lip snagged on her front teeth) and said, "I'll bet you say that to all your one-armed girlfriends."

The record producer lit a cigarette and tilted his head back, exhaling the smoke toward the ceiling.

"I can understand your need to joke like that. It took a long time for my sister to believe that she might be considered attractive to the opposite sex." He inhaled again and this time directed his exhale straight ahead. "She's been married now for four years, to a man who absolutely adores her."

Violet couldn't figure out if Mr. Zeller was patronizing or mocking her; either way, she didn't like it, and leaned forward to let him know she wanted to listen to the music and not him. Then, smarting from his impudence or whatever it was, Violet thought, No, I'm not going to be a namby-pamby about this— and she turned to him and said, "Mr. Zeller, I'm not the type to put up with any shenanigans!"

"And what shenanigans are we talking about?"

"Oh, come on," said Violet. "I look forward to doing business with you and DeLite Records, but just because I'm female and you might feel sorry for me doesn't mean you have to flirt with me."

Mr. Zeller flicked the ash of his Camel in the square crystal ashtray on the side table. "Who says I feel sorry for you?"

Violet wished for supernatural powers; specifically, one that would allow her to disappear and regain form and shape in a place far, far away. Seconds passed before she grimly accepted her wish was being ignored and that she was still seated on the slippery leather couch in Phinnaeus O'Reilly's music room.

"It's just that . . . it's—"

"Why is it unreasonable to think I might be attracted to you? Because you were unfortunate enough to be in a terrible accident?"

"Yes!" said Violet, her voice so forceful that she glanced nervously at the band, certain they had heard her. "Yes," she repeated, whispering. "Yes, because of my arm and, oh yes, because

I'm so ugly that the only way I'll get a husband is if I visit a school for the blind—and that's a direct quote from my cousin Byron!"

"Your cousin Byron's an idiot," said Mr. Zeller. Stubbing out his cigarette, he leaned back into the couch. "Anyone else can see what a striking woman you are."

Tears flashed in Violet's eyes.

"Why are you doing this to me? I don't understand the joke."

For the first time, the smooth Mr. Zeller looked rattled.

"Violet, honestly, I'm not joking. I suppose if my sister hadn't lost her arm, I might be uncomfortable that you're an amputee; but even if I were, it wouldn't blind me to your other qualities."

Violet was stumped. "My good business skills?" she offered finally, her voice wavering. "My sense of humor?"

Mr. Zeller pressed his lips together, and Violet had the odd sense that he was going to cry himself. They both listened as the band played "Coyote Lou," from the movie Mr. O'Reilly had starred in. This version, thanks to Dallas's mournful harmonica playing, was more like a lament than a ballad.

"Yes," said Mr. Zeller finally. "I am attracted to your business skills—I like a strong woman who knows what she's doing, and yes, I am attracted to your sense of humor. If you want to go down the list, I'm also attracted to your body, Violet. Do you know how many short dumpy women would love a long lean graceful body like yours? And then there's your beautiful black shiny hair. And of course, your face, your bright eyes—"

Like a bully, laughter rose up inside her, muscling aside all other emotion.

"Okay, really, the joke's over," said Violet, dotting the corners of her eyes with a finger. "I might have gone along with the long lean body—well, I don't know about the graceful part—and the black hair business, but—"

"Violet, listen to me. You're no Paulette Goddard and you're no Carole Lombard—"

"Gee, tell me something I don't know."

Mr. Zeller sighed. "But why would you want to be? Why would you want to be just pretty when you could be something striking, something unusual?"

Violet was beginning to lose patience with the whole sorry conversation.

"A girl doesn't aspire to be 'striking' and 'unusual'—which we both know are just polite ways to say 'strange' or 'homely'— a girl wants to be 'just pretty' *because it makes everything a whole lot easier!*"

Again she looked at the band, afraid she was being too loud, but the musicians were oblivious to everything but their own music.

"Tell me," said Mr. Zeller—and from his voice, Violet knew that the nonsense wasn't over. "Aside from your arm, what do you think is so strange or homely about yourself?"

"Are you crazy?" she said, spitting words. "Just look at me! Look at the size of my chin, for crying out loud!"

The record producer, his head slightly tilted, regarded Violet for a moment.

"You have a strong chin, certainly, but it's a far cry from either strange or homely."

"Ha! Tell that to my mother! She told me I had a man's chin on a six-year-old girl's face."

Lawrence Zeller made a face. "Your mother said that?"

Violet nodded, her shoulders rounding with sadness. "Before she ran off and left me, she did."

"With a mother and a cousin saying things like that to you, I hope you had other family members who were telling you differently."

Violet shook her head. "I didn't."

The record producer looked wounded, but he didn't have a chance to reply.

"Larry—did you hear that?" shouted Phinnaeus O'Reilly. "I want to re-record that song with this arrangement!"

"It's certainly possible," said Mr. Zeller.

They listened to the rest of the jam session in silence, until

Mr. Zeller looked at his watch and asked if she'd mind talking a little business in another room where it was quiet.

"Look, Violet," he said, rising, "we're going to be working together a lot with the Pearltones and I'll respect your wishes to keep it strictly professional. As far as I know, you and Kjel are a couple anyway"—Violet inhaled her surprised gasp—"but if you ever think you might find me a hair as interesting as I find you, just let me know."

Before the show, Kjel asked Violet what she and "the big shot record producer" were talking about all afternoon.

"You sure looked like you were having an intense conversation."

"Just business," said Violet, feigning nonchalance.

"I know what *business* he was interested in," said Kjel.

Laughing, her face the same color as the band's pink jackets, Violet waved her hand.

"And then when you left! Where'd you go, anyway? Somewhere to seal the deal with a kiss?"

"Kjel," said Austin, "quit teasing her."

"Yeah," said Elwin. "Who Violet kisses is none of our business."

"I didn't kiss anyone!" said Violet. "All I did was agree that in a mere three weeks we'll all be in New York City in the DeLite recording studios!"

She was suddenly lifted in the air by several pairs of arms as shouts of "New York City!" and "Delite Records!" bounced around the walls of the small dressing room. Even Dallas, leaning against the wall on a metal folding chair, was cheered enough by the news to push aside his perpetual sneer and smile.

Chapter Nineteen

I WAS THRILLED THAT AFTER PLAYING A FEW MORE DATES WE *would be heading north. The nights were especially hard, what with worrying about Austin and Dallas—had they gotten to their rooms okay? Had anyone followed them?—and my sleep was restless and tainted with bad dreams. One night I woke up sweaty, my breath coming in little puffs. I had been dreaming I was going to get ice cream at a soda fountain, only to find the shop window papered with signs reading, "Whites Only," "No Credit," "Catholics Not Allowed," "No Unchaperoned Women," and finally, one in the corner that read in heavy print, "Absolutely No Amputees."*

Lawrence Zeller had gone back to New York, but he asked me to telephone him and let him know what was going on with the band. I knew he had spoken kindly about me to his secretary because whenever the operator asked her if she'd accept charges from a Violet Mathers, she said, "Of course; we'd be delighted."

Mr. Zeller liked to hear about the crowd count, the song lineup and any changes that were made in it, and if "You're My Gem" had been the audience favorite or if they'd responded more to "A Miracle Like You."

The guys teased me about these calls; especially Kjel, who said I came out of the phone booth looking like I'd just been in a heat wave.

Oh my—I love when a diner can surprise you. Who would have thought they had a daily special dessert and that it would be apple crisp like this?

Anyway; it wasn't as if I'd fallen for Lawrence Zeller or anything, but I had to like him for the mere fact that he liked me. And this is really strange; a sweet little dream poked up through those nightmares I was having. I dreamed it at least a half-dozen times and it was always the same, a dream featuring Lawrence Zeller in a tuxedo and I in a gown slathered with petticoats and kid gloves buttoned with pearls. And both gloves had hands in them, and with my left hand I reached out to Mr. Zeller and we began dancing a waltz and in an accent deeper than my Kentucky one, I thanked the man "for seein' the whole Violet."

Several hours before the band's performance in Pine Bluff, Arkansas, Violet went to get her sewing kit—the sleeve of Kjel's jacket was ripped—out of Elwin's panel truck. When she opened the door, she expected, among the boxes of provisions, the fishing poles, and various detritus, to see the thin mattress. What she didn't expect to see was a naked Dallas pumping away on top of a naked blond woman, both of them, judging by their cries, in the throes of a religious experience.

She gasped and quickly turned away, hoping her entrance/exit went unnoticed, but apparently the Almighty was too busy being summoned by the lovemakers to grant Violet her prayer.

"What the—"

Violet closed the door as Dallas shouted and ran into the theater, revising her prayer to "Please let him think I was Elwin."

He didn't say anything to her before or after the show, but that wasn't unusual, Dallas most often acting as if he were the king and everyone else part of his serfdom: *he* decided when and if words were to be exchanged.

Two days later a delivery boy from Western Union knocked on the dressing room where they'd all gathered for a meeting.

"Telegram! Telegram for Mr. Dallas Sykes!"

Austin admitted later that his heart took a dive toward his lower intestines; surely this was bad news from Odessa; news about their mother.

He saw the tremble in Dallas's hands as he opened it, and he knew for a moment his brother must be thinking the same thing, but relief smoothed his features after a quick scan with his eyes.

"It's not . . . it's not about Mama?"

Dallas shook his head. "It's from Frenchie."

"Frenchie," said Kjel. "What's she say?"

"She says 'congratulations.' She heard about our record deal."

"How'd she hear about that?" asked Elwin.

"A little thing called the telephone."

"You called her *long distance*?"

Dallas laughed. "It wasn't the first time."

"That's true love," said Austin with a theatrical sigh. "When you're willing to spend the money on long distance."

"Heck," said Kjel, "Violet calls our record producer person-to-person *collect*."

"So tell me, Dallas," said Austin, frowning at Kjel. "What else does it say in there? 'Love you madly. Stop.' " He continued in a high-pitched French accent. "Or, 'Can't *wait* to love you madly. Don't stop.' "

"Ooh-la-la," said Kjel. "I'll bet on that one."

Laughing, Dallas rubbed his earlobe, and as he looked up, he made eye contact with the one person in the room whose spirits weren't as high as everyone else's.

"What are you looking at?" he said, the snarl back in his voice.

"Nothing," said Violet, and deciding the business of the meeting could be taken care of later, she got out of her chair.

Moving like a panther, Dallas was across the room, grabbing Violet by her stump before she had taken two steps to the door.

"Don't you judge me, you nosy little bitch!"

"Dallas!" said Austin. He and Kjel and Elwin had risen together, none of them understanding what Dallas was doing but knowing that he had to be stopped.

***

"Understand?" He pushed Violet against the wall so hard that the autographed pictures of Guy Lombardo and Chick Merton rattled.

Austin grabbed his brother by one arm and Kjel by the other, but he flung their arms off, pointing his finger at Violet's face. Violet couldn't have been more scared if he were holding a switchblade.

"If you knew one damn thing about what a man needs, you—"

He was grabbed again, and in the wrestling, was nearly knocked over.

"You don't know anything about love!" he said as Austin pushed him out the door. "Stumpy bitch don't know anything!"

The three remaining in the room listened until the brothers' angry words and footsteps faded.

"What on *earth*?" said Elwin, his voice a raspy whisper.

"Violet, are you all right?" asked Kjel.

She nodded, but she wasn't.

"It's all right," he said, wrapping her in his arms. "Good heavens, you're shaking like a leaf. Come and sit down on the sofa, Violet. Did he hurt your arm?"

Aware that he was talking to her, but not quite certain of the words, Violet kept nodding, letting herself be led to the sofa, and it was only when Kjel sat on one side of her and Elwin on the other that she heard the chattering of her teeth.

"What do you need, Violet?" asked Kjel, his voice soft. "Should we get you something to drink—some whiskey, maybe? Are you warm enough? We can get a blanket out of the truck—or there's probably one around here someplace."

He got up and went to the dressing-room closet.

"Bingo," he said, reaching up for the blanket on the top shelf. "Although I'm not seeing any bottles in here."

After sitting under the blanket for several minutes, Violet finally stopped shivering.

"Violet, what was *that* all about?"

"I . . . I saw him with another woman. In Elwin's truck. But that's all. I didn't say anything and he didn't say anything and I thought that was it . . . until now." Violet felt the rise of phlegm in her throat and tears in her eyes. "I really don't know; he got the telegram and you guys were joking and—"

The knock on the door was tentative, as if it belonged to a bill collector who'd come to collect on a debtor known to be in possession of a mean streak and an underfed Doberman.

"Yes?" Kjel said, and the door opened.

"Dallas has got something to say," said Austin. The door opened wider, and seeing Dallas behind his brother, a shiver spasmed through Violet's body.

Austin stepped aside, as if he knew by standing close to his brother he was supporting him. To Kjel, it seemed Austin looked more ashamed than Dallas.

"I'm sorry, Violet," said Dallas, and he looked in her general direction but his eyes could not make the trip all the way up to her face to look into her eyes. "I . . . I don't know what got into me."

The brothers stared at the floor; Dallas's arms behind his back, Austin's crossed in front of him. Violet stared at her lap and Elwin stared at his folded hands.

Kjel stared at Dallas. "So where'd this apology come from?"

Dallas jerked his head up. "What do you mean?"

"Did Austin make you say you're sorry?"

Dallas looked at his brother, who continued his captivation with the floor.

"Austin can't make me do anything."

"Well, even if he did," said Kjel as he stood up, "I don't think it would matter much. Even if it came from you, it wouldn't matter much. You're out of the band, Dallas."

"What?"

"Kjel, let's talk about—"

"He said he was sorry—"

As the protests pummeled him, Kjel remained standing, his eyes on Dallas, until it was quiet. Dallas stared back, his chest puffing out with each breath. To Violet, they looked like two bulls deciding whether to charge each other.

"Who said you're the boss?"

"No one," said Kjel. "I just happen to think attacking *our manager* is a good enough reason to be kicked out of the band."

Embarrassed, Dallas ducked his head. "I didn't attack her, I was just—" He looked to his brother for help, but Austin offered none. He looked to Elwin, but Elwin was not done viewing his hands. Dallas felt his shoulders sag, felt his life and what seemed like its great possibility begin to swirl down the drain, just as it had when the bald pompous judge had banged his gavel after sentencing him to three years for attempted robbery. They were just after a little cash and some cigarettes, for Christ sake!

Shame and anger filled his head like a migraine; he could feel the heat of it inside his head, and then he thought of Frenchie and how she had said this band was his destiny; he saw her small, birdlike face and couldn't bear to think of the look on it when he told her he'd been kicked out of the Pearltones.

"I know," he offered, trying to keep the pleading out of his voice. "Let's take a vote. That's only fair, right?"

Kjel rubbed his throat. "Yeah, I guess that's fair. So who thinks Dallas should—"

"Wait!" said Violet. The bees in her ears were so frenetic she was surprised she could hear her own voice over them. Things were happening much too fast; she felt as if they were all in the panel truck careening toward a cliff and suddenly discovering the brakes were bad.

"Just wait a second," she said, standing up. She felt small sitting on the beat-up couch and wanted to remind them how tall she was. "There's not going to be a vote."

Dallas looked as if he were going to throttle her all over again, and she held up her hand, not only signaling him to stay back, but to stop all dissent before it began.

"And here's why." She was surprised when emotion churned up inside her; she pretended she had a sudden itch she couldn't ignore and slapped at her shoulder, killing the nonexistent mosquito and the existing need to cry. Scratching, she collected herself. She tossed her head and her black hair fanned out in the quick short motion. "Say you vote him out, Kjel, and say Dallas votes for himself. That's a tie vote, leaving it to Austin and Elwin to decide. You don't want to force something like that on them, Kjel." She turned to Austin. "And if you voted against him, Dallas would never forgive you, and I can't have that on my conscience." She looked back at Kjel. "I can't have the band breaking up on my conscience. There's just too much at stake right now."

Kjel looked pained. "But he—look at your arm, Violet!"

She didn't need to look at her stump to see the bruises; she could feel them. Instead, issuing an all-points bulletin for any and all courage that might be hiding in the cracks and crevices of her psyche, she leveled her gaze at Dallas.

"I know you won't ever touch me again," she said. "Will you?"

Shame was a wind that bowed Dallas's head. "No," he said, and when the wind passed he raised his head and after clearing his throat said louder, "No. I will never touch you again, Violet."

"You better not," said Kjel, pointing his finger at Dallas. "Because next time you won't get a second chance."

He pushed past Dallas and out of the room.

"And I . . . I guess I should . . . uh . . . go check on the instruments," said Elwin.

Wordlessly, Dallas followed him, and the two men couldn't get out of the room fast enough.

"I can't say how sorry I am," said Austin in the silence that followed the men's departure. "But as sorry as I am, I can't say as I would have voted him out."

"Don't worry about it, Austin. I understand."

The man's eyes widened. "You know, Violet, I believe you do." He stepped toward the door. "I better go . . . do whatever it is they're doing. So . . . *arrivederci.*"

Violet laughed at the awkward good-bye. "Arrivederci."

His hand on the door, Austin turned around. "Violet, I just thought of the word of the day."

"What is it?"

Austin smiled. "The word of the day is *largesse*."

✴

AFTER THE SHOW, Kjel followed the taillights of Elwin's truck. Lately they had been following the brothers to whatever motel or auto-park cabins they were allowed to stay in. As usual, Dallas was humiliated by the escort service.

"Don't he think we can take care of ourselves?"

In the dark, Austin rolled his eyes. First correcting him on his grammar, he then corrected him on Kjel's motives.

"Concern is not a belief that we're unable to take care of ourselves. And besides, it's Violet's idea. She told me she sleeps better knowing we're safe."

"She tells you a lot, doesn't she?"

"We're friends," said Austin, feeling his face warm. "Friends tell each other things."

Dallas laughed, and if anyone could make laughter sound mirthless, it was he.

"You'd like to get into that skinny cripple's little white drawers, wouldn't you, bro?"

Contempt became a component of Austin's blood and he could feel it pulse through his veins. He lit a cigarette to give his hands something to do other than striking his brother.

After exhaling a long column of smoke, he said, "I'd think you'd appreciate Violet after what she did for you today—and may I say, Dallas, that if you indeed do ever touch her again, I will personally kick you out of the band and then out of my life."

"See, you didn't deny it, Austin." Dallas laughed again, and this time it actually sounded as if he meant it. "You didn't deny it."

While his brother slouched against the passenger door, smoking, Dallas began to whistle. Getting a rise out of Austin inevitably improved his spirits, and he tapped the steering wheel with one finger, keeping time. Then too, it was a starry-night sky and cool air swept through the opened windows, air that smelled of the wide-opened countryside. That there was also a bottle of whiskey waiting to be opened back at his cabin lightened his mood, and his whistling broke into singing.

> *"Jimmy crack corn, and I don't care,*
> *Jimmy crack corn, and I don't care—"*

Austin was not one to nurse his own bad mood as if it were a wound, protecting it from anyone's attempt to make it feel better; he butted his cigarette in the ashtray and joined his voice in harmony.

> *"Jimmy crack corn, and I don't care—*
> *My master's gone away!"*

Dallas thumped his palm on the steering wheel and Austin beat a rhythm on the edge of the dashboard and their repertoire expanded to include "Swing Low, Sweet Chariot" and "Dixie." They sang "In the Evening by the Moonlight," mimicking the hammy, exaggerated minstrel voice of Al Jolson singing "Mammy," and when they were done they hooted and hollered until Dallas held up his hand, imploring his brother to stop.

"Ah's gwine drive off the road," he said in a deep voice. "An if's ah drive off dat road, da mastuh be awful mad."

"Yes suh, da mastuh whip your black hide," said Austin.

"Oooh, in dat case, maybe ah'll drive off the da road afta all."

Behind them, Kjel honked his horn.

"What, I'm going too slow for you?" Dallas asked, accelerating.

The horn honked again.

"He's turning," said Austin. "He wants you to follow him."

Muttering, Dallas turned the car around in the middle of the road and followed Kjel's truck down a dirt road.

"Where the hell is he taking us?" asked Dallas.

"I'll bet it's the Clamshells," said Austin, seeing a bonfire. "They said they were having a party."

"Parties," said Dallas as he parked the truck behind Kjel's. "White people don't know shit about throwing parties."

He was wrong. The Clamshells were thrilled when their heroes joined them.

"Oh, my goodness, sit down, sit down," said Birdie, the unofficial leader, flapping her hand, a signal to the half-dozen others to make room for the Pearltones on the logs that were situated around the fire.

"We're . . . we're so honored you're here," said Alice, and as Kjel sat next to her, she felt the heat of his body and reminded herself that she was too near an open fire to swoon.

"Honored to be here," said Kjel, looking around. "Hey, looks like your numbers are dwindling."

"I'll say," said Birdie. "I think at one point—Peoria, I believe—there were over thirty of us."

The remaining Clamshells looked glumly into the fire.

"Hey," said Kjel, "are you sharing those?"

Several bottles within the circle were quickly passed toward Kjel and intercepted by the other Pearltones.

"Drink up," said a pipe-smoking woman with a face wizened by both age and sun. "There's plenty more where that came from."

"This is Pansy," said Birdie, gesturing toward the woman who'd just spoken. "This is her land, and her liquor."

"Only because my husband died," said Pansy with a laugh. She took a swig from the bottle and showed her teeth in either a smile or a grimace. "He was a bastard, but he did leave me a nice chunk of property, and he did know his way around a still." She took another swig and this time there was no confusing her grimace with a smile. "Although some batches are better than others."

"Pansy was at the show," said Birdie. "We told her all about us and about how blue we were, knowing it's our last time being together—"

"What do you mean?" said Kjel. "You can always come and see us after we make the record."

———

The campfire made its usual noises, but those seated around it were silent.

"Summer's over," said Palmer finally. "I have to get back to work. I'm plumb broke."

"We all are," said Alice. "Well, of course except for Birdie."

The heiress shrugged and raised a bottle. "To Howe Steel."

Alice's eyes teared up as she stared at Kjel. "But even though I'm broke . . . I wouldn't trade these past months in for all the money in the world!"

The other Clamshells asserted as much.

"We can't tell you how much your music has meant to us," said Nell, her voice choked.

"And when you're rich and famous," said Clark, "we'll be able to tell everyone that we knew you when!"

Gwen sniffled. "I don't know how I'm going to go back to my regular life. You made me forget about it . . . how hard it was."

"I thought I loved teaching," said Alice, "but it's going to be awfully hard correcting papers after this."

Kjel took Alice's hand, causing a chain reaction. Even Dallas didn't protest when Nell took his right hand and Birdie his left. Violet was saved embarrassment over breaking the circle when Austin encircled her stump with his hand.

Staring into the hypnotic fire, people didn't speak, but they did clear their throats, sniffle, and muffle little gasps and sobs.

Finally Dallas sighed, let go of the hands that were holding his, and turning toward his brother said, "See, I *told* you white people didn't know shit about parties."

Dallas's words, and the continued passing of bottles, set the party in the right direction.

"Well, I don't know about the rest of you," said Alice, whose low tolerance for liquor was evident in her tight, precise speech and rogue giggles (even those who prided themselves on their high tolerances were surprised at the wallop a few sips of this hooch packed), "but I think after all the entertainment the Pearl-tones have given us, it's time we gave back."

———

"It was more than entertainment," said Palmer glumly.

Violet nudged Palmer with her elbow. "Ye gads, man. Cheer up."

Violet rarely drank, but rarely didn't mean never, and whenever the bottle came around, she helped herself to it. She was sad to realize that the Clamshells would be leaving, and more than willing to lighten her gloom with the liquid that gave meaning to the word "firewater"; now that it had burned and cauterized her esophagus, she could hardly taste it.

"So you're going to sing us a song?" she asked Alice.

"No," said the young teacher. "But I am going to dance."

She stepped over the log and out of the circle and proceeded to shimmy as if she'd just stepped on a live wire.

"Lord in Heaven," whispered Kjel, which was a fair encapsulation of the feelings of the all the men in the group.

"Well, I can't jiggle," said Clark after the spent and breathless Alice staggered back to the log. "But I can juggle."

As he unlaced his boots, he asked for a volunteer to donate a shoe, and armed with two boots and one of Birdie's expensive Italian leather flats, he began to throw them up in the air and, to the astonishment of the group, catch them.

"Now that's coordination," said Pansy. "I like a coordinated man."

"You like coordination?" said Kjel. "I know somebody who can show you coordination. Elwin, go get your fishing rod."

"There's no water around here," protested the big man.

"You're not going fishing," said Kjel. "At least not for fish."

While Elwin stumbled off into the dark to get his fishing pole out of the truck, Clark tried to get fancy with his juggling, stepping on and off the log as he threw the shoes into the air. He was impressive, and the audience rewarded him with several bursts of applause. Inspired, he jumped up, clicking his heels together, successfully, and then repeated the motion, unsuccessfully. He tripped, falling over the log with an *Oof!* and sending Birdie's Italian flat into the fire.

"My shoe!" said Birdie. "My shoe that I had made in Florence!"

There was a whirring sound and a motion in the fire that made sparks fly. After a vague clicking, the shoe suddenly emerged from the fire, wiggling and waggling and looking for all to see like an apparition; the Invisible Man—or judging by the shoe, the Invisible Woman—doing a crazy jig in one visible shoe.

Amidst the screams and gasps of surprise, Kjel doubled over laughing.

"It's Elwin," he said as the big man walked toward the group, holding his fishing pole and a shoe attached to the line.

"Looks like those Eye-talians were biting," he said, blushing with pleasure when his joke was received with laughter.

"See, Elwin can just about catch anything with his fishing pole," said Kjel. "Anywhere you tell him to land the hook and sinker, he will."

"Really?" said Palmer, throwing his hat over his head. "Catch that."

"Well, he's got to see it first," said Kjel.

Pansy picked up her flashlight, strafing the ground with a streak of light until it landed on the worn derby.

Jutting his lower lip out, Elwin studied his target. It lay on its side in the dirt, and he knew if he could position the hook beneath the brim and tug, it would probably catch hold. With the Clamshells and the Pearltones watching, he took a few practice swings without releasing the line. Finally satisfied, he drew the pole back, let go, and, to the delight of the crowd, snared his catch.

"Bravo!" said Palmer. Unhooking his hat, he noticed the special hook. "Hey, that's a lot bigger than a fishhook!"

"He custom-made it," said Kjel.

"It's my catch-stuff-other-than-fish hook," said Elwin. "My grandmother—she raised me—wouldn't let me have a rifle, so I'd target-shoot with my fishing rod."

"Your grandmother sounds like a wise woman," said Birdie.

"Imagine if soldiers were sent to war with fishing rods instead of rifles."

"There she goes again," mumbled Clark, staring up at the sky.

"Here," said Gwen, standing up and backing away from the log ring. "See if you can get my handbag."

Pansy directed the flashlight on the target, and after studying it, Elwin took a few practice runs.

Before taking final aim, Elwin was distracted by Dallas, who was mouthing words and waving a finger at him. Understanding what his friend was saying, he laughed and shook his head. Dallas nodded, mouthed the words again, and repeated the gesture.

"Are you going to share your joke with the rest of us?" Austin asked his brother.

"Just giving the man some encouragement," said Dallas.

Stopping his chuckling with a shake of his head, Elwin concentrated one last time on his target and let the line fly. He missed Gwen's purse, but it wasn't his intended target. The hem of her skirt was, which he snagged and pulled up.

"Elwin!" shrieked the young woman, pushing down her skirt with her hands.

Birdie jumped up to unhook her friend, scolding the lecherous fisherman.

"Elwin, I'm surprised at you," she said, trying to keep her voice stern but having difficulty.

"Dallas told me to do it," said Elwin, and Nell registered her protest by shoving Dallas's shoulder. Austin leaned over and did the same to his other shoulder.

"I said lift up her *spirits,*" said Dallas, "not her *skirt!*"

"You're terrible," said Birdie, but she scolded him the way a mother scolds a mischievous child of whom she's secretly proud. She sat back beside him and swatted his maligned shoulder. "Just terrible."

The spirits of those assembled didn't need a boost with a fishhook, and had gotten to the level by which a good party is defined; there was much laughing and joking, and more talent exhibitions: Palmer did his Jimmy Cagney and Cary Grant impressions (Violet thought his Cagney sounded more like Marie Dressler, although his Cary Grant was serviceable), and Nell showed such a flair for dramatics with her recitation of "The Highwayman" that every time she came to the part, "And the highwayman kept riding, riding, riding . . ." goose bumps collectively mottled the forearms of her listeners.

When Clark announced that it was time to square-dance, Austin pulled out his harmonica to play "Turkey in the Straw," and Clark called out moves.

> *"Bow to your partner, then take her hand,*
> *Tonight we'll dance to beat of the band."*

Tipsiness had erased the inhibitions Violet and any of her partners felt about her stump; she thought it was the height of comedy that while alamanding or do-si-do-ing, a partner would pretend to grab her nonexistent hand, until she was ready to sit down, her laughter interfering with her ability to follow the calls. She was hardly alone; laughter made everyone clumsy, made them gasp and stumble and bump into one another.

The din of their laughter covered the sound of horse hoofs, so they didn't know they had company until the two apparitions were upon them.

"Stop!" shouted one. "I command you to cease all activity!"

All activity ceased as the group stared up at the white-robed men whose faces were hidden behind what looked to Violet like oversized dunce caps with eyeholes. Austin felt his mouth go dry and a certain rubbery quality overtook his knees. There was no moisture left in Dallas's mouth either, but he felt his muscles winch tight and he cased the two men, trying to find the more vulnerable target. Kjel too felt his body go on alert and was wondering who would get hurt and how bad when Pansy, her voice amused, said, "Hey, Lester, hey, Carney. You fellas having one of your little dress-up parties?"

Lester or Carney pointed a finger at Pansy, who, making herself comfortable, sat back down on the log.

"Silence!"

With a smile, she took a puff on her pipe. "Oh, silence yourself."

"These nigras must leave your property, and they must leave now."

Pansy took the pipe out of her mouth and stood up.

"You've got one thing right, Carney—this is *my* property. And I say who gets to be on it and who doesn't. So I'd appreciate it if you and Lester would just turn yourselves around and *leave.* And tell the rest of your little knitting club that if they choose to continue to meet on *my* property, there'll be consequences to pay."

"But, Mrs. Littlefield, we've always met here!"

"That was when Winston was alive," said Pansy. "If you haven't noticed, Lester, that's no longer the case."

One of the horses danced a little as its rider leaned toward the other to speak to him. Violet watched as the points of their hats met, like the beaks of two birds greeting each other.

"You better watch what you say, Pansy Littlefield," said the bolder of the two. "You cross one of us, you cross us all."

With that, he turned his horse around, as did his partner, and they rode away from the campfire and the circle of people. All eyes were on their departure and not on Elwin, so no one noticed when he reached for his fishing rod. What they did notice was what appeared to be magic: the quick backward tug of one of the clan members' hood.

Reflexively, the man turned, wondering what had grabbed ahold of him, and when Elwin reeled in the line, he had to direct his horse to move in the direction he was being pulled.

"What's got hold of me!" he cried as the hood, lifted at its hem, moved up his face. Grabbing hold of the fabric, he let his displeasure be known.

"It's a hook, Carney! They've got me hooked!" Trying to unsnag himself, he lost his balance, nearly sliding off his horse. "Easy, *easy!*"

To his friend, he said, "Help me!"

As the group by the fire watched in rapt attention, Elwin kept reeling in the line while Carney tried to pull the hook out of the fabric.

"Damn it, y'all gonna pay for this!"

The two horses fidgeted and snorted as they were forced to move backward as Elwin kept winding the reel. Finally, exasperated and embarrassed, the man pulled the hood off his friend and threw it to the ground.

"Carney!" said Lester as his sweaty pink face was revealed. He had the look that a boy facing a bully often wears; the panicked, outraged look that often precedes tears.

"Giddyup, Trixie!" ordered Carney, inspiring his partially defrocked friend to command his horse to get moving too.

"Giddyup, Buttercup. H'ya!"

Chapter Twenty

IN SMITH LAKE, MISSOURI, A PRETTY LITTLE TOWN WITH RED AND
gold asters in the window boxes of its Main Street businesses, I sat in a
phone booth (remember when people sought privacy for their telephone
conversations and weren't blathering into cell phones?) recapping our es-
cape for Lawrence Zeller.

"We drove all night, swilling coffee from a thermos and checking the
side and rearview mirrors about every half second."

"Oh, Violet," said Lawrence, his voice scolding in its concern and
worry.

"Then we got kind of silly—you know how you get when you're
nervous and tired—and Kjel put his hand to his mouth like he was talk-
ing into a police radio and said, 'Calling all clans, calling all clans, be on
the lookout for a group of black and white musicians. Armed with guitars
and considered dangerous.' "

I laughed but there was silence on the other line.

"And then Elwin wondered if the women wore the same outfits, and
I said sure, except that maybe they jazz them up with a little lace around
the hood, a pleat or two in the robes—"

"Oh, Violet, the sooner you get to New York the better—"

"We even figured out how they came to wear those hoods. Most of them had the dunce caps they'd worn throughout school so they decided they may as well be thrifty and use them in their costumes. Never say the KKK is full of spendthrifts!"

"Violet, how is everyone now?" said Lawrence, failing to appreciate my story. "How are Dallas and Austin holding up?"

"Fine—they went with Elwin to find the lake this town's named after. No doubt we'll be eating fish tonight."

"Well, you be careful."

"Don't worry, we are," and at that moment I looked up, glancing at the sign on the forest green awning of the pharmacy across the street: Gladstone Sundries.

"Chaw," I said, "I've got to go."

"What's the matter, Violet?"

"Nothing," I said lightly, adding to myself, yet.

So I did have a little foresight, see? Nothing was wrong yet, but once I crossed that street and walked into the drugstore, I knew there was a possibility of trouble.

What I had no way of knowing was how much, and it still haunts me, that pretty little town of Smith Lake and all that happened there.

Kjel was sitting on one of the benches with which the town council had thoughtfully furnished the business district sidewalks.

Watching a wide-eyed Violet race across the street, he swallowed the last of the candy bar he was eating.

"Violet," he said, standing up, "what's the matter? What'd Larry say?"

Waving her hand in reply, Violet went to the pharmacy window, moving her head this way and that as she looked past the Geritol and Vigor Vitamin displays.

"Looking for someone?" asked Kjel, sidling next to her, and when Violet turned to him and he saw her ashen face, he said, "Violet, you're acting like you've seen a ghost."

"Maybe I have," whispered Violet. "Or maybe I will."

A white-haired woman leaving the store smiled at the couple.

"Welcome to Smith Lake," she said. As the mayor's wife, she

believed it her duty to be friendly, especially to good-looking men. "It's not every day that we get visited by such a handsome couple."

She said this while staring into Kjel's eyes because it would be too bold to say what she was thinking: *it's as if God couldn't decide which color was prettier so He gave you one of each.*

"It's not every day that we get to visit such a handsome town," said Kjel, and when he smiled, the mayor's wife touched the window ledge behind her; not that she really thought she would swoon, but just in case.

"Well," she said, experiencing a hot flash; odd, since she had gone through the change two decades earlier, "you need any help with anything, just visit the mayor at his office down the street." She patted her permanent-waved curls, inadvertently snagging her hairnet with a fingernail. "I'm his wife, Minerva Haskell."

Kjel bowed, doffing an imaginary hat. "Pleased to meet you, Mrs. Haskell."

Remembering the many unchecked items on her to-do list, the old woman said, "The pleasure is all mine!" and as she continued her way down the street, she thought, *If anyone could make smelling salts come back in fashion, that man could.*

Violet had welcomed the brief encounter with the mayor's wife; it gave her time to collect her thoughts. Now, thoughts collected, she took a deep breath and before pushing open the pharmacy door turned to Kjel.

"Please stay here. I'll be right back."

Taking a step back, Kjel shrugged his shoulders, indicating that it was fine with him.

The wood floor creaked as Violet walked down the center aisle, her body filled with a mad percussion, from the buzzing bees in her head to her wild, drumming heart. She noticed everything; the orderly, dusted shelves holding jars of Noxzema stacked in a little blue pyramid, tins of talcums, tooth and foot powders, pomades, ointments and salves; a magazine rack, a stand labeled SHOE AND HAT CARE, filled with polish and saddle soap and brushes. To the side of the pharmacist's window was a counter and cash register, and seeing the woman standing in front of it, Violet felt as if her internal organs were suddenly flash-frozen.

Was that her mother? Her sister? What was the matter with her nose? As quickly as the questions blinked on in her mind, the answers blinked back: *No, I'd recognize my mama anywhere, and that's not my mama, and even if my mama had another daughter, that woman's too old to be my sister and, well, she obviously broke it.*

"May I help you?" said the woman at the counter, whose knotted, easterly leaning nose had less to do with the childhood fall that broke it than the clumsy-fingered doctor who set it.

"I . . . uh . . . well," Violet said, a blush painting her face. On the other woman's face, the look of concern grew as she regarded the strange-acting, one-armed girl.

Violet blew air out of her mouth, hot and clammy at the same time.

"Well . . . I . . . I don't see where it is you keep your chewing gum."

Pursing her lips until they were outlined in white, the clerk pointed to a small candy counter. Violet studied the rectangles of Wrigley's and Black Jack and Cloves gum like a jewelry appraiser looking at diamonds, finally selecting a package of Doublemint.

At the counter, she fished for pennies in her coin purse, clearing her throat, and when she still couldn't talk, clearing it again.

"Could you tell me," she said, her words finally dislodged, "could you tell me if this pharmacy is owned by a *Yarby* Gladstone?"

"May I ask the nature of your inquiry?" said the crooked-nosed woman, trying to disguise her excitement. She was a person who spent her spare time reading detective novels and was thrilled by the intrigue and suspense that had suddenly visited her own life vis-à-vis this strange, one-armed girl.

"I . . . uh, there was a Yarby Gladstone back in my hometown."

"And what hometown was that?" asked the woman, squinting her eyes the way Philip Marlowe might during interrogations.

———

"Uh, Mount Crawford, Kentucky," said Violet, wondering if the clerk had an astigmatism.

"I see." The woman nodded slowly, mulling over the clue.

"*Is* this pharmacy owned by a Yarby Gladstone?" asked Violet, when it appeared the clerk might never stop standing there, nodding.

When the woman stopped nodding, there was still a sense of motion about her face because of the nose that looked as if it had careened around a corner.

"As a matter of fact," she said, "Yarby Gladstone *is* the proprietor of this establishment." She watched with great interest as the color drained out of the one-armed girl's face.

Two quick breaths jumped up out of Violet's throat. "Is . . . is he here?"

Nervous, scared, near tears, noted the amateur sleuth.

"Why, no he's not," she said. "Mr. Gladstone always takes his afternoon break at this time." And because she was a fan of suspense, she slowly collected the pennies on the counter, rang up Violet's purchase, and looked at her watch before adding, "He should be back in twenty minutes."

✳

"WHERE'S MY YELLOW DRESS?" said Violet, clawing through her carpetbag.

"Violet, what's going on?" asked Kjel, breathless from chasing her to the truck, parked around the corner.

"How'm I ever going to iron this thing?" she wailed, shaking out the hand-sewn dress with the eyelet bolero.

"Violet," said Kjel, stressing her name the way a doctor does when checking a patient for consciousness. "Violet, what's going on?"

When she looked at him, her dark eyes were so full of pain and fear that he put his arms around her, and crying into his shoulder, she told him who the owner of the drugstore was.

_____

✦

"A ONE-ARMED GIRL?" said her employer as the clerk breathlessly relayed the events of Violet's visit to him. "I don't know any one-armed girl from Mount Crawford. Didn't she leave a name?"

"She wasn't exactly forthcoming," said the clerk, passing the blame onto the mystery girl rather than her own negligent sleuthing.

The druggist clicked and unclicked a Gladstone Pharmacy pen; he didn't like surprises and he didn't like being told about a one-armed girl by his crooked-nose clerk; it made him uneasy, he felt he had wandered off sunny Main Street and into a dark alley. God knows he couldn't find a better or more loyal employee than Janeen Jenkins, but sometimes just a glance at her gnarled and slanted nose put him in a bad mood that lasted hours.

When the bell over the drugstore door tinkled, the clerk, checking the stock of corn plasters and moleskins, looked up and shivered: it was the return of the one-armed girl, and she knew a mystery of some sort was about to be solved.

"Is Mr. Gladstone back?" asked Violet, her husky voice a whisper.

"Why, yes, I'll go get him," said Janeen, taking in the young woman's male companion, who was, anyone could see, quite a lot to take in.

Kjel squeezed Violet's arm and assured her, "It's okay, Violet, it's okay," but when the tall man in the white coat walked out of the pharmacy and into the store, Violet leaned into Kjel, light-headed and not so certain it was.

"Yes?" he said, his balding head cocked, his clean pharmacist's hands held in front of his stomach.

When silence greeted his semigreeting, Kjel patted the small of Violet's back, and it was enough of an impetus to propel her forward.

"Mr. Gladstone," she said. "Mr. Gladstone, I'm Erlene Mathers's girl."

———

LORNA LANDVIK

"Let's talk in my office," said the pharmacist, moving faster than his bulk would suggest; he was at Violet's side in a moment, leading her through the low swinging door that led behind the counter and through the door into the pharmacy and his office.

"Oh, my," said the clerk, turning her sharp eye to the handsome blond stranger, hoping he might help provide more clues as to exactly what was going on.

✴

YARBY GLADSTONE HAD the reputation of a gentleman, and it was deserved; he would have rather invited Franklin "the damn socialist!" Roosevelt into his office than Violet Mathers, but he gestured toward a chair as he sat heavily on his own.

"So what brings you here, Violet?" he asked, wishing mightily for a tall glass of whiskey.

"You remember my name!"

"Of course I do—I used to tease you and call you 'Bouquet of Flowers,' and you'd say, 'My name's Violet!' "

A pang of memory pierced her; she had known only cruel teasing, and his kindly banter had made her feel special.

"What happened to your arm?"

"It got cut off," said Violet crossly, and suddenly she reached across his desk, grabbing a framed photograph. "That's not her!" she cried. "Why don't you have a picture of *her*?"

"For God's sakes!" said Mr. Gladstone, rising up from his chair, and after he pried the photograph from her hand, they stood staring at each other over his desk, breathing hard.

Her breath was on the verge of turning into sobs, but before it did, she asked the question she'd been waiting to have answered for years. "Mr. Gladstone, where's my mother?"

Looking at the door, he shushed her. "Do you want the whole town to hear you?"

"Where is she? Where's her picture? Is she with you now?"

The furrows of the pharmacist's face were deep. "Violet, I'm going to have to insist you lower your voice."

"Answer my question!" she cried, and then, tears stinging her eyes, she whispered, "Please."

As Violet sat back down, so did Yarby Gladstone, panting, frightened at his impulse to overtake the young woman, to make her stop shouting.

Watching her weep, he felt a bile of disgust and pity rise in his throat and swallowed hard, ashamed of himself.

"Violet," he said softly, wishing he could give her a different answer, "Violet, I don't know where Erlene is. I haven't seen her in over ten years."

Violet hung her head, unable to face the world in front of her.

"She . . . I . . ." Struggling with the words, Mr. Gladstone took a deep breath, knowing the sooner they were out, the sooner this would be over. "Violet, Erlene left me not two years after we left Mount Crawford. We had traveled for a while—'on the run and in love,' is what she called it—but—"

Here Violet gasped, and Yarby Gladstone got up and moved his chair next to her because he knew she needed someone to hold her up, even if it was the man who was knocking her down. She didn't resist when he took her right hand in his own; it felt as limp and dead as a snared fish.

"We wound up in Atlanta," he continued, wanting to cry out when he felt her tears splash on his hand. "I have a cousin there who set me up in his store—there's a total of eleven Gladstones in the pharmacy business." This fact, one he usually recited with pride, now made him feel silly. "Then one day . . . one day I came home and Erlene was gone. She didn't leave a note, but a neighbor told me she'd left with a fellow who'd been coming around the apartment while I was at work."

Violet felt his sigh more than heard it.

"I won't lie to you, she broke my heart, but—" Yarby Gladstone looked at the picture of his wife and little boy, taken at the Rotary picnic last spring, and even as he hated that it was lying facedown on his desk, it made him feel, for the first time in his life, how minor his heartbreak was compared to the little girl's whose mother he'd taken away.

"Violet," he said, his voice thick, "I'm so sorry."

Feeling short of breath, Violet lifted her head and tilted it back, so that her chin pointed to the ceiling. She sat like that for a long time, eyes closed, listening to the hum of bees.

When she lowered her chin, it felt as if her head was made of lead.

"Do you know where she is now?"

Yarby held up his clean hands, his fingers splayed. "I stayed in Atlanta for another year but I never saw or heard from her again. My neighbor said the man she left with was from South Carolina, if that means anything to you."

Violet shook her heavy head. "It doesn't."

The sun was filling the west window with a golden after-noon light, and the daughter and the lover sat thinking about the woman who had deserted them both.

"Thank you for your time," said Violet presently, and as she stood up, Yarby Gladstone felt a near-desperate need for atone-ment.

"Violet," he said, "do you need money? Work? Anything at all?"

"No thank you. I don't need a thing."

"So you're doing all right?"

Her hand on the doorknob, Violet turned around.

"Mr. Gladstone, I'm doing better than I ever imagined I could."

The pharmacist nodded, his mouth twisting to one side. "I'm glad," he said, when he could get the words out. "I'm glad, Violet."

After they had walked away from the drugstore, Kjel opened his jacket to Violet and, laughing, revealed the bounty of items tucked into his waistband and wallet pocket: candy, gauze, soaps, postcards, bobby pins, combs, and even a hot-water bottle.

"I thought this might make you feel better," he said, but as soon as he saw Violet's face, he turned around and went back to the pharmacy.

"I seem to have taken some things without paying for them," he said to the crooked-nosed clerk as he unloaded the items in his jacket on top of the counter. "I'm returning them now."

The armchair detective nodded, if only in recognition of the strange and mysterious.

✳

THEY TOOK THE ROAD out of town whose sign directed them to SMITH LAKE, 12 MILES. Violet had rejected Kjel's offers of seeing a movie ("Look, Violet—*Robin Hood* is playing—you like Errol Flynn, don't you?"), of fabric shopping ("You can spend as long as you want Violet, and I won't say a word"), and of bowling ("Let's make a wager over who gets the most strikes!"), nodding only when Kjel said, "Should we just head out?"

It was a golden September afternoon; the air was still warm and the trees were still green but in a breeze were hints of the cold, the yellow and red to come.

Kjel was worried about Violet, slumped in her seat, staring out the window with vacant eyes, and he kept up a chatter of words to distract her.

Finally, tired of the sound of his own voice, he closed his mouth and they drove several miles, the silence interrupted only by the pinging noise of gravel hitting the underside of the truck.

He was wracking his brain for a way to make Violet feel better, and when inspiration appeared, he sent up a thank-you and pulled over.

Turning off the ignition key, he jumped out of the truck and raced over to Violet's side, opening the door.

"Come on, Violet," he said, offering her his hand, "we're going on a field trip."

"I . . . I'd rather—"

"Oh, you don't know what you'd rather," he said, taking her hand and pulling her out of the cab. "Now, come on, out of the car."

"Why?" she asked, but he didn't answer until they had walked down the slight incline of a ditch and through the tall grass that led to a thicket of trees.

"Ta-da!" said Kjel, gesturing toward a massive black walnut tree whose limbs reached out in all directions, as if making dibs on every inch of space around it.

Kjel smiled at the question on Violet's face.

"Look at how low that branch is," he said. "Look at that fork there. It's the perfect climbing tree."

Violet sighed. "So I suppose you're going to climb it."

"No, *we're* going to climb it."

Patience was leaking out of Violet like air out of a slashed tire, and she waved her stump.

"Oh, I'm not going to buy that old excuse again. If you can sew, you can climb a tree. Especially this tree—*babies* could climb this tree." He looped his hands together. "Now step up, Violet, then grab hold of that branch there."

She leveled a sour look at him but that only made him laugh.

"Come on, it'll be fun. You get a whole different perspective of things when you're sitting up in a tree."

Violet knew Kjel would not let her back in the truck until she had climbed the tree, and so she stepped into the stirrup of his hands and grabbed the branch.

"Okay, now use your stump," he said, further boosting her by giving her rump a push. "And use your feet to climb up."

Violet did as she was told and managed to hoist herself up.

"Okay, now move over a little—I'm coming up."

Kjel scrambled up like a monkey and sat down on the seat a wide branch offered.

"Come on," he said, patting the space next to him, "sit next to me."

Violet did as she was told, and Kjel smiled, happy to think this might just be the tonic, to sit up amidst this greenery, with a nice view of a meadow and a blue sky—

"Oh, Violet."

Her face was scrunched up and tears found their way down the crumpled topography of her face.

He put his arm around her and both of them wobbled for an unbalanced moment.

"Whoa," said Kjel, steadying them both. "Sorry about that." He wiped a line of tears off her face with his thumb. "I'm sorry about everything, Violet. Just when you think you might finally find your mother . . ."

Violet's sigh was deep and long. "Even though I found Mr. Gladstone, a part of me knew she wouldn't be with him. And I'd bet anything she's not with that guy from South Carolina either. She probably got tired of him and ran off with somebody from Virginia. Or Texas. Or Idaho."

"Maybe she got tired of the local talent," said Kjel. "Maybe she ran off with someone from England or Scotland—yeah, a burly bagpiper in a kilt!"

A trace of a smile appeared on Violet's face. "Or maybe China. Maybe she ran off with a rickshaw driver."

"Well, a person doesn't really need to run off with a rickshaw driver. I mean, he could pull her away."

Considering this, Violet's smile took on length. "A sea captain could sail her away."

"And a broom salesman could whisk her away."

"And a hosiery salesman could sock her away."

"And his partner selling pumps could shoe her away."

"That was bad," said Violet, shaking her head, and the motion seemed to return her to her sadness.

"Aw, Violet," said Kjel, tightening his arm around her.

"Say she was still with Yarby Gladstone," said Violet, "what would she have thought of me after all these years? Would she have taken me in her arms and said how she missed me every single day? Would she have cried seeing me?"

"I bet she would have, Violet."

"Yeah, but they might not have been tears of joy." Violet's laugh was bitter and she swung her legs, looking at the leafy branches above her. "Did I ever tell you, Kjel, about my special relationship with a tree? An old river birch down by the creek behind my house that I used to run to when my daddy was mean to me, that I used to hug, that I used to pretend hugged me back, that I even called 'Tree Pa'?"

"Oh, Violet."

She leaned against the shield of Kjel's chest, crying hard, and Kjel held her hard, one foot shoved against a forked branch to balance himself. Thinking of the motherless Violet seeking shelter in the arms of a river birch tree because the arms of her own father weren't open to her sent a wave of sadness rolling over him. How many times had his own father touched him with affection? Countless times. How many times had he been held by his always present mother? Countless, countless times.

Pressing his cheek to Violet's, he felt her tears and wondered how her face couldn't be covered with tears every single day.

"Oh, Violet," he said again, his mantra, and wanting to wipe her face of tears, of pain, he kissed her cheek, her forehead, and when he kissed her lips, she drew back her head, her eyes and mouth open with surprise.

"Kjel!"

He leaned toward her and her face met his, and he kissed her again, his mouth determined to kiss away that pain, that fear.

Violet was in a kaleidoscope of emotion; sadness was sliced up by surprise, which fragmented into longing, which broke into a hundred sunbursts of pleasure. His body against hers was so warm it felt fevered, and Violet wanted to be full in that fever, wanted to be consumed by it, and his lips on hers were soft then hard and when his tongue was in her mouth she would have cried out if there had been room for a cry to escape, and her stump pressed against his shoulder, her arm around him and feeling his hard muscled back, the kaleidescope burst into passion, shards and shards of passion, and she felt she was flying, and in a way she was, right out of the tree.

Kjel accompanied her in flight and they both landed hard enough so that the breath was knocked out of them.

They lay there for a while, looking up at the sky beyond the green clusters of leaves and the tree limb from which they'd fallen, and when her breath came back to her, Violet started laughing. It seemed the only response to her passionate interlude with Kjel and their subsequent tumble.

Lying on the grass, Kjel answered her laughter with his own before asking Violet if she was all right.

"Fine," she said, sitting up. "How about you?"

He struggled to sit up, his fingers probing his upper arm. "I might have done something to my shoulder."

Kjel rotated it, or tried to, grimacing so that his mouth was a narrow rectangle.

"We didn't even fall that far," he said, regarding the low bough that minutes earlier had been their perch.

"I don't know," said Violet, "I think we're pretty lucky."

Their eyes met and the kaleidoscope began twirling inside Violet, but holding his shoulder, Kjel got to his feet.

"I guess we better get going, Violet," he said, wincing as he dusted off his backside. "See what kind of fish we're going to have for dinner."

✴

WHEN VIOLET WOKE UP, the moon overhead was so bright and glowing it looked like a stage prop. Disoriented, she thought for a moment she might be dreaming and that her dream featured an artificial, back-lit moon and loud, laughing, drunk people. She sat up, her back reminding her that she had been asleep on the ground, and realized that both the moon and the loud, laughing drunk people were real.

Across the campfire she saw Kjel and Austin sitting up, rubbing sleep and their own dreams from their eyes.

"Dallas?" said Austin, his voice furry.

He had left the campsite several hours earlier, asking Elwin for the keys to his truck.

"I'll be gone a half hour," he'd said, pocketing the keys Elwin tossed at him. "I'm just going out for one beer."

Austin knew "one" and "beer" was a combination his brother was incapable of putting together, but it had been such a great day, a rare day in which he and his brother had not only gotten along, but had fun, and he was reluctant to spoil it by acting like Dallas's parent.

As the campfire dwindled down and Elwin won another round of penny ante poker, Austin did notice that Dallas had not returned a half hour or even an hour later; and two hours later, when Kjel added wood to the fire and Violet yawned and asked if anybody minded if she took the spot under the hickory tree, he noticed that Dallas had still not returned.

Kjel knew, by the position of the bright gaudy moon, that it was at least two o'clock in the morning, and when the doors of Elwin's truck opened and shut and one loud voice said, "Shit, you spilled all over me," and another loud voice answered, "Nah, you must have pissed yourself," he said, "Looks like we've got company."

Three men staggered to the fire, and the air suddenly was filled with the smells of beer and tobacco and engine grease, and although she couldn't smell it, Violet sensed the raging testosterone with which young men arm themselves when entering strange situations.

"This is my younger brother, Austin—yes, like the city," Dallas said, and as he gestured, beer sloshed out of the bottle he was holding. "This is Kjel—like in 'sea*shell*.' That's Elwin as in Elwin, and over there, that's Violet. Like the color . . . or the flower."

He didn't slur his words but Austin heard the drunkenness behind Dallas's easy gregariousness.

"And I'm Frank . . . as in hot dog," said a gaunt man whose cheeks were nubby with both acne and fight scars. "And this here is Andy . . . as in *asshole*."

"Shut up—you're the asshole," said Andy, a short round man in bib overalls.

Rather than sitting, the men seemed to collapse to the ground, and Violet immediately sat up as straight as she could, positioning herself so her stump wouldn't be so noticeable. The bees in her ears grew feisty.

"Austin," said Dallas, leaning into his brother, "you don't look so happy. Don't worry—these guys are okay." He looked at his new friends; Frank had mashed a late-season mosquito and was examining the bloody pulp on his fingers, while Andy was chugging down his beer the way a hungry baby takes a bottle. "Right? Ain't you guys okay?"

"Hell, yeah," said Frank, wiping his hands in the dirt. "We're a-okay."

"Swell," said Kjel. "I'm glad everyone's okay. But you mind moving your party? We were all sleeping."

Cupping his hands around his mouth, Dallas whispered, "The man needs his beauty rest. As you can see, he's a dish. At least that's what all the girls say."

"For crying out loud, Dallas—" began Austin.

"That's what all the girls say, right, Violet? She's in love with him," he explained to his drunken pals. "Isn't that right, Violet— you and every goddamned woman in the whole goddamned world!"

"Okay, that's enough," said Austin, and as he stood up, he grabbed Dallas by the arm, attempting to pull him up.

"Get your goddamned hands off me!" said Dallas, and Frank and Andy tensed; on sudden, eager alert that there might be a fight.

"Hey," said Elwin, and even as he scrambled to his feet he kept his voice light, "why don't I show your friends my little fishing trick?"

"Yeah," said Frank, who wasn't about to argue with a man who had a foot in height and at least a hundred pounds on him. "Yeah, let's go fishing."

Violet released a slow breath of relief as the three drunks sidewinded their way to the panel truck. *Good old Elwin,* she thought as he got his fishing pole and softly instructed his charges to follow him down the road a piece.

"But the lake's right there," said Frank, pointing in the opposite direction.

———

"But we're going target practicing," said Elwin.

"Target practice," said Frank. "What the hell are you talkin' about?"

"You'll see," said Dallas, laughing. "Elwin here's a sharp-shooter with a fishing rod!"

"Yeah?" said Andy. "Well, I'm a sharpshooter with a gun!"

In the bright gaudy moonlight the men looked like blue shadows, and Violet saw the short drunk man reach into the pockets of his bib overalls, saw him raise his arms to the sky and heard a *pop!*

"I'm Wyatt Earp!" he cackled. "I'm Buffalo Bill!" He twirled and aimed, as if surprised by a band of outlaws pushing their way through a saloon door.

Pop! Pop! Pop!

"Put down the fuckin' gun, Wyatt!" said Dallas.

There was a frenzy of activity, and as people shouted and hollered, Violet squinted, trying to understand what the blue shadows were doing. As Elwin tackled Andy, Frank jumped on his back, and Austin leaped up, running to help Dallas pull Frank off Elwin.

Frantically searching the ground for a weapon, Violet grabbed a stick, ready to join the fray.

"Come on, Kjel, we just can't sit here!"

She would forever regret the tone of her voice—the tone that accused Kjel of babying his sore shoulder, of being timid at best and cowardly at worst—but at the time, she couldn't tell him she was sorry; she couldn't tell him anything. When she looked at him, her throat closed like a pneumatic door through which no words could pass. Kjel was the one who spoke.

Slumped over to the side, he smiled the way people do when their surprise is so strong they can barely comprehend what's going on.

"Violet," he whispered, "I think I've been shot."

Chapter Twenty-one

THANKS. I THINK IT SAYS NICE THINGS ABOUT A PERSON WHO *carries tissues: you're like a good Scout—prepared for anything.*

Whoo! It still gets to me, thinking about that night and what I could have done to change its outcome. How could we have let our lives be shattered by a dumb stupid drunk in bib overalls? A great tragedy shouldn't be preceded, shouldn't rise out of moments so banal, so dim-witted and brainless; it makes the tragedy seem all the more senseless.

In the truck, driving out to Smith Lake, Kjel had cleared his throat.

"Violet, you know I love you, but what happened—"

I had shushed him then, his words like a clanging door slamming shut all those wild hopes in me, and I knew with a sickening feeling that what had fueled Kjel to kiss me was pity, not passion. He had meant to console me, not romance me, and hurt and angry, I was barely civil to him at the campsite. Austin passed me some looks that asked, "What's going on?" but I ignored them and was in a snit the whole night. When I was lying out my bedroll and Kjel said, "Good night, Violet," I didn't even answer him. I still feel bad about that.

For a long time after that night—years, really—I was mad at the moon. A crescent moon, a harvest moon, a blue moon—I thought each phase of the moon was a traitor; not only a witness to what had happened but an accomplice, shining its big glowing light on everything. Maybe if it had been dark, things would have been different. Maybe, maybe, maybe. Those maybes can be like moths to your sanity, gnawing away.

Well, looks like I've used up all your Kleenex. Thank goodness for the napkin dispenser.

"Did Kjel know he was sick?" Violet asked nodding toward the Lutheran minister asleep in his bed.

"Yes," said Leola, dabbing at her eyes. Her apron pockets always held handkerchiefs now, and by noon they were full of damp wads. "He had telephoned us in August and we told him then. We had just found out."

"But that was last month!" said Violet. "Why didn't Kjel tell us about him then?"

Leola shrugged. "Maybe he didn't think it was so serious. We didn't at first, but now Dr. Oberg says he'd be surprised if Esben sees Thanksgiving."

"Doctors aren't supposed to say things like that!"

Leola allowed herself a wan smile. "Esben and Dr. Oberg are old friends, Violet. And Esben says he has enough hope of his own; he doesn't need false hope from the doctor."

Sadness had found a cavity in Violet's chest and filled it with a weight that made her feel as if she had caved in around it; she was surprised when she passed a mirror and saw that she wasn't hunchbacked. How could Pastor Hedstrom be so yellow and emaciated, wasting away from liver cancer? How could the God he had dedicated his life to permit this to happen to such a fine man, *on top of everything else*?

Pastor Hedstrom urged her to be frank with him, to feel free to discuss her real feelings. With his permission, Violet let loose a litany of tortured questions, most of which were prefaced with the question, "How could God . . . ?"

"God doesn't do these things," the pastor said.

"Oh, sure. He can *cure* but He doesn't *cause*? That sort of lets Him off the hook, doesn't it?"

"Life is full of mystery, Violet. There is no way we can understand one-billionth, one-*trillionth,* of all that makes up this world and beyond. That's what faith is for. It holds you up when everything is conspiring to push you down."

"How many times have you used that in a sermon?" said Violet, ignoring the polite part of herself that shushed her. "How many times have people listened to that and thought the same thing I'm thinking now: that's bullshit!"

Fading back into his pillow, exhausted from his preaching, exhausted from everything, Pastor Hedstrom nevertheless found the strength to chuckle.

"I'm glad you were never a member of the church council," he said weakly. "There would have been anarchy in the pews."

✦

AUSTIN FELT NOW that he too was an amputee, that part of himself had been as clearly severed as Violet's arm. Every word of the day was the same, and it was *misery.* His sadness was as deep as Violet's, but mixed in it was guilt, and it ate away at him like a corrosive agent. *Dallas.* The very syllables of his brother's name burned like bile in his chest; he could barely stand to think of him, and yet he could hardly think of anything else.

Not satisfied with destroying everything, Dallas had lit off on that terrible night, not even waiting around to see what he had wrought. Austin's daydreams were plagued by reenactments of that night—the screams and shouts, carrying Kjel to the open bed of the truck and racing, flying blindly through the night to the nearest town with the nearest hospital. The waiting, the sheriff's interviews, more waiting.

Austin hardly took note when Dallas announced he was going outside to take a walk.

"I'm going crazy in here," he told his brother, giving a little salute as he stood in the door's threshold.

Hours later, when the doctor had solemnly told them the news, Dallas was not around to hear it, and it occurred to Austin that his brother might be taking more than a little walk.

He was right; Dallas never returned, and neither did half of the General Fund—nearly $3,500 that had been in a strongbox in Elwin's truck.

"I can't believe a relation of mine could do such a thing," Austin told Violet. "I am so sorry . . . and so ashamed."

"I can't believe he'd do such a thing either," said Violet, and she put her arm around Austin and he put his around her, and with their foreheads fused together they cried.

The townspeople of Pearl, North Dakota, who were in sorrow themselves over their terminally ill and beloved minister, knew not to make a stink when Violet and Austin came into town, even though it was a shocking sight to see a Negro man and a white woman—a white, one-armed woman—shopping together, or sitting at the Parisian Café counter together, talking in low urgent voices.

"Remember what Pastor Hedstrom says," they reminded each other, "that God doesn't make inferiors."

They didn't quite know what to make of the suited city slicker, or the group of four women and two men who filled every room in Cletis Warren's rooming house; as one woman who went by the name of Birdie explained to the postal clerk, "We're the Pearltones' biggest fans. And if they need help, well, we're happy to do what we can."

"Uff-da," said Minnie Bjornberg, driving out to the Hedstroms' to deliver several hot dishes and pies the Deborah Circle had made, "I had no idea they were causing such a stir with their music!"

"You know I've always thought those colored musicians had a good sense of rhythm," said Vera Iglehard. "And really, with your eyes closed—music is music."

The Clamshells made themselves indispensable to the Hedstrom family; Birdie was more than happy to run errands in her fancy Duesenburg, stocking the larder without being asked; Gwen and Alice thought nothing of scrubbing the kitchen floor or washing basket loads of dirty sheets and laundry; and Palmer helped Austin and Elwin with the heavy chores and in taking care of the few animals that were still on the farm.

They quietly disappeared at mealtimes, until Leola asked Violet—rather sharply—why they hadn't been invited to join them at the supper table. "Honestly, all the work they do as well as cooking half the food anyway, and we let them drive into town to eat?"

It had taken Leola a while to warm to them; she didn't mind eccentricities but these people were *odd;* grown men and women giving up their regular lives to traipse after a band of musicians?

She expressed these thoughts at the first dinner they shared together, and rather than offend the Clamshells, she amused them.

"My mother asked the same thing," said Birdie, whom Leola could tell was the boss of the outfit. "And I've asked her, 'When were you a part of something that was changing the world?' "

"Changing the world?" said Leola. "Uffda-mayda. It was just music."

The Clamshells' reflex was to roll their eyes at such ignorance, but they would never be so disrespectful to Kjel's mother.

"Everything about the Pearltones was magic," said Gwen with a sigh. "I don't know where I'll find magic like that again."

"It was music played in a new way, by people who normally don't play together," said Palmer, leaning over the table so that the fabric of his shirt nearly grazed his cabbage salad. "I never would have expected that I could do something like this—become a 'Clamshell,' for pity's sake—after all, I own my own insurance agency!"

"My law," said Leola. "Who takes care of it for you while you're gone?"

Palmer colored. "My wife. We . . . we love each other, but honestly, she seems to enjoy running the business all by herself, with no interference from me."

"I grew up on a farm," said Gwen. "Not like this one . . . my father . . . well, we were taught Negroes were on the same level as . . . animals." Tears gathered in the young woman's eyes. "Sorry, Austin."

His mouth bunched, Austin nodded. "Apology accepted."

"I might have always thought that way if I . . . if I hadn't become a Clamshell. I thought it was about the music, but it was about so much more!"

The devotion that had initially struck Leola as odd now touched her; she could drink all day at the well of their love for her son and his music.

Gwen was good with Esben too; she was fluent in Norwegian, and sat in the bedside rocker, talking to Esben in Norske, at his request.

"It's all coming back to me," Esben told his wife of his first language, the language soon abandoned by his parents in their quest for assimilation. "When I speak it, it reminds me of them . . . and how big the world is." He paused, giving in to a rattling cough. "And besides, who wouldn't want a beautiful young woman to sit and *snakke Norske* with him?"

"I *snakke* a bit myself, don't forget," said Leola, whose grandparents emigrated from Trondheim.

"Not enough to understand the dirty jokes we tell."

Leola pretended to swat him.

✸

THAT THEY COULD STILL joke was an immense comfort to Leola and gave her a tiny sliver of unreasonable hope that, yes, if Esben could still laugh in his predicament, maybe he was going to make it after all.

It was the same splintered hope that Violet clung to; if she could still make *Kjel* laugh, if he still could make her laugh, then the universe would surely reward them for generating laughter; cultivating patches of vibrant green in the parched and dour landscape in which they now lived.

"That's all right," Violet might tell him upon entering the room, "don't get up."

Austin joined right in, asking Kjel, "Are you going to lie around all day?" or "On your back as usual, hmm?"

Berit, who drove down from Bismarck every weekend to help her mother, disapproved of the teasing.

"It's disrespectful," she said. "How can they make fun of Kjel the way he is now?"

At times like these, Leola wondered from which ancestral fuddy-duddy her daughter had inherited her humorlessness.

"What are they supposed to do? Cry twenty-four hours a day? It never hurts to laugh, no matter how bad things are."

Berit pursed her lips, one of her many physical signals of disapproval.

"Not everything's funny, Mother."

"No," said Leola, "so I guess when you can laugh, it's all the sweeter."

Leola didn't like to admit it, but she was ashamed of her daughter at times; Berit was so stern with her father and brother, as if blaming them for their predicaments and for no longer being what she wanted them to be. She read aloud to both of them, but the way an impatient teacher might, one who wanted to get to the next item on the curriculum. Leola knew that her daughter believed that by appearing strong, she would be strong, but she couldn't help but compare how Violet and Austin were with Kjel, how they seemed more his siblings than Berit did.

All the help Leola was getting from them and the Clamshells allowed her moments of escape, when she'd take an hour to drive without destination, past the fields where she and her husband "sowed their seeds," past the old one-room schoolhouse that was closed when they built the big high school in town, past farmhouses in which she and her husband had been invited for suppers, baby showers, and graduation parties. She was glad for the great wide flatness of the North Dakota landscape; it gave her room to think and gave perspective to her thoughts, and she'd park the car next to the ditch and cry and beat the steering wheel, asking God big questions: "Why Esben *and* Kjel? How am I supposed to deal with both of them the way they are? How am I supposed to help them?"

Answers were whispered so quietly that she wasn't sure she heard them; driving home she might look at the bristly fields of harvested wheat, thinking how they would be blanketed in snow in a few months, and in a few months after that, freshly tilled and ready for planting. It was the most fundamental, most obvious example of every season having its purpose.

So now You're answering me in Bible verses, Leola thought, but that was enough; enough so that she knew she could face what needed to be faced with a glad heart. Or if not glad, at least open, and an open heart was a gift that in all of this she hadn't expected.

Chapter Twenty-two

LOOK, I'VE GOT PICTURES. BEFORE AND AFTERS. ONE OF THE *Clamshells* took this one, at a gas station somewhere in Illinois. Oh, you don't have to tell me he's handsome; my gosh, the sun rose and set on that face. And look at his body, look at those beautiful shoulders and his shapely forearms! Forget Speedo swimsuits—all a man needs to do is roll up his sleeves to get my attention.

Yes, I look happy; wouldn't you be if a man like that had his arm around you. What? Striking? Me? Actually, it's not the first time I've heard that, but I'm fully aware that you can be homely and striking at the same time. Yup, that's Austin; I think his smile is the biggest of all of ours. Like he often said, he was just happy to be here.

This is an after picture.

That's Kjel on the chair. Lawrence Zeller and Austin had carried him into the living room. Can you believe the difference—I mean here he is, the picture of health, literally, and here he is, frail and thin. I can barely stand to look at it, but this was Kjel too. This was my brave and beautiful Kjel, heir to Thor and Odin, busy wrestling lightning, tempering tornadoes, and calming the warring factions of the underworld from the chair in his parents' living room.

You've probably figured out by now what's been so hard for me to say: Kjel, great dancer, mover, shaker, hopper, jumper, was paralyzed. The bullet from the gun of that stupid drunken fool in the overalls hurtled into the center of Kjel's back, right above the tailbone, stopping forever any movement from his waist down. Stopped forever the world as we knew it.

We all held out hope that the doctors were wrong, that his immobility was only a temporary condition; nobody moved like Kjel and therefore he'd heal differently—his uniqueness would now manifest itself into curing what ignorant doctors said couldn't be cured. But even the miracle that was Kjel couldn't figure out how to reknit his spinal column; Kjel had taken a big fall, and all the king's horses and all the king's men, couldn't put him back together again.

He howled in anger when the doctor told him there was no chance he'd ever walk again; the small halls of the hospital echoed with his animal cries until sedatives were ordered.

"Violet, is it true?" he asked me, and when I nodded, nearly blind from the tears flooding my eyes, he said, "Then do me a favor, will you? Get a gun and shoot me."

I stood by his hospital bed, blubbering, and he looked at me the way many had, but never him: with disdain, and the hurt I felt from that look was almost physical.

"If you can't do it, tell Austin to," he said. "Or Elwin. I mean it."

He was in a terrible, dark mood, barely speaking to any of us, and when he did it was only to ask if we'd brought the gun to kill him with— but when we got to Pearl and he saw how bad Esben was, the blackness disappeared—or was pushed aside—and the old Kjel began to emerge.

"He doesn't want to worry his dad," said Austin one day out in the barn. He liked to help with the farm chores, including feeding Kjel's old horse, and loved the simplicity of filling buckets with grain and water, loved the gratitude of the old horse who, after being curried, would push his head against Austin's shoulder, an equine pat on the back.

"But when his dad goes," said Elwin, who made himself useful by acting as the family's chauffeur, driving to town for food and supplies, "he'll probably be twice as mad—still mad about himself and then mad about his dad dying."

Austin stroked old Mo's velvety nose. "Maybe. At least he's laugh-

ing a little bit now. I was worried I might not hear that sound again." He turned his head to hide the tears in his eyes.

Elwin left to run an errand for Mrs. Hedstrom and I sat on the hay bale, watching the dust motes drift in the streams of light that pushed through the cracks in the barn walls.

We were all hit hard by what happened to Kjel, but Austin carried—literally—burdens we didn't. He was the one called upon to lift and carry Kjel, and therefore understood the depth of his injuries; he could feel the frailty, the finality, the dead hollowness of bones and muscles that didn't work anymore. The remorse he carried was immeasurable; grief is heavy but there's nothing harder to carry than guilt, and Austin was loaded down with it.

"Why'd Dallas have to hook up with those hooligans?" he asked, turning away from the horse and toward me. It was a question I'd heard before, and the only answer I had was to shake my head.

"I wish it had been Dallas. Honest to God, Violet, he's my own brother, but I wish it had been him." There was a franticness in Austin's eyes, as if his own words were scaring him. "And if the bullet had struck Dallas, I wouldn't have wanted it to paralyze him because I would have had to take care of him and I'm sick of taking care of him! If the bullet had struck Dallas, I wish it would have killed him!"

His cry was like an animal's who'd just stepped in a steel trap.

"I wish my own brother was dead and I wish . . . I wish Kjel was up and moving and playing his guitar because we could have gotten someone to replace Dallas—I know it would have been hard but Dallas is replaceable, whereas Kjel is not—and then the Pearltones would have gone on and we would have made music and records and—" He gasped for air and the intake of oxygen acted like a blow across the face, and when he staggered, I stood up and caught him.

"I can't bear it," he said, sobbing, choking the words out. "He's the best man I've ever known."

"I know, I know," I said, stroking his head, his back, whispering softly. "He's the best man any of us has ever known."

We were pressed against each other so tight that I wasn't sure if I felt his heart beating or my own, and the tears on his cheek were mixed with the tears on mine and we held each other and stroked each other's hair and *rubbed each other's backs and I can't tell you when the comforting, the stroking and the patting, rose to a higher level, but it did. Austin kissed a tear off my face, and as my grief began to change into something else, I remembered sitting in that walnut tree with Kjel and the shifting kaleidoscope of my emotions—*

"No!" I said, wrenching myself out of Austin's arms. "No, I'm not going to do this again! No one kisses Violet Mathers out of pity!"

As I raced out of the barn, Mo snorted in her stall as if offended by my behavior; I can only imagine what Austin thought.

During Berit's first visit home to see Kjel, ingratiating herself to Violet had been the last thing on her mind, her first words spoken to her being, "How long are you going to stay here?"

As an inferno of a flush blazed through her, Violet could only manage a mumbled "I don't know." She felt her old insecurity rise up and she hated Berit for its return, hated Berit for making her remember what it used to feel like to be herself.

She's not Marjorie Melby, Violet reminded herself, *and I am not the lice-infested kid I used to be.*

"I'll be here as long as your mother wants me to be here," Violet said, gathering up the shards of her new, confident self and pasting them back together, "as long as Kjel needs me."

Berit's laugh was bitter. " 'As long as Kjel needs me'?" she mocked. "When did Kjel *ever* need you?"

Leola had come through the kitchen door then, and seeing the faces of her daughter and Violet, she knew she had walked into something unpleasant. Worse, she knew that Berit was its cause.

"Berit, dear, sit with your father awhile, will you? I need to get supper started."

Spots of color had risen on the blond woman's high cheekbones; she knew she was being excused and she didn't like it.

"Why don't I help you out here?"

Leola took a pan out of the cupboard. "That's okay, honey, I'd rather you sit with your dad. He'd love the company."

After she huffed out of the kitchen, Leola wrapped her arm around Violet.

"Some people are good in calamity and others aren't," she said. "Berit unfortunately is in the latter category . . . unlike you."

"Unlike me?" said Violet, surprised. "You think I'm good in calamity?"

Chuckling, Leola squeezed the thin young woman. "Good in calamity? Violet, you're a rock. I don't know what I'd do without you here."

"Really?" said Violet.

"Absolutely. Anyway, I hope Berit didn't say anything to hurt your feelings; all of this—her dad, her brother—it's a little hard for her to take it all in."

Violet nodded, feeling ashamed of how harshly she'd judged Berit; of course Berit must be hurting in ways she couldn't even fathom. She vowed then and there to be as kind as possible to Kjel's sister, whether or not Berit cared to reciprocate the kindness.

It didn't take her long to see that Berit's bad behavior wasn't a response to life's punches, but an inherent personality trait. Austin might as well have been the Invisible Man as far as Berit was concerned; she never looked at him, let alone made eye contact with him, and if he should be so uppity as to speak to her, she would respond with a curt answer, before rushing out of the room as if pushed by a strong foul wind.

A week before he died, Pastor Hedstrom illuminated the differences between his children to Violet, who, hearing him moan late in the night, had come to sit with him.

"It's all right," she said, taking his dry papery hand as she sat in the bedside chair. "I'm here."

"Leola?"

"No, Pastor Hedstrom, she's asleep." Normally, Leola heard and responded to every whimper, every sigh of her husband's, but tonight she snored softly in the chair on the other side of the bed. "It's Violet."

"Violet," said Esben as if greeting one of his own beloved children, and the young woman felt her throat swell. "Violet, you always were my favorite."

Violet drew in a short quick gasp.

"Yes," he said, his voice a whisper. "I don't think there's a flower in the world as cheerful as a violet. It's small and spunky and who would have thought purple and yellow and white would be such a dazzling color combination?" He took a deep breath and it had a trailing, raspy echo.

"Can I get you anything?" Violet asked. More than his pallor, more than his emaciation and more than his smell, it was the vagaries of his breathing that scared Violet the most.

The minister's head quivered no, and after a moment his breath steadied enough so that he could speak.

"It's sort of relaxing now that Berit's gone, isn't it?"

Esben didn't see Violet's eyes widen but he sensed her surprised reaction and chuckled.

"God knows I love my children, but even one's own children can drive a person crazy. Probably one's own children can drive a person the *craziest.*"

He tried to push himself up into a sitting position to better converse with Violet but he could no more manage that than he could have hoisted Isalee the adagio dancer over his head.

Violet reached underneath his arms and gave him a little boost upward, shocked at the lightness of his frame and how close his bones were to the surface of his skin. He smiled at her as she tucked a pillow under his head.

"Thank you for not yelling at me for trying to do too much," he said. "Berit would have yelled at me."

Violet patted his arm, not knowing what to say.

"Berit's trouble is she's used to perfection. She's a beautiful girl, isn't she, Violet?"

"She certainly is, Pastor Hedstrom."

"The trouble is, when a person's blessed with beauty, sometimes they forget it's a blessing and instead think it's a privilege, and unfortunately I think Berit has come to expect the same privilege across the board."

Leola made a snuffling sound as she turned her head to the other side. Esben looked at his wife, and in his recessed eyes there remained an undeniable twinkle.

"Of course, look at the kids' mother and you can see where they got their good looks. Isn't she the loveliest thing you've ever laid eyes on?"

The pastor didn't let her respond. "Well, now I guess that's a silly question—I'll bet Kjel's the loveliest thing you've ever seen."

"I can't say as I'd disagree with you, Pastor Hedstrom," said Violet, feeling no need to deny the truth.

Esben's gasp was followed by a gurgling sound, and Violet realized he was crying. So did Leola, who woke up.

"Esben, what's the matter, darling?" she asked, rousing herself.

He waved his hand feebly.

"He was . . . we were talking about Kjel," said Violet.

Leola nodded, stroking her husband's hand. "It is something to cry about."

"Did you know, Violet," he said after he had gathered himself, "that he used to wake up every morning and say, 'Oh my stars'?"

"He still does," said Violet, thinking that at least he had before the shooting.

"Can you imagine having a son who greets the morning like that? Can you imagine the blessing?"

"I imagine that blessing is huge," said Violet, her voice wavering. "I imagine so many blessings from Kjel are huge."

Esben smiled at Leola. "She knows our son," and the girl who for most of her life had no reason to believe in God said, "and *that* has been a blessing."

Chapter Twenty-three

WERE YOU CLOSE TO YOUR DAD? DID HE HOLD YOU WHEN YOU *needed holding and give you a little boost when your reach wasn't long enough? Did he laugh at your jokes and listen seriously, his brow furrowed, when you thought you had something important to say?*

Can you imagine how sane we'd be if we had fathers like that?

A few days before he died, I'd been reading to Esben when Austin brought Kjel in, and after Kjel struggled onto the bed, the pastor took his son's hand in his.

"Sing me one of your songs. A Pearltones' song."

Kjel looked as if the air had been punched out of him, but after a moment he began singing, "You're My Gem," and after another moment Austin took the harmony and the bees in my ears whined and for once I was grateful for their presence, for making it a little harder to hear. Pastor Hedstrom was pleased; he sat back against the pillows, a smile crawling over the sunken planes of his face; but me, I had to force myself not to run out of the room screaming. To hear that song sung a cappella, without the guitars and the harmonica and the stand-up bass, was hard enough; what was worse was remembering how Kjel used to move while singing it, how he'd shimmy his shoulders and shake one leg as if it was wet, and how the girls in the audience would cry and stretch out their arms, pleading with him to come closer, closer; remembering that look of glee on his face when Dallas would speed up the chorus, forcing Kjel to move faster and faster until it seemed the stage was a bed of hot coals his feet could barely stand to touch.

Perched against the pillows, Kjel finished the song, and for a long time it was quiet in that sickroom, until Esben moved his head to better look at his son.

"No," he said, his voice faint, "you're my gem."

Pastor Hedstrom died a week before Thanksgiving, and at his funeral Nils gave the eulogy and Berit read from Psalms and when the presiding minister asked if anyone wanted to say a few words, Kjel said quietly, "Thank you."

By the time the weather turned cold and the deep North Dakota winter set in, most of the Clamshells had left. Palmer was going to give the insurance business and his wife one last chance, and Gwen was going back to her parents' farm.

"Winter's the best time to go back," she told Violet at the train station, tying her scarf. "There's no fieldwork."

Only Birdie Howe and Alice O'Neill remained, and Alice was planning to leave at Christmas, when she would introduce her family to her new fiancé, Elwin Sather.

When Elwin had shared the news earlier with him, Austin said, "So you're not going to hold out for the adagio dancer?"

Elwin sputtered a laugh. "Well, I figure if Alice can settle for me instead of Kjel, I can settle for her instead of Isalee."

"I don't think either of you are settling."

"Thanks, Austin. I guess I don't either—at least not in my case. It was nice to have a dream girl, but it's nicer to have a real one."

When the couple announced the news to everyone, Kjel was the first to offer his congratulations. "Let's get out the champagne!"

Leola *tsked*. "Kjel, we don't have any champagne."

"Well, let's put it on the grocery list." He smiled at Alice. "Do I get to kiss the bride?"

Without answering, Alice bent down to receive her kiss, and when she stood up, she was flush-faced and teary-eyed.

"Aw, look what you did to her," said Elwin. "She never looks like that after I kiss her."

Alice swatted his arm as her blush moved into a deeper color spectrum.

"Where are you going to live?" asked Leola, who was knitting a blanket for the baby Berit had announced was coming that spring.

"Well," said Alice, "we were thinking of going to Chicago—my folks live near there—but I was talking to Prudence at the café and she told me the junior-high English teacher was moving to Minneapolis and so I talked to the principal and—"

"And they hired her!" said Elwin. "And I'm pretty sure I've got a job lined up at the grain elevator after the new year and so it looks like we'll be staying in Pearl for a while!"

This was all news to Violet—good news. The thought of any more separation from anyone affiliated with the Pearltones was one she did not like to consider. Apparently Kjel felt the same way.

"That's the best news I've heard in a long time," he said. "And deserving of a party."

"Yes, a party," said Leola. "We could all use a party."

"An engagement/staying-in-Pearl/Christmas party," suggested Violet.

"*Definitely* a Christmas party," said Kjel, "so the rest of us can get some presents."

Dark came early to those winter afternoons, painting long blue shadows across the fields of snow and drawing its nightshade over the sky before the clock read four.

Leola combated the gloomy weather by making a pot of hot chocolate that she'd serve every afternoon in the parlor, while Violet read aloud. Austin would light a fire, and for the hour that Violet read, everyone's problems were pushed aside so they might concentrate on those of the fictional characters.

———

"Was it this dark this early last winter?" Violet asked one afternoon. She had been reading *Wuthering Heights* aloud and the light was getting so dim she could barely see the page.

"Why, Cathy, it's always dark on these moors," said Austin in his high British accent. "Isn't it Lytton?" he asked, turning toward Kjel.

"Lytton?" said Kjel with a scoff. "I'm Heathcliffe." He looked out the window at the gathering darkness. "We're a lot farther north than we were last year, Violet, but I remember it getting dark." He closed his eyes. "Remember when we were at those sisters' house? Dottie and Jeannie or something or other?"

"Dottie and Ginny," said Violet, nodding.

"We left in the late afternoon to get to the show and I remember it was pretty dark then." He paused for a moment. "Remember that night's show, Austin? You dropped your harmonica and when you picked it up you shook it and played it like you were mad at it." He paused again, for a longer moment. "Man, that was a good show."

"They all were," said Austin.

Kjel sighed then, a sound that always froze Violet's heart for a moment because she could hear the sadness in it; a well of sadness so deep that if you dropped a stone in it, you wouldn't even hear it hit the water.

"Why don't I finish this chapter," she suggested, "and when I'm done, let's talk about what we're going to get Elwin and Alice."

❋

THE PARTY PLANNING brought a cheer into the house, a cheer everyone leaped into as enthusiastically as those on a sinking ship jump into lifeboats.

The kitchen was fragrant with the smells of mince pies and cookies—gingerbread and shortbread and the toffee bars that were Kjel's favorites—and the parlor and hallways added the Christmassy aroma of pine from the big spruce tree Austin and Elwin had chopped down ("You wouldn't believe how far we had to travel to find this tree!" said Austin), and the boughs placed above the doorways and on the fireplace mantel.

It was the kind of Christmas Violet always dreamed about, her sewing machine furiously humming as she made robes for everyone—matching ones for the bridal couple, terry cloth for Leola and Austin, and a fine lined smoking jacket for Kjel, who had more use for a robe than anyone.

Keeping busy was the antidote for keeping, if not happy, then at least off the precipice of grief.

When the big evening arrived, Violet's hair fanned out with static electricity when she brushed it and little shocks pricked at her fingers when she touched most surfaces. She had heard of air crackling with electricity but had never seen such an obvious display, and it tickled her that excitement and hope could agitate the very components of the atmosphere.

Elwin and Alice shared the sofa, and at their feet sat a pile of opened presents. Birdie had given them a set of china with place settings for four; Leola had given them a hand-embroidered tablecloth; and Austin and Kjel gave them a signed and framed copy of the photograph of the Pearltones they had taken in Memphis.

"Violet said you'd probably like a mixer more," said Kjel.

"I did not!"

Elwin's mouth moved back and forth as he looked at the picture for a long time, and when he said "Thanks," his voice had a little crick in it.

"Actually, we have ordered you a mixer as well," said Austin. "We ordered it through the Sears catalog."

When Alice opened the "his" and "hers" robes Violet made them, she gushed, "Oh, they're beautiful! Look, Elwin, she monogrammed them and everything!"

"Those are nice," said Kjel with a whistle as they were passed around the small circle. "Violet, you really ought to figure out a way to market what you sew."

"I would imagine the clamor for your designs would be exceptionally loud," added Austin.

"I know I'd pay good money for a dress out of the Fashions by Violetta collection," said Leola.

"All right," said Violet, not liking the attention paid to her, "whose turn is it for a present?"

"I'd say it's yours," said Birdie, handing her an envelope. "Here. Open this one from me."

Violet fumbled opening the envelope, but no one offered to help her; only sat watching her, expectant looks on their faces.

She read the slip of paper out loud, not understanding what the words meant. "One Year Lease on the Property Formerly Known as Rawlson's Appliance."

"Oh yes," said Leola, "I knew they'd be selling that store after Harold Rawlson's heart attack."

"That's why we had to order the mixer from Sears," said Austin.

Violet's teeth scraped the middle of her upper lip. She didn't like when everyone was in on a joke except her.

"Oh, come on," said Kjel finally. "Somebody tell Violet what that's all about."

Birdie was squirming in her seat, clearly waiting for the assignment. She folded her hands in front of her and leaned forward like someone ready to do business.

"Violet," she said, and when the grin she tried to rein in broke lose, she took another moment to compose herself. Giving her head a little toss, she began again. "Violet. What you're holding in your hand is a lease to what is to become Fashions by Violetta. The offices and the design studio."

Violet knew there had been liquor in the eggnog, but she didn't think she had imbibed enough to feel as drunk as she felt now.

"What?"

Everyone laughed as if she had just delivered a punch line.

"It's your Christmas present, Violet. A chance to do what you always wanted to do—design clothes."

Violet bit the center of her lip—hard—and stood up.

"Excuse me," she said, and left the room.

Austin found her in the kitchen, sobbing into a dish towel.

"Violet," he said after sitting down across the table from her. He laughed, a low and soft laugh that made her cry harder.

"I'm sorry," he said, but his sincerity was questionable after another burble of laughter escaped from him.

"Violet," he said, "we thought you'd be so happy. What's wrong?"

She looked up at him, her face pinstriped with tears. "It's not a joke?"

"No, Violet, it's not a joke. It's a vote of confidence, is what it is. Birdie Howe feels you've got the talent to make something of yourself, and you know Birdie Howe—she's got the money to back up someone she believes in."

He had taken her hand in both of his—a bold move, as since that day in the barn, Austin had assumed his touch was nothing Violet wanted—and rubbed it as if trying to better its circulation. Violet ignored the little shimmer she felt when his hand squeezed hers, ignored it to the point of convincing herself she felt nothing, only the comfort of a friend consoling her.

"It's too big a present," said Violet. "What if I made a bunch of clothes and nobody wanted to buy them? What if Birdie lost all her money?"

Austin shook his head. "Even if Birdie lost every single penny she's putting into this little venture, it wouldn't put a dent in the huge money machine that she drives; secondly, people love your clothes—anytime you wear one of your skirts or blouses, twenty people ask, 'Where'd you get that?'—and thirdly, the big present isn't the store lease, it's Birdie's confidence in you. It seems to me the really big present would be giving yourself a little bit of the confidence all of us have in you."

Humbled, Violet bowed her head.

"That's the word of the day, Violet: 'confidence.' And 'gratitude.' "

"If you're going to give me a word of the day," mumbled Violet, "give me a *word*. Not two."

"Oh no? Here are two more: shut up." He stood, pulling her

up by her hand. "Now come on, just tell Birdie thank you and let us get on with the rest of the presents, okay? I'm dying to see what Leola got me."

✹

IT HAD BEEN PAINFUL for Violet to watch Kjel's reaction to his presents; although he smiled and commented on the quality of the item sewn or knit, his presents had been ones a person gives to a bedridden old man; things to cover his body: Violet's robe, a sweater his mother had knit, a piece-quilt Alice had bought at the dry-goods store. Austin was the only one who thought to forego practicality and get something Kjel the *person* would like.

"A bugle," said Kjel.

"I just thought you might get a kick out of learning another instrument," said Austin with a shrug. He was embarrassed, unable to tell from Kjel's voice—half exclamation, half question—whether he liked it or not. "It was either a bugle or skis."

One tense moment passed as his joke settled on the others, and when Kjel laughed, everyone else felt they'd been given permission to.

"Well, I would have preferred the skis," he said, lifting the bugle out of its case. "But you've always been a man of practicality." To the applause of his mother and friends, he blew one long, loud note.

"Thank you," said Kjel. "It's a great present." He looked out of the window. "But you know what I'd really like?"

Everyone in the room asked the same question. "What?"

Kjel's smile was sly. "To go sledding."

✹

THE HIGHEST HILL IN PEARL was behind the school building; it was a hill that would have made those from more voluptuous landscapes laugh, but it had an incline that gave a sledder enough speed and distance for a good ride.

Leola had wanted to protest that Kjel wasn't up to such activity, but she knew she couldn't throw a wet blanket on a man nearly drowning under them.

Instead, she supervised his clothing, reminding him to put on long underwear, and when he was dressed, Austin carried him downstairs and into the parlor.

Leola wrapped Esben's favorite scarf around his neck and told him not to do anything foolish.

"Ma, how can I do anything foolish?" he said. "I can hardly move."

He sat in the backseat of Birdie's Duesenberg, between Violet and Austin.

"This is going to be so much fun," said Birdie, backing out onto the road. "I haven't gone sledding since I was a little girl."

Elwin and Alice, having carted the toboggan and sleds in the panel truck, met them at the hill. The sky was swathed in clouds, and a bonfire built by sledders who were leaving, burned at the top.

"All right," said Elwin, after the men had set him on the toboggan. "Who's going to ride with Kjel?"

"I will!" volunteered Violet, her heart thumping.

"I was thinking it should be either me or Austin," said Elwin. "Maybe after we see how it goes, you can take a turn."

"Violet, we can both go together," said Austin. "You sit at the bottom and hold his feet and I'll sit behind him."

Austin set Kjel in the middle of the toboggan and sat down behind him, putting his arms around his chest. Violet sat down at the bottom and lifted Kjel's legs over her knees.

"Is everybody ready?" asked Elwin.

"Fire away!" said Kjel, and at a count of three, Elwin and Alice pushed the heavy wooden toboggan and sent it sailing down the hill.

Sprays of snow pelted Violet in the face and the wind screamed, and behind the noise of the bees in her head, she heard laughter.

It was Kjel's laughter and it lasted even after they reached the bottom of the hill and the toboggan slowed to a stop.

"Oh, man, that was fun!" said Kjel, and when Alice and Elwin swooshed beside them on the old Radio Flyer, he started laughing again.

The trip back up the hill hauling Kjel was arduous, but it was worth the effort just to hear Kjel's stream of laughter on the way down. They made the trip eleven times—Violet counted—until Elwin said it was time to go; he and Alice had a long drive facing them tomorrow morning and they were bushed.

Kjel was exhilarated from the speed and movement, and on the way home he relived the trips down the hill, remembering how if he shut his eyes it seemed he was moving faster. But he had to forego the sensation of greater speed, choosing instead to see the snow fly up from under the sled runners, the tassle bounce on Violet's hat, to see the sprawl of stars in the winter sky. He had always loved winter, the deep, still cold of it, its wildness manifested in blizzards and whiteout winds, loved its physical reaction to human and animal warmth—how it made their very breath visible. He couldn't wait to get out his skates, his cross-country skis . . .

His stomach felt as if it had lost its bearings, plunging in a free fall. Whenever he thought things were normal, when he pictured lacing his skates, imagining the first scrape of his blades on the ice or how he'd push off across the snow, his skis making a trail alongside the fields, his stomach was the first to remind him of what was no longer possible. His mind reeled then with the sickening truth, stunning him so completely that for a moment everything was as paralyzed as his legs.

When his breath came back, he'd remind himself of all he still had and he could almost drown out the whisper that told him what he had lost: *my legs, my legs,* could almost but not quite echo—*my legs.*

Chapter Twenty-four

HAS ANYONE EVER WRITTEN A SONG FOR YOU? PICKED OUT EACH *note, thinking,* Yes, a G here or should it be a G sharp?" *and stringing all those notes together as if tatting lace or crafting a ruby necklace? And then adding words that fit the music, that fit the person? Did you ever get a present like that?*

We were back from sledding, red-cheeked and laughing, filled with the best holiday kind of happiness, when Kjel asked us all to go into the parlor; he had one more present he wanted to give. Austin helped to settle him on the big wing chair and Elwin handed him his guitar and after strumming a few chords, Kjel looked at me and smiled.

> *"When the night is lonely and it seems the dark will stay,*
> *When Life doesn't love you and pushes you away,*
> *When despite how hard I try, I still can't see the sun,*
> *In comes my Violet, who helps to get the hurting done."*

I searched Kjel's face for the joke that had to be there—he couldn't be serious singing those words about me!—but there was no mockery in his beautiful face, and before I could stop myself, I was crying like a baby whose lollipop had just been snatched away.

"Violet!" said Kjel, with a little laughter in his voice. "I know the rhyme scheme needs work but I can change it."

"Oh, Kjel!" I said, leaping onto his lap, and if his legs had feeling, they would have felt crushed. He set his guitar on the floor so it wouldn't get crushed and I wrapped my arms around his neck like a lasso and cried until I hiccuped.

To soothe me, he began singing the Violet song again, this time slower and softer, like a lullaby, and Austin hummed a harmony and Elwin tapped a beat on the piano bench, and in my ragged inhales I smelled the pine boughs and the hot cider Leola had served and I thought to myself, So this is Christmas.

"I love it," said Myrva Peasley, pirouetting in front of the mirror. "What do you think, Ralph?"

"It's real nice, honey," said her husband, whose discomfort in being in a ladies' dress shop was tempered by the fact that his wife did indeed look nice. Myrva had kept her figure even after four sons (the last one eleven pounds at birth!), and the dress she had tried on accentuated her trim waist and still fairly round bottom.

"Would you like to wear it home or shall I box it up?" asked Jean Copenhaver, who, with the blessings of her father, had left the bar at Ivar's Place and come to Pearl to help run VIM.

"Oh, I can't take this off," said Myrva, swishing the skirt in her hands like a flamenco dancer. "Ralph's going to take me out for lunch in it, aren't you, Ralph?"

"Whatever you say, dear."

Violet's store had been open for two months and already she had more orders than she could fill. There were three machines in the back room, and Birdie said she was going to buy another, and a young woman and a church friend of Leola's—both of whom could sew seams like nobody's business—had been hired to help Violet, president and namesake of VIM.

Birdie thought long and hard about the business's name. "I

know you're partial to Fashions by Violetta," she said, "but it sounds a little . . . well, it's a name a young girl would think of. We need something that projects sophistication and modernity." Birdie looked around at the shop, which had been, at Jean's suggestion (who knew Jean had a flair for decorating?!) painted a cream color on two walls and a deep violet on the others. "Violet Wear . . . Mode by Mathers, VM Fashions . . . what's your middle name, Violet?"

"Idell. After my mother's mother, I'm told, although they never did get along."

Birdie gave a quick nod. "Well, that's it, then, your initials. VIM Fashions. It's short, it's snappy, it's punchy, and it's kind of like V.I.P."

"V-I-M," said Violet, sounding out the letters the way Birdie had. "I like it."

"I'll call a sign painter and then the printer for some cards." Birdie believed there was no time like the present.

Violet worked half the time at the store—she loved the bustle of women busy at work, consulting with customers; talking to Elise Jacobsen about "the dress I've always wanted," or to Thelma Schmitz, the first woman from Pearl to have ever gone to law school, who wanted a suit that "slims and yet says I mean business." More than anything, of course, she loved that she was doing what she had wanted to do all her life—and loved that she was getting paid for it!

"I expected the first couple months to be bumpy," said Birdie, who had funded the whole enterprise, "but according to Mr. Maxwell, we're going to be in the black in no time at all!"

Mr. Maxwell was employed by the Howe family and often dispatched to assist and advise Birdie in whatever enterprise caught her interest. It was a job he enjoyed—Birdie had a good eye for businesses (unlike her brother Tern, who couldn't seem to hold on to a dollar if you sewed it into his pockets), and the candy company she'd backed in Chicago was producing a steady stream of Rai-lates ("Chocolate and raisins all rolled up in sweet and tasty goodness!") *and* cash, and the bookstore in Rockford, while not a huge moneymaker, was not a money pit either, and had been honored twice with the Civic Award by the city's mayor. (Some griped that "The Book Store," as Birdie simply named it, was a gathering place for leftist pinkos and that's why the mayor—a leftist pinko himself, according to these unhappy constituents—honored it so often.) Mr. Maxwell appreciated the passion Birdie brought to her businesses—her grandfather, who founded the company, had brought a similar passion toward steel; goodness knows she could choose to live the life of a dilettante, as her younger sister Chickie had.

Mr. Maxwell had been with the firm for nearly forty years and never questioned the Howes' penchant for nicknames, especially those having to do with flight, although as he told Mrs. Maxwell, "Give children a strange nickname and it's likely they'll live up to them. Tern and Chickie—they're a couple birdbrains, but Birdie—Birdie's got sense."

AS HAPPY AS SHE WAS working in the shop, Violet needed to be near Kjel more than a full-time job would have allowed her, and so she worked at home, which, thrillingly, was how she referred to the Hedstrom house. Elwin and Alice had rented a small apartment in town, and Jean was staying with Birdie at the boardinghouse; but Violet and Austin had remained, and Leola and Kjel made it plain that they never had to think of moving.

"What's that the Mexicans say?" said Leola. " '*Mi casa* is your *casa*?' Well, that's how I feel about you two; in fact I don't even like to think what I'd do without you." Violet had taken over Nils's old room as her own (Berit was apparently unfamiliar with "what the Mexicans said," telling her mother under no circumstances were any of "Kjel's strange crew allowed to take over *my* room"), and it had a nice southern exposure. She liked to draw there in the late mornings on the days she stayed home, or work on her Featherweight, which Austin had set beside the window. (Austin himself slept in Kjel's room, the better to respond to him should Kjel need anything.)

In the afternoons, Austin and Kjel might accompany her on VIM errands, or they might play Crazy Eights in the parlor, or visit in the kitchen with Leola as she baked.

"Violet, I hope you're not getting so successful that you won't have time to be our manager," said Kjel one February afternoon as they traversed the aisles of a new fabric store in Valley City. To buy Kjel a wheelchair, the congregation of Pastor Hedstrom's church had planned several fund-raising events, but the spaghetti supper brought in enough money so that the others weren't needed. Kjel, whose naturally muscular arms were now bulging from the weight-lifting exercises he performed every morning, manipulated the wheels of the chair effortlessly, and now he maneuvered through the store aisles as easily and precisely as a marching band.

Violet wondered if she should speak to the store manager about who their wholesaler was—to keep up with business, she knew she had to start buying in bulk and no longer could afford the luxury of buying a few yards off this bolt and a few yards off that one—when a tall young man approached Austin.

"Might I ask what you're doing here?" he asked, stroking what he called his goatee and his mother called "those seven hairs on your chinny chin chin."

"I beg your pardon?" asked Austin, his voice surprised, always willing to give someone the benefit of the doubt.

"We'd like you to take your business elsewhere."

"Who's we?" asked Kjel, wheeling over.

"Management," said the man.

Kjel sidled up closer to the man, forcing him to take a step back until he was pressed against a bolt of green-and-white seersucker.

"I suppose you're the manager?" said Kjel, and when the man nodded, he added a derisive, "Figures." He looked to his left and to his right, as if waiting for the right time to cross an intersection. "And why is it you'd like my friend here to take his business elsewhere?"

"We have a certain clientele here," said the man, whose dream was to someday manage a fine department store—maybe Dayton's in Minneapolis or Marshall Field's in Chicago. "And your *friend* is not a part of it."

Violet's right arm was clutching a bolt of royal-blue jersey, and her instinct, which she did not act upon, was to hurl it at the man, who she felt shouldn't be managing a dog kennel, let alone a fabric store. Kjel had the same instinct but he *did* act upon it, reaching out with both arms and pulling down one bolt of fabric after another until a small pile of jersey, garbardine, cotton, and corduroy rose before his wheelchair.

The manager, mortified, shook as if a low but steady dosage of electricity was being routed through his body.

"You will pick those up now!"

"I'll pick those up," said Kjel, backing up in his wheelchair, "when you pick up some manners, *asshole.*"

He turned the corner sharply and Violet and Austin fell in step behind him, knowing that whatever victory Kjel had claimed over the store manager, in the scope of things, it was a small one.

✸

THE CITIZENS OF PEARL had accepted the presence of the black man mainly because the Hedstrom family had.

After the bus crash, when the minister and his wife hosted both a Negro and a one-armed girl, there had been a flurry of talk among the church congregants, the majority of it unapproving.

"I don't know, Geraldine, it's just not right, our pastor opening his house up to those types of people. It just doesn't look good."

"Well, Frances, Jesus consorted with prostitutes and lepers!"

"That's different—those prostitutes and lepers weren't Negroes!"

When Pastor Hedstrom took sick, there was no question that everyone would do what they could to help, and when Kjel—the golden boy of Pearl Lutheran, as well as the entire town—came home crippled, and they were forced to interact with Violet and Austin, a shift began.

"Why, Frances, that Austin fellow not only carried my pies into the house, he said they looked like they'd take the blue ribbon at the state fair!"

"Leola says he's one of the nicest people she's ever met, and if he's all right by Leola, he's all right by me!"

Those who weren't members of the church also held Pastor Hedstrom and his family in high regard (except for Father Brady, who thought preaching the word in a town that was twenty percent Catholic to seventy-five percent Lutheran had to be a lot like purgatory). Esben and Leola were involved members of the community, helping out not only as clergy but as neighbors (it was no secret the poor Doyle family was as close to atheists as a family could be in rural North Dakota, and still every spring, Esben helped Laslo Doyle put in what few crops his puny chunk of land could hold), and were involved as citizens (Leola serving on the school board and Pearl Beautification Council for years, and Esben providing the baritone voice for Pearl's Barbershop Quartet). As a consequence, it didn't take long for the statement, "If the colored fella's all right by the Hedstrom family, he's all right by me," to be heard over and over again, until people didn't shake their heads or mutter under their breaths when they saw Austin filling a prescription at the drugstore or opening an account at First National.

And the amputee; the fact that her devotion to the care and tending of the Hedstroms matched that of Austin's was appreciated, but what made the denizens of Pearl embrace Violet was the realization that someone with a special talent had chosen their town in which to practice it.

Sheriff Flore's wife Rita, who had a reputation of being Pearl's most stylish dresser, said if a gal wanted to be chic, she didn't have to shop in Fargo anymore.

"With VIM we've got haute couture right on Main Street!"

"What's hote cot-er?" Axel Swenson asked when his wife repeated the quote to him.

"I'm not really sure," said Stella Swenson, "but if Rita Flore's glad we have it on Main Street, then so am I!"

✳

"WE'LL COME BACK to the store with signs," said Kjel angrily on their way to the truck. "We'll picket them! 'Regal Fabrics Unfairly Discriminates!' 'Regal Fabrics Employs Assholes!' "

Austin laughed. " '*Fucking* Regal Fabrics Employs *Fucking Assholes*!' If we're going to protest, we might as well *protest*."

Before they crossed the street, he held on to the wheelchair handles, tilting the chair up and then gently down.

"Fucking curbs," said Kjel, and then, his wheels mired in the wet snow, he added, "Fucking slush."

The sky was the same gray as the snow, and Violet didn't have to look at Kjel to see the fury in his eyes; didn't have to look at Austin to know his mouth was pressed tight, his jaw muscles flexed.

"Fucking *everything,*" she said, understanding when misery could use a little company.

✳

THAT EVENING AT DINNER, Kjel reiterated his hopes that Violet would still have time to manage the Pearltones.

"Kjel, whatever are you talking about?" Leola asked, exchanging looks with Violet as she passed the platter of pork roast.

"You don't have to look at Violet like I'm crazy," said Kjel, and Leola, caught, held up her hands.

"The thing of it is," he said, and now it was his turn to trade knowing looks with Austin, "well, the Pearltones are ready to perform again."

As the moon peered in the skylight like a big yellow eye, he and Austin had made plans, talking late into the night as Kjel lay in his boyhood bed and Austin in the cot by the closet. His bed was the most peaceful place in the world for Kjel; lying down, his fingers laced behind his head, looking out at the sky, he was reminded of his father, and even let himself think that now, along with the stars and the moon, his pa was looking down on him too.

Austin aided and abetted his hope, another reason—among the many—that Kjel loved him.

"You feel more like my brother than Nils ever did," he said late one night after a particularly successful songwriting session.

Austin turned on his side, resting his head on his open palm.

"From what I saw, you and Nils seemed to get along pretty well."

The window above Kjel offered a picture of swirling snow.

"We get along all right, but I can't say I *know* him. I mean the guy wanted to get into banking ever since he was little."

Austin chuckled. "When you started playing guitar, didn't he want to play too?"

"Nah. Interested in sports, interested in his grades, but never interested in music."

"Man, Dallas and I would get into fistfights over whose turn it was to sit at the piano. And when we started playing guitar . . . we were like two scientists awed by the same discovery."

"I would have loved that. Loved sharing something like that with Nils."

"It was . . . *sensational*. I never loved Dallas more than when I was playing music with him." The heavy feeling that always accompanied thoughts of his brother settled in Austin's chest. "The hard part was when we weren't playing music."

"How so?"

"Oh, come on—you know Dallas. He's always been hot-headed and looking for something that's going to get someone in trouble. We had a big thing in common—our music—but not a lot else."

Kjel sighed. "Nils would never carry me around like you do.

Well, he would, out of obligation, but he'd make sure I knew what a burden I was."

"Hey, wherever you need to be carried, I'll carry you. I know you'd do the same for me."

"I'd at least give you a ride in my chair."

Austin smiled in the dark. "Thanks, man."

"Don't mention it."

★

AFTER THE DISHES WERE DONE, Violet, Leola, and Alice, who'd arrived with Elwin and a pan of fudge for dessert, were invited into the parlor.

They sat on the big sofa facing the three men: Kjel in his chair in the middle, Elwin to his left, and Austin to his left.

"Ladies," said Austin, "we'd like to welcome you to the first performance by the newly reconstituted Pearltones." He smiled at the audience of three, and then to his bandmates, he nodded and said, "And a one, two, one, two, three, four."

The sounds of two guitars and a stand-up bass played by Elwin with more energy than proficiency filled the air, and Violet strained her ears above the bees' buzz to recognize the tune. She didn't; it was brand-new, its notes bright as specks of sunshine and woven together like a lightweight cotton. It was a summer song, fresh and playful, and Violet closed her eyes, thinking, *I could be on an ocean beach listening to this, wearing a straw hat and drinking lemonade through a straw.*

It was a love song, but not a pining one; the kind of love song a pixilated groom might sing to his bride.

The audience clapped their approval, Leola adding a four-fingered whistle. "Thank you," said Kjel, leaning over his guitar in a bow. "We've always heard Pearl, North Dakota, has a good ear." Nodding toward Elwin, he asked, "So what do you think of our new bassist?"

The applause was louder, and Elwin's balding head turned pink.

———

"He's been practicing like crazy," stage-whispered Alice.

"And it shows," said Kjel. He cleared his throat and smiled, and in that dazzling, welcoming, seductive smile, Violet felt the same tug deep in her belly that hundreds of women who'd seen Kjel play felt: pure and simple desire.

"Now we're gonna heat things up a little and play a new song called 'Abby.' "

A flare of jealousy ignited in her chest—wasn't there a girl named Abby who Kjel spent a few nights with? Yes, Violet remembered her, a wide-hipped thing with dyed hair and over-plucked eyebrows.

The tempo was fast and raucous, and even as Violet steamed over this Abby who was not her idea of inspiration for a song, she couldn't help but be carried away by the excitement of the two guitars and the pounding bass. She could imagine how Kjel would have danced to this song, how his shoulders and hips and legs would be working together in one long tease, but the image only made her sad and she tried to push it out of her mind.

They played seven more songs, closing with the ever-popular "You're My Gem." They were right in describing the band as "reconstituted," because they weren't the same without Dallas's guitar and harmonica; without that mocking, sullen, speedy guitar played by that mocking, sullen, fingers-flying guitarist, the Pearltones were missing its edge of danger. Kjel had provided the sex and Dallas the danger, and Violet knew that's what made the band's fans scream, even if they couldn't articulate it.

Still, any band that featured Kjel in any shape or form was a cut above what was on the top of the radio charts, and when Kjel flicked the sweat from his head and said, "Whew!" Leola, Violet, and Alice stood up to applaud.

It was a smaller audience than the Pearltones were used to, and the cries of "Bravo!" weren't the impassioned screams that young women lobbed at them like hosannas, but the band members' happiness at playing together again in front of a live audience shone on their faces like a spotlight.

"Well," said Violet, "it sounds like the Pearltones are back in business."

"That's right," said Kjel. "But this time no juke joints, no dives, no small-town bandshells."

"That's right," said Austin. "We want to start off in New York and then on to London, Paris, and Rome."

"Didn't you guys hear?" Violet asked. "There's a war going on."

Kjel shook his head. "Always worrying about details."

Chapter Twenty-five

IT WAS THRILLING TO THINK OF THE PEARLTONES BACK ON THE road; thrilling to think of making arrangements and negotiating with club owners; and most thrilling, to be in the presence of that music again. I loved VIM—who wouldn't love a childhood dream come true?—but I loved being a part of Kjel's and the Pearltones' dream, loved the idea of recapturing the magic that had been a part of our daily lives just months ago.

"We can keep VIM running," I told Birdie. "I could mail in my designs and patterns, and with you running things and Madge and Esther sewing, well, I probably wouldn't even be missed!"

"Me running things?" said Birdie with a cough. "No offense, Violet, but if the Pearltones are going back on the road, so am I!"

I didn't arrange the first gig—the Pearl High School principal did, asking if the band would mind playing for a retirement benefit for Miss Eide, the drama and debate teacher—but I did arrange for the surprise guests.

Lawrence Zeller had hired the pilot and the chartered plane that flew us back to Pearl after the shooting, and he had stayed two days, helping us settle Kjel in.

"I'd stay longer if I could," he said as I waited with him in the bus station, "but Belle DeLisle starts her recording session Friday, and if I'm not back for it—well, not everyone's as easygoing an artist as Kjel was."

His voice cracked then, and as that now constant guest—sadness— settled in between us, he took my hand.

"I still can't believe it happened," he said, and when I agreed, he said, "So how long will you stay here?"

"I . . . I don't know."

He played with the top button of his beautifully cut coat.

"Well, if Kjel ever needs anything that I might be able to help him with, will you let me know?"

I nodded.

"And if you ever need anything that I might be able to help you with, will you do the same?"

I nodded again, thanking him as I pulled my hand away.

I knew some of the Clamshells would show up, but I was flummoxed when Lawrence Zeller brought the Irish Cowboy into the teachers' lounge that served as our dressing room.

"Phinnaeus O'Reilly!" said Kjel, his face flushed with happiness and surprise. "Man, you've got better things to do than listen to a high-school concert!"

"Not if you're playing, my friend," he said, bending down to embrace Kjel in his wiry little arms.

The gym was packed, and when Miss Eide, tiny and bent with arthritis, introduced the band, I thought the bleachers would collapse from all the foot stomping.

She kissed Kjel after he rolled out onto the makeshift stage ("Hey," he said, indicating his chair, "if it's good enough for the president, it's good enough for me"), and then waving both knotted hands in the air, she cried, "He tastes as good as he looks, ladies!"

Kjel tucked his hand inside his shirt and moved it up and down to simulate a beating heart. "So does she, men!"

They had to stop their first song three times because no one could hear it through the applause. Finally, Kjel shouted something unintelligible into the microphone, and the audience, curious as to what he said, quieted.

"Thank you," he said, "We're very happy to be here—"

"We're happy you're here too, Kjel!" someone shouted.

"As you know, we've gone through some tough times—"

"We're with you all the way, Kjel!"

"—but those times are over and now it's time to have a good time!"

They ripped into "Wishin'," not stopping for the applause, which made the applause stop, once the audience realized they'd rather hear the band than themselves. When the song was over, the Pearltones nodded, accepting several moments of the wild clapping and cheering before launching into their second song, thus setting the pattern for the night.

I stood offstage with Lawrence Zeller and Phinnaeus O'Reilly, watching the band and watching the audience, my excitement a vibration in my body as strong as the one in my ears. Their reception was everything and more I could have hoped for—there was the lead singer sitting in a wheelchair, and still the men watched the band intently, like a pack of wolves watching what the leader's going to do with the deer carcass, and the female portion of the audience swayed in a collective swoon.

"They've still got it," said Phinnaeus.

"Violet," said Lawrence Zeller, "I think we're going to have to start discussions about a new recording contract."

When Kjel told the crowd there was a special visitor in the house and Phinnaeus came out onstage and joined Kjel and Austin in singing "A Miracle Like You," the clapping and stomping sounded like a stampede of a herd of elephants chasing a herd of rhinos chasing a herd of wildebeests.

Outside, it was a cold March evening, with waves of old crusted snow pushed against the school building, but inside, I saw the school janitor touching the radiator, a look of confusion on his face, as if wondering how the cool radiator could be pumping out so much heat.

After so much darkness, those in the Hedstrom farmhouse were once again living in light.

Kjel and Austin hunkered down for intensive songwriting sessions, emerging only for meals, and then offering those at the kitchen table big smiles and samples of lyrics and melodies.

Before he left Pearl, Phinnaeus O'Reilly asked shyly if he

could play on their new record, "because it would be my great honor."

"*Your* great honor," said Kjel. "*Our* great honor."

"Our *incomparable* honor," added Austin. "Our *inestimable* honor."

The components of air moved aside to make room for happiness. Hearing Kjel and Austin practice made Violet and Leola laugh and dance together, made Elwin practice extra hard on his bass with hopes of becoming a real Pearltone, made Birdie telephone the Clamshells to gleefully exclaim, "We may be back in business again!"

But light—especially such bright, intensive light—fades, although no one expected it to extinguish itself so fast, plunging them into the nadir of darkness.

❉

KJEL KNEW THAT Austin had a library card from the Pearl Library (he claimed it was one of his proudest possessions) and that he replenished his stack of books—all read—every week, but he didn't know that the current pile on Austin's bedside table was unread, collecting dust as if they were nothing but knickknacks.

He didn't know exactly why his mother was cleaning so much—Leola washed the kitchen floor every morning, and when she was done, her knees sore and red, she scrubbed the sink with bleach. The routine was repeated in the bathroom, and before bed she slathered her raw hands with Vaseline, hoping to neutralize the smell and the tight ache in her fingers. What Kjel knew was that the Vaseline wasn't working, and when she touched his face, he smelled the cologne of the washerwoman and the maid.

He did know that a buyer from a fancy women's apparel store in Minneapolis came into VIM and left her card with Birdie, asking that she have "Miss Mathers" contact her regarding the possibility of designing a line for the store. What he didn't know was that Violet received the news with so little enthusiasm that

Birdie, piqued, almost shook her, asking, "For the love of Mike, Violet, don't you know what this means?"

His ears brought news to him, but sometimes he was uncertain whether the voices he was hearing belonged to real people or were conjured up by his fevered imagination. He was assuming his imagination was fevered; everything else seemed to be: someone had lit a match to his chest, and the heat radiated throughout his entire body. He could even feel the fire in his legs, which would have thrilled him if it hadn't burned so much. He called out for ice, for cool cloths, but no one heard him, or if they did, they did not respond, which hurt his feelings, but more than that, convinced him that something was profoundly wrong.

He didn't remember when the sickness had descended upon him, hovering inside his chest like a storm front. He didn't remember when the energy began leaking out of him so that he wanted nothing but sleep, nor did he remember the first words he said to Violet, who with Austin and Leola sat around his bed like sentries: "Hello . . . good night." He didn't remember the cough so vicious that it was punctuated with spatters of blood.

He didn't remember Doc Oberg's glum diagnosis—pneumonia—although a sound—his mother's sob—had imprinted itself on his brain. He hated that memory of his mother's cry and thought his brain cruel for remembering it when he forgot so many other things.

He felt he had missed out on so much, on great chunks of moving, pulsating, bright and gorgeous life, but whether those chunks represented minutes or hours or days, he could not tell.

Just ask someone! he begged himself, but his mouth could not be bullied opened. *Look around—look at the calendar, look at the clock!* But his eyes were uncooperative and wouldn't open despite his effort. Only his nose seemed capable of doing its job, helping him to recognize the people around him. Bleach: Ma. Cigarettes and wood: Austin. (Why his friend smelled like a piece of newly sawed oak was a puzzle to him, but underneath the cigarette smoke, that was what his nose smelled.) To his left, smelling of soap and starch, smelling so *brisk,* was Violet. He smiled; *brisk* was not the way Violet smelled that long-ago morning she had pressed herself against his back as they rode old Mo back to the house. She had smelled of old clothes that needed washing and last night's rain in her hair, and Kjel remembered thinking, *She smells sad. She smells like the color of her name.*

The Violet who sat beside the bed bore no traces of sadness in her scent, and Kjel bet, more from the whiff of starch than the soap, that she was wearing the intricate blouse she had made with all the pleats, the thin white voile blouse through which he could see the scallop of her brassiere. Kjel smiled again; with its promises of sex and mystery, the shadow of a bra under a woman's blouse was one of his favorite views in the world.

Kjel smiled again. *That's what I'll do; I won't worry about this blood of mine blazing through my veins, I won't worry about the anvil some sadist put on my chest* (this particularly bothered him because he didn't know any sadist who would do something like that). *Until my eyes and ears and mouth start working again* (a picture of the see-no-evil, speak-no-evil, hear-no-evil monkeys came into his head) *I'll just float on all these nice things, these soft pillows.*

He remembered a night with a high-strung girl in Springfield—Colleen? Corrinne?—who raked her long fingernails across his neck when he told her he had to leave.

"Everyone leaves me! Everyone leaves me!" she cried, and Kjel, hustling out of her apartment, his hand cupping his wounded neck, thought, *It's not hard to see why.*

When he slunk back into the campsite, Violet awoke, and looking at him in the firelight, she asked, "Who'd you sleep with? A polecat?"

Violet. He had had a lot of fun with a lot of women, but never more fun than with her. He had laughed harder with her and been more impressed by her—she could do more with one arm and fifty cents than a two-armed person with a dollar could do—she could do more than any other woman, and yet for all that she had given him, he had not been able to give her what she wanted: himself.

"That girl would lay down in front of a moving train for

you," Dallas once told him, a sneer souring his smile. "If a pack of wild dogs was ready to jump you, she'd get between you and the first open jaw. If a lightning bolt had you in its sight, she'd push you aside and take the hit herself. If a—"

"Okay, okay," Kjel said. "I get your point."

"I like that kind of devotion in a woman," Dallas said, and then with a laugh, he added, "or I should say from the *right* kind of woman. From a woman like Violet, I 'spect it's some kind of irritation—like a fly that won't quit buzzing around your head, like the flies that buzz inside her ears."

"It's bees," Kjel had said ineffectually.

He knew the chivalrous thing would have been to wipe the smirk off Dallas's face, but how could he, hearing more than a wisp of truth in what Dallas said?

Violet, Violet, Violet. Her name bubbled in the lava that flowed through his head. When his vision came back, when he could hear and speak again, he would touch her black hair and tell her how pretty and shiny it was; he would run his hands down the sides of her neck and around the curve of her shoulders and tell her that Birdie was right in her opinion that Violet cut an elegant figure ("She's got the kind of body we low-to-the-ground women dream about"); he would take her hand and press it against his chest so she could feel his heart beat and tell her, "I love you, Violet Mathers."

I do love you, and I know that's what you want, Violet, but it's not what you need. Wise up to what you need, Violet, he's right in front of you.

It occurred to him that he was trying to put things in order. *Are these the thoughts of a dying man? Is that what's happening to me; am I dying?*

For a moment fear turned the fire inside him to ice, and the change in temperature stunned him and he cried out. As the shock of the ice waned, melted, the cool was such a blessed relief that he thought, *This is all right. If dying takes away the fire, then it's all right.*

Moments passed, or maybe hours, and the fire had returned, evaporating the ice as well as the fear that had caused it. What remained inside him, flickering inside the flames, was a curious astonishment. *Can it be that I won't see my twenty-fifth birthday? That I won't see 1940?* He loved the changing of a decade, the sense that a new age was dawning. He remembered the midnight of a new year when the youth group had gathered for a party in the church basement, stealing Delores Shumway away from the chaperones to kiss her.

"Nineteen thirty, Delores! Nineteen thirty! Has anything ever sounded so modern?"

He knew war was a part of the new decade, but surely people living in 1940—*1940!*—would figure out a way to stop it soon after it started.

If he got better, maybe he'd enlist.

No, you won't, and whoever or whatever it was that taunted him reminded him that people who couldn't move their legs didn't make effective soldiers.

Even as he thought he wouldn't want to be a soldier anyway, his sadness added even more weight to the anvil on his chest. He often forgot that he was that awful word, *paraplegic,* and that he'd never again move his legs, would never walk or run or dance or lie on top of a woman, his legs undulating with the rest of his body like a wave.

He had wanted to die, when the doors of his old life clanked shut and he discovered the prison he was in.

Once he realized his hate and outrage weren't making him any stronger, weren't turning on switches in his body that had been forever turned off, he came to believe what his father and mother, what Violet and Austin, told him.

"You've got so much to live for—why, in the tally of what you have and what you don't, the first column has so many more entries than the second!"

"How would you feel?" he asked Austin on a day when the credit side didn't seem much more substantial than the debit. "How would you feel if you had to wear *diapers?*"

"That would stink," said Austin somberly, and it wasn't until he heard Kjel's huff that he realized his pun. "Sorry."

"It does," said Kjel after a moment. "It stinks to lie in piss and shit like some fuckin' baby. Fuck." His voice broke as he repeated the word over and over. "Austin, how would you feel if you couldn't *fuck* anymore?" Under the blanket, his hand cupped his penis. "I can barely get it to do anything! I thought it was just my legs that couldn't move! I'm supposed to lie here with legs that don't work and a dick that doesn't work either? What kind of life is that?"

"Sounds a lot like mine," said Austin. "I'm serious," he went on, figuring that Kjel's snort might be something close to laughter, and a snort was better than nothing. "I have not experienced connubial relations since . . . why, my memory fails me."

"I'd rather my memory fail me than my dick," said Kjel, and Austin was heartened by the tiniest bit of cheer in his words.

"I think man would rather *anything* fail before his dick," said Austin, and Kjel nodded, his soft laughter real.

He convinced himself many times over that what he had—his music, his friends, his family—was enough, and those times when his confidence in the belief faltered, he felt guilty and small. He still whispered, "Oh my stars," but like a child reciting the Pledge of Allegiance whose words mean nothing to him, it was more out of duty than sincerity.

"I feel bad that everything I have isn't enough," he told Violet a week or two before Christmas, "but it isn't."

"Not enough for what?" asked Violet, pushing words past the tight claw of fear that gripped her throat. They were sitting in front of the fire, stringing popcorn and cranberries for the tree, and Violet had been filled with a happiness and contentment as sweet as the candy canes tied with ribbon to the pine bough above the mantel. She had assumed—or hoped—that the same happiness and contentment had settled in Kjel—hadn't he been laughing and joking with her just a moment ago? Hadn't he started singing "O Tannebaum" in a German accent thick enough to ice a pan of strudel?

"Enough to live like this," he said, his gaze falling on the bumps that were his knees, under the plaid blanket.

"Will it ever be?" Violet asked, her deep voice suddenly high and thin.

"Well, it better be," said Kjel, and when he flashed his smile, Violet felt a jolt of relief. "Because I can't hardly run away from it, can I?"

The only thing that could work in his favor—time—was working, and by the time of their concert at the school gym, Kjel had come to believe that music was going to save him.

He had closed his eyes while he sang "Waiting for You," and in that darkness, he saw himself dancing onstage, every note of music escorting each step, each move. In his mind's eye he saw himself jump when Elwin thumped a high D on his bass, saw himself bound across the stage like a kid riding a broomstick horse, saw his fancy footwork, his feet sliding and tapping and kicking, and when he opened his eyes at the song's end to see and hear the crowd burst into applause, he thought, *Maybe it is enough.*

He smelled bleach as a hand pressed against his forehead.

Ma, he thought as a tumble of gratitude and regret filled his head.

His beautiful mother who, to keep him occupied during church, let him buff her fingernails with his spit and her hanky. Ma, who'd made a raft out of sofa cushions on the parlor floor, and read *Huckleberry Finn* when he was sick with the measles. Ma, who'd warm up supper for him when he was late from basketball practice, and sit at the kitchen table, chin in her hand, smiling as she watched him devour it, smiling as if shoveling food in his mouth was an act of wonder.

Why had he eaten the Jordan almonds—her favorite—that he bought for her birthday, giving her instead a bouquet of tulips he'd yanked from Mrs. Ghizoni's garden? Why did he wave her off when he'd come home one day from school to find her listening to a waltz on the radio, when she held out her arms to him and said, "Madam requests a dance"? Why didn't he write her more when he was on the road?

How could a son ever pay back his mother for the kindnesses she heaped upon him; how could he ever thank her long enough and loud enough for that constant, shining light? Space and distance were meaningless; he knew without doubt that light was always lit, that his mother's love was like the sun or the moon, always there, his own personal sextant, showing him where home was.

Why can't I open my mouth to tell her thank you?

The unidentified sadist had come back, putting more weight on his chest, and he wished someone would push it off before his lungs were crushed.

There were more smells than usual: Berit's lily-of-the-valley perfume, the metal of Nils's cuff links, Elwin's hair tonic—why would a man with so little hair use so much tonic? He smelled ink—it must be Jean, who always had a pen clipped to her pocket; chalk dust from Alice's classroom; and powdered sugar—had Birdie been to the bakery? *Thank you, Berit, for setting me up with your cute friend Brenda! Thank you, Nils, for the marbles, especially that cat's-eye shooter! Thank you, Elwin, for your steady beat. And for your loyalty, I thank you, Clamshells!*

The fire was fading. He didn't feel he was burning up, and yet something was consuming him. Every part of his body, his aching, compressed chest, his inert and heavy legs, every muscle and every organ was strained and on alert, not knowing whether to flee or fight, or *what* to flee from, to fight.

He smelled cigarettes and wood, soap and starch.

Austin! Violet! How can I ever thank you?

The deep consciousness of each single cell and fiber finally understood, finally recognizing the power that was taking him away. Of course! Music! It wasn't a band of angels—unless angels hummed in a one-hundred-part harmony of horns and winds and strings and drums. Music filled every inch of him, pulsing through his veins instead of the flaming blood, an avalanche of sound thundering through his head and to his fingertips, his toes. The darkness he hadn't been able to open his eyes against now parted as a curtain, and the light it revealed was part of the music. The illuminated music was now a tidal wave, so bright and shimmery that as it swept him away, he yelped with pleasure.

Oh my stars!

———

Chapter Twenty-six

YEARS LATER, AUSTIN AND I SAW ELVIS PRESLEY SING AT A FAIR *outside Memphis and we both looked at each other, our jaws hanging open as if someone had taken a screwdriver to the hinges. It was as if we were watching Kjel—both he and Elvis had that same ache in their voices, that same wild joy in their moves, both had faces that made a person think the whole universe is a big juicy apple, ready to bite into. And of course, they both had their audiences screaming and swooning. Not that we were keeping score, but Austin and I reminded each other that Kjel wrote his material and that he was a better guitar player. On Mr. Presley's side, he did have a slightly sweeter voice, with that yodelly, wide range. And they both had that wonderful sense of humor about their effect on the audience; those boys knew how to* tease.

When I heard that the King had a twin brother who died at birth, I thought he also had a twin who was born twenty years before him.

So that's what the world lost. What we lost was so much more.

March ended and April began, and before anyone noticed how much the earth had changed, it was already May.

On her way to the coal bin in the washing house, Leola noticed, *My lilacs are out!*

She reached out to steady herself on a fence post, her mind reeling. *How can my lilacs be out this early?*

Too impatient to go to the shed for her shears, she picked a flock of lilacs, wrestling with the thicker stems, turning them and twisting them until they broke. She was not so much moved by their beauty as she was their *existence,* and she wanted to show the others this unprecedented premature bloom.

Her arms loaded with the frothy white-and-lavender flowers, she looked past the bushes, noticing for the first time the green velvet of new grass that had replaced the gray expanse of old snow, saw that the maple was no longer bare, but fully dressed in the latest spring attire.

Well, I'll be . . .

In the kitchen, she planted herself in front of the calendar tacked to the wall and studied it. There in big print—below a picture of lilacs, no less—was the word MAY. She turned to Austin and Violet, who sat at the table, and asked, her voice harsh with accusation, "Did you two know it was May already?"

"Uh . . . I knew," said Austin, and Violet nodded meekly, wondering why this knowledge might upset Leola so.

"I . . . I also knew it was the twenty-first," said Violet, thinking if they were confessing to the crime of knowing the date, she might as well tell all she knew.

Leola stared at them, the lilacs in her arms trembling. For a moment she thought she was going crazy again, going to that place she'd visited for so long after her baby Lena died, but a protective impulse, like a practiced security guard, stepped up and pushed aside her fear and she laughed.

Her laughter was a door opening, and both Violet and Austin went to it and the three of them laughed together, and when it was over, they bobbed for a long time on waves of sighs, savoring the aftertaste of that laughter, a succulent they had long gone without.

"Oh, my," said Leola, taking a deep breath, the lilacs damp

and drooping in her lap. Violet smiled at her expectantly, hoping she might say something else that would make them laugh all over again.

"It . . . it almost felt as if Kjel was here," she said, and as she smiled, tears flashed in her eyes and her face seemed to melt into an expression of woe, and she covered it with her hands and sobbed.

Grief felt to Violet like a big black dog; a mangy Labrador who fooled her sometimes by its good behavior, walking placidly next to her, present but quiet. Other times it yanked and strained against its leash, pulling her into shadows darker than night. During those times, she would go into her room, almost choking from her tears, her throat filled with mucus and moans.

Several days after Kjel's death, as she was racing up the stairs to her room, she bumped into Austin, who was racing down them. To Violet, his face looked like she felt, and to Austin, her face looked like he felt.

"Excuse me, I—"

"I was just—"

"Are you—"

They spoke quarter sentences until Austin blurted, "Violet, would you come and walk with me?"

She wanted to collapse on her bed and hold Jellycakes to her until the doll was as damp as a washcloth from her tears, but the need in Austin's voice was so evident that Violet simply nodded.

Turning around, she descended the staircase with Austin. They dressed in their outerwear by the back door, and when the cold March wind blew its frost in Violet's face, she thought, *Good*. That the weather was miserable too gave her some comfort; it was as if the whole world was in mourning for Kjel.

They walked along the road in silence, alongside the fields with their random stubble of crop poking through the old snow. They walked until the cold and damp seeped into Violet's boots and she said, "Maybe we should turn around."

Austin nodded, and Violet took two steps forward before realizing he had turned abruptly around.

———

"I hated the way he cracked his knuckles!" Austin said, almost shouting. "I couldn't stand that sound, but he kept cracking them anyway!"

Violet drew in her breath, fast as a hiccup.

"I hated the way he used to always help himself to whatever food was on your plate!" In her mind's eye, she could see Kjel's fork or fingers, coming after her food.

"I hated his stupid candy—not so much that he *stole* it, but that he was so cheap about sharing it," said Austin. "Bastard sure liked his candy."

"The bastard sure did."

They were both crying now, and the wind blew in their faces, trying to turn their tears to ice.

Violet was riffling through memories in her mind, remembering Kjel onstage, offstage, at a campsite or a café counter, in big cities and in the countryside, but she could not think of one more thing she hated about him. Austin was as quiet as she was, apparently having the same problem, and they walked and walked in the windy silence.

"I loved how he sat on a chair," said Violet when they were crossing the yard to the house. "I loved how he'd lean forward with his forearms resting against his knees and how his fingertips would barely touch one another."

"Oh, Violet, don't even start," said Austin sadly. "I don't have the time and energy for that list."

✳

LEOLA WAS LESS SURPRISED by June than May, and didn't gasp when she drove into town in July, thinking, *Where did that corn come from?,* and she knew by the heavy heat that pressed her down onto the couch for an afternoon nap and how quickly the wash dried on the line that it was the middle of August. When September drew its amber curtain across summer, she neither thought the time had passed too fast or too slow, only that it had passed.

To her children, who visited as often as they could (this

meant once since Kjel's death for Nils, and once a month for Berit, who was nursing a new baby as well as a resentment that Violet and Austin were still taking up space in her house), the memories of how Leola closed down after their baby sister died were still painful ones, and as long as she wasn't taking to her bed, it was their opinion that she was handling the deaths of her husband and son well. She wasn't her old self, more a muted self, but who wouldn't be?

Knowing how important it was for her children to think she was all right, Leola censored her behavior for them, writing cheerfully of the nest of owlets in the barn rafters and of the Doyle's rooster who terrorized all relief-seeking interlopers who dared enter his domain, chasing and pecking at them until they had safely slammed the outhouse door.

Except that Mrs. Doyle's sister, who was visiting from Iowa, found when she sat down that she was looking into the beady eyes of her tormenter, who had beat her into the privy!

While Berit visited, Leola slapped on smiles like a loose woman looking for business and busied herself in the kitchen—baking was a sign of sanity in her daughter's eyes—and pried her grandson out of her Berit's arms as much as possible.

The five-month-old boy was fat and blond and beautiful, drool spilling from his mouth like water from a rainspout in response to the two white pearls of teeth breaking through his bottom gum. She loved to hold him—it gave her a rare peace and contentment—and for the same reason, she hated to hold him, for it was too painful giving him back to Berit, or setting him in the cradle they had dragged down from the attic; her empty arms magnified a life full of gaping, empty spaces.

The baby was christened James Edward, and nothing Berit had ever done had hurt Leola more than failing to name the baby after Kjel. It wouldn't have had to be Kjel James, but couldn't she have at least called him James Kjel? Or James Kjel Esben?

"James is Lloyd's maternal grandfather," Berit had explained on the telephone when she called to announce the happy news of his birth, "and Edward is his paternal grandfather."

And Kjel was your brother, thought Leola, feeling a tiny piece of her heart harden against her daughter.

"He never disappointed me," Leola blurted out one night as she and Violet and Austin sat in Kjel's truck, watching a hockey game on Shaeffer's Slough. The threesome found some solace in watching people—particularly young people—at play; they attended several Pearl High football games (Go, Thrashers!) in the fall and were regular fans of both the girls' (half-court) and boys' basketball games.

Leola had filled a thermos with cocoa, and with a heavy car blanket across their laps, they were cozier than most people managed to be in minus-fourteen-degree weather.

Violet sipped her cocoa, but neither she nor Austin said anything, waiting for Leola to say whatever it was she had to say.

"He could be a naughty little boy," she said, with a two-syllable chortle, "giving his sister a *Last of the Mohicans* haircut—my land, you should have heard Berit bellow when she looked in the mirror!—and he put one of those rubber things—those whoopee cushion dealies, on Nils's chair when he brought his first girlfriend home for supper."

The idea of Nils, who could be somewhat of a gasbag anyway, sitting down only to let loose a volley of fabricated flatulence made them all laugh.

Leola sighed. "But his naughtiness was never . . . prompted by malice, understand? It was only curiosity, and how could a boy's curiosity disappoint anyone?"

Austin looked out at the skaters on the ice; mostly farm kids and a couple of adults whose energy hadn't been completely crushed by the daily grind.

"You are exactly right, Leola. He never disappointed me . . . except by dying."

Chapter Twenty-seven

NINETEEN FORTY CAME AND WENT AND THE WAR ON THE OTHER side *of the world heated up. Austin sat at the kitchen table reading aloud from the* Fargo Forum, *articles headlined,* HITLER INVADES NORWAY *("Norway!" worried Leola, "I've still got relatives in Trondheim!"),* CHURCHILL NEW PRIME MINISTER, *and* TROTSKY ASSASSINATED.

"The world's on fire," he would say, folding the paper up into a sharp-edged rectangle and slapping it on the table to punish it for its bad news.

VIM was going great guns. It still makes me catch my breath to think how women scrambled to wear something I designed. But scrambling they were; so much so that we had expanded, moving into the livery stable, re-modeling it and turning it into a regular factory, outfitting it with cutting tables and sewing machines and a real live reception area where a pretty farm girl named Lorraine answered the phone and greeted whoever came into VIM's doors. If it sounds like things moved fast, they did, but not on my account.

"There's no time like the present," Birdie liked to say, a counter to all my procrastination and uncertainty.

"What if you invest all this money and things don't work out? What if you lose everything?"

"Haven't we been over this too many times already?" said Birdie, pushing aside the frizzy fringe of her bangs. "You seem to underestimate the depths of my wealth, Violet, which is fine, but don't underestimate the depths of your talent."

So I didn't. I let her pour money into the factory and advertising and salaries, and I sat every morning in Kjel's old room, under his skylight, designing. I took the train to Minneapolis several times a year to go fabric shopping and read about myself in a story Ladies' Home Journal *did about women-owned businesses. Leola framed the article and hung it in her "Braggart's Gallery," the wall that boasted her children's school achievement awards and athletic honors.*

Seeing it hanging next to Nils's Salutarian Certificate and her own 4-H Blue Ribbons (one for her oral report on Betsy Ross, the other for knitting argyle socks), during one of her no-longer-frequent visits, I heard Berit pout, "Mama, she's not your daughter."

"Maybe not by blood," said Leola, "but I love her and I'm proud of her."

Can you see why we stayed on there?

I never happened to come upon (okay, eavesdrop on) a conversation with Leola and Berit where I heard Leola say those same things about Austin, but she didn't have to; her actions shouted out her love and respect.

And my actions, well I guess you could say they were doing some shouting themselves.

The first long walk Violet and Austin took after Kjel's death led to another walk, and that one to the next, until they were meeting every morning before breakfast to exercise their legs (and, Violet said, to exorcise their demons). Conversation was minimal by choice, and usually words exchanged had to do with the walk itself: "Are you tired?" "Shall we go farther?" "Do you want to turn back?"

One morning Violet slipped on a slick of ice and Austin reached out to her and held on to her arm. She didn't resist and they walked the two miles back to the house, his hand curled around her bicep. The next day she didn't have to slip before he took her hand, and from then on they were incapable of walking with each other without touching. Weeks passed, and as they walked hand in hand every morning, their hikes became less sad, less heavy-footed trudges across the countryside, and as their pace increased, so did their conversation; they talked so much that neither could remember the long silences that had filled their walks earlier.

They started from the beginning, sharing stories of their lives before they knew each other.

"When I learned cursive, my teacher, Miss Long, let me stay after school and practice my handwriting while she corrected papers," said Austin. "Man, I thought writing out 'cat' and 'dog' and 'jump' was something akin to magic."

"I don't know that my daddy ever learned how to read," said Violet. "He sure seemed to hate the fact that I could."

They shared their most painful or embarrassing stories from adolescence (what a deep well to draw from that was!).

"Dorthea Maxwell—to think I wasted my admiration on that snaky little girl—had the job of reading the Top Five—the names of the outstanding students during our eighth-grade graduation—and when she got to my name—this was not just in front of the whole school, but parents and grandparents—she cleared her pretty little throat and read, 'Buggy Sykes.' That was my nickname—because of my eyes, obviously—but no one's nickname was ever used during the Top Five before." Austin shook his head. "First there was a gasp, then you should have heard the laughter."

"They called me Froggy," said Violet. "Or Olive Oyl. Or Stilts. I don't know what they called me after I lost my arm, because I quit school the first day I went back after the accident."

"You quit school? I never knew that, Violet."

"There's a lot you don't know, Austin."

But as months passed and more and more stories were told, Violet couldn't say that anymore. She learned enough about Austin, and he about her, that they both could have written each other's biographies. It made her feel safe that Austin knew so much about her, and she welcomed every question of his, happy that instead of turning away, he wanted to know even more.

One cold November morning when the air was wild with snow, he asked her if she ever thought of moving to New York City to be with Lawrence Zeller.

"*Lawrence Zeller.* Why would I go to New York City to be with Lawrence Zeller?"

"It's obvious, Violet, that he's sweet on you."

Violet had to laugh. "Well, I'm not sweet on him."

"That makes me very happy."

Now that he had gotten his toe wet, Austin felt he might as well jump in, and he asked her what she had meant when she pushed him away in the barn, saying nobody was going to kiss her out of pity.

"Because for me, pity never entered the equation," he said, and after Violet told him the story of Kjel kissing her in the walnut tree, he said, "And maybe it didn't enter the equation for Kjel either."

"Oh, *please.*"

"I mean it, Violet. Kjel knew how I felt about you—"

"How you felt about me?"

Austin readjusted the muffler around his neck. "Yes, Violet. He knew I was interested in you even before I did—or at least before I was ready to admit it."

Violet's mind reeled.

"You know how Kjel could read people. As for the kissing . . . it probably ended because he didn't want to take something that I wanted so badly."

"It ended because we fell out of the tree."

"I'll tell you again Violet: however it started, however it ended, it wasn't because of pity."

In the snow then, on the road a quarter mile past the Doyle farmhouse, Austin reached for Violet and she reached back and it was easy for Austin to think that the mad and swirling snowflakes were provided for their personal benefit, as if the sky was throwing confetti, joining in the celebration.

And kisses, Austin learned standing there, his arms wrapped around the frame that even in a bulky wool coat was thin and narrow, were a celebration he intended to partake in as often as possible; no special occasion was needed for kisses, as they *were* the special occasion.

"Oh, my," said Violet finally, turning her head. "Let me catch my breath."

"I think I swallowed it," said Austin. "But I'd be happy to return it."

He blew the lightest puff of air in her mouth and sealed it in with a kiss that sent a wave of weakness through his body, weakness that settled in his knees.

"Good heavens, Violet," he said, pulling back his head, "you make me light-headed."

"It's sort of my signature."

❋

THAT THE ENERGY AND EXCITEMENT of new love could flower in the bleak landscape that life had laid out heartened Leola, and when Austin came into the room, she'd watch Violet's face change, her features out of control for a brief moment as she squirmed with pleasure. Hearing the way Austin said "Violet," Leola remembered how Esben said her name when they were courting, with a breathy wonderment, as if to say the name was to have been given a gift. Seeing Violet and Austin reach out for each other's hand at the same moment brought back happy memories of her children's first loves. How could she forget Richard Abramson, six-foot-seven at fourteen years of age, and with feet to match, when he and Berit won the honor of "Best Dancers" at the eighth-grade graduation party; or Judith Igelhart, who according to Nils "is not just pretty, Ma, but she likes math as much as me!" And Kjel! All the girls who dropped by to visit him, claiming they were "in the neighborhood" ("What neighborhood?" Leola wanted to ask them. "We live on a farm!"); all the Valentine cards he collected from girls in classes above his and below; all the love notes she found crumpled in his pants pockets when she did the wash.

Berit was not so enamored of this love, and told her mother in no uncertain terms, why.

"For Pete's sake, Mother, it was obvious to anyone with eyes how much Violet loved Kjel—it was embarrassing just to watch the way she looked at him!—and pathetic too because there was no way a guy like Kjel could ever—"

"Berit, don't speak of her like—"

"—be the slightest bit attracted to a girl like her. And now that he's gone, instead of mourning him *like a lady,* she suddenly turns to the first guy who's available, not caring that he's a *Negro,* not caring that in most states it's *illegal* for them to be a couple, not caring—"

"Berit!" she said, making her voice as sharp as a slap since she couldn't strike her (and at that moment, Leola's inability to hit her child seemed a policy borne more of weakness than of strength). "Berit Ann Hedstrom Glattie! You will not speak of Violet and Austin ever again unless it's with the love and respect they deserve! Do you understand me?" Leola was so full of anger that she shook with it. *"Do you?"*

Berit folded an antimacassar—she'd been helping her mother reorganize the linen closet—and placed it on a shelf. Without answering, she turned and walked down the hallway to her room, shutting the door behind her quietly, even though Leola knew something had irretrievably been slammed shut.

Neither Violet nor Austin had to overhear that conversation to understand that it had taken place; *civil* just barely described their relationship to Kjel's sister, whom they avoided the way a bite victim will stay clear of dogs.

"Not only will I write, I'll telephone you every night," said Austin, gathering Violet in his arms.

"Remember the party line," warned Leola. "You might not

want to whisper sweet things to Violet with eight other people rubbering in."

"I thought only you did that," said Violet, teasing Leola about her habit of quietly picking up the phone even when it wasn't their ring.

Austin was going to St. Louis for his mother's funeral.

"Oh, my real mother died long ago," he said, reassuring Leola, who was worried that Austin might break under this new blow. "It's a relief she finally let go of her body."

They drove him to Jamestown to take the train, and because they were getting more stares than they were already comfortable with, they didn't do what they wanted to do, which was to embrace, to kiss good-bye.

They were bold enough to shake hands, and it was a long, unmoving handshake that not even the huffy "Well, I never!" issued by a woman in a tweed suit could make them drop.

"I've got a word of the day for you," said Austin, moving his long fingers against Violet's palm. "But it'll have to last you the entire time I'm gone."

"What is it?" asked Violet, batting her long black eyelashes, enjoying her coquettishness.

"It's 'I'll miss you.' "

Violet laughed. "Once again, you've overshot your mark."

"Brevity's the soul of wit," said Austin as the porter called out to board the train. "But it's not the soul of the word of the day."

"And I'd have to say, neither is logic."

They stared into each other's eyes for a long moment, wishing they could do more, and then Austin turned and, getting on the train, the porter greeted him, letting Austin know with a drawn-out, "Good morning, sirrrrrr," just what he thought of brothers cavorting with white women.

Austin tried to be soothed by the gentle rumble of the train but he was anxious and out of sorts, knowing that his dead mother was waiting for him in St. Louis, as well as his live brother. He had spoken to Dallas only once since that terrible night and that had been two days earlier, when he and Odessa telephoned him with news of Eula's passing. It was news he'd been expecting; what he hadn't been expecting was hearing his brother's voice.

Dallas had offered his condolences concerning Kjel.

"Dessa told me about Kjel. Man, that's tough."

"Tough?" Austin couldn't contain his fury. "No, this was tough: you bringing those drunken fools into our camp, you running away, you stealing our money, you being the sorriest, lowest brother—"

"Hey, man, this is long distance. Save your insults for when you see me."

✸

AUSTIN WASN'T HUNGRY, but needing a distraction from his thoughts, he opened the lunch bucket Violet and Leola had packed for him. There wasn't enough food to feed an army, but possibly enough to feed a regiment.

And two pieces of rhubarb pie.

Leola knew Austin loved her rhubarb pie, just as Kjel had, and looking at the slices wrapped in wax paper, he thought of his own mother in the kitchen, proudly presenting him with her "famous" orange chiffon cake or sweet potato pie.

"The secret's in the sugar," she'd say, kissing his cheek, "lots and lots of sugar!"

He'd act appalled, fighting her off, but in truth having his mother's arms around him, her kisses stamped all over his face, made him feel as if he were a prince and that everyone in the kingdom was raising their glasses, their swords, to salute him.

Well, it's a good thing she's dead, he thought, *because she wouldn't make me feel like a prince anymore.*

"Less you have to do with the white world, the better," Eula Sykes counseled her children. "They ask you a question, you'd better answer, but don't get into no conversation with them. They always figure out a way to bite you."

His mother thought black men who consorted with white women were to be pitied; "men not man enough to know what a real woman's all about." When her husband Mokey told her about which musicians brought their white girlfriends to the club, Eula would clamp her mouth shut and shake her head.

"Oh, I used to like him, but not anymore. Now I wouldn't use his music to wipe up my kitchen floor."

He had absorbed her lessons well and never ever would have imagined himself with a white woman, but then Violet, well, who cared about color when you met someone like her?

I don't need her to feel better about myself as a colored man, or even as a man, Mama; I need her to feel better about everything.

In his mind, Austin could hear his brother's taunting voice: "A man doesn't need any woman to make him feel better about *anything*. Especially a woman like Violet."

In his mind, Austin slugged his brother full in the mouth, and then because it felt so good, doubled up his fist and slugged him again.

Chapter Twenty-eight

ONCE WHEN WE WERE CLOSING THE SHOP, BIRDIE ASKED ME IF *Kjel had lived, would I have ever fallen for Austin? Austin had asked me this himself, and I gave Birdie the answer I'd given him.*

"I don't know," I said, my eyes focused on the store window and reading backward the words that still sent a thrill through me: VIM, FINE WOMEN'S APPAREL.

"Loving him would have been enough for now, but who knows how long I could have been satisfied with not being loved back?"

Birdie nodded. "I think that's how all of us felt—we loved him more than anything but knew that the likelihood of becoming 'Mrs. Kjel Hedstrom' was pretty remote."

"You loved him? I thought it was the music, the movement, that the Clamshells loved."

Birdie's eyes teared up but she sniffed quickly, a signal that she was not going to put up with what she called "any of this crying nonsense."

"It was all those things . . . but come on, Violet—who didn't fall in love with Kjel?"

I believe in romance; hearts and flowers and poetry recited on a grassy bank with a jug of wine, a loaf of bread, and thou, but never underestimate the importance of ease in the love department. Austin made me feel so comfortable, made me feel that the real Violet Mathers was not just all right by him, but . . . special. Who would have thought plain old sharp-tongued, one-armed me was special?

I'm pretty certain if Kjel had lived, he would have pushed us toward each other; I think he was doing that already.

We were so tender with each other. Austin treated me as if it were his mission to do everything in his power not to let anything else hurt me, least of all himself. I found I had answered the same calling; both of us knew what it was to be bruised and ragged beggars knocking on doors; now we had the opportunity to open each other's door with open smiles and a pot of soup on the stove.

Leola gave us the time and space to move as fast or slowly as we wanted, and slow seemed to suit the both of us. Our courtship was mostly walking and talking, sweetened by a bouquet of garden flowers presented in a mason jar, a book purchased at The Wise Reader Book Store (it was right across the street from VIM, and Austin visited it nearly as much as he did the library), a handmade shirt with topstitching decorating the collar, the placket, and both pockets.

What I remember best is holding hands. His skin was so dark against mine, and even as I admired the beautiful contrast and geometry our entwined fingers made, a swell of disbelief washed through me—this is what all the fuss is about? Two different colors?

The goodwill the townspeople had for the Hedstroms went a long way in their acceptance of us as a couple, but I also believe that for many, the shock of a white woman and a black man together was dulled somewhat by my stump. I was flawed, you see, and therefore not attractive to most eligible white men. I'm sure it would have been another thing entirely if I looked like Berit and was fully armed (pun intended). That VIM was doing such great business and that we had hired eight townspeople (as well as four Clamshells who were still loyal to the idea of the Pearltones even though the band no longer existed, as well as to the friendships they'd made with one another) certainly increased my stature, and then there was Austin himself, who with his music was ingratiating people all over again.

There had been several choir directors since Leola had last led a tone-deaf tenor and the bald soprano, and when the last one resigned due to a painful case of shingles, Leola suggested Austin fill his place.

"But does he know 'traditional' music?" Edith Solvedt asked.

"We can always warn him to keep the African rhythms to a minimum," Leola answered. "And besides, he can help us bring in new members."

This was true; once Austin agreed to "audition" (meeting with the choir members as well as the church board to talk about and demonstrate his grasp of "regular" church music) and passed (wowing them with a soulful "Abide With Me" on the piano), Alice and Elwin joined, as did Gwen, who was now working for VIM as a saleswoman. Gwen brought along Stella, another VIM employee, and Stella brought her boyfriend Henry, who'd heard the Pearltones' last performance at the school.

"I feel like I really missed out in not seeing them before the accident," said Henry.

We all nodded, and Gwen said, "You did."

Since the death of Mr. Eclesson, Pearl's children had been deprived of a private music teacher; this too was a mantle Austin willingly picked up. He taught piano and guitar and came home from each lesson not grousing about talentless brats but excited about how quickly Freddie Peasley picked up reading the bass clef or Beulah Doyle's reach. He was a natural teacher who loved sharing what he knew, and sometimes he'd come home from teaching and I'd come home from VIM and we'd grab each other in happy hugs, eager to talk about how we spent our days.

Who could have predicted this man would turn out to be the love of my life? It's as if Cupid was cross-eyed and fired off a quiver of arrows helter-skelter, in the craziest of directions, and Austin and I got in the way. Crazy old Cupid.

They got married on a late summer's day, in the barn, by the cow. As Violet liked to tell people, "I don't mean we stood by the cow during the ceremony, I mean the cow officiated."

It wasn't the sort of wedding in which invitations were sent; it wasn't a wedding that entailed weeks of planning; in fact the bride and groom didn't even know there was going to be a wedding until Maisy mooed.

Up in the hayloft, Austin lifted his head.

"Violet," he said, out of breath from their frantic kissing, "let's get married."

She laughed; they had talked about it, but the odds of doing it had seemed fairly insurmountable. Still, she was willing to humor him. "Okay, Austin."

"No, Violet, I mean now." He pulled her into a sitting position by her shoulders. "Down in the barn."

"What?"

A pall of seriousness fell over the delight that had animated Austin's face. "Cows are sacred in India, Violet."

Violet stared at him, assuming there was more to the story.

"The Puranas think there's no gift more sacred than the gift of cows."

Violet continued to stare. "So you've been reading up on India, hmm?"

"On world religions, actually." He picked up a piece of straw and began chewing on it. "Hinduism is fascinating. We close our hearts and minds to so much, Violet."

"I'm sure we do," she agreed. "Now what did you mean about going down into the barn to get married?"

"In the Hindu religion, cows are cleansers and sanctifiers. Let's go have Maisy sanctify us in marriage."

He pulled her so they were standing, their movement stirring up dust motes in the beams of light that shone through the cracks in the wood.

Austin descended the ladder first; it was a bit tricky for Violet to negotiate the rungs, and he liked to be in a position to catch her if she fell.

When they reached the ground, Violet batted the pieces of straw out of her hair. She felt shy and silly and a part of her wanted to cry.

"Violet," he said, taking her hand in both of his, "I'm not

making fun of you or us and it certainly is not my intent to mock the institution of marriage."

"Florid alert," said Violet. The more purple his language became, the more nervous she knew he was.

Austin smiled and kissed her hand. "All right, then I'll lay it out for you this way: they won't let us get married in our home, then we'll find our own way of getting married."

"But we talked about going over to Minnesota—"

"Violet, we live here! Here in North Dakota! We're good citizens, we pay our taxes, and yet if they want to keep us apart, or punish us—well, fuck 'em!"

"Austin," teased Violet, "now you're beyond florid!"

Maisy mooed.

"Come on, Violet. She wants to get this show on the road. If we can't have a legal marriage, we can have a blessed one, and that's what really counts, isn't it?"

He led her over to the big brown Guernsey, who twitched her tail and blinked her long-lashed eyes.

"See, she's telling us she's never seen a couple more suited for each other."

Violet laughed. "Smart cow."

"Sacred cow, remember? *Sanctifying* cow. Now put your hand on her back."

Violet did as she was told, and Austin, stepping around to the other side of the cow, lay his hand on top of hers.

"We are gathered here today," began Austin, and Violet's breath caught in her throat, "in the presence of God and Brahman and Allah and Buddha—"

"My goodness, you *have* been reading up," said Violet.

"Like I said, it's fascinating stuff." He cleared his throat. "And the Great Spirit and every other deity in this unfathomable world of ours, gathered here to profess our love and unite in marriage. Isn't that right, Maisy?"

The cow's flank shuddered as a fly landed on it.

"And so, Violet," Austin said, and there was no way Violet could look anywhere but into his deep brown eyes, "do you take

Austin to be your spiritually wedded husband, to love and to honor him, through richer and poorer, sickness and health, till death do you part?"

As her throat closed, Violet nodded, and when it seemed it had opened a trace, she whispered, "I do."

In the farm cologne of sun-warmed hay and dung, they stood standing, the cow between them, smiling at each other in the excited, hopeful, and grateful way of brides and grooms who know without doubt they've found exactly who they were supposed to find.

Violet inhaled, filling her lungs, and after she exhaled she began to speak.

"Austin, do you take Violet to be your spiritually wedded wife, to love and honor and obey—"

"Hey, that was supposed to be my line!"

"Finders keepers, losers weepers," said Violet as Maisy lowed. "All right, she's telling us there's a time and place for jokes."

"If this isn't it, I don't know what is," offered Austin, and when Violet's face fell, he said, "I mean that in the best way!"

Pressing her lips together, Violet nodded; she knew he did. Emotion was a stampede of rhinos and hippos, birds and butterflies, charging through her, and the bees in her ears droned a frenzied accompaniment.

She gulped for breath, like a swimmer who'd been underwater for too long, and then because saying the words was the most important thing, she began.

"Do you promise to sing to her and play your guitar for her and talk to her so she'll always know how you're feeling and never have to guess and hold her in your arms as much as she needs holding?"

Austin's eyes glittered with tears. "I do."

"Through richer and poorer and sickness and health and whatever else Life might throw at us, because we know Life *likes* to throw things, till death do us part?"

"Death won't part us."

"But that's not your line."

"I do," said Austin, squeezing her hand. "I do, I do, I do."

"Then with the powers vested in Maisy—"

"She now pronounces us man—"

"—and wife."

They waited for Maisy to top off the glorious moment with a moo, a tapping of hooves, but the old cow, big and brown and patient, only swished her tail.

"Then by the powers vested in me through her," said Austin, "I demand that I kiss the bride."

Had it been a different world, Violet might have proceeded up the aisle in a white wedding gown while the organist emitted faint clouds of talcum powder as she forcefully pedaled "Trumpet Voluntary." She might have joined her betrothed in standing before a preacher, lit from behind in the colored mellowed light of a ten-foot stained-glass window, and maybe a soloist would have sung, "Ave Maria." Still, Violet could hardly imagine any ceremony meaning more or feeling more holy than her wedding in the barn, with its simple choir of cooing pigeons up in the rafters, its ushers of mice racing guests of spiders and flies to their seats, its dusty sunlight, and as she smiled at Austin and over the bony ridge of Maisy's back, they leaned toward each other and shared their first kiss as man and wife.

That night at supper, they told Leola what they had done.

She turned around, dabbing at her eyes with the corner of her apron, calling out a dozen silent prayers.

"Well then," she said, after she had collected herself, "I'm glad I made a cake!"

As the coffee percolated, she got the Brownie camera Nils had given her and Esben and took photographs of the couple feeding each other the chocolate layer cake.

"And what will be the bridal suite?" she asked before they went to bed, and red-faced, Violet shrugged, looking at Austin.

"Where would you like to have us?" he asked gently.

"Well, your room's bigger," she reminded them, and it was settled, and when they got there, scrubbed clean and smelling of soap, they found that Leola had scattered rose petals on the bed under the skylight, in the room that used to be Kjel's.

★

FOUR MONTHS LATER Pearl Harbor was attacked, and that the world was going to hell seemed less Austin's disgruntled analysis of newspaper headlines than a terrible reality.

When winter turned into spring, nothing changed that truth, especially when Austin told Violet he was enlisting.

"April Fool's is two days away," said Violet.

"And I do have an April Fool's joke for you," said Austin, "but this isn't it."

Bearing a lunch of two egg salad sandwiches and chocolate malteds from the Parisian Cafe, he had come for lunch in Violet's office (never had she dreamed she'd have her own office—with a VIOLET MATHERS nameplate on the desk and a drawing table with an adjustable top!) and they were seated on the settee Birdie had brought in for "customer consultations."

Violet swallowed a sip of her malted, the ice cream suddenly sour in her throat. "Austin, don't," she said. She wasn't asking him to stop teasing her—she could tell by his voice that he wasn't—she wanted to stop what he said he was going to do.

"I've got three more music lessons tomorrow and then I'll be leaving on Saturday," said Austin as if he hadn't heard her. "I'm going to sign up in St. Louis and see my sister while I'm there."

Fear was a cold clammy hand reaching up from Violet's stomach to her heart.

"Why?" she said, the one frozen word she managed to cough up.

Austin's big barrel chest rose in a sigh as he chewed his bottom lip.

"I feel it's my duty."

Violet let out a whoop that Birdie heard out in the showroom.

"We're a happy lot," she explained to the woman, who'd come all the way from Pierre to place an order for two suits.

———

"Don't you want to be with me?" asked Violet. "I thought you loved me!"

"I do love you, Violet, more than anyone or anything. But my country's at war."

Violet stared at Austin, her mouth agape. When had the man she thought she knew so well gone crazy?

"*Your* country?" she said, feeling dizzy as she stood up. "What has this country ever done for you?"

Looking at his wife—his tall and elegant and beautiful Violet—the speech he was ready to give was blocked by the lump in his throat. He loved his wife, his life—didn't she know that? Didn't she know how hard it was to leave them?

Violet stood looking out the windows, but everything she saw swirled; she didn't see Sheriff Flore chatting with Mac McDonald outside his barbershop as much as she saw them spinning, like the unwinding red-and-white colors of the barber pole. She squeezed her eyes shut, willing the twirling colors to stop.

"Violet," whispered Austin, encircling her from behind with his arms. She shook as if stricken with bodywide tremors, and he tightened his arms around her. "Violet, I don't want to go, but I have to go."

"You don't have to go," said Violet, and she broke the circle his arms made so she could face him. "Nobody's making you go."

Austin's face wore the exaggerated sadness of a little lost boy's or a clown's. "I'm making myself go."

"*Why?*" asked Violet again. "You want to fight for someone's freedom when you don't even have your own?"

"Who says I'm not free?" said Austin, his voice cross.

"Almost every state in the country! According to them, you're not free enough to marry me!"

"But we're still married, aren't we? No matter what the stupid law says, we're still married, aren't we, Violet?"

Violet nodded as the tears began streaming down her face. She couldn't understand why her husband would do such a stupid thing, and yet she knew Austin wouldn't do anything stupid and her fear and anger was at war with her confusion.

Like an earnest Boy Scout, Austin escorted his wife back to the settee, sitting down first and pulling her to his lap. As she cried on his shoulder, one hand rested on the small of her back and the other smoothed her shiny black hair. When her erratic snuffling had settled, Austin spoke.

"You ask me what my country has ever done for me and I have to answer: it's given me everything. My country is its people, Violet—and so my country is my family, all those great musicians who used to play at my dad's place—"

Lifting her head up, Violet said, "This sounds like a speech, Austin."

Relieved that she felt better enough to tease him, Austin smiled. "Well, if it is a speech, will you at least allow me the courtesy of giving it?"

As Violet nodded, he repeated what he had said about America being the home of the people he loved.

"People like you, Violet! People like Kjel, and Leola and Birdie and Elwin and the Clamshells—people like Geraldine Knox, who played a song today she had written especially for me! It was called "Teacher O Mine," and I swear, Violet, Cole Porter'd better beware that a little twelve-year-old lyricist is hot on his trail!"

"What about the melody?"

"Her skills in that department are slightly more rudimentary." He offered another smile but Violet could see the wistfulness in it.

"Tell me the rest of your speech, Austin. I promise I won't interrupt anymore."

"The thing of it is, Violet, it's not really about *my* country and what it has or hasn't done for me or to me." A little cry rose in his throat, surprising him and surprising Violet, who reflexively gasped back.

"I can't just sit back in my beautiful life with my beautiful wife when . . . when . . . well, you've heard those terrible stories coming out of Germany . . . of a monster loose, Violet!"

"But what about the monsters here?" asked Violet, her voice small.

"This is the one that needs fighting now," he said, shaking his head, "and I'm going to fight it. I have to fight it." He took her face in his hands and they looked into each other's eyes, each searching for something, but neither was sure exactly what.

Chapter Twenty-nine

IF I WERE STARRING IN TWO BROADWAY SHOWS AT THE SAME time, I couldn't have had more drama in my life. The same week Austin was shipped overseas, I realized that I was pregnant. I didn't need Doc Oberg to tell me the news; my period was the Big Ben of menstrual cycles, always exactly on time.

I shared the news with Austin in a letter, and in response to my confession that the ratio of being terrified to being delighted was about eighty to twenty, he wrote back, "Mine's three to ninety-seven!"

I loved that he didn't say he was one-hundred-percent delighted; his three-percent terror fortified me.

As my condition became obvious to the rest of the world (Birdie said I looked like a peashooter that had accidentally swallowed a peach), I braced myself for all sorts of reactions, but like that other percentage, only three percent expressed outrage, compared to the ninety-seven who seemed relatively happy for me.

"My grandpa says it's illegal for you to have a mulatto," said Wesley Breyer, one of Austin's students. "What's a mulatto?"

It's nothing like the idiot your grandfather is, I said in my head, but aloud I exercised more restraint.

"It's a word to describe a baby who has a mix of two different skin colors."

"A mix of two different skin colors," repeated Wesley with awe in his voice, "like that?"

He pointed to my skirt, which was a black-and-white houndstooth, and I had to smile.

"Yup, just like that," I said. "Although it might come out polka-dotted or it could be checkered."

Ivy Patterson, the wife of the owner of the Pearl Gazette, a paper that had published many articles about VIM and its impact on the town's economy, threw a shower for me. Thirteen-year-old Belinda Peasley offered her babysitting services at half price, "on account of Mr. Sykes being in the war and all." Gaylord Bentson, the carpenter/electrician who had done much of the retrofitting work at VIM, told me that genetically our baby might be (I braced myself here) "a talented artist or a talented musician, but for sure, he'll be a nice person."

I was often on the brink of tears during my pregnancy, not because of the meanness of people, but because of their kindness. I knew that Pearl's goodwill toward me and Austin was an offshoot of the great goodwill they held for the Hedstroms, but even so, that little town in the middle of North Dakota was so accepting it almost seemed enchanted. Maybe a tooth fairy, carting an extra heavy bag of teeth, eased her weight load by dropping a ton of fairy dust on the sleeping villagers; maybe the cows ate a clover so sweet that it gave anyone who drank its milk a peaceable state of mind; maybe the severe winter cold froze things like cruelty and intolerance as easily as it froze slough water and fingertips.

Austin and I have traveled far in this wide world, and never, not in the most cosmopolitan of cities, have we ever been accepted the way we were in beautiful Pearl, North Dakota.

My more sophisticated friends laugh when I tell them that; they think everyone in a small town is either a rube or a figure of no consequence, but I just quote from the Pearltones' "The Be-Boppin' Dakotan": "It ain't where you're from, it's where you're at."

In the flurry of letters that passed between Violet and Austin, it was decided that should the baby be a boy, he'd be called Kjel

Montrose (Austin's father's nickname was Mokey, but his given name was Montrose), and if the baby was a girl, she'd be named Miracle, after Kjel's favorite song.

Miracle Leola Sykes was born under the skylight in Kjel's room, and when Doc Oberg laid the mewling baby in her mother's arms, the whispered words out of Violet's mouth were, "Oh my stars."

She was a tiny little thing, measuring in at six pounds and was eighteen inches long, but when she nudged her way to Violet's nipple, Violet was glad she was already lying down, because the weight of the baby would have knocked her down.

Assuming it was the bees in her head, it took Violet a moment to realize she wasn't hearing a roar so much as feeling it, and that roar was the potent and primal announcement: "You're my baby and I'm your mother!"

Her father wrote:

Dear Miracle,

Happy Birthday! No child should come into the world while there is a war going on, but unfortunately the powers that be have yet to grasp this simple truth and enact appropriate legislation. Oh my; your mother always says I get florid when I get emotional, and I suppose the preceding sentence is evidence of that. I'm just so excited to have you here! I have not seen you or touched you and yet your existence has filled me with a pride and joy that causes me to check to see if my feet truly are touching the ground because it certainly feels as if I'm walking on air!

You are a miracle, Miracle, made out of a love that's a miracle, named after a man who was a miracle, and a song that, while not exactly in the league of miracles, is awfully tuneful.

I wish more than anything I were home with you, but I am fighting this war in the manner they see fit—i.e., I am typing out forms in a requisition office in our country's capital. Apparently the army considers me capable of this duty; their belief in me flags, however, when it comes to duties concerning a gun or bazooka. I've heard there are black soldiers training for armored warfare in Fort Knox, but whether or not they get beyond the training and into combat remains to be seen. It's a funny thing, Miracle, a person wanting to serve their country and their country telling them it only trusts them in certain limited capacities.

However, dear Miracle, I have come to realize that true service to my country probably doesn't involve shooting at someone; I lay awake nights thinking what that true service might be. Here are some of my ideas: Reading aloud the great philosophers to world leaders in a group story hour. Insisting that the presidency be served by a male/female team. Inviting a Grand Dragon into my house for a weekend. My list is long, baby girl, and I am not holding my breath that any items on it will soon be implemented.

Your mother is happy that I am not throwing hand grenades or dodging Messerschmitts, and I guess I am too, for it means I have a far better chance of seeing you, holding you. I pray for all those out there who are doing what I thought I should be doing; I pray for an end to all this madness, and most of all, I pray for you and the family you have made for me and your mother.

Love and Peace for future birthdays, Miracle,
Daddy

The townspeople of Pearl threw a Welcome Home party for two of its returning veterans, Austin and Arnie Iglehard, who came back from his tour missing two fingers and the ability to sleep without all the lights on.

There were macaroni and cheese hot dishes and eight different cakes and all the ginger ale punch anyone would care to drink and the mood was festive, except that Arnie Iglehard seemed to flinch a lot and Austin wouldn't let go of his baby daughter.

"You'd better let Mrs. Flore hold her," Violet whispered, laughing. "We want to stay in the sheriff's good graces!"

"I've got three months of holding to make up," said Austin,

looking into the small circle that was his daughter's face. "And I'm not giving her up to the sheriff's wife, the mayor's wife, the governor's wife, or Eleanor Roosevelt herself!"

✳

MIRACLE'S INFANCY PASSED IN A blur; it seemed to her parents that a day passed not in hours, but in milestones; at five months Miracle sat up, at six months her first teeth poked through her bottom gums, at seven months she was crawling, earning the praise of Leola, her honorary grandmother.

"My gracious, I've never seen a baby crawl so fast and so far at such a young age!"

Violet and Austin thought, as most parents do, that theirs was the most advanced child to grace the planet Earth, their only complaint that these milestones passed in microseconds.

One night, after the usual struggle putting Miracle to bed ("Don't wanna sleep!" the two-and-a-half-year-old would scream. "Wanna stay awake all night!"), Austin and Violet were sitting in the parlor with Leola, watching the color and shape permutations of the fire and listening to the radio. As the evening settled in, this was the time when Leola most missed Esben and Kjel, but thanks to her housemates, her melancholia had long ago softened from a deep purple to lavender.

"That song reminds me of—" said Leola, and before she got her words out, Austin shushed her.

"Austin," scolded Violet, but her ears suddenly picked up what Austin's already had: a familiar voice and familiar lines. "Friday night is for cats like me to go and find some kittens."

The three all leaned toward the radio, as still as statues as they listened to the radio.

"And that was the Dallas Sykes Band playing 'All Night Cattin,' " said the radio announcer. "This is a combo that's starting to get a lot of attention across the country, and we're pleased to let our loyal listeners throughout the music-loving Dakotas have a listen. And now let's listen to a song requested by a navy man just back from his tour of duty—by the way, we thank you, as we thank all our men who have served and are serving—yes, a song by the maestro himself, Mr. Bing Cros—"

Austin had lifted himself off the davenport and, still squatting, turned off the radio.

"That son of a bitch," he said, his voice full of surprise.

"Kjel and Austin and Dallas wrote that song," Violet explained to Leola. "It was one of the Pearltones' most popular numbers."

"Yes," said Leola nodding, "I remember Kjel singing it at his last performance."

A pang of longing struck the three of them, and their individual memories were also a collective one, a picture of Kjel sitting in the school gymnasium playing his guitar.

"That son of a bitch," said Austin, rising.

"Where're you going, honey?" asked Violet.

"I'm going for a walk," said Austin. "A walk that takes me by Kampa's Tavern."

He got home an hour and a half later—the three-mile walk taking up most of his time, as he never drank more than one beer—and welcomed the milk and slab of apple pie Violet had waiting for him.

"I apologize for my abrupt departure," he said. "I just had to get some air."

Sitting at the table, Violet's right hand cupped her stump. "What are we going to do?"

Austin stared at the pie like a tea reader studies leaves, but the golden pastry crust offered no answers.

"Maybe we should call Lawrence."

"That's a good idea," said Austin, looking at his watch. "I'll give him a call tomorrow morning." He shook his head, and picking up a fork, cut into the pie. He ate for a while, taking his time with each mouthful, as if the act of chewing helped him think. Finally he wiped his mouth on the gingham napkin and said, "If he's using that song, I'll bet he's using others. It's not fair that no one knows Kjel wrote them too."

"And you," said Violet. "Give credit where credit is due."

Shaking his head, Austin wiped his mouth again. "You'd think Dallas would have figured out something that simple, wouldn't you?"

✳

SEVERAL WEEKS LATER a registered letter was delivered to Austin.

" *'Dear Brother,'* " he read aloud to Violet and Leola, his voice slick with sarcasm:

"Imagine my surprise when old Larry Zeller tracked down my lawyer (imagine that, I've got a lawyer and he's not appointed by the courts!). It hurts me to know that you think I wouldn't give you and Kjel songwriting credit—what do you take me for, man?

So you and Violet are still up in the boondocks, huh? I got a place in Hollywood, California, now with a sweet fox named LaNae, although I don't see much of either one, as we're on the road so much. Thank God for all the girls out there willing to ease my weary load. Ha!

The Dallas Sykes Band! There's six of us, but if you'd ever want to step aboard, there's always room. We had eighty gigs last year and looks like we'll almost double that this year.

So things are good, bro, and I hope next time you contact me you'll do it yourself and not have some lawyer do your dirty work.

Still yours,
Dallas

P.S. Dessa's got a fella now—can you believe it? I met the guy, and looking at his mug, I could tell what they mean by 'love is blind.' "

He didn't read the P.P.S., in which Dallas had added, *"But I guess you know that."*

———

"What does songwriting credit mean anyway?" asked Leola.

"It means our names would be on anything published," said Austin.

"Oh, I'd like that," said Leola.

Several months later another registered letter was delivered, this one with a check enclosed.

Our first royalty check, bro! The money is for you and Kjel, so pass his portion on to whoever . . . more where this comes from—"You're My Gem" is a hit!

A bile of sadness rose up in Austin. Kjel and Austin wrote that song; Dallas had nothing to do with it.

It was a shock every time they heard one of the Pearltones' songs on the radio, and if Miracle was in the room, she sensed the charged emotion. Sometimes she cried, sometimes she laughed, other times she ran to her mother, her father, or Leola, putting her small hands on each side of their faces, offering comfort.

"I don't like this song because it makes you sad, Nana Lee," she said.

Leola enveloped the small girl in her arms. "I'm a funny kind of sad," she said. "Sad because the song reminds me of someone I loved very much, and happy because I like to be reminded."

As Miracle got older, she understood that her father not only taught other people music, but had once played in a band, played and wrote songs that she now heard on the radio.

"It's funny that you can *write* music, isn't it?" she asked her father. "People write books, but they don't write paintings."

Austin laughed, picking up his daughter and setting her on his lap. "I know—when you hear music, it doesn't seem like something that can be written. But thank goodness it can—then we don't forget it, and then other people get to play it too."

"Still, it should be called something else."

"It is. 'Composing.' If you make up music, you're a composer composing music."

"Composing music; that sounds much better." She touched Austin's cheek. "You know what else I wish would sound better, Daddy?"

"What, sweetheart?"

"My name," said the little girl. "I don't like being called Miracle. It sounds like I'm bragging."

Thereafter she was known as Miri.

Austin had read about reincarnation, and he didn't mean to be smug, but it did seem as if he had lived some pretty good past lives to get to this present one. He was in love with a fine woman, he loved teaching music, and he had a daughter who convinced him that being a father was the highest calling a man could answer.

"I'd give up my music for her," he told Violet. "I'd give up my life."

"I'd give up your life for her too," said Violet solemnly.

"Just as long as she doesn't inherit your sense of humor."

"If she doesn't inherit mine, whose is there to inherit?"

Austin wasn't successful at suppressing his laughter. "All right, truce. Let's just sit here and look at our beautiful girl."

It was a favorite activity of theirs to watch Miri sleep; to stare at her lovely face in respose. It dazzled both of them how beautiful their daughter was; certainly neither of them was of the belief she had inherited her looks from them.

"Nonsense," said Leola. "She's the perfect mix of you; she's got the best from both of you."

And her looks were just one facet of the diamond that was their girl.

"She's the brightest student I've ever had," Alice Sather told Violet and Austin at Miri's third-grade conference. "She's so curious—goodness, the questions she asks me! I've taken to writing them down." Alice flipped a few pages of the notebook in front of her. " 'Why do people say Columbus discovered America if the Indians were already here?' 'Do you think the person who discovered short division was just lazy and didn't want to do it the long way?' 'How fast would the earth have to rotate before we all got dizzy?' " Alice's teacher's smile was almost as proud as those of Miri's parents.

"She loves having you as a teacher," said Violet. "She thinks it's pretty special that you and Elwin are such good friends of ours."

Having been an excellent student herself, Violet was thrilled at Miri's success. Sitting in a classroom diffused with late afternoon sunshine, the cursive alphabet bordering the wall, the chalkboard mottled with erasure marks, filled Violet with a happiness that even manifested itself in her posture; she sat ramrod straight, holding Austin's hand, exchanging squeezes of pride over each excellent report.

She was a favorite of her music teacher's too. Miri had inherited her father's and uncle's musical talent, and it was a great joy of Austin's to teach her to play the piano. It was an even greater joy when her talent outgrew his teaching ability and he had to drive her to Jamestown to practice with Mathilda Mount, a classical pianist who had played with the Chicago Symphony.

"She has such a depth of soul," Miss Mount would tell the proud parents, "it's as if she not only reads the music, but the composer's meaning behind each note."

Her childhood was a time of great happiness for her parents, but every child turns into a teenager, and the turbulence of Miri's adolescence was compounded by her awareness of just how different she was from her peers.

She often came to the shop after school and did her homework at Violet's drawing table, or if she didn't have homework, acted as Violet's assistant, cutting out or pinning fabric.

One afternoon as she helped her mother drape yards of satin over a mannequin, Miri said, "Mom, remember that field trip we took to the Corn Palace?"

Violet nodded, pins in her mouth.

"Well, we took the tour with these kids from Bismarck, and guess what they kept asking me?"

Steeling herself, Violet shook her head.

"What kind of Indian are you? And then they put their hands to their mouths and go 'whoo, whoo, whoo, whoo.' "

"Oh, sweetheart," said Violet, taking the pins out of her mouth. "That field trip was over a month ago. Why didn't you tell me about it then?"

"I don't know," said Miri impatiently. "Anyway, I said I'm not an Indian, and even if I was, what would be the problem with that?" She picked up a pin that had fallen on the floor and jabbed it into her wristband pin cushion. "And then this one fat kid says, 'The problem with that is if you're not an Indian, then you might be a nigger. Are you a nigger?' "

"Oh, Miri!"

"I hate who I am! I hate being part nigger! I hate that my father's not white!"

Violet's impulse to slap Miri was overtaken by her impulse to hug her, and she held the weeping girl to her, kneeling on the satin fabric that had puddled to the floor.

When Miri was in eighth grade, her English teacher called Austin and Violet in for a conference.

"Lord have mercy," Austin whispered, looking at the title of the neatly handwritten paper Mrs. Harper set in front of them.

"My Family Tree," it read, "By Miri (Mulatto) Sykes."

"I'm very concerned by this," said the kindly teacher.

Reading the paper, so were Violet and Austin.

There is not one person in the whole town of Pearl, not one person in LaMour County, not one person in the whole state of North Dakota (I'm pretty sure) who's like me! I don't say that in a "gee, I'm special" way either; I say it in a "I hate being a freak" way!

As far as my family tree goes, it's one I'd rather not climb! My mother is estranged from her side and doesn't seem to know much about her lineage, but they're from Kentucky and before that Georgia which means if you went far back enough, they probably owned slaves—maybe my mother's side of the family owned slaves from my father's side of the family! Isn't that something of which to be proud!

And so the story of my family tree is going to be short—the story of a family shrub is more like it—because it is a story I do not care to investigate further. It is a story of which I am sad to be a part.

"Chaw," whispered Violet.

"I know, I felt awful reading it," said Mrs. Harper. "She's always struck me as such a well-adjusted girl." She watched helplessly as Mr. Sykes put his arm around his wife, as Mrs. Sykes blinked back tears, and because she was the type of teacher whose glass was not merely half full but brimming, she said, "Well, she certainly knows where to place her prepositions."

"Baby, you're a pioneer," Austin told his daughter later that evening, "and pioneers have got to blaze trails. You've got to blaze the trail through people's ignorance."

"That's such a stupid thing to say!" said Miri. "I don't want to blaze trails! I don't want to be a stupid pioneer!"

Austin tried telling Miri stories, he tried lecturing her, but all of his words fell on deaf ears; his daughter was hurting and she wanted to share that hurt with him.

"You can come to the home games," she said when she began playing high school basketball. "But I'd appreciate it if you didn't come when we play away."

"Miri, you can't—" began Violet, but Austin interrupted her.

"I will happily attend your home games," he said, "and I will wait with bated breath to hear the results of your away games. Will you at least share them with me when you get home?"

"Oh, Daddy!" said Miri, throwing herself on her father. "Oh, Daddy, I'm sorry!"

That she was sorry didn't prevent her from lashing out at Austin, telling him where he could or couldn't go and what he could or couldn't do.

"Daddy, when you drive me to Jamestown for my piano lesson, I don't want to stop for lunch anymore!"

"Daddy, when Mom goes to Chicago, don't worry about picking me up after play practice—I can get a ride with Bonnie Roeg."

———

Violet watched in despair as Austin seemed to shrink before her eyes.

"You can't put up with this Austin! You've got to talk to her!"

"Violet, I have talked to her, you know that! But at this point, she's not listening to anything I have to say!"

"So what do we do?"

Austin's head shook in little moves. "I'm hoping the time will come when she starts listening to herself, and hears how wrong she is."

"But what if she never listens to herself? What if she never hears how wrong she is?"

"Miri's got a good brain, Violet," said Austin, sighing deeply. "And she's got a good heart. We've got to trust that she'll use both."

Chapter Thirty

WHEN SHE WAS SIXTEEN, MIRI RAN AWAY. SHE WAS GONE FOR TWO *days and I was as frantic as I'd been when my mother ran off; no, more so, because a mother's love is so much more knowing than a daughter's. When she called us from Fargo and she was fine, I just about burst with euphoria.*

Leola went with us to pick her up, and I saw her lips press together and her nostrils flare when she saw Miri pushing away her father's hug.

"This nonsense has got to stop," she told Miri when we were all in the car.

Miri looked stricken; her dear Nana Lee was not one to criticize her.

"Now, I know it's not easy being of a mixed race in this world we live in, but you are of mixed race and there's nothing you can do to change it. So you'd better learn, little girl, that your allies are the ones who love you. You're not responsible for how other people treat you—and there will be idiots who treat you badly—but you are responsible for how you treat other people, and I for one can't take this running away, this cruelty toward the people who love you best."

I'm not sure Leola's words changed Miri—really, Austin and I had been saying the same version of them all along—but maybe the beginnings of an epiphany began in the interior of that Ford Fairlane.

It was music that finally brought Miri all the way back to her father, back to us. She was accepted into Juilliard (Juilliard!) and wasn't there three weeks when the phone rang.

"Mom," she said, "put Dad on the phone."

It was a conversation that lasted nearly two hours, and after Austin hung up, he began to cry.

"She was writing a piano exercise for her composition class," he said, wiping away tears with the heel of his palms. "And she said she could feel me; with every note she wrote she felt as if I were there, as if I were guiding the song!"

For parents, there's nothing sweeter than seeing your child fight her demons and win. Miri embraced her musical and ancestral heritages. She graduated from Juilliard and began a career as a pianist, and a few years later decided she needed to go to law school "if I really want to effect change." When the black power and women's movement asked for volunteers, she signed on as a dedicated and hardworking member. I have a photograph my future son-in-law (a lovely man, a clarinetist from Albany) took when we joined Miri on a "Free Angela!" march—in the middle is our beautiful caramel-skinned daughter, her arms linked with her black dad and her white mom.

I don't know how we could have been happier. Austin and I spent a lot of time in New York, having bought an apartment during Miri's sophomore year at Juilliard. VIM had sixteen stores nationwide, and the one we opened in Manhattan got a lot of attention; I was written up in Women's Wear Daily *and* Vogue *and movie stars called me to design their gowns for the Oscars.*

"Violet!" said Austin, looking stupefied as he cupped his hand over the telephone receiver. "It's Elizabeth Taylor calling!"

When we weren't in New York or traveling for business, we might fly to London or Paris or Rio, and as thrilling as that was, we still couldn't wait to go back to Pearl, to meet the new child Elwin and Alice had adopted and to sit at the kitchen table after supper and play Scrabble with Leola.

When Violet was fifty-four years old, the buzzing in her ears stopped. She had slept uneasily the night before, a deep cough and nightmares rattling her awake.

———

She dreamed that Miri—who was having a difficult pregnancy with her first child—ḥad miscarried and that she was trying to stanch the river of blood that flowed from her daughter. She dreamed she was a little girl, sitting on the crumbling front steps, waiting for her mother. She couldn't understand why everyone passing the house gasped and screamed until she looked at her wristwatch and realized she had no skin; she was a skeleton. She woke up after each nightmare breathing heavily, sweat dampening the roots of her hair.

Leery of slumber and what it might bring, she was nevertheless too tired not to succumb to her great weariness and she fell back asleep near dawn, and when the nightmares stepped aside, there was Kjel.

"Hello, Violet."

She looked up; she was outside, not in Pearl but in a tree-filled place that reminded her of the corner of Minnesota they'd camped in.

"Kjel!" she cried to the figure crouched in what she realized was Tree Pa. "What are you doing?"

"Just sitting up here with the birds. Learning some new songs."

"I've missed you so much!"

"Have you? I'm always around, you know."

"No, you're not—you're dead!"

Kjel laughed, and his bird teachers were now the students and they ruffled their feathers and clucked, jealous of the sound.

"I'm as alive as the sunshine, Violet. I'm as alive as the shadows."

Overwhelmed, Violet sat on the ground and began to cry, and in one swoop Kjel was out of the arms of Tree Pa and next to her.

"Why did you take so long to talk to me?" she asked. "You've been dead over twenty years!"

"Violet, please. Let's agree to disagree about my dead status. And how do you know I haven't been talking to you?"

"Because I would have heard you! Because I've been waiting for a sign from you for all these years!"

"A sign of what?"

"I . . . I don't know—a sign that you're all right; that everything's all right."

————

Kjel smiled, and Violet gasped, remembering the gift that was his smile.

"Violet, you of all people should know that everything's all right. Look at your life! Look at all you've done! Look at Austin, look at Miri!"

"You know about Miri?"

"Of course I do. What a beautiful young woman. Running for city council in New York, isn't she?"

"Wow. You have kept track of things. We're so proud of her, but she's pregnant now, and still working for the law firm and playing an occasional concert and—"

"All will be well, Violet. You just have to trust that all will be well."

"That seems strange, coming from you. I mean, considering what happened to you."

"Violet, many things happened to me."

"I know but—"

Kjel laughed, and Violet begged her mind to freeze the picture of his face at that moment.

"And all is well."

He was off the ground in a movement so quick that Violet couldn't comprehend it, and then he was a color, a touch of velvet, a scent of wild-flowers, a breeze tinged with music, and that breeze blew in one of her ears and out the other.

She woke with a gasp and lay unmoving, staring up at the ceiling. *I don't want to be awake! I want to go back there!*

Austin grunted in his sleep and rolled to his side, and Violet frowned, irritated at the volume of noise he made; the nasally grumble, the rustle of sheets, like paper being shuffled.

Confusion batted her head. *Why was everything so loud? Every-thing except*—Violet's eyes opened wide as the full realization of what was happening hit her: the bees in her ears were gone.

For a moment she panicked—where were they?—and scrambled up to sit against the headboard, pulling the blanket up to her chin.

"What the—" mumbled Austin, waking up and reaching for the commandeered covers. He was shocked into full conscious-ness upon seeing his wife's face.

"Violet! Violet, what's the matter?"

Staring ahead, Violet pressed her finger to her lips. She waited one minute, two minutes, until Austin interrupted her.

"Violet, what—"

They still had not come back, and the panic drained from her—what did she care *where* they were?

"They're gone," she said finally.

"What are gone?" asked Austin, looking around the room for clues.

"The bees," said Violet. "The bees in my ears. Kjel took them away."

"Kjel?"

"He came to me in a dream—or maybe it wasn't a dream. He . . . oh, Austin—it was so beautiful! He knows about you and me! He knows about Miri! He was so . . . so *Kjel*!"

Violet was crying now, and Austin opened his arms to her, holding her for a long time as she snorted and sobbed and told him all about her dream.

"He said all will be well! He said all is well!"

Austin wasn't the type of man who prided himself on stoicism; he had long ago learned that it was easier to feel what he felt, and what he felt now was an amalgam of grief and happiness, loneliness and joy, despair and hope. This is what got him crying, as hard as his wife in their bed under the skylight; that even dead, Kjel continued to give them what he always had: hope.

Chapter Thirty-one

ONE OF THE BEAUTIES (YES, PLURAL) OF LIVING A LONG LIFE IS *that you get to see how everything turns out. What scares me most in this world full of scary things is the thought that if I'd been successful at taking my swan dive off the Golden Gate Bridge, none of this would have happened.* I would have missed out on my own fabulous life. *What a loss for me, and for all those who knew me. It's not that I'm becoming vainglorious in my dotage; no, the more you live, the more you see that your own story is interdependent on the stories of others. And you can't work with fabric as long as I have without appreciating the importance of every single thread.*

Remember that dream I had about Miri's miscarriage? It didn't come out of nowhere—I'd had three myself and didn't want her to go through what I had—but she did miscarry and there was an awful lot of blood. She recovered, though, and a year and a half later gave birth to just about the most amazing little boy that ever came onto this earth. They named him Austin Gregory, for his two grandfathers, a name you can bet sent his maternal grandfather to the moon, around Jupiter, past Mercury, and back. Miri continued her political career; she served on a school board, two city councils, as a state assemblywoman, and now she's running for governor of

New York State! Imagine that—the sad teenager who signed a junior-high paper, "Miri 'Mulatto' Sykes" is running for governor of New York State! And that polls show her leading the race! She incorporates her music into her politics; she and David write her campaign songs, which are so catchy people still sing ones she wrote fifteen, twenty years ago. The dinner at The Waldorf-Astoria I'm going to tomorrow night? It's a campaign fund-raiser for Miri. Care to make a contribution?

Back to my grandson—he's a beautiful boy—well, man now—who inherited none of his mother's musical gifts but a lot of his grandmother's artistic ones. He's worked for VIM since he graduated college and is responsible for our very successful men's line: VIGOR. He and his wife are expecting their first child next month, the grace of which takes my breath away.

Leola lived until she was ninety-nine years old, and we all would have been at her bedside had we known she was dying. But she didn't know it either; one minute she was sitting by the fireplace with her cup of cocoa and her knitting needles, the next minute she was bathed in white light, or hitching a ride on angels' wings, or standing at the Pearly Gates, reciting a password she didn't know she knew. Austin was jamming with Elwin and one of his old students and I was seeing a movie with Jean in Pearl's new movie theater, and when we got home, there sat Leola, a smile on her face as if she were dreaming. It's a blessing to die with a smile on your face; Austin sure didn't. He did not want to go, did not want to go, and argued with a Grim Reaper that only he could see that it most definitely was not his time.

"You're confusing me with someone else," he said in the ambulance, and then he looked at me, his eyes wild. "Violet, please, tell this Apostle of Doom fellow that the reason he's in such a foul mood is that he has the wrong man!"

I was laughing—so was the paramedic attending Austin—I mean how could a guy be making jokes like that if he was truly on his deathbed?

I felt bad for a long time that I had laughed, that I hadn't trusted the man I trusted most in the world to be telling me the truth at that most crucial juncture in his life. But I thought it was just a bad case of indigestion—that's what he had been complaining about in the New Orleans airport—how was I to know that the poison from his burst appendix was already seeping through his body?

He was only sixty-three years old, and I had been foolish enough to believe that I would have him forever. I know, I know, the people you love are with you forever in your heart, but I wanted Austin with me forever here on earth. I wanted to look up and see him staring at me with his beautiful bug eyes and to ask him, "What're you looking at?" and have him answer, "Pure loveliness"; I wanted to talk about Miri with that full-chested wonderment and delight that is reserved for parents of the same child, and I wanted to listen to him talk about her in the same way.

We held hands all the time—his became the partner my hand had so long ago lost, and more than anything, I wanted those beautiful long fingers forever entwined with my own.

But somehow . . . you soldier on. Memories do become salve and bandages, and ultimately—surprisingly—a perfume. It's my signature fragrance and I wear it every day: Eau de Austin with trace notes of Leola, of Esben, of Kjel.

Another one of those beauties of old age I was telling up about is that generally you wise up with regard to reconciliations.

Now I don't think all bridges should remain upright—I did burn one with my daddy, but it had been so rotted and rickety it had to go. And my mother—well, I felt as if she'd burned the bridge we stood on and it was up to her to rebuild it, not me.

And truly, I am fine with that. You can't have everything, so you have to go after what you really want.

Unfortunately, Austin didn't get to be old enough to decide that whatever hurt his brother had caused him wasn't worth the pain of es-trangement, but I did.

After Austin died, I was too lonesome to stay in Pearl or our New York apartment where I was so reminded of him, and so I started travel-ing around the country. My first trip was on a train to Missoula, and find-ing it comforting to travel with other people, I got aboard a bus to Los Angeles, which reminded me of my bus ride out of Mount Crawford. I traveled for thousands of miles—if buses gave mileage points the way air-

lines do, I'd have a free trip around the world. Traveling by bus got me reintroduced to diners, and, during a trip through Tennessee, reintroduced me to Dallas.

I went to see him play in Memphis—not two blocks from the club (now a Blockbuster video store) the Pearltones had played in. Dallas had a big following, and I sat in the back of the crowded club, next to a table of people one-third my age, who shut their eyes and moved their heads while Dallas went off on one of his fancy guitar riffs. I don't know how he could have seen anything through the dark and smoke, but if anything, Dallas had always been full of surprises.

"This next song is for a woman who was fine enough to be married to the best musician I ever knew: my brother."

He lifted his sunglasses up to wink at me, and then after softly counting to four, began singing, "You're My Gem."

After the set, the head-bobbing young people who had given me dirty looks when I sat next to them wanted to buy me drinks, and I gave in to the temptation of liquid courage—but only one glass full.

In the dressing room, Dallas hugged me hard.

"Violet Mathers, it's been too long."

I pulled away from him, offended. "Violet Mathers Sykes."

"Oh, come on, you never made it legal."

I knew immediately that the years had done nothing to soften his sarcasm, and my old snippy self had jumped into position, ready to scratch, when Dallas put down all his weapons and began to cry. Cry big, so big that someone knocked on the door asking if he was all right.

We had dinner at a rib joint and then Dallas asked if I'd like to go along to visit Frenchie.

"Frenchie? My goodness, is she still alive?"

"No, but I still like to visit her."

His music made him young onstage, but in his big Cadillac, Dallas drove like the old man he was.

"I know I should have come to Austin's funeral, but you know I was on—"

"Yes, on tour in Germany," I said, wishing he'd choose the middle of the lane rather than the side to drive in. "I got your telegram."

"Nobody sends telegrams anymore," said Dallas. "They're like hats and handkerchiefs—remnants of a classier time."

Even as I was anticipating a certain collision, I had to laugh. "That sounds like something Austin would have said."

"Does it?" said Dallas, as if I'd complimented him.

The graveyard was on a small hill of a small church on the outskirts of town. Dallas drove up the gravel road that ringed it and parked.

"Oh no, don't get out," he said when I opened the door. "It's too damp for my knees." He pointed to a monument and I peered out at the scattered granite markers and cones of flowers that looked blue in the night. "That's Frenchie, over there."

"What happened with you two anyway?"

Dallas's sigh could have put out the candles of a septuagenarian's cake.

"The usual," he said, and his fingers trembled as he lit a cigarette. "I had something I really liked but I thought there had to be something better."

"And was there?"

"Maybe. But I never found it. Didn't mean I stopped lookin', though." Dallas aimed a smoke ring out the open window and it rose and circled in the darkness like a lariat of mist. "Hey," he said, forcing brightness into his voice. "Tell me something I don't know."

"Well, my ears don't ring anymore."

"No shit! What's that like?"

I thought for a moment. "It's on the list of the best things that ever happened to me."

"Along with?"

"My daughter . . . Austin . . . Kjel . . . the Pearltones."

"Austin . . . Kjel . . . the Pearltones . . . they'd be on my list too."

We sat in a long moment of silence, and I could tell by the way he worked his jaw that Dallas was trying not to cry again.

"Well, I've got some other news for you," I said, my voice bright "Remember Birdie, ringleader of the Clamshells?"

"Our devoted fans," said Dallas, his laugh a guttural sputter. "The Clamshells beat those Dead Heads by thirty years."

"The Pearltones were always ahead of their time. Anyway, Birdie's the one who bankrolled my business and she finally just retired last June. Then she took off on a singles cruise—seventy-eight years old and she's dancing the night away with Greek and Corsican bachelors!"

"Well, listen to this—I lived up in Seattle in the sixties, and guess who hosted the afternoon movie on TV? Isalee Bailey, that little adagio dancer!"

"No kidding!" I said, infused with a tickle of delight. "So she had a showbiz career after all."

"And how about Elwin?"

I told him about Elwin and Alice and how they'd adopted seven children from around the world.

"He was a good man," said Dallas, nodding. "I still think it was Elwin who kept us out of a lot of trouble."

"How do you mean?"

"Dude was so big! Anyone who wanted to mess with us knew they had to mess with Elwin, and most of them said 'No thanks.' "

"Except for that fight . . . the one right here in Memphis, remember?"

" 'Course I remember. But that, as Austin would say, was an anomaly. Along with everything else about the Pearltones."

A breeze stirred through a chinaberry tree next to the road and we listened to the dry rattle.

"Yeah, Violet, I've been with a lot of groups since the Pearltone days, but none of 'em, not one, had that magic onstage, and for sure none of 'em had those guardian angels offstage."

"Guardian angels?"

Dallas's voice was as open and guileless as a boy's. "Someone or something was watching out for us then. How we managed to play in the places we did without getting lynched or killed is beyond me."

"Don't forget what happened to Kjel," I said, suddenly angry.

"Oh, I don't, Violet. I can't." He butted his cigarette in the ashtray and asked me about Miri, and grateful for the change of subject, I told her all about her.

"And you have a child, don't you?"

"Two," said Dallas, "that I know of." He smiled at the old joke, and the flag of his sly handsomeness still waved in his tired old face.

"My son Dante's a session musician in L.A. and my daughter Beverly's a costume designer. Sorta like you, Violet. Although she's never made anything as fine as those Pearltone jackets."

"Ha! Remember how hard you fought against those?"

Dallas shook his head. "I still got mine, Violet. I can't button it anymore, though—musta shrunk over the years."

"Austin's shrunk too," I said. "But Kjel's never did—in fact he was buried in it."

The night seemed a breathing thing, its pulse the crickets' chirp, and we sat quietly in the car, listening to it. Dallas looked at me for a long time and I could see that despite his bravado and his basic Dallasness, the man was nearly pickled in regret.

"I was scared more than anything," he said finally. "And the fact that I ran has been chasing me all my life. I'm always running, Violet, always tired."

It was 3:00 A.M. when Dallas dropped me off at my hotel, bumping into the curb with his front tire and braking so hard my forehead nearly made purchase with the windshield. I leaned to kiss him on the cheek, but he grabbed me and I was scared for a moment, remembering the young Dallas. But this old Dallas only wanted to hold me and Austin and Kjel and everyone else we had shared, and when he finally released me, he kissed me on the lips and said, "Violet Mathers Sykes, you're a hell of a woman."

If I had a dime for every time someone's told me that, I'd be in a higher tax bracket than I already am. I know you understand that I say that not as bragging, but as encouragement. Who'd have ever thought a shunned, husky-voiced, one-armed, big-chinned girl with a hive of bees in her head could live a life so full of miracles?

But we all have, when you think of it. I'd love to hear about yours; the big ones, the little ones, and those miracles you haven't even recognized yet.

Look, the waitress is putting on another pot of coffee.

Come on, your turn.

Oh My Stars

Lorna Landvik

A Reader's Guide

A CONVERSATION WITH LORNA LANDVIK

Alex Schemmer is a writer living in Los Angeles.

Alex Schemmer: Can you describe your writing process?

Lorna Landvik: A book usually starts with the appearance of the main character(s) in my head. I don't know much about them, but am given enough of a glimpse (as well as their name; they always come named) to begin writing about them. The more I write, the more I learn the story. When the characters decide they don't want to do what I have them doing, they rebel, and they almost always win in determining their fate. I write forward; I learn something that I didn't know and then I go back and change things. My writing process is always a little dance—forward, then back, forward two steps, back one. I don't write from an outline and while I sometimes get an inkling of what the ending is going to be midway through the book, often as not, the ending surprises me.

AS: How did the idea for this book come to you? Was the genesis a specific character, a place, an image?

LL: Violet came into my head while I was sitting on my porch and she immediately let me know she was from Kentucky, she had suffered a terrible accident, and the bulk of her story would be told in the Great Depression.

AS: How did you create and develop the character of Violet? Do you base your characters on real people, or are they entirely imagined?

LL: I don't consciously base my characters on any living people but I can't say they're fully imagined. I think that everyone I've met in my life makes some sort of impression on my subconscious and it's from that stew that I create my characters. My mother, who died shortly after I delivered the book to my editor, does seem to infuse this story, however. Like Violet, she grew up in the Depression and was an excellent seamstress and clothes designer, and like Kjel, music was a big part of her life. Something I recently learned was that when she played House with some of her sisters, they had names they called themselves—hers was Violet Robinson. That was a strange coincidence.

AS: What did you do as research to create the world of the Great Depression?

LL: I've always been interested in the Great Depression and throughout my life have read books about this time. I've always been fascinated by the New Deal and the programs that were initiated to put people back to work. I also heard stories of my parents and relatives who went through it.

AS: How about the music industry of the 1930s? Did you use any historical groups as models for the Pearltones?

LL: I'm a big fan of all kinds of music—about twenty-five years ago I stumbled upon a Stanley Brothers album and was immediately captivated by their harmonies. Their music drew me into bluegrass. That's how it's often been for me—one great song or one great album can make me want to explore not only that particular musician or group's music, but the genre in which they're playing as well.

AS: You are also an actress and a comedian. Do you find that your experience as a performer aids you as a writer?

LL: I think performing has given me more of an ear for the rhythm of the language—how, by the mere placement of one word, you can get a laugh or you can get dead silence. I think I'm also more aware of the importance of dialogue and will often say dialogue out loud after I've written it to make sure it flows right and that it's in character.

AS: Each chapter begins with the elderly Violet addressing the reader in the first person, while the action is recorded in the third person. Was this always the plan? What made you decide on this format?

LL: This format wasn't always the plan—I rarely *have* a plan. I began writing Violet's story and *bam-bam-bam*—I realized all sorts of bad things happened to her and that her early life was pretty grim. Maybe to let the reader know that things worked out for her, I decided to have her looking back at her life from the perspective of old age.

AS: Music and laughter seem to be saving graces that propel your characters through adversity. Is this informed by your own life experiences? Are laughter and music restorative?

LL: I'm a big fan of music and a big fan of humor. I love to sing (I'd like to think my limited range is off-set by my ear for harmonization) and play a few instruments with varying degrees of skill. I don't intentionally look for the humor in life but can't seem to escape it (nor would I want to). And yes; laughter is restorative—there's no way you can feel bad after a good laugh. Music can play to all your emotions but I guess anything that helps you feel more is a good thing.

AS: In the book, the elderly Violet claims that she is in the nature camp of the nature-vs.-nurture debate; upbringing can refine but not reshape a personality. Where do you stand on this issue?

LL: I have to say Violet and I are like minds on this subject. I really do believe that we enter the world with a certain personality and while nurturing can make its mark, the basic personality is already there.

AS: In the same vein, certain events and adversities change the course of Violet's life. Do these events shape her personality, or does her personality influence how she reacts to them?

LL: I'm sure it's a combination. She remarks on her upbringing, saying that she feels she was born with a sense of humor but that her mother's abandonment and her father's meanness sharpened her humor and made her use it more as a weapon. But when she is invited into Kjel and Austin's world, her tight heart opens again, but only because she's willing to let it flower. Austin and Dallas had the same background and faced the same prejudice, yet Austin wasn't bullied by his pain; he didn't submit to it, while Austin did, burying his real self.

AS: If Violet had reached San Francisco, do you think she would have committed suicide? Do you consider Violet a born "survivor"?

LL: I'm assuming she would have killed herself had she gotten there; that's why I'm so glad she didn't. Initially, it took a person like Kjel—big-hearted, his arms wide-open to the world—to get her to see the value of life, and then it was others—Austin, Leola, Esben, et cetera—who showed her the value of her own life. I don't know that she was a "born" survivor—I think she survived the way all of us do—with the help and love of others.

AS: The natural world (Violet's name, her paternal affiliation with a tree, Kjel's fascination with the heavens) registers strongly as a motif throughout the book. As an author, do you consciously think about themes or motifs when writing? Or do they spring up organically?

LL: I try to tell a good story with engaging characters and whatever themes my readers find in my writing is okay by me.

AS: Dallas and Selma French seem like an unlikely pair, yet they fall in love. Is love blind? Do you believe in soulmates?

LL: I believe love is blind, deaf, and dumb; I also believe love is all-seeing, all-hearing, and all-knowing. Why a person falls in love with another is beyond easy analysis. I believe that we have many soulmates, and are lucky if we find just one of them.

AS: What are your thoughts on beauty? Violet starts out as a homely, awkward girl, but becomes, in her own way, a beautiful woman; do you think beauty is dependent on bone structure? On attitude and confidence? Or is it purely subjective?

LL: Oh man, there isn't time or space to answer these questions! I certainly appreciate the kind of beauty that comes with good bone structure and fine features but I know that lasting beauty has much more to do with the things unseen than seen. (Guess I'm channeling *The Little Prince* here . . .) I'm disgusted by the culture that thinks beauty cannot exist without youth, or at least without the appearance of youth. In the end, it's not how the world sees you, but how you see yourself.

AS: Will we see Violet again in any of your work?

LL: I doubt it; I think Violet's story has been told.

AS: When you're not writing yourself, whom do you read? Do films and music inspire you as well?

LL: Some of my favorite writers are Anne Tyler, Michael Malone, Mark Twain, Charles Dickens, Robert Girardi, Kaye Gibbons . . . I could go on and on. I see a lot of movies—we've got a great big palace of a movie theater near us that still serves real butter on its popcorn and my husband and I are regulars there (sometimes more for the popcorn than for the movies). Some of my favorite movies were made decades ago—I love Preston Sturges; his movie *Mad Wednesday* is a comedy classic. As in books, I prefer character-driven movies above all. And music— who isn't inspired by music?

AS: In the book, one character claims that the Pearltones helped change the world. Do you think art (big "A" or little) has this power?

LL: I do. Its effect may take years; but a good painting, a good song, can inspire someone else to do something even greater that in turn inspires someone else. I think the world is saved by people trying to reach out, trying to inspire.

AS: Their enjoyment aside, do you want your readers to take away anything with them after this book?

LL: I spoke to a reader who asked me about "Tree Pa." She wondered if I knew a person who actually sought out a tree to hug and hold as Violet did, or if I just made the situation up. I told her I just made it up; she then told me she knew a man who had no family and few friends and had his own tree he went to for solace, to hold when no one else would hold him. She said she got goosebumps reading about Violet and Tree Pa because it reminded her so much of her friend and how he didn't seem to need the tree as much the more their friendship grew. I would love readers to close my books thinking that as long as we all are in this world together, we might as well do all we can to help one another out; to stand in and substitute for that tree. And then of course, I'd like them to think, "Hmmm, I wonder if the bookstore is open so I can buy some more Lorna Landvik books."

READING GROUP QUESTIONS
AND TOPICS FOR DISCUSSION

1. *Oh My Stars* begins in highly unusual fashion, describing Violet's horrible accident in the opening passages. Why might an author introduce a character this way? What sort of tone does it establish for the novel?

2. Consider the book's portrayal of Depression-era America. Why has the author selected this particular time and place for her story? How does the setting complement the action?

3. Music-making is one of the central dramatic tropes in *Oh My Stars*. What is the thematic significance of music for these characters? How, if at all, is musical expression preferable to the spoken or written word?

4. Violet longs for recognition: Even when jerking her arm from industrial equipment, she thinks of the birthday party she ought to be enjoying instead. What different kinds of attention does she seek from others? How are her expectations fulfilled or disappointed? Ultimately, does anyone "see the whole Violet"?

5. Violet explicitly weighs in on the nature-vs.-nurture debate in chapter 5. What are your views on this issue? Is the cake in fact already baked at birth?

6. Various sorts of families appear throughout the story: the Hedstrom clan, Violet and her father, the band. What defines a family? What are its obligations, and what determines its success?

7. Despite its subject matter and the bleak circumstances of its setting, *Oh My Stars* maintains a relatively upbeat tone. Would you describe the book as funny? How does the author use humor? How do the characters use it? Does humor represent a solution to problems, or merely a diversion from them?

8. The narrative employs a flashback structure, braiding the events of the Depression with more recent commentary. Why did the author choose this technique? How do you think it contributes to the story? Do you feel Violet's perspective (as presented in the italicized paragraphs that introduce each chapter) enhances your own understanding of the events she describes?

9. Throughout the book, certain events and adversities change the course of Violet's life. Do these events shape her personality, or does her personality influence how she reacts to them? What about Kjel? Austin? Which characters are the most impressionable? Which are the most indomitable?

10. The characters in *Oh My Stars* are, by and large, a celebratory group. What does the book celebrate? Does the author, in her narrative, impart any lessons distinct from the messages Violet shares?

PHOTO: © BRIAN VELENCHENKO

LORNA LANDVIK is the bestselling author of *Patty Jane's House of Curl, Your Oasis on Flame Lake, The Tall Pine Polka, Welcome to the Great Mysterious, Angry Housewives Eating Bon Bons,* and *Oh My Stars.* She is also an actor, playwright, and proud soccer mom.